SONS OF THUNDER

Look for these exciting Western series
from bestselling authors
William W. Johnstone and J.A. Johnstone

The Mountain Man

Preacher: The First Mountain Man

Luke Jensen: Bounty Hunter

Those Jensen Boys!

The Jensen Brand

MacCallister

The Red Ryan Westerns

Perley Gates

Have Brides, Will Travel

Will Tanner, Deputy U.S. Marshal

Shotgun Johnny

The Chuckwagon Trail

The Jackals

The Slash and Pecos Westerns

The Texas Moonshiners

Stoneface Finnegan Westerns

Ben Savage: Saloon Ranger

The Buck Trammel Westerns

The Death and Texas Westerns

The Hunter Buchanon Westerns

SONS OF THUNDER

WILLIAM W. JOHNSTONE
and
J.A. JOHNSTONE

KENSINGTON
PUBLISHING CORP.

www.kensingtonbooks.com

KENSINGTON BOOKS are published by

Kensington Publishing Corp.
119 West 40th Street
New York, NY 10018

Copyright © 2022 by J.A. Johnstone

PUBLISHER'S NOTE
Following the death of William W. Johnstone, the Johnstone family is working with a carefully selected writer to organize and complete Mr. Johnstone's outlines and many unfinished manuscripts to create additional novels in all of his series like The Last Gunfighter, Mountain Man, and Eagles, among others. This novel was inspired by Mr. Johnstone's superb storytelling.

All Kensington titles, imprints, and distributed lines are available at special quantity discounts for bulk purchases for sales promotion, premiums, fund-raising, educational, or institutional use. Special book excerpts or customized printings can also be created to fit specific needs. For details, write or phone the office of the Kensington Special Sales Manager: Attn. Special Sales Department. Kensington Publishing Corp., 119 West 40th Street, New York, NY 10018. Phone: 1-800-221-2647.

Library of Congress Card Catalogue Number: 2021951536

The K with book logo Reg. US Pat. & TM Off.

ISBN: 978-1-4967-3589-8

First Kensington Hardcover Edition: May 2022

10 9 8 7 6 5 4 3 2 1

Printed in the United States of America

SONS OF THUNDER

Chapter 1

Thunder rumbled like angry gods bowling with boulders. Witches' fingers of lightning poked across the firmament, intermittently lighting up this rain-tortured Rocky Mountain canyon, which had been turned by the late-summer monsoon storm into howling bedlam.

Between lightning bolts, the Colorado night was as black as the bottom of a deep well save for the buffeting gray curtain of wind-lashed rain that seemed to have no letup in it whatever.

Hunkered low inside his oilskin rain slicker and seated in the driver's box of the stout Pittsburg freight wagon, holding the sodden harness ribbons tight in his gloved hands, James "Slash" Braddock turned to his long-boned partner seated beside him and shouted, "Good Lord, Pecos. I do believe we have a good chance of drowning out here, sittin' in our consarned wagon no less!"

He looked down at the ankle-deep rainwater churning on the floor of the driver's box. It had soaked his boots and socks and damn near frozen his feet.

"If the river keeps rising," returned Melvin "Pecos Kid" Baker, pausing as another peal of near-deafening thunder hammered down around them, "we might be swimmin' for it, Slash!" He turned his head to regard the Poudre River where it churned and pounded loudly in its rocky bed off the trail's right side. "It looks to me like it's starting to swell out of its banks!"

"We have to find shelter soon!"

"That old ghost town of Manhattan should be dead ahead. Last time we passed through there, a saloon was still in operation, remember?"

"I do! And I also remember, if my memory hasn't gotten even cloudier than I think it has here on the downhill side of my allotment, the fella that ran the place was a big Swede everybody called 'the Dutchman,' who served a thick dark ale and cooked a mean T-bone steak!"

"And he piled up a whole passel of greasy fried potatoes around it, too! Cooked to a crispy brown, just the way I like it!"

"Oh, Lordy, you're killin' me!"

"I'll be hanged if I ain't killin' myself!"

"I hope Manhattan is as close as you think it is!"

"Hey! Look there!" Pecos straightened in his seat and thrust out his right arm to aim his pointing index finger over the two stout, rain-silvered mules hitched to the wagon. "I think I see a light!"

Slash gazed straight ahead, around the steady stream of rain sluicing down from the crease in the crown of his black Stetson. Sure enough, a pinprick of soft amber light shone in the gauzy darkness.

"Well, well, looks like you had it right!" Slash said.

Pecos grinned and pressed a finger to his temple. "Yours might be gettin' murky, but my thinker box is workin' just fine, Slash!"

"I suppose you think that means you oughta be doin' the thinkin' for both of us." Slash chuckled and wagged his head as he shook the reins over the lumbering mules' backs. "Lordy, I shudder at the thought!"

"I'm too cold an' wet to kick your scrawny behind, so I'll let that one go!"

Slash laughed.

The mules quickened their pace despite the sodden trail, which had become a shallow stream churning with muddy water that shone amber when the lightning flashed. They climbed the gradual grade on top of which the ghost town of Manhattan sat in a wide horseshoe bend of the river.

A loud crashing boom sounded, cutting through the stormy din, making mules and men jerk with starts. Slash and Pecos turned to see a lightning bolt strike a thumb of rock on the far side of the river. A lone pine rose like a sentinel from the top of the rock. It glowed brightly, as did the entire thumb, against the darkness of the mountain wall, sizzling loudly.

The pine exploded, and the thumb broke loose from the stone wall from which it jutted and tumbled down against the wall with several more explosive roars. Burning tree and sizzling rock tumbled away in the stormy darkness.

The scorched-stone aroma of brimstone peppered the air.

"Yikes!" Pecos said.

"Yeah!" Slash agreed, again flicking the reins over the mules' backs. "Come on, you mangy broomtails. Pick it up less'n you wanna get roasted alive out here!"

Mules, wagon, and men flattened out at the top of the rise; and the two rows of mostly vacant and eerily dark business buildings of old Manhattan, a rollicking gold camp just a few short years ago, pushed up around the wagon. The only building with lights in its windows shone dead ahead, on the street's left side. That would be the Dutchman's place.

"Should be an old barn up here, on the right," Pecos said.

Slash swung the mules over to the large log barn standing tall and dark and doorless on the right side of the street, between a boarded-up bordello with a tumbledown front stoop and a boarded-up barbershop, its once colorful pole having faded to gray. Slash hazed the mules on into the barn, and as the wagon followed them in, the rain stopped lashing him and his partner, though the storm, hammering the old building and echoing around inside the cave-like interior.

The smell of moldy hay and ancient ammonia touched the two men's nostrils.

The mules brayed uncertainly.

The two men, former outlaws turned freighters—when they weren't working as unofficial federal lawmen for the devilish scalawag Chief Marshal Luther T. "Bleed-'Em-So" Bledsoe, that was—clambered stiffly down from the wagon. In their late fifties, neither man was as young as he used to be, and they felt the weight of their years—especially during cold, rainy spells like the one they were enduring this night in the Front Range, west of their hometown of Camp Collins, in northern Colorado.

They'd delivered a load of supplies to a gold mine at the west end of Poudre Canyon, and they'd expected to be home by now. The storm had slowed them down considerably.

As the two men unhitched and tended the mules, first rubbing them down and then feeding and watering them, Slash couldn't help thinking of his lovely bride, the former Jaycee Breckenridge, who was waiting for him back in their second-floor suite of the saloon/gambling parlor/brothel that Jay owned in Fort Collins.

"What're you grinnin' about?"

Slash turned to his partner, who was opening a stall door at the rear of the barn. "Huh?"

"What're you grinnin' about?"

Slash led the second mule toward where Pecos was leading the first mule into the stall, the clomping of the mules' hooves on the hard-packed earthen floor all but drowned by the rain, wind, and thunder battering the old barn, making the roof leak in places and the timbers creak.

"I didn't know I was grinnin'."

"Like a jackass with a snoot full of cockleburs. Never mind. I know what you were grinnin' about. Or, should I say, *who* you were grinnin' about," Pecos amended, then gave a wry snort as he stepped out of the stall. "Don't worry. You'll see her soon enough."

"Who?" Slash said, playing dumb, as he led the second mule into the large stall, then set down a bucket of parched corn for the second mule, just as Pecos had done for the first mule.

"Your newly betrothed, fer cryin' in the queen's ale! You don't have to be embarrassed about bein' eager to see your wife, you know, Slash. There ain't no shame in it." Pecos placed his hand on his longtime partner's shoulder and leaned toward him, as though to impart a closely held secret. "There ain't no shame in missin' your woman. Especially when that woman happens to be one Miss Jaycee Breckenridge!"

"Ah, hell," Slash said, sheepishly brushing a fist across his chin. "It was that obvious, huh?"

"It was that obvious. Let me repeat—there ain't no shame in it."

"I know there ain't no shame in it, you big lummox!" Slash said, removing his hat and batting the excess water from it against his leg. The truth was, however, that despite having been married to Jay for a good six months now and having learned to open up more about his feelings, he still found himself falling back into his age-old natural habit of being reluctant to show those feelings to his male pards.

Or his male *pard*, as the case was. About the only friend the middle-aged former outlaw still had on this side of the sod was the Pecos River Kid himself. In fact, Pecos might have been the only true friend Slash had ever had, Slash being more than a tad on the contrary and solitary side. It still surprised Pecos that his friend, who was shorter and darker than Pecos's gray-blond six feet four, was finally married, since the only women he'd ever kept company with before Jay had come along were percentage gals.

Whores.

Pecos grinned slyly. "What were you thinkin' about?"

"Huh?" Slash said, indignant.

"Come on. What were you thinkin' about that made you grin that big horse fritter–eatin' grin?"

"Hah!" Slash said as the two men walked back toward the barn's front opening and the gray curtain of rain and flashing light just beyond it. "Wouldn't you like to know!"

Pecos chuckled. "I suppose she's gonna be worried when we don't show up tonight."

He and Slash stopped to regard the storm, neither one overly eager to brave it again, even though they hoped they'd find a surrounding of good hot food inside the saloon, if the Dutchman hadn't closed up on account of the storm. The wavering lamplight in the windows told them he hadn't. The Dutchman, an ex-prospector, lived on the building's second story.

"I reckon she will, but it's probably raining in Camp Collins, too, so she'll likely know why we're delayed." Slash winced, adjusted the set of his hat. "She'll still be worried, though. I don't much like worryin' the gal," he found himself openly admitting. "It's the one thing about marriage . . . in fact, it's the *only* thing about marriage . . . I've so far found disagreeable."

"Must be nice, though," Pecos said with a wistful sigh. "Havin' somebody back home worryin' about you."

"You know what you need to do, don't you?" Slash said. "You need to get down on your hands and knees and ask ol'

Bleed-'Em-So's queenly secretary to hitch her star to your wagon. Then you'll have a worrier of your own at home, pinin' for ya an' singin' sad songs when you're away."

Pecos had recently become right friendly with the jade-eyed, golden-haired Nordic beauty Abigail Langdon, though they'd both so far kept that fact from the owly chief marshal himself. Bledsoe had hired Slash and Pecos to do his dirty work—the assignments he didn't feel comfortable saddling his bona fide deputy marshals with, mostly because said assignments were off the books for being in part or in totality *illegal*. Rather, he'd coerced them into working for him, under threat of being hung or sent to prison for their past sundry indiscretions.

But their working for him didn't mean he approved of either former cutthroat.

As a deputy U.S. marshal once himself, Bledsoe had chased the pair and their former gang, the Snake River Marauders, from Canada to Mexico and back again several times without running any of them to ground. He had also taken a bullet from Slash several years back. It had been an inadvertent bullet, a ricochet, but the blue whistler had confined the nasty old gent to a push chair, just the same.

When and if Slash and Pecos went down in a hail of hot lead during the implementation of one of the chief marshal's dangerous assignments, the colicky old federal would shed no tears at their funerals.

"If Bledsoe ever found about me an' Abigail—and if we tied the knot, he would—he'd shoot us both," Pecos said. "Me? I deserve a bullet. Hell, a bullet's too good for me. But I wouldn't want that fate to befall dear Abigail." Pecos gave his big head a sad wag. "Nah, we'll just have to keep meetin' in secret until she finds someone younger and more upstandin'."

"Well, that shouldn't be too hard." Slash grinned.

"You're damn lucky I'm too cold and wet and hungry to whup your ass."

"You'd have to catch me first, ya big lummox. Speakin' of hunger, come on, partner," Slash said, pulling his hat down tight and lifting the collar of his rain slicker. "Let's go say hi to the Dutchman!"

The two former bank and train robbers ran into the rainy street.

Chapter 2

Slash and Pecos entered the Dutchman's saloon in the nick of time, for even though it was only nine o'clock, the big, blond, long-limbed, and bony Scandinavian had written off any further business this stormy night and was about to blow the lamps out and head upstairs to his living quarters.

He was all smiles to see some company and badly needed business, however, for it had been a quiet several days. After giving the two freighters the key to a room they would share upstairs, where he had five to rent, he hustled back into the kitchen to stoke his stove and fry up a couple of big T-bones and a cast-iron skillet of his signature potatoes, which he cultivated himself in an irrigated garden behind the saloon.

Slash and Pecos chose a table close to the fully stoked and pleasantly ticking potbelly stove, draped their rain slickers over their chair backs, and sat down to nurse the two frothy dark ales the Dutchman had drawn for them.

"Ah, shelter from the storm!" Pecos intoned, lifting his mug to suck some of the froth from the rim of his mug.

"Nice quiet one, just how I like it," Slash said. "The older I get, partner, the more peace and quiet I like. Less'n, of course, I'm snuggled under the bedcovers with that good-lookin' gal of mine. Then forget the peace *and* the quiet!"

"Sure, sure, rub it in," Pecos groused before taking another sip from his dimpled schooner.

"Sorry about that," Slash said with mock chagrin.

"No, you're not."

"No, you're right. I'm not," Slash said and chuckled. He loved nothing more than to torment his partner out of sheer deviltry.

He sank back in his chair, enjoying the heat emanating from the stove and soaking deep into his cold bones, loosening the age-tender muscles. Now that he was inside and out of it, sitting by a warm fire, he even enjoyed listening to the drumming and whooshing of the storm, the dribbling of the rain down the sashed windows, and watching the intermittent flashes of the lightning.

Peace and quiet, at last. Good beer. Even better food on the way. And a couple of warm beds waiting for him and Pecos upstairs.

Yessir, Slash remarked silently to himself, *you just can't beat it.*

Presently, the drumming of horses rose from the street, as did the shouting of several men. Neither Slash nor Pecos could make out what the men were saying, but the newcomers' tones told them they were pleasantly surprised to have found a still open sanctuary in this otherwise boarded-up, cold, and uninviting ghost town.

"There goes our peace and quiet," Slash said before taking another sip of his beer.

"Oh, well," Pecos said, hauling out his makings to roll a quirley, "the Dutchman will be pleased as punch for the business."

"I reckon."

When the Dutchman brought two smoking and loudly sputtering platters out from the kitchen, and Pecos informed him of the added business he was likely to get when the newcomers had stabled their mounts, the big, blond, red-faced man rubbed his big, fleshy paws together greedily.

"*Jah*, it is a good night, after all!" He clapped his hands together as he ambled around behind the big mahogany bar with an ornate backbar complete with leaded glass mirror. "*Jah! Jah!* Now we're talking!"

He rubbed his big hands on his apron and adjusted a couple of the glasses arranged in a pyramid on the bar before him. Meanwhile, Slash and Pecos tucked cloth napkins into their shirt collars and hunkered over their platters, eating hungrily. They were both a little over halfway through their steaks and potatoes when shouting sounded from outside again—men exclaiming in jovial tones, as though in celebration.

A woman's cry was added to the din.

Then another.

Slash and Pecos looked up from their meals and exchanged curious frowns.

"Hmm," the Dutchman said, waiting behind the bar and now frowning toward the door, as well.

Boots thumped on the stoop.

"Last one inside's a rotten egg!" a man shouted just outside the door.

The door opened abruptly, fairly flying open, as a man entered with a young woman draped over his right shoulder. She wore a sodden dark blue dress, which clung to her legs like a second skin. She was kicking those legs desperately, struggling inside the grasp of the man who carried her on his shoulder as though she were a fifty-pound sack of oats. The dress's hem was pulled up to reveal soaked pantaloons, also clinging to the young woman's slender legs.

The man was grinning beneath the brim of his high-crowned black hat, from which rain dripped liberally. He was a short, broad-chested man in his middle twenties, with a red mustache and side-whiskers and twin Colts holstered on his hips, beneath a pale linen duster as wet as the dress of the girl on his shoulder.

Another, taller man followed him into the saloon, with yet another young woman draped over his own right shoulder. Both girls—yeah, that was what they were, girls of maybe sixteen or seventeen, Slash judged—complained loudly and kicked their legs and futilely slammed their clenched fists against the backs of the men carrying them. The men only whooped and laughed.

The smaller, red-mustached gent glanced at the Swede standing behind the bar and said, "Hope you got beds upstairs, partner, 'cause that's where we're headed!"

The taller man whooped loudly and followed the small man and his own unwilling cargo toward the narrow staircase rising at the room's rear.

"Stop!" bellowed the plump blonde in a lemon-yellow dress who was draped over the taller man's shoulder. "Put me down! Oh, please put me down this instant. You're *hurting* me!"

As the men and the two complaining girls passed Slash and Pecos's table, the two cutthroats-turned-freighters shared expressions of mute exasperation. Slash, seated facing the front of the room, started to rise from his chair and protest the girls' ill-treatment but froze halfway up from his chair when he saw several more men enter the saloon, all wearing either soaked canvas dusters or rain-beaded oilskin slickers.

They kept coming in, talking and laughing and swatting their hats against their legs, dislodging moisture, until a total of eight men had entered, including the two now mounting the stairs behind Slash. What had stayed Slash's rise from his chair was not only the number of men entering the Swede's watering hole, but also the fact that three of the newcomers were carrying Winchester carbines. The others were armed, as well. Slash could see a few holstered guns and even a couple of sheathed knives inside unbuttoned dusters, or he could see the telltale bulge of said armaments behind buttoned dusters and slickers.

These fellas were armed for bear!

Not possessing a suicide bent, Slash sank back into his chair as the other men favored him and Pecos with passing glances. The last newcomer to enter slammed the door on the continuing storm and followed the others to the bar.

"Gotta be fifty thousand dollars, fellas," announced one of the six heading for the bar, patting a swollen pouch of the saddlebags draped over his shoulder. "Fifty thousand dollars if there's a dime!"

"Sure enough," said another. "I couldn't believe my eyes when we blew the lock off that strongbox and opened the lid. Holy thunder! What a mother lode of greenbacks and coins!"

The speaker slapped the shoulder of the portly, shaggy-headed, bearded man bellying up to the bar beside him. They turned to the Swede, who was eyeing them with an uncertain smile on his broad mouth, and, slapping the bar, loudly ordered whiskey and beer.

Slash and Pecos shared another look. This time a *knowing* look. Pecos still held a thick bite of steak and a couple of crispy potatoes impaled with a fork halfway between his plate and his mouth, having frozen in that position when he'd first heard the girls yell.

It was obvious to both former train and bank robbers that the newcomers were outlaws who'd recently taken down a stage, plundered the strongbox, and kidnapped the two young women—a pair of unlucky passengers aboard the coach when the tough nuts had struck. Now those unlucky girls were upstairs with two of the outlaws, with the rest no doubt soon to follow, and the girls' luck was likely heading even farther south.

The obvious question was voiced by Pecos, albeit in a register that couldn't be heard above the celebratory outlaws' jovial din over their run of good luck: "What're we gonna do about this, Slash?"

Slash winced as he cut into his meat with a serrated knife, trying to at least make a casual show of continuing his meal. "I'm open to suggestions." He cut his eyes to the men at the bar, who, with the exception of two standing sideways to it, had their backs to him and Pecos. "The roughtails ain't payin' us any attention at all."

Pecos swung his head for a quick look. "That's 'cause they're young and we're old. They ain't afraid of us."

Slash glanced sidelong at the celebrating firebrands, one of whom had poured the loot out onto the bar and was loudly counting it with the help of one of his pards. "No damn respect," the former robber said through an angry snarl. "Probably think we been freightin' all our lives." He gave a caustic laugh. "If they only knew!"

Pecos jutted his jaw and hardened his eyes at his partner. "Slash, will you keep your damn voice down? If they knew who we were, they'd likely have opened up on us by now, filled us so full of lead we'd rattle when we walked."

"A little respect—that's all I ask!"

"What are we gonna do about those two poor girls up there?" Pecos raised his eyes to the ceiling, from which emanated, beneath the din coming from the six at the bar, the other two outlaws' raised voices and the girls' cries, as well as a good bit of stomping around.

Slash forked potatoes into his mouth and chewed, sliding his furtive gaze between Pecos and the six men at the bar. While he continued to eat, he was no longer hungry, and the food no longer tasted good. "Well, there's eight of them. Two of us."

Pecos stiffly forked more food into his mouth. "Tall odds."

"Maybe too tall."

"You thinkin' if we stick our noses in, you're liable to make Jay a widow after only a half a year's worth of marriage?"

"That might be soon enough for her, after spendin' six months with me . . ."

"You can say that again!"

"But six months ain't long enough for me with her . . ."

"Slash, I do believe you've grown a heart."

"That bein' said, we can't sit here and listen to what them two girls is goin' through upstairs without at least tryin' to do somethin'."

"Which brings us back to what?"

"True enough." Slash switched his gaze to the bar again and inwardly flinched when he saw that one of the six tough nuts was looking straight at him. Slash feigned a smile and nodded at the man, whose expression grew wistful. He opened his mouth and ran a thumb pensively along his jawline, then, scowling curiously, turned back to the bar.

Slash turned back to Pecos and cursed.

"What is it?"

"One of 'em looked right at me. Like maybe he recognized me."

Pecos shuttled his own gaze to the bar. "Which one?"

"The oldest one of the bunch. The one who carried in the saddlebags."

Pecos studied the man of topic in the backbar mirror, then turned back to Slash. "Ah, hell, you know who that is?"

"Who?"

"Scratch Lawson. We had a run-in with him about ten years ago, when he was still wet behind the ears but meaner'n a stick-teased rattlesnake."

Slash took another quick glance at the man in the mirror. He was of medium height, with curly pewter hair tufting out from beneath his battered, funnel-brimmed cream Stetson. He was long faced, cow eyed, and wore several days of pewter stubble on his narrow jaws. His sodden duster bulged where two pistols were holstered on his hips.

"Ah, hell!" Slash said.

"Yeah."

"Our gang got crossways with his gang down in Mexico, when we robbed that *rurale* supply depot. Turns out his bunch, led by Loot Wiley from Galveston, had targeted it, too. We got to it first, and they came after us."

"We killed two of theirs, and they wounded one of ours."

"Bo Gleeson . . . Yeah, I remember."

"I reckon if we're gonna do somethin', we'd best get down to it," Pecos said. "Before Lawson puts names to our faces."

Too late.

The outlaw of topic, Scratch Lawson, suddenly slapped the bar and whipped around to face Slash and Pecos, yelling, *"Slash Braddock and the Pecos River Kid!"*

He grinned and slid both flaps of his wet duster back behind the bone handles of his matched Smith & Wessons.

Chapter 3

A cold, wet stone dropped in Slash's belly.

He turned to Scratch Lawson, who was standing with his back to the bar, grinning, and said, "Scratch? Scratch Lawson, is that you, you old polecat? Damn! How long's it been, anyways?"

"Too damn long, Slash." Lawson switched his cow-stupid, snake-mean eyes to Pecos. "Pecos," he said, the smile fading from his lips. "Too damn long! I been waitin' to run into you two old dogs for the past ten, twelve years."

The five other outlaws at the bar turned toward Slash and Pecos, frowning, also sliding the flaps of their dusters or oilskins back behind their guns, revealing an amazing amount and vast array of firepower.

"You happy now, Slash?" Pecos asked his partner out of the side of his mouth. "You're finally gettin' the attention you been longin' for!"

Lawson stretched his lips back from his teeth and bellowed, "*Kill them!*"

As he and the other outlaws started to slide their hoglegs from their holsters, Slash said, "Shut up and go to work, or we're wolf bait, partner!"

"Don't tell me to shut up!" Pecos returned as he and Slash threw themselves from their chairs.

This was neither man's first rodeo.

Over their long and storied careers as outlaws, both men had found themselves in similar situations. Of course, they were older now, so throwing themselves so suddenly out of their chairs while skinning their six-shooters, then striking the hard wooden floor with their fifty-plus-year-old bodies was a more challenging and regretful maneuver than it had been when they were, say, twenty-two or twenty-three years young.

Necessity, however, even at the ex-cutthroats' ripe old ages, was often the mother of painful maneuvers.

Both men struck the floor on opposite sides of their table as bullets fired by the outlaws plunked into the table itself as well as the backs of the chairs Slash and Pecos had vacated. Lead also tore splinters from the floor around where the two men landed, groaning and grunting and raising and cocking their hoglegs and taking hasty aim at the men lined up like tin cans on fence posts before them.

Quickly, they went to work before the outlaws, bleary eyed from drink and apparently shocked by the two old farts' acrobatic maneuvers, could recock their pistols and readjust their aims.

Boom-boom!

Boom-boom! Boom!

The outlaws screamed as lead ripped through their soaked duds to plunder chilly flesh.

They continued yelling, and a few even managed to return fire, albeit wildly, as Slash and Pecos continued cocking and triggering their revolvers, the wheels of Pecos's Russian .44 and both of Slash's handsome, matched, bone-gripped Colts spinning quickly in their iron frames, orange flames lapping from the three maws and the squint-eyed faces of the two former outlaws aiming along the barrels.

The rickety building fairly leaped with each blast of the thundering barrage, and the flames guttered in lanterns swinging from ceiling wires.

Finally silence.

Then, as though in afterthought, Slash's second Colt sent another bullet into Scratch Lawson's lanky frame where it was being held up by the man's elbows hooked over the edge of the bar behind him. The others were already sprawled in ragged, bloody piles at the base of the bar, to each side of the outlaw leader.

Boom!

Lawson screamed as the bullet drilled a third hole through his brisket. Stretching his lips back from his teeth, he glared at Scratch and bellowed, "*You go to hell!*"

His elbows unhooked from the edge of the bar, and he dropped straight down to the floor, where he lay quivering as his ticket was punched. Next stop—*hell*!

Slash stared at the man's corpse through the gray curtain of wafting powder smoke. "I'll likely see ya there, but not tonight, amigo!"

"Reload, Slash!" came Pecos's strained cry from where the bigger man lay unseen on the other side of the table between them.

Slash remembered the other two outlaws upstairs, from where the only sounds emanating now were those of running boots pounding floorboards, and these were growing in volume as the runner approached the top of the stairs. Slash got one of his Colts loaded and snapped the loading gate closed as the runner stopped. He aimed the pistol up the stairs just as a head appeared on the right side of the second-floor landing, at the mouth of the second-floor hall.

A head and a pistol, rather.

The pistol barked, flames lapping from the barrel.

As the bullet tore into the floor to Slash's right, Slash and

Pecos both returned fire, and the bullets hammered into the door casing up there just as the shooter pulled his head back into the hall.

"Damn!" Pecos said on the other side of the table from Slash.

A gun barked again. Slash flinched and prepared to return fire up the staircase but held fire. No head or pistol appeared at the top of the stairs. The gun's bark had been slightly muffled—fired from a ways down the hall.

Slash frowned, curious. Then his heart thudded.

Had the stage robbers shot one of the girls?

Pecos must have had the same dark suspicion, because Slash heard him say, "Damn!"

But then a man staggered out of the mouth of the hall atop the stairs and onto the landing. It was the same man who'd fired into the saloon hall. It was the shorter of the two rapists. Wearing only long handles and socks, the long handles unbuttoned down to his pale, bulging belly, he still held his pistol, but he held it straight down along his right leg. He was walking funny, like a man in a trance.

Another gun barked. Or maybe the same one as before.

The outlaw jerked forward on the landing, grunting and throwing his head back on his shoulders. He stumbled forward, triggered his own pistol into the floor of the landing. He pitched forward over the stair rail and turned a somersault in the air before striking the floor with a thundering boom and a deep sigh.

"Damn!" Pecos said again.

"I'll second that," Slash muttered, staring in mute befuddlement up at the now-empty landing.

A shrill wail issued from the hall. It was a long, high-pitched scream of unbearable agony. Not one of the girls. This was a man's scream.

More heavy, stumbling foot thuds issued from the hall until the second outlaw, the taller, leaner man, appeared at the top of the landing. The second outlaw and one of the girls, that was. This man, too, wore only long handles and socks. Still wearing her soaked blue dress, which was badly twisted and torn, the brunette sat on the outlaw's shoulders, looking down at the hand she held over the outlaw's right eye. Her feet, which hung down to the outlaw's waist, were small and pale and bare.

Slash frowned again, his incredulity building.

No. The brunette wasn't holding her hand over the outlaw's eye. She was grinding the neck of a broken whiskey bottle into that eye.

Blood oozed out around her hand and the large brown shard of broken glass and dribbled down the outlaw's face. The outlaw screamed again and turned toward the main saloon hall. He started stumbling down the steps, the girl remaining on his shoulders, looking down, wet and tangled brown hair hanging to her exposed shoulders. She stretched her lips back from her teeth as she continued grinding the broken neck of the bottle into the outlaw's eye.

The man took three stumbling steps down the stairs, stopped, threw his head back, looked up at the girl on his shoulders, and screamed again, then tumbled forward.

As he did, the girl, almost gracefully, leaned out away from him, grabbed the stair rail to her left, slid back off the man's shoulders, dropped lithely onto the stairs, then stood there, watching the outlaw fall forward and tumble wildly and loudly down the steps before piling up on the floor in front of the staircase.

The girl's dress and right hand were covered in blood. Even her hair was streaked with blood as it hung in tangles to her shoulders.

She stood staring through the thin screen of her hair, one corner of her upper lip curled, one nostril flared.

The man lay moaning and writhing.

"Damn!" Pecos said again.

"Yep," Slash agreed.

Soundlessly, the second girl—the plump blonde—appeared at the top of the stairs. She held a big silver-chased revolver in both hands straight down in front of her. Her yellow dress was also torn and hung to her shoulders. Her long hair also hung in tangles.

Her face was eerily void of expression.

She slowly raised the big pistol, clicking the hammer back. She aimed it down the stairs, to the right of the other girl, who was standing with her back to the stair rail, shuttling her gaze from the blonde above her to the groaning, sobbing outlaw below her.

The chubby blonde narrowed one eye behind the wet screen of her hair, tucked her lower lip beneath her upper teeth, and squeezed the trigger.

Thunder filled the saloon.

The bullet thumped into the outlaw's chest, making his body jerk from side to side. The man said, *"Oh!"* in surprised grief as he dropped his chin to look down at the hole over his heart. He raised his hands to the blood-oozing wound, then dropped them back down to the floor. His head fell back.

He turned his bloody face to one side, blinked once, said, *"Crap!"* and gave a last, long, rattling sigh.

Silence filled the saloon.

The blonde slowly lowered the silver-chased equalizer behind a wafting cloud of pale powder smoke.

"Damn!" Pecos said again, still on the floor on the other side of the table from Slash.

Again, Slash agreed as he stared in slack-jawed fascination at the two girls on the stairs. "Yeah . . ."

Outside, hooves thudded—several riders entering the yard.

Slash could hear them clearly, and he realized then that the storm had stopped. Lightning no longer flashed in the windows. He and Pecos both climbed to their feet and looked at each other over their bullet-pocked table, on which the remains of their meals sat. Both men turned to the door at the front of the room.

"Now, who's that?" Pecos said.

As if in response, a man called, "Nancy! Polly!"

In response to the man, both girls, who were still standing on the stairs behind Slash, said at the same time, "*Poppa!*"

They both ran down the stairs, brushed past first Slash and then Pecos. and headed for the door. The brunette opened it. A man in a ten-gallon Stetson stood just beyond it, holding a rifle and wearing a yellow oilskin. He was craggy faced, and a thick salt-and-pepper handlebar mustache mantled his broad mouth.

"Poppa!" both girls exclaimed again and threw themselves into the man's arms.

"Girls!" the man said, wrapping his arms around his daughters, hugging them tightly. "We've been worried sick about you!"

Slash and Pecos saw several other men standing in a semicircle behind him, all dressed similarly and holding rifles, casting hard gazes around the man and the girls at Slash and Pecos standing inside.

Suddenly, the girls' father looked up to cast his own hard gaze at the two men standing in the saloon. He turned his head to see the dead men piled up at the base of the bar as well as the one lying at the foot of the stairs.

He turned to the girls again, nodded at the brunette's right hand, and said urgently, "Polly, is that your blood?"

The girl shook her head and gave a vaguely devilish grin.

The man sighed in relief, then shoved the girls to one side and, his clear blue eyes acquiring a hard, wary cast, returned his gaze to Slash and Pecos. The other men stepped forward and to each side of the older man, who had the look of a rancher, and a wealthy one, judging by his clothes.

Pecos holstered his Russian and raised his right hand, palm out, in supplication. "Stand down, gents. Me an' my partner here are as pure as the mountain snows." He glanced at Slash. "Leastways in this situation . . ."

The rancher and one of the younger men—a tall, long-legged gent with a thick brown mustache, probably the older man's underling—walked into the saloon. They stopped, looked at Slash and Pecos, then at the Dutchman, who was standing behind the bar with a stricken expression. He must have cowered behind the bar when the lead had started flying, Slash silently opined.

The younger man walked over to inspect the dead men piled up near the bar. The older man walked back into the saloon's shadows to inspect the two men lying back there, then returned to the front of the saloon to stand with the younger man and to turn and face Slash and Pecos once more.

He scowled his skepticism, looking first Pecos and then Slash up and down. "Did you two take them *all* down?"

"We took care of the ones down here," Slash said. "Your daughters took care of the other two."

A smile flickered across the man's mustached mouth. He gave his head a single shake, then explained, "When the stage didn't show up at the ranch, I led my men out looking for them. My ranch sits along the stage line. We found the coach. The driver, shotgun messenger, and three passengers were dead. My Nancy and Polly were gone. We tracked the gang here. I'm Walter Benjamin. I own the Circle Six up Dogleg Canyon, north of here." He frowned curiously. "Who might you be?"

Slash and Pecos exchanged glances.

Slash shrugged, grinned. "Just a couple of raggedy-heeled old freighters takin' shelter from the storm, Mr. Benjamin."

Benjamin frowned doubtfully. He glanced at the two bedraggled girls, now standing in the doorway behind him, with his men, then turned back to Slash and Pecos. He smiled, pinched his hat brim to the pair, then turned and stepped back out the door. The younger gent followed him, glancing dubiously over his shoulder at Slash and Pecos.

"Come on, Nancy, Polly," the rancher said to the girls. "Let's get you home and into hot baths!"

When they'd thundered on out of the yard, Pecos turned to Slash and said, "Damn!"

"Yeah."

They'd returned to their meals, which had gotten cold during the melee, and the Dutchman was busy going through the dead men's pockets with a greedy little grin flashing in his eyes, when hoof thuds again sounded from beyond the closed door.

Pecos looked up at Slash. "Hope that ain't more trouble. I've done had my fill for one rainy night."

They were just finishing their cold meals and ales, which had miraculously survived the melee, when several hard thumps sounded on the stoop. The door opened a few inches, shuddering in its frame. More thumps from the stoop and then a grunt. A raspy voice said peevishly, "Come on, Donahue, ya damn weakling. *Push!*"

The door flew wide, and a cotton-headed, bespectacled little man in a wheelchair was pushed into the room by a tall, dark, mustached hombre in a long rain slicker and high-crowned black Stetson.

Slash and Pecos gaped at the little man in the push chair. They were tongue-tied for several stretched seconds before they said at the same time and in similar tones of shock and awe: "Chief Marshal Bleed-'Em-So Bledsoe, *what in holy blazes are you doing here?*"

A broad smile blossomed across the little man's cadaverous face, and his rain-splattered spectacles slid down his nose. "Nothin' like a night ride in a high-mountain lightning storm. No, sir, nothin' like it at all!"

The chief marshal, the bane of Slash and Pecos's existence, clapped his spidery hands together, threw his head back, and howled.

Chapter 4

Slash and Pecos shared another skeptical look. Neither man was yet convinced that what his eyes were telling him was true. That the devilish little cripple who doubled as their boss had really tracked them down way up here in the high and rocky, and during a frog-strangler, no less!

Still grinning like a mule eating briars—in fact, the chief marshal did resemble nothing so much as a mule, and an ugly one at that—Bledsoe looked at the carnage piled along the base of the bar to his left. He looked at the Dutchman, who was crouching over one of the dead, holding a gold pocket watch in one hand, a small coin pouch in the other hand, gazing back at the chief marshal guiltily.

Bledsoe turned to Slash and Pecos again. "Your handiwork?"

"Yeah, but we can't take the credit for them other two at the back of the room," Slash said, hooking a thumb over his shoulder.

"A pair of sisters cuter'n speckled pups took care of them," Pecos added.

Bledsoe shook his head and smiled in amazement. "Trouble dogs your heels like hungry curs, don't it, boys? Just like hungry curs." He waved his hand and was promptly pushed on into the room by the big flint-eyed deputy U.S. marshal, whom Slash and Pecos both recognized as Clifford "Skeet" Donahue.

The chief marshal and Donahue were followed into the room by two more deputy U.S. marshals, who, save for their hair and eye color, could have been Donahue's twin brothers. Both were equally flint eyed and expressionless.

Both men held rifles, and after one of them had kicked the door shut, they stood against the wall to either side of it, holding the rifles at port arms, as though ol' Bleed-'Em-So were royalty worth assassinating. On the other hand, the colicky little gent, who'd been a lawdog for the past thirty years—and a notoriously bellicose one, at that—probably had several prisons full of men who'd like nothing better than to turn him toe down and kick him out with a cold shovel.

You could throw Slash and Pecos into that category, as well.

The only reason they worked for the feisty little turd was that if they refused to, he'd have the president rescind the pardon he'd granted them when they'd agreed to work off the books for Bledsoe. They knew this because Bledsoe had told them so. It was open blackmail. The little lawdog loved nothing more than gloating over the fact that he held the fates of the two former cutthroats, whose trails he'd shadowed for most of his career, in his pale, skeletal hands.

He could cut the rope suspending the sword of Damocles over their heads any ol' time he pleased. Hell, he could do it just for fun, if he wanted to. Neither Slash nor Pecos would put it past him. But he was likely waiting for both former outlaws to die bloody while in his employ. That would give the chairbound lawdog—chairbound due to Slash's own bullet, albeit a ricochet—no end of satisfaction.

After rather aggressively kicking a chair out of the way, Donahue deposited the chief marshal at Slash and Pecos's table. He crouched to light the fat stogie Bledsoe had produced from inside his suit, then, waving out the match, retreated to a nearby table, turned a chair around, and slacked into it before crossing his long legs and digging his makings sack out of his coat pocket.

As he did, he kept shuttling his heavy-browed, owly gaze between Slash and Pecos with customary disdain for the two ex-bank and ex-train robbers. None of Bledsoe's bona fide federal lawmen approved of the two former owlhoots. Who could blame them? After all, Slash and Pecos had handed their hats to the feckless lawdogs for many a year, eluding them at every turn—until that last turn two years ago, when Slash and Pecos had tried to pull one more train robbery to fund their retirement. That there was bad blood between them was not surprising.

Slash and Pecos didn't care for the federals, whom they saw as witless civil servants, either.

Slash regarded the chairbound little man skeptically through the thick cloud of cigar smoke wreathing the air around Bledsoe's head. "You didn't ride out here just to enjoy the lightning."

"Nah, nah, of course not," Bledsoe said, waving his spidery hand again and chuckling. "But it's not all business, either. I rode to Camp Collins yesterday, figuring I'd find you there. I inquired with your lovely wife, the former outlaw queen Jaycee Breckenridge," he said, looking at Slash and grinning ironically, "and she told me you two were delivering mining supplies up the Poudre Canyon but should be headed back to town tomorrow—which, of course, is now today. Since I was headed up this way, anyway, paying a political and social call on a mine-owner friend—sort of taking an extended *working* vacation, you know?—I proceeded, figuring I'd run into you, there being only one main trail."

"And here we are," Pecos said, pitching his voice with his own brand of irony.

"And here you are."

"Don't tell me you got a job for us," Slash said, grimacing. "We're all booked up with freight runs for the rest of the summer. This is the busy time of the year for us freight jockeys, Chief."

The chief marshal turned his head toward the door and yelled, "Miss Langdon, are you coming?"

"Coming, Chief!" called a resonate female voice from somewhere out in the yard.

Slash kicked Pecos under the table and grinned.

Pecos glared at him.

Turning back to Slash and Pecos, Bledsoe said, "She slept on the way up here and wanted a moment to compose herself. I don't know why—she knew it was only you two old cutthroats we were going to see, since I had Donahue scout the barn for your wagon."

Again, Slash kicked Pecos under the table and smiled.

Pecos gave him a hard, threatening look, using only his eyes. Slash wasn't sure what would happen if ol' Bleed-'Em-So found out that Pecos and Miss Langdon had been meeting regularly in Denver and checking into the Larimer Hotel under assumed names, meeting up in each other's rooms, and behaving most unprofessionally.

So unprofessionally, in fact, that each time Pecos had returned to Fort Collins after one of their trysts, he'd slept ten hours straight and still yawned all the next day.

Now, with Slash bedeviling him in Bledsoe's very presence, Pecos's ears burned with rage. With only his eyes, he told his partner, who was grinning jeeringly across the table at him, that once they were alone again, he'd pay in a big, big way for the fun he was having at Pecos's expense.

Why, he'd kick the stuffing out of both the smaller man's ends and set it on fire!

If he got the message across, it didn't show in Slash's still mocking eyes, which he just now switched to the door as boots thumped on the stoop. The latch was tripped, and the door opened, revealing the apple of Pecos's eye—Miss Abigail Langdon, her own bewitchingly beautiful self.

"Sorry for the delay, Chief," she said in her sexily husky voice, lowering her chin demurely as she strode forward wearing a long, hooded fox-fur cape and carrying a large leather valise in her right, brown-gloved hand. She turned her head toward the bar, saw the dead men lying there in pools of their own blood, raised her brows, then turned her only mildly curious gaze to Slash and Pecos as she continued walking toward their table.

"Good evening, gentlemen," she said. "You've been busy, I see."

"Good evenin', Miss Langdon," both Slash and Pecos said at the same time.

Pecos felt his ears turn red as he watched his forbidden lover stride toward him—a big-boned Viking queen of a gal with long lake-green eyes, like a cat's eyes, and the thickest, shiniest golden hair Pecos had ever seen, now curling out from the cape's raised hood to trail down across her nicely curved bosom, which was pushing out from behind the dead fox. She was a big gal, but no gal ever wore her size better or in a more beguiling, fairy-tale-like fashion. A fella with a good imagination could picture Miss Langdon with her long golden locks in braids that tumbled down from a spiked iron helmet; her cheeks painted for war; her supple, shapely body clad in furs and leather; and with a shield in one hand, a war axe in the other.

"If you made a play for that cat-eyed beauty," Slash had once warned Pecos, "Bleed-'Em-So would throw a necktie party in your honor and play cat's cradle with your ugly head!"

Oh, how Slash had laughed!

Pecos knew he was silently laughing now at Pecos's discomfort, aggravated to a dangerous degree by the strong male pull the woman had on him. That was why he purposefully kept his eyes off Slash and tried desperately to keep a flush from rising in his cheeks and giving him . . . and the beguiling Miss Langdon . . . away to Bledsoe as the lovely golden-haired Norse-Celtic goddess approached. She walked around behind Pecos, heading for the opposite side of the table, where the chief marshal was seated, and for the life of Pecos, he did not know why he did what he did next, but do it he did—he rose abruptly from his chair. Impulsively as well as clumsily, he reached for a chair for Miss Langdon—yes, it was still "Miss Langdon," never "Abbie" or even "Abigail," even now, in the depths of their carnal mischief—and rammed his shoulder right into the poor woman.

He'd just been trying to be a gentleman, since none of the other men in the room seemed inclined to, but Pecos was a big man, considerably bigger than even the large, Nordic-boned Miss Langdon. He knocked her back and sideways as she gave a startled "Oh!"

"Oh, Lordy. I do apologize, Miss Langdon!"

Pecos grabbed the young woman's arm and pulled her toward him—again, clumsily and using too much strength. He pulled her right into him! She stepped back, blushing and looking up at him with those long jade eyes, saying, "It's quite all right . . . uh . . . Mr. Baker." She smiled and shook her head, as if to clear the cobwebs.

Pecos again attempted to pull out the chair for her, and again, in his nervousness and sudden self-consciousness, feeling that dreaded blush burning in his cheeks, he pulled it out too fast and with too much vigor and rammed it right into his leg. "*Oh!*" he grunted as the hard wooden seat barked against his knee.

To top it all off, he got his left boot caught inside the chair's left rear leg and damn near tripped and fell down, nearly pulling the chair down on top of him! "*Damn!*" he said, fighting to maintain his balance, grabbing the back of the chair with both hands.

He looked down to see both the chief marshal and Slash looking up at him skeptically, though a mocking grin was still tugging at one side of Slash's mouth and a devilish gleam shone in his eyes.

"Careful, Mr. Baker!" Miss Langdon said, grabbing his arm.

She glanced at Bledsoe and, color rising in her own beautifully sculpted cheeks now, as well, glanced at her hand on Pecos's arm and promptly removed it.

Bledsoe turned to Slash and, scowling incredulously, said, "How much has he had to drink?"

"I don't know about him," Slash said, lifting his own nearly empty schooner, "but I haven't had nearly enough!" He chuckled and polished off his beer.

Pecos composed himself and, adjusting the chair for the woman standing beside him, said, "Here you are . . . uh . . . ma'am. Take a seat right here."

"Thank you," Miss Langdon said, glancing up at him quickly, then quickly looking at Bledsoe and then down at the table as she sank into the chair. Taking a deep breath, she straightened her back and reached up with both her gloved hands to remove the cape's hood from her head.

She shook out her hair, making all those thick golden tresses fly with captivating messiness across her shoulders and down her chest. Flushed as though in the heat of war, perhaps lopping off a Roman head with a double-edged battle-ax, she was especially beautiful.

Pecos watched the distinctly alluring female maneuver, the removing of the hood and the shaking out of her hair, and for a moment Slash thought the big man was going to swallow his own tongue. The flush on Pecos's face receded, though his ears turned redder, as he sank down into his chair and looked down at the table, hoping against hope that his overenergetic attempt to play the casual gentleman hadn't exposed his and Miss Langdon's proscribed high jinks to their employer.

Slash chuckled under his breath, then cleared his throat to cover it, turned to the chief again—Bledsoe was studying Pecos a little too closely—and repeated his previous grievance. "Like I was sayin', it's a busy time of the year, Chief. Besides, I'm a married man now. I ain't gonna be able to take on as many assignments as you've been givin' me an' that big galoot yonder."

Again, he kicked Pecos under the table.

Again, Pecos hardened his jaws at him.

Miss Langdon caught the expression on Pecos's face, and again, her cheeks flushed and she stared down at the leather valise, which she'd placed on the table before her, running her thumb absently across the monogram.

Safely distracted, Bledsoe looked at Slash and gave a wolfish chuckle. "Oh, you think so, do you?"

"Sorry, Chief," Slash said, opening his hands, "but we've risked life and limb for you a good many times now. Gonna have to cut back. Ain't as young as we used to be, neither. Hell, Pecos over there is gettin' so damn old, he almost kills himself just tryin' to pull a chair out for a pretty lady!"

"Slash," Pecos said, keeping his voice low with menace, "you an' me are gonna have us a little powwow tonight."

"Me?" Slash said. "I don't have any Injun blood, an' neither do you, so take off the war paint."

"Gentlemen, gentlemen," Bledsoe said, glancing back over his shoulder at Donahue and rolling his eyes, as if to say, "Why in the blazes do I put up with this pair of cork-headed tinhorns?" Turning back to Slash, he held up his cigar and said, "Miss Langdon, would you please produce that amnesty from the president of the United States? My cigar went out."

"Oh, hell!" Slash said, glaring now at the marshal. "This

sorta thing was outlawed at the end of the War Between the States, Chief!"

"No, this kind of thing was not outlawed at war's end." Bledsoe placed a spidery hand, splay-fingered, on the table and leaned so close to Slash that Slash could smell his breath, which reeked of the cigar and the brandy he'd likely sipped on his journey through the storm. "If by 'this thing,' you mean you two old scalawags are mine, all mine, *to do with as I please*, or you're both going to be the guests of honor at your own necktie party!"

Chapter 5

The chief marshal pulled his head back and closed his fingers together on the table.

"Now, then, let's get down to brass tacks. I have a brandy and a good cigar waiting for me at Grant Mitchell's place over at Storm Mountain. The job I have for you is embarrassingly simple as well as easy, so don't get your drawers in a bunch. Should take you a week at the most. It's *so* simple and easy that I would send one of my junior deputies, but I have all of them chasing counterfeiters out Utah way. These three have their hands full keeping vengeance-seeking ex-cons from feeding me pills I can't digest. So, I am sending you and the dancing bear over here."

Pecos glanced at Miss Langdon and flushed. Miss Langdon averted her gaze and tucked her fetching lower lip under her equally fetching upper lip to cover a smile.

"A week, huh?" Pecos said, miffed by the old bastard's jibe. "That's what you always tell us, Chief."

"Well, this time I'm not lying. I promise." Bledsoe chuckled at his own wit. "All you have to do is ride up into the mountains, to a town named Frisco in the Sowbelly Mountains, and kidnap a showgirl away from her acting troupe. Her name is Hazel Leadbetter, though she performs under the name Fannie Diamond. You're to issue her a subpoena and escort her back to Denver to testify at a murder trial."

"Who's on trial for murder?" Slash asked as Miss Langdon stood her valise on the table and opened it.

"Her beau's first cousin and fellow gang member, Chaz 'the Knife' Lutz. Her gentleman friend—and I use the term *gentleman* very loosely, if not inappropriately altogether—happens to be the notorious outlaw Duke Winter. Winter and the Knife are close as brothers. I want her to testify against Lutz and spill the beans about where Winter and the rest of his gang are holed up. They're some of the nastiest bank robbers in the whole damn territory . . . since you two hung up your flour sack masks, that is, and—"

"We weren't nasty!" Pecos objected, casting another quick, furtive glance at the golden-haired object of his desire, who looked at the table again. "In fact, we were right polite."

"Yeah," Slash chimed in. "We always said, '*Please* open the vault, Mr. Banker, before we blow your lights out,' didn't we, Pecos?"

"Sure 'nuff did!" Pecos glanced at Miss Langdon and winked.

Slash would be damned if she didn't blush again, beautifully, and look shyly down at the table. He was starting to get a little worried that Pecos was going to leap out of his chair and onto the gal, and that it would take him and all three of Bledsoe's deputies to separate the fairly salivating lovers.

"Now, then," Bledsoe said with an air of irritable impatience, "shall we get back to the matter at hand?" He glanced at his assistant. "Miss Langdon, the photo of Fannie Diamond, please."

"Yes, Chief Marshal." The Viking beauty dipped a pale, long-fingered hand into the valise and pulled out a photograph. She handed it to Bledsoe, who examined it first, then held it up before him so that both Slash and Pecos, sitting to either side of him, could study it.

In the photograph, a fetching young woman posed between a fake rock and a fake barrel cactus in some photographer's studio dressed up to look like the Sonoran Desert. The fetching young woman, with a heart-shaped face and long, flowing black hair, was decked out in some non-Indian showman's idea of an Indian dress, though neither Slash nor Pecos had ever seen an Indian maiden wearing anything half as gaudy as the frock on this gal, or wearing a single string of what appeared to be pearls encircling her fair-skinned neck. A big bone-handled knife resided in an ornately beaded sheath rested on her right hip.

"This is Miss Diamond in a theater photograph for a production of *Apache Jane*."

"*Apache Jane*?" Slash asked with a chuckle.

"*Apache Jane*. Apparently, Jane tumbles for a soldier, is kicked out of her tribe by her Apache family, and comes to a sad end after a skirmish with a mountain lion while on the run from her soldier lover in the desert after finding him in the arms of her saloon girl!" Bledsoe laughed and slapped the table. "Who do they find to make this stuff up?" He chuckled again and shook his head. "Anyway, she's currently in a production of *Madame Margueritte: Portrait of a Courtesan* at the Frisco Opera House. Right popular show, I hear. You shouldn't have any trouble tracking her down. Just follow the horde of drunken miners, an' they'll likely lead you right to her!"

"What?" Pecos said doubtfully. "You want us to pull her off the stage in the middle of a performance?"

"I don't care what you have to do to get her here. Just get her here. She's apparently fallen under Duke Winter's spell, for she's been his *close friend*, shall we say, for several years. He started sparking her when she was just a kid in pigtails runnin' loose among those gold camps up thataway, before she went to some theatrical school in St. Louis, returned to the mountains, and became famous. I've sent lawmen up there to get her to inform on Winter, but she denies knowing him. We know she's his sweetheart, because they've been seen together many times—even right here in Denver, the actress on Winter's arm. We think he holes up somewhere in the mountains above Frisco, but those rugged peaks are a maze.

"We need the girl to tell us where we can find him and to testify against 'the Knife' Lutz. We've learned that she saw him murder the owner of an opera house in Idaho Springs. Apparently, the man refused to allow Miss Diamond to perform on his stage due to the way she worked up the crowd. Winter and Miss Diamond were present. An old swamper saw the killin' through a crack in the door and reported it to the local sheriff, who reported it to me. I sent several federals up that way to arrest both Lutz and Winter, but they could find only Lutz. He was whorin', as usual, and three sheets to the wind.

"Winter, the slipperiest of the pair, had returned to the gang's outlaw lair, wherever in hell that is. We have one witness who saw her witness the murder. That witness will testify against Lutz, but since she's old and rather feeble, we want Miss Diamond to seal the deal, as it were. Threatened with prison if she doesn't, for aiding and abetting known outlaws, I'm guessing she will."

"So you want us to kidnap a showgirl," Slash said, sharing a dubious glance with Pecos.

"*Actress*," Bledsoe said with an ironic smile before puffing his stogie.

"Sounds like a sorry business to me," Pecos said. "Why don't you send Donahue?" He glanced at the tall federal badge-toter sitting back in his chair, legs crossed, smoking.

Donahue responded with only a wry chuff.

"Donahue's a senior deputy," Bledsoe said. "Such menial labor is beneath him. Besides, he watches my backside."

Slash and Pecos shared another look—a sour one this time.

Bledsoe looked at Miss Langdon. "Miss Langdon, do you have the railroad tickets as well as the other documents I wrote up for these two?"

"Of course." She dipped a hand into the valise, extracted a large manila envelope, and set it in the middle of the table. Slash and Pecos stared down at it as though it were a dog turd.

"The tickets inside that envelope are dated day after tomorrow," Bledsoe said, wheeling himself back away from the table. "There's sundry other documents you'll need to read . . . if either one of you *can* read . . . before you reach Frisco." He gave a caustic snort, then glanced at his secretary. "Miss Langdon, shall we? You're probably ready for a hot bath. And I am ready for a brandy and one of Grant Mitchell's fine cigars." He looked distastefully at his own half-smoked stogie and dropped it on the floor.

He glanced over his shoulder. "Donahue."

Donahue donned his hat, lifted his big frame from his chair, and began pushing the chief marshal toward the door. "Good luck, gentlemen," Bledsoe called, with a brief wave of his spidery hand. "Not that you'll need it. An easier job I can't imagine. Not even you two should screw this one up." He laughed raucously. "Good night!"

With that, Donahue pushed the chief marshal out the door.

Pecos rose quickly as Miss Langdon rose from her chair. Slash rose then, as well.

Miss Langdon glanced up at Pecos, whose ears had pinkened again when Bledsoe had mentioned Miss Langdon's hot bath. She glanced at the chief marshal being pushed outside by Donahue, then gave Pecos an intimate little smile and whispered, "I'll see you when you get back." She brushed her hand across his.

"Yes, you will," Pecos returned, keeping his own voice at a whisper, so the two marshals still standing on either side of the door wouldn't overhear.

Miss Langdon strode out the door. The two remaining federal men in the saloon each gave Slash and Pecos snide glances before they followed her out into the night.

"You two are cuter'n speckled pups," Slash said to Pecos.

"Oh, shut up!" Pecos returned, slacking back down in his chair. "I oughta bust your butt!"

"You'd have to catch me first," Slash said, sagging back down in his own chair.

"Do you think ol' Bleed-'Em-So suspects me an' Miss Langdon?"

"You're still alive, aren't ya?" Slash turned his head to yell, "Hey, Dutchman, how 'bout a pair more beers?"

Pecos reached under the table to caress his shin. "I didn't appreciate those kicks under the table, you blackhearted son of Satan!" But then Pecos dipped his chin and smiled from beneath his brows. "She likes me, though, don't she?"

"I thought she was gonna pass out from the vapors," Slash said, chuckling.

The Dutchman had retreated from Bledsoe and the other federals to a back room. Nothing like federals to make a mountain man nervous. Now he surfaced and headed back behind the bar. When he'd drawn two beers, he set a schooner down in front of each man, then returned to his work of looting the dead still piled up at the base of the bar.

Slash sucked the foam off the top of his glass and grinned at his partner. "What've you two been up to in Denver, anyway, to put such high color in that gal's cheeks?"

"A gentleman don't share his secrets . . . especially with a fork-tailed devil like you." Pecos blew foam from his beer and sipped. "It ain't gonna last, though."

"Bledsoe?"

"Him an' . . . Well . . . let's face it, Slash. She's twenty-some-odd years younger than me. Sooner or later a younger man's gonna wander into her life. Just like he should." Pecos stared glumly into his beer.

"Ah, hell," Slash said, crouched forward to trough an Indian Kid rolling paper between his thumb and index finger and to dribble Durham onto it from a leather pouch. "Enjoy it while it lasts. Me? I'm feelin' steamed about havin' to leave Jay again just as soon as I get back to town."

"Oh, well," Pecos said. "If that old devil ain't lyin', it'll be short work for good money."

"It better be." Slash snapped a match to life on his thumbnail, touched the flame to his quirley, and inhaled deeply, smiling dreamily, pretending the smoke was the perfume of his lovely bride waiting for him back in her warm boudoir in Camp Collins.

Chapter 6

In fact, at the same moment, the former Jaycee Brecken-ridge, who had become Mrs. James "Slash" Braddock six months ago, was just then yelling: "Scully Fieldbottom, if I've told you once, I've told you a thousand times to keep your *cotton-pickin' hands off my girls!*"

She punctuated the admonition by smashing the hide-wrapped bung starter, which she'd grabbed from behind the bar in her House of a Thousand Delights in Fort Collins, against the back of the big, long-haired miner's head. The beefy gent released the scantily clad girl he'd practically been mauling in the saloon's main drinking hall, but to Jay's astonishment, despite the wallop she'd just given him, he remained on his feet.

He shook his shaggy head, as if to clear the cobwebs. His long, greasy, tangled hair flew around his head, sending out an odor that burned Jay's eyes. He swung around to face her. She stood a whole head shorter than the big, ugly bruiser, who now strode heavily toward her, squeezing his hamlike hands into red fists.

His flat, feral eyes blazed with drunken anger.

"Look out, Miss Jay!" yelled one of the check-suited male customers standing at the bar. "When Scully gets like this, he'll tear you limb from limb!"

Jay knew that was true. Scully Fieldbottom had been thrown out of every respectable saloon in town, including hers multiple times. Still, though she'd banned the big, smelly, buckskin-clad man long ago, he somehow managed to skulk in from time to time, usually after he'd put a load on in one of the less respectable watering holes in town, and grab one of Jay's girls.

Which was what he'd done tonight.

Jay backed away from the man, noting that though the place had about fifteen male customers in it, none of them seemed in a hurry to rush to her rescue. They were all aware of Fieldbottom's reputation for mindless savagery. Jay's two bouncers, the Chinaman Ki-Lin and the Irishman O'Connell, would have rushed over with their own batons, but she'd given both men the night off—Ki-Lin because he was sick, and O'Connell because it was his fiancée's birthday.

As Fieldbottom stumbled toward her, lower jaw jutting with fury, Jay realized she might have bit off more than she could chew. But this wasn't her first rodeo. She saw two townsmen start to walk reluctantly toward her, feeling compelled to play the role of her shiny-armored knights, but she thrust out her left hand at them, palm out.

"Stay there, gentlemen. I can handle Mr. Fieldbottom here just fine on my own."

A couple of the customers grimaced, while a couple more sucked air through their gritted teeth in dread.

Fieldbottom's broad, pitted, savage face crinkled with a smile as he drew within four feet of Jay, who stopped backing away from him now and reached behind the red silk belt encircling her narrow waist and plucked out her ace in the hole—a brass-barreled, over-and-under Lady Derringer with an alluringly attired young doxie engraved, cameo-style, in the grips.

She raised the handsome little popper, aimed at Fieldbottom's broad forehead beneath his moth-eaten watch cap, and clicked back one of the two hammers.

"Out," she said crisply, narrowing one eye as she aimed down the stubby barrel. "The next time I see you in here, I am going to drill a bullet through your big, ugly head. Do you understand? Grunt twice if you understand."

The bearlike man glowered down the double-bore's barrels, slid his enraged eyes to Jaycee, and curled his nostrils. He stared at the two barrels, and then he raised his gaze to her eyes. They were a bear's eyes, flat with mindless rage as well as drink.

He flared both big nostrils at her, gave a guttural cry of deep frustration, then turned and ambled off toward the front of the room, turning his head to cast his owly gaze over his shoulder at Jay. He climbed the three steps to the door, stopped in front of the batwings, and looked at Jay over his shoulder again, giving her one more threatening parting glare.

Fieldbottom pushed out through the batwings, and before the louvered doors had stopped swinging back into place, the room erupted in congratulatory applause. Jay's working girls, stationed here and there with men around the room, applauded loudest. The one who called herself Texas Tina, though her real name was Dora Muldoon, stuck two fingers between her lips and whistled loudly.

"Thank you!" Jay called into the din and, folding her right arm across her waist, gave a courtly bow. She had to admit, though, if only to herself, that the giant man's last glare at her had chilled her. "After all that," she said, "I think I need a breath of fresh air." She looked at the middle-aged, bald, livery-attired barman standing behind the bar. "Man the store for me, will you, Pete?"

"Sure will, Miss Jay," Pete returned, running a towel around the inside of a cut glass goblet. "By the way, I'd have come to your rescue, but I remembered the Lady D in your belt." He winked at his boss.

"Rest assured, I know you would have, Pete!" Jay called

with one of her usual winning smiles and a wave as she walked up the steps to the batwings.

She pushed through the batwings and stepped out onto the saloon's broad front veranda, which was wedge shaped, as the front of the building faced the corner of the town's main drag. It was high summer, but there was a chill in the air, as there often was in the evening here on the Rocky Mountain Front Range.

She peered to her right along the street, to where Slash and Pecos's freight yard sat off the street's left side, where the otherwise east–west-running street doglegged to the south. All dark over there, which meant the two former outlaws turned freighters weren't back yet from their freight run up the Poudre Canyon. It had rained a little earlier here in town, which meant it had probably rained harder up in the mountains. The men had probably decided to hole up for the night and give the storm a chance to move out over the plains before they resumed their journey.

Jay supposed she should be happy that that was what they'd probably done. They'd be safer that way, as the narrow Poudre Canyon was always a flash-flood risk during mountain downpours, which usually came nearly every afternoon this time of the year. Still, she missed Slash. Since they'd been married, they'd been apart only a few times—when Slash and Pecos had been off on freight runs and when they'd been sent out on a dangerous mission by the deplorable chief marshal Bledsoe.

Jay had gotten used to having her man around, and she liked going to sleep at night with his arms wrapped around her, his chin resting on her shoulder. She'd missed that after her former lover, Pistol Pete Johnson, was killed by one of Bledsoe's men in a box canyon in the San Juan Mountains—something Slash wrongly blamed himself for because he'd led the Snake River Marauders into that canyon, which had only one way in and one way out. In the wake of Pete's death, she'd spent six years alone in a remote mountain cabin, and while she'd grown accustomed to a solitary life, she preferred sharing her days and nights with a man she loved and who loved her in kind.

She hated to admit it even to herself, because she saw herself as a stouthearted gal slow to scare even during the most trying of times, but her encounter with the big bruiser Scully Fieldbottom had shaken her. If he'd had his way, he'd have broken her like a matchstick. Those cold, feral eyes still burned into her, and she felt a cold knot in her belly.

Something told her that her encounters with the brutal giant were not over. Well, she knew very well what had told her that. The man had promised as much with his ominous gaze. Reflecting on that dark look, she suddenly realized that she was alone out here and that the street beyond the lamplight angling out of the windows of her own establishment was nearly as dark as the inside of a glove.

Fear touched her. What if Fieldbottom was on the prowl out here, maybe lying in wait for her? Crossing her arms on her breasts, she turned toward the batwings. She started forward, toward the welcome light and reassuring hum of conversation just beyond those louvered doors, but stopped when hoof thuds rose in the street to the west.

Three or four horseback riders were trotting toward her.

She turned back to the street, frowning with interest, as three man- and horse-shaped shadows appeared in the darkness to her left—one man in a cream hat on a cream horse and two other men on darker-colored horses. As they approached the Thousand Delights, they swung their horses up to one of the four hitchracks, at which three other saddled mounts stood hang-headed. One of those mounts lifted its head and gave a loud, echoing whinny, which made Jay, in her current anxious mood, jerk with a start.

She jerked again when the tied horse's whinny was answered in kind by the cream, which was just then nosing up to the same hitchrack.

Astride the cream was a tall, broad-shouldered man in a high-crowned cream Stetson, corduroy jacket, and string tie. Long gray side-whiskers framed his broad, sun-seasoned face, the features of which Jay could now make out since the lamplight from the saloon's windows illuminated all three newcomers.

"Hello, Grant," Jay said, recognizing the tall man astride the cream as a prominent local rancher, Grant Balldinger, who also sat on the city council and just about every other council in the county. He was also on the school board and was president of the local stockmen's association. "What brings you to town this late?"

Balldinger swung his head toward Jay, whom he likely hadn't seen in the veranda's shadows, and said, "Oh, hello there, Jay. The boys and I decided to ride in for a late supper. Been at it hard on the range all day and didn't feel like cooking." Being from Texas by way of Louisiana, he had a mossy-soft Southern accent.

"Hello, Miss Jay," said one of the other two men, Balldinger's son, Todd, who'd drawn his horse up to Balldinger's right. The other rider, Balldinger's foreman, Ace Calloway, had drawn his horse up to the rancher's left.

"Hello, Todd. How are you?"

"Just fine, ma'am."

"And you, Ace?" Jay asked the foreman, a tight-lipped, cold-eyed man whom Jay had never warmed to, though he, as well as father and son Balldinger, were loyal customers.

"Just fine, ma'am," Calloway said through a grunt as he and the other two men swung down from their mounts.

"The beer cold, Miss Jay?" asked Todd Balldinger The rangy lad, dressed nearly all in black save the pearl-gripped six-shooter holstered in a black holster on his right thigh, attested to the fact that the young man, all of twenty or twenty-one, fancied himself a bit of a pistolero. He hurried up the porch steps, pinching his hat brim to Jay.

"Isn't it always?" Jay asked genially. "I pay good money for that ice, so it had better be cold!"

Todd chuckled and spur-rattled his way across the veranda and through the batwings, followed closely by the expressionless foreman, who passed Jay with only an all-business nod of his head before pushing his own way through the batwings.

"Jay, I lied." Grant Balldinger had come up the steps behind Calloway but stopped now, placing one hand-tooled leather boot on the veranda and keeping the other one on the first step below it. He looked up at Jay, smiling broadly beneath the wide brim of his crisp Stetson banded with braided rawhide. His brown eyes, which always seemed a little flat and cold, despite the fact that he always smiled a lot—a businessman's slightly unctuous smile—flashed in the amber light pushing out from over the batwings. "I didn't come just for supper and suds."

"You . . . didn't . . . ?" Jay asked uncertainly.

A widower, Balldinger had once pursued Jay before she'd married Slash, but she hadn't been interested. She hoped that wasn't what he was up to now—especially given the fact that he was well aware that she and Slash had tied the knot.

"Oh, don't worry," the man said, broadening his toothy smile. "I didn't come to ask you out again. No, no. I can't say I've ever approved of Slash Braddock—in fact, I think that that old outlaw is much too far beneath you for you to have hitched your star to his wagon—but what's done is done. You chose him over me, and I've done licked my wounds."

"Grant, please," Jay said, frowning her disapproval at the impropriety of the man's remarks. What business did he have voicing his disapproval of the man she'd chosen to marry?

What nerve! She was about to tell him that very thing when he blurted out suddenly, "Jay, I've come to make you an offer on the Thousand Delights."

"Oh!" Jay said, shocked and befuddled, splaying her fingers across her chest. She gave a strained, uncertain smile, chuckling throatily. "But . . . Grant . . . the Thousand Delights . . . It's . . . it's not for sale. I have no intention of selling."

The rancher smiled more broadly at her, his eyes determined. "Come on." He winked, closed his hand around her wrist, stepped forward, and gave her arm a firm tug. "Let's go inside and talk about it."

She frowned with bewilderment. Why would the man think she'd entertain an offer on her business, which, next to Slash, was the light of her life? Everyone in Camp Collins knew that. Still, she followed him, haltingly, feeling another bout of anxiousness. Nothing like what Fieldbottom had evoked. But still . . .

She hadn't liked the hard, determined look in Balldinger's eyes.

Just before she stepped through the batwings, she cast her gaze toward the still dark freight yard again. She sure wished Slash were here.

Chapter 7

Slash and Pecos pulled their freight wagon into Camp Collins around noon the next day.

Pecos was driving. He swung the wagon up in front of the county sheriff's office—a two-story wood-frame building that housed not only the sheriff's office but the tax assessor and the county attorneys, as well. There was a jail extension in back, between the sheriff's office and the county courthouse, which wasn't much larger than this older building.

"Home, sweet home," Pecos said as he set the brake.

"For a few hours," Slash grouched. He'd been dozing, but now he lifted his head and cuffed his black hat up off his forehead.

"Ah, hell. It'll be a quick trip, Slash. You'll be back in that fancy suite of rooms of yours an' Jay's in no time."

Slash turned to his partner with a scowl of deep aggravation on his sun-seasoned, darkly handsome features. "I sure wish ol' Bleed-'Em-So would let us out of this deal. How long does he think we can keep troubleshooting for him, anyway? Look at us, Pecos. We ain't young men anymore!"

"Tell me about it. Hell, I'm reminded of that as soon as I set my gimpy old feet on the floor every morning. Then, again, I don't have a carpeted floor like you an' Jay do!"

"Well, move over to the Thousand Delights. Hell, Jay'll set you up in style—likely for free!"

"Ah, hell, I couldn't ask her to do that. Besides, someone has to keep an eye on the freight yard. Now with Myra havin' moved over to Ma Ellison's boardinghouse, I'm the only one there."

"Did I just hear my name?" said a young woman's pleasant-sounding voice.

Slash and Pecos turned to see Myra Thompson herself step out of the sheriff's office with her arm hooked through that of the tall, lanky, bucktoothed deputy Delbert Thayer, who, in his early twenties, was close to the age of young Myra, who was twenty. She'd been living with Slash and Pecos at the freight yard, where they'd hired her to keep the account books and do the billing, though she did far more than that, including securing freighting contracts. In fact, they both doubted they'd stay in business without the orphaned, former outlaw girl's practical and parsimonious oversight.

After Slash had moved over to Jay's saloon, Myra had moved into the boardinghouse. It hadn't been exactly right and proper for her to be living with two bachelors even before Slash had moved out. But afterward, her living with just one had seemed even less proper. She'd begun dating young Deputy Thayer, and she'd wanted to make a good impression on the young man's family, and her living with another man—especially one so much older than she, and a former notorious outlaw, no less—would likely give the wrong impression altogether.

Pecos didn't mind. She'd once set her hat for him, and while he loved Myra like a daughter, that was the only kind of love he felt for her. She was even younger than Abigail Langdon. He'd been relieved when she'd started stepping out with Delbert. He had to admit it got a little quiet these days around the freight yard, however.

"Well, hello there, honey," Pecos said. "I was just tellin' Slash why I can't move over to the Thousand Delights with him an' Jay. Someone needs to keep an eye on the freight yard."

"Ain't you lookin' spiffy?" Slash said.

It was true. The slender gal, pretty with auburn hair, a cute little figure, and a brown-eyed, heart-shaped face, appeared to be wearing a new red dress with a wasp waist and white lace at the neck and sleeves. Leastways, Slash had never seen her in it before. The little straw hat pinned to her hair owned a natty spray of silk flowers and a black bow.

Myra lowered her head demurely, blushing, two endearing dimples showing in her cheeks. "Why, thank you, Slash."

"And I'll be hanged, Delbert, if you're not wearing a suit coat and a string tie!" Pecos chimed in. "Where you two headed, anyways? You ain't lightin' out to elope, now, are you? I, for one, wanna come to the weddin'!"

It was the young deputy's turn to color up like a Colorado sunset. "Ah, heck, no," he said, customarily shy and awkward. He glanced down at Myra, who stood a whole head shorter than he, and laughed through his buckteeth.

"Del is taking me to the new hotel for lunch," Myra said. "He even reserved us a table in the Colorado room."

"Well, I'll be hanged," Slash said. "What's the occasion, pray tell?"

"No occasion," Del said, beaming down at his blushing girl. "Don't need to be no special occasion to take the purtiest gal in all of Colorado out for a fine fried-chicken lunch with all the surroundin's!"

"You got a point there," Pecos said. "You two run along an' have fun. We just stopped to drop off a pair of saddlebags loaded with stolen money we come upon up in the Poudre Canyon last night."

"Stolen money?" Myra said with brow-raised interest.

"Who stole what money, an' how did you two come upon it?" Suddenly, she clapped a white-gloved hand to her mouth with a gasp and widened her eyes. "You two didn't have a weak night and slide back to your former ways, did you? Oh, please tell me you haven't!"

Slash and Pecos chuckled.

"Nah, nah. Now, don't worry, honey," Slash said. "I gotta admit, it wasn't real easy to haul that loot all the way down the canyon without considering, for a time or two, how much fun we could have with it. But it was only a time or two, and we talked ourselves out of it."

Pecos reached down and picked the saddlebags up off the floor of the driver's box. "Here they are right here, and all the money that was in there when we come upon 'em is there, though it pains me to say so, right enough! The money belongs to the Poudre River stage line, which was robbed last night up the canyon, driver an' shotgun messenger and three passengers killed, don't ya know?"

"I'll take 'em inside and lock 'em up," Del said, releasing Myra's arm and stepping forward. "The sheriff ain't in just now, but I'll tell him about the loot after lunch." He glanced at Myra, his eyes suddenly all business. "He'll probably want me to ride up there with him this afternoon and do a thorough investigation of such a travesty!"

Myra turned to Slash and Pecos and tucked her upper lip beneath her lower teeth. "I just swoon when he talks like that!"

Again, Slash and Pecos chuckled.

"You're a gentleman and a scholar," Pecos said, handing the bags down to the string bean. "Slash is in a hurry to see his sweetheart, don't ya know? Me? I'm ready for lunch my ownself."

"The sheriff knows where to find us if he needs a statement or some such," Slash said. "You'll find all eight outlaws lyin' toe up at the Dutchman's place ten miles up the canyon."

"The Dutchman's place, eh?" The young deputy's eyes widened. "Did you fellas take 'em *all* down?"

Slash and Pecos glanced at each other.

"Nope, can't claim that," Slash said. "We had help." He couldn't help chuckling as he remembered the little blond gal's handiwork with that big silver-chased Colt.

Del gave a snort as he glanced at Myra. "I was gonna say you two are gettin' a little long in the tooth for tangling with that many owlhoots!" He chuckled.

Myra gave Slash and Pecos an apologetic smile for her socially awkward beau. "Del," she said, "why don't you take those saddlebags inside, hon? I'm gettin' awful hungry."

"Be right back, sweetheart! See ya, fellas."

When the deputy had hauled the saddlebags inside, Myra turned to Slash and Pecos and said, "Sorry about Del, fellas."

"Nah, hell," Pecos said. "He's right."

"We are a little long in the tooth, and that's a natural fact," Slash said, pinching his hat brim to the girl as Pecos shook the ribbons over the mules' backs and the wagon rolled forward.

"It ain't easy gettin' old," Slash said as Pecos steered the wagon along the bustling main drag, heading for the Thousand Delights.

"No, it ain't, but at least your purty gal's waitin' for you to help take your mind off it." Pecos nodded to indicate the beautiful Jaycee Breckenridge was standing on the broad front veranda of the Thousand Delights.

Jay was like a sailor's wife, waiting for her man on a pier stretching into an ocean, gazing seaward.

Slash feasted his eyes on the lovely gal, the thick tresses of her copper hair framing her pretty oval face and spilling down over her bare freckled shoulders. She wore a gown nearly the same green of her eyes, and a neck choker adorned with three sequins in a diamond pattern.

Seeing the two men on the wagon trundling toward her, Jay raised her arm and waved heartily, smiling beautifully.

"Darlin', if you ain't a sight for these sore eyes!" Slash said as Pecos angled the mules up to the base of the saloon's broad porch steps.

"Slash! Pecos! I've been worried!"

"Weather held us up," Pecos told her.

"That's what I figured, but I was still worried about this handsome fellow of mine," Jay said, hiking her skirts up as she walked down the steps, the hair bouncing on her shoulders glinting in the midday sunshine, sequins flashing at her neck. "And you, too, of course, Pecos. That goes without saying, you big lug!"

She smiled up at the taller of the two former outlaws, and then, when Slash had climbed quickly down to the street and turned to her, she threw herself into his arms, kissed him passionately and then buried her face in his chest. "I've missed you!"

Slash laughed as he rocked his pretty wife in his arms. "I've missed you, too, honey!" He glanced at Pecos. "Partner, you mind puttin' the mules an' the wagon up yourself? I'll do it next time."

"Sure, sure, partner. Not a problem. Well, I'll be leavin' you lovebirds alone," Pecos said, shaking the ribbons over the mules' backs.

Jay turned to him as he swung the mules out into the street. "Pecos, don't hurry off. Come in and have lunch with us."

"Nah," the big man said, swinging the mules and the wagon around and heading back in the direction of the freight yard. "You know what they say about fifth wheels. Hy-yahh!"

Jay looked up at Slash, frowning. "What's the matter with him?"

"Not sure," Slash said, staring after his friend of almost forty years, dust lifting behind the wagon's rolling wheels. "I think he's . . . I think he's *lonely*, Jay."

* * *

Pecos drove the wagon into the implement barn at the freight yard, then unhitched the mules, fed and watered them, rubbed then down, and curried both animals carefully.

That job took him close to an hour.

Afterward, he looked at the long, low clapboard shack on the other side of the yard, which he and Pecos and Myra Thompson used to live in together. The place glowed new-penny copper in the lens-clear Colorado sunshine, but it looked as lonely as a mausoleum. Rather than head inside right away, he doped each of the wagon's wheels from the jockey box residing beneath the driver's boot, then spent some more time—longer than the job really needed—soaping harness leather.

By the time he'd swept out the barn and turned the mules into the corral, it was getting late in the day, shadows bleeding out from the toothy ridges, including the prominent local landmark Horsetooth Rock, west of town, and angling over the growing, bustling town itself.

He went inside and drank several dipperfuls of water, then threw a sandwich together from salted beef and a wheel of cheese from the keeper shed. After that he boiled water for a bath and soaked for a good long time, sipping whiskey and smoking a quirley and watching the light fade in the windows.

He looked around the wooden-floored hovel.

Slash was gone and Myra was gone. Myra did most of her freight company work from the boardinghouse now, coming here only when she needed Pecos to sign something. Few signs of her and Slash remained.

Just Pecos here now.

Over his long years on the frontier, the Pecos River Kid had always had a woman. Or nearly always, anyway. That was how he and Slash had been different. Slash had been a solitary soul. Pecos had always had a big, tender heart, and he'd tumbled for one woman after another. He'd always tumbled hard and ached like hell when he and the gal forked trails. He wasn't sure why, but he'd never been able to stick with just one long enough to get married.

But, then, hell, he'd been an outlaw. He'd been married to the outlaw trail.

And to Slash Braddock, if the truth be known. Not in any weird way. But he'd always been—hell, *still was*, despite Slash's having gotten hitched—closer to Slash than to anyone else in his life.

Now he supposed he had Miss Langdon. But not really. She was too young for him. Oh, she obviously enjoyed his company, but what she and Pecos had wouldn't last. It was just for kicks and giggles, mostly. Eventually, she'd find herself another, younger man, and she'd move on.

And right she should. Pecos was too old for her.

"Ah, hell," Pecos said, scolding himself for feeling sorry for himself. Leaning back against the tub, he blew smoke rings at the shaded brown ceiling.

He wouldn't admit as much to Slash, but he was looking forward to getting back on the trail again with his partner tomorrow. That seemed the only place he was happy anymore.

When it was just him and Slash.

Chapter 8

"Slash, did you see that?" Pecos asked his partner the next day, as they rode the narrow-gauge Buckhorn line into the mountains west of Denver, heading for the little mountain mining town of Frisco, in the Sowbelly Range.

"I saw it."

"What'd you make of it?"

"Twelve-gauge double-bore. Both barrels sawed off just above the forestock. Each has one. Saw 'em both as they both sat down."

"Concealed by their dusters."

"Because they don't want anyone to see 'em?"

"Why else would you wear a gut shredder inside your duster?"

"Exactly," Slash said, raking his thumbnail down his jaw, which he'd cleanly shaven in the wee hours of the morning, while listening to his lovely bride, Jay, snore softly in the warm bed he'd pried himself out of at 4:00 a.m. and cursing Chief Marshal Bledsoe under his breath.

Slash turned to Pecos where they sat roughly three-quarters of the way down from the front of the hot, smoky passenger car, on the car's left side, tailbones grinding into the thinly velour-upholstered wooden seats. Both freighters-turned–Bledsoe's actress nappers sat next to the window, Slash facing forward, Pecos facing Slash, their war bags and rifles piled on the seats beside them.

Pecos glanced over his right shoulder once more at the two men who'd just taken seats on the other side of the aisle from them and one row up toward the front of the car. Pecos turned to Slash. Keeping his voice low, though it was so noisy in the car, what with the squawking of the couplers and the clacking of the heavy wheels over the rail seams, he'd have to have practically yelled for the two gents to overhear him, he said, "Wouldn't the joke be on us if us two old train robbers got robbed on a train?"

"I wouldn't be laughin'."

"What're we gonna do?"

"I don't know. While I've robbed many a train, I've never been robbed on one."

"Well, we got the advantage of knowin' how it's done, at least."

"Yeah." Slash looked around. "There's gotta be more than those two men. We usually put four men in a car: One up front, near the front door, the other one near the back, by the rear door."

"Don't look around so damn much. They'll think we're on to 'em!" Pecos wheezed, scowling.

Slash turned his head back forward. "I think I picked out the one at the rear. See the fella in the bowler hat sittin' by himself, readin' the paper, on the aisle seat?"

Pecos swept the rear of the car with his gaze, beyond the ten or so regular folk asleep or palavering with bored airs in the seats between him and the rear door ahead of him. An old lady had a wicker chicken cage on the seat beside her. The barred rock hen inside the cage was clucking at the old lady, like a dog wanting a treat. The old lady, who wore a brightly patterned scarf over her gray head, was asleep sitting up, her jowly head lolling a little to one side, her eyes closed but fluttering, as though the chicken were keeping her from dropping into a deeper snooze.

Pecos picked out the man Slash had indicated. Again, he scowled at Slash. "What makes you think it's him?"

"What? You think it's the old lady or the priest?"

"Could be the fancy Dan in the checked suit, wearin' a pinky ring."

"He's a gambler. Besides, who wears a pinky ring to rob a train?"

Pecos chuckled, glanced cautiously over his left shoulder, glad the two men with the shotguns hadn't seemed to notice him and Slash. They both sat with their hatted heads bowed, as though in prayer, catching a few winks.

Or wanting to appear to be.

"Who wears a pinky ring to do *anything*?"

"You can say that again." Slash shook his head. "Nah, it's one of the two I picked out." He was gazing toward the front of the train over Pecos's left shoulder, sweeping his gaze from left to right and back again. "I'm trying to pick out the other one."

It wasn't easy going, however, because all he could see were the backs of the twenty or so passengers' heads. There appeared to be several cowpunchers, a few businessmen, two old ladies sitting together, both with their heads down as they slept, and an old man and a little boy sitting together, looking down, as though they were playing cards or checkers.

"All right, I'm gonna say it's the one sittin' alone and wearin' a ratty hat with a feather stickin' out of its band. He's seated on the aisle, which would make sense. Has the look of a train robber about him."

"What do train robbers look like, Slash? Us?"

"Most ain't nearly as handsome as us. As me, anyways." He gave a wry snort. "Most look stupider'n us, too—even dumber'n you—which is the reason most have much shorter careers than the ones we had." Slash looked at the man ahead of him in the aisle seat on his and Pecos's side of the car. He sat up near the door. Slash could see part of his profile. "Yeah, this fella looks dumber'n a bag of hammers. Dumb and mean. He's a train robber, all right."

"You mean one of *today's* train robbers."

"Right. One of *today's* train robbers."

Pecos cast another cautious glance over his shoulder. "Now that that's settled, how is pickin' out the other two going to help us avoid gettin' robbed? We gonna just stand up and start shootin'?"

Slash winced. "Best not. Bledsoe would frown on that, most like. Might pink a passenger."

"Well, then . . . ?"

"I don't know," Slash said defensively. "Maybe it just makes me feel better!"

As though to punctuate his exclamation, the doors at each end of the car burst open and two men shot through each like bulls through a chute, rocking and raising rifles and firing into the ceiling. The explosions were nearly deafening in the close quarters.

"All right, this is a holdup! Everybody just remain seated and calm, and you won't be hurt! Me an' my boys are gonna send bags around, and ever'body's gotta make a contribution to the cause or get your consarned heads blown off!"

Slash and Pecos swiveled their heads, eyes wide, jaws hanging, and took in the two robbers at each end of the car. All four were dressed in three-piece business suits complete with boiled collars and foulard ties. One wore a cream Stetson, while the other three wore bowler hats. One wore gold-framed spectacles and had muttonchops and a handlebar mustache with waxed and twisted upswept ends.

Slash and Pecos shared a scowl.

"They don't look like any kinda bank robber I've ever

seen!" Pecos exclaimed beneath the din of the frightened crowd. The chicken was clucking loudly, and a baby and its young mother were wailing.

"Please, don't shoot me!" the young mother cried, hunkered down over the baby, squeezing her eyes closed. "Please don't shoot me! Please don't shoot me!"

"They're kinda loud, too," Slash said. "Who bursts in, firin' rifles into the consarned ceilin'? You wanna keeps folks calm—not *peein' their drawers*!"

"Hey, you two!" said one of the bank robbers making his way down the aisle from the front, passing bags up and down the rows like collection plates. He was the big, beefy gent in the crisp Stetson, and he was glaring at Slash. "Shut up over there and empty your damn pockets, or you're crow bait!"

Slash looked at Pecos, his lower jaw dropping still farther with astonishment, and the burn of rage lifting in his cheeks. "I'll be ding-dong-damned if these rubes is gonna rob *Slash Braddock*!"

Slash reached for his rifle.

At the same time, the two men wearing linen dusters on the other side of the aisle and one row up from Slash and Pecos leaped to their feet. One swung around to face the rear of the car, and both threw the flaps of their dusters back and raised their sawed-off twelve-gauge shotguns.

"Freeze and drop the rifles! We're Pinkerton agents!"

Slash froze with his Winchester raised halfway to his shoulder. He and Pecos gaped at the two men with the shotguns and slid their incredulous gazes to the four bank robbers.

The beefy one in the crisp Stetson said, "Like *hell*!"

He swung his Winchester toward the Pinkertons. The one with his shotgun aimed toward the front of the car tripped one trigger. The double-aught buck ripped through the big man's chest and belly, picked him up and threw him back and over the seat of the old man and the boy. He fired his rifle into the ceiling again before disappearing over the old man and the boy and tumbling to the floor at their feet.

"Holy cow, Gramps!" the boy cried in astonishment. "Did you see that!"

"Kill the pinks! Kill the pinks!" cried the old lady, flinging the chicken cage aside, bounding to her feet, and raising a long-barreled Smith & Wesson. She aimed the gun straight out from her shoulder and expertly fired it, sending her bullet into the forehead of the Pinkerton who'd been facing the back of the car. The other Pinkerton swung toward her, shouting, and cut loose with the barrel of his second gut shredder. Smoke and flames roiled from the barrel as the concussive report hammered around inside the coach car like rocks in a rolling steel barrel.

The buckshot picked up the old lady and flung her like a rag doll back toward the priest, who cried, "Good Lord!" and flung himself wide of the flying missile of the old lady.

"*Ma!*" cried one of the outlaws, rushing up from the rear of the car.

He stopped and slid his horrified gaze from the old lady to the second Pinkerton, who was just then tossing his shotgun aside and reaching for both the walnut-butted Colts holstered on his hips. He didn't get either weapon clear of the leather before the old lady's train-robbing son punched a .44 Winchester round through his throat, sending him flopping backward, eyes bulging, clawing with both gloved hands at the hole in his throat, which was oozing blood.

Slash racked a round into his Winchester, took hasty aim, and drilled the outlaw who'd just drilled the second Pinkerton a third eye above and between the other two. He stumbled backward, pitching from side to side, as the train kept trundling along the tracks on a slight upgrade. He burst through the back door, flipped over the vestibule rail, and disappeared onto the rails between the cars.

A rifle thundered near the front of the car. A bullet whizzed between Slash and Pecos to plunk through the window right of the now-open back door. Slash and Pecos turned to see the fourth outlaw—or the fifth one, if you're including the old lady, and you'd better since she'd just killed a Pinkerton—glaring at them while gritting his teeth and cocking his Winchester.

"I got him!" Pecos said, raising his Colt's revolving rifle, dragging the hammer back, and firing.

The fifth outlaw pitched with the sway of the car just as Pecos fired, causing the bullet to slide a tad wide and merely kiss the nap of his right broadcloth coat sleeve. However, the bullet startled the gent. He dropped the rifle as he stumbled backward along the car's central aisle. He stumbled sideways into a blond-headed young lady who was maybe seventeen years old. She screamed and cowered in her seat, lowering her head over the cardboard hat box on her lap.

The fifth outlaw—long faced, with a high dome-like forehead, which had been revealed when he'd lost his hat when he stumbled—grabbed the girl brusquely up out of her seat. He thrust her in front of him, drew a knife from a sheath on his hip, and held it to her throat.

She screamed but pinched off the scream when the curved point of the knife pressed up against the underside of her chin. She lifted her head, sobbing, tears rolling down her cheeks.

"Stay where you are, or I'll cut her throat!" the man shouted above the din of the distressed passengers and the clacking wheels. He backed down the aisle toward the door.

"Help me!" the girl screamed through her tears. "Please, don't kill me, mister! Please, don't kill me! I'm getting *married in two days*! Oh, please . . ." Her pleas choked off as the sobs took over, her tear-soaked lips fluttering.

"*So help me!*" the outlaw spat out sharply at Slash and Pecos, his eyes wide and glassy.

"You hurt her, you're a dead man!" Pecos yelled as he and Slash stood aiming their rifles at the blackhearted cuss.

The man fumbled the door open and backed through it, half dragging the sobbing girl.

Pecos glanced at Slash as he lowered his rifle, then took off running down the aisle toward the front door. Slash ran close behind him, both former outlaws weaving slightly with the swaying of the car. Pecos pulled the door open and turned to his right just as the outlaw, one arm wrapped around the crying girl's waist, leaped off the vestibule and into the air. The girl's sausage curls and pink ribbons blew up, and she screamed a half second before she and the outlaw dropped down out of Slash's and Pecos's sight.

"Damn!" Pecos bellowed into the wind.

"You can say that again!"

They both stepped to the far right side of the vestibule to see the outlaw and the girl rolling wildly down the grassy embankment and falling away behind the coach car as the train continued chugging up the grade.

Pecos whipped his head toward Slash, eyes wide and jaws hard. "I'm goin' after that devil!"

With that he thrust out his arms and leaped off the vestibule.

Slash followed, yelling, "I'm right behind you, partner . . . *I reckon*!"

They struck the grassy embankment roughly ten feet apart and rolled wildly toward the pine and fir forest twenty feet below the rails. As soon as they'd struck the ground and started rolling, both men instantly remembered why they no longer did that sort of thing—leap from moving trains.

Hell, they took care not to leap from trains sitting still!

Even though the ground was softened by fairly deep grass, it pummeled both middle-aged men without mercy. They grunted as they rolled, their old bones being painfully assaulted. Their heads and shoulders, too. Not to mention their creaky hips and knees.

Oh, what misery!

When they rolled to a stop at the bottom of the bank, they gritted their teeth against the sundry aching bruises and looked over to where the outlaw was just then climbing to his feet. The girl lay sobbing, nearly buried in the grass.

"Hold it right there, amigo!" Pecos yelled, reaching for the Colt's revolving rifle, which he'd lost in the fall but which had come to a stop beside him.

Rising to one knee, he aimed the long gun straight out from his right shoulder. Slash grabbed his Winchester, swept a lock of his disheveled gray-streaked dark brown hair back from one eye, and racked a round into the rifle's chamber.

The outlaw turned to Slash and Pecos, the feral glint returning to his eyes. His three-piece suit was rumpled and flecked with grass, and his necktie hung askew.

The girl lay between Slash and Pecos and the outlaw. Now she heaved herself to her feet, using her arm to toss her thick blond curls back over her head. She turned to Slash and Pecos and wailed, "Don't shoot! Please don't shoot me! Oh, please don't shoot!"

"Get down, little lady!" Slash yelled, for she was now partly blocking his and Pecos's view of their target.

The outlaw grinned, bounded forward, and grabbed the girl's arm. He pulled her up hard against him and raised the bowie knife again to her throat.

"Drop those rifles, you two old fools, or I'll cut her damn head off!"

Pecos glanced at Slash, who was standing beside him and aiming his Winchester at the outlaw. Slash returned the look with a frustrated one of his own.

Pecos turned back to the outlaw and narrowed his right eye, aiming down the Colt's barrel. "Go ahead!"

Slash turned to him, stricken. "*What?*"

"I warn you—I will!" the outlaw spat through gritted teeth.

"I said go ahead!" Pecos said.

"Pecos!" Slash said, scowling at his longtime partner, wondering if he'd gone off his nut.

"I just will!" the outlaw yelled louder, hunkering over the girl and touching the curved tip of the knife to the underside of her chin.

"Go ahead!" Pecos said, grinning shrewdly down the Colt's barrel. "Cut her head off!"

Horrified, Slash said, "Pecos, I got me a big suspicion he'll do it!"

"No, he won't," Pecos said, still aiming down his rifle's barrel.

Scowling his own frustration, deep lines carved across his dome-like forehead, the outlaw said, "I'm warnin' you! This is your last chance!"

"Go ahead," Pecos said again.

Suddenly, the girl threw up her right arm and swatted the man's knife hand away from her throat. "Oh, forget it, Vernon. That one's not buyin' it." She spat to one side, then returned her suddenly hateful gaze to Pecos. "Must be smarter than he looks!"

"Ah, hell!" said the outlaw, dropping his knife hand to his side.

Both he and the outlaw blonde stood slump shouldered, weary looking, beaten, the girl in front of the man.

"I'll be damned," Slash said, turning to Pecos. "How'd you know . . . ?"

"That they were in it together? I don't know. Musta been the way she carried on so in the car. 'I'm getting married in two days!' And then, out here, how she rose up to block our aims at ol' Vernon."

"Vernon Wade!" yelled a man behind and above Slash and Pecos. "Vernon Wade and Kitty Tuttle!"

Slash and Pecos turned to see two men in suits and dusters, and with Wells Fargo shields pinned to their vests, slip-sliding sideways down the embankment from about fifty yards up the grade. Each man held a rifle. The train had stopped at the top of the grade, maybe a hundred yards beyond, and black coal smoke curled from the locomotive's diamond-shaped stack.

The engineer and fireman had poked their heads, topped in pin-striped caps, the fireman puffing a fat stogie, out of the locomotive's big open side and were gazing back toward where the Wells Fargo men were making their way at a slant down the grade, heading for Slash and Pecos.

"Sure enough, it is them," said one of the Wells Fargo men— taller than the other one and wearing a gray soup-strainer mustache. He was the older of the pair, the other man being in his late thirties and a little shorter and with a more determined expression. The older gent mostly looked amused. "We sorta figured Ma Brewster's Bunch was due to make a hit," he said to Slash and Pecos as he and the other man approached.

"They were seen in the area, and a former gang member spilled the beans on 'em," said the younger man, moving past Slash and Pecos and aiming his own Winchester at the crestfallen outlaw pair. "On your knees—both of you! Hands behind your heads. You're under arrest for murder and attempted robbery!"

The older gent, also holding his Winchester on Vernon Wade and Kitty Tuttle, who were now dutifully and regretfully dropping to their knees, glanced at Slash and Pecos. "We was holed up in the express car. Two Pinkertons were in the passenger coach."

"They still are," Slash told him. "Dead."

The older Wells Fargo man grimaced, nodded. "We saw. After the engineer got the train stopped, we checked it out, while you two were taking down this pair here." He glanced at Slash and Pecos again, while the other Wells Fargo agent was closing the cuffs on Vernon and Kitty. "Who are you two, anyway?" He frowned, lines of curiosity corrugating his tanned, leathery forehead beneath the brim of his crisp brown Stetson.

Slash glanced at Pecos and shrugged. "Just a coupla good Samaritans, I reckon."

"Well, you sure handled these two with aplomb. Are you all right? That tumble you both took down the bank had to hurt!"

Pecos winced and lifted his arm. "It sure did!"

"Yeah," Slash said, stretching the kinks out of his neck and walking up the bank to retrieve his hat. "Next time I'm gonna think twice before I pull a stunt like that."

As he and Pecos headed back up the bank toward the passenger coach, Slash glanced at his partner. He'd be damned if Pecos wasn't smiling.

"What're you smiling about?"

"Huh?" Pecos said, as though surprised by the question.

"You're smilin'."

"I am?"

"You were." Slash regarded his taller partner suspiciously, one eye narrowed. "You know what I think? I think you enjoyed yourself, nasty tumble an' all!"

Pecos looked off with a speculative air. Then he turned to Slash and grinned again. Yeah," he said, frowning, as though it puzzled even him. "I think I did." He clapped Slash on the back. "Ah, come on, partner. Ain't it nice to be out ridin' the long coulees again, gettin' into dustups—even if it is for ol' Bleed-'Em-So Bledsoe? Don't it get your blood up, your ticker *pumpin'*?"

Slash scowled at him, shook his head, and sighed. "We gotta get you hitched before you kill us both!"

Chapter 9

"This time, I'm gonna wait till this sucker stops before I get off," Slash said.

It was the following morning, and they were pulling into the little mountain mining town of Frisco several hours late due to the depredations of the Ma Brewster's Bunch.

"That's a good idea, Slash."

"Well, I'm a thinkin' man."

"You are. I'm gonna follow *your* lead this time."

Both men chuckled as they stood on the passenger car's rear vestibule, saddlebags slung over their shoulders, rifles and war bags in their hands, and watched as the train pulled up to the little log depot building with a sign chained beneath its porch roof announcing FRISCO, COLORADO TERRITORY.

Both men had had a long, uncomfortable night's ride through the mountains. They'd tried to sleep sitting up on the uncomfortable train seats, with every joint and muscle barking like a rabid dog. They had shared a flask of whiskey, which had helped, but no amount of whiskey helped when two men on the downhill side of fifty leaped off a moving train, even if said train was moving at only ten or so miles per hour.

Pecos might have enjoyed the dustup, despite his aches and pains, but Slash did not have that luxury. He wished he could go home and have Jay rub liniment into his sundry aching parts.

But now he and Pecos had to face the unenviable task of kidnapping a showgirl. *Actress.* The actress sweetheart of a hard-bitten, savage outlaw, but a showgirl just the same. Slash wondered how much Pecos was going to enjoy *that* aspect of Bleed-'Em-So's bitter deed.

He knew *he* wasn't. But what choice did he have? It was either kidnap a showgirl or stretch the hangman's hemp.

After he and Pecos had saddled their horses and led both mounts down from the stock car, they mounted up and rode around the little depot building, on the front stoop of which a salt-and-pepper bearded gent in a blue wool coat and leather billed hat—likely, the depot agent—sat in a chair, stroking a liver-colored cat and smoking a pipe. The town of Frisco lay before them, on either side of the broad main drag, down which they clomped, Slash on his sleek Appaloosa, which he merely called "Horse," and Pecos on his stocky buckskin, which he'd unimaginatively dubbed "Buck," looking for the town constable's office.

That was their first stop.

According to the papers in the envelope Miss Langdon had given them, Bleed-'Em-So had wanted them to check in with the town constable and show the man their orders and a letter from the chief marshal himself, explaining why Slash and Pecos were about to haul a young showgirl away on the train. Slash and Pecos thought that was a good idea. Neither one wanted to get drilled by the local law, who might mistake the performance of their official . . . er, uh, *unofficial* duties, as it were . . . for kidnapping.

Besides, the man would likely know where they could run down the actress, the former Hazel Leadbetter, now performing as Fannie Diamond.

Frisco was a raucous place, as could be attested by the drunks staggering from saloon to saloon, even though it was still fairly early in the day. But that was a mountain mining town for you, where men finished up their shifts at the surrounding mines at all hours, their nights spent toiling in the earth's bowels dovetailing into days spent swilling tangleleg and playing slap 'n' tickle with the local parlor girls, of which there appeared to be plenty.

Several of the colorfully, albeit scantily, clad young ladies hailed Slash and Pecos from second- and third-story saloon and parlor-house balconies as they rode along, weaving their way through the pedestrian traffic as well as that of ore drays and prospectors' buckboards drawn by mules and jackasses. There was the steady, monotonous din of stamping mills making big rocks into small rocks on the stony, mine-honeycombed ridges surrounding the settlement.

Beneath the hammering sounds of the mills was the pattering of pianos inside the tent shacks and false-fronted drinking, gambling, and whoring establishments that Slash and Pecos rode past on each side of the street. Included in the cacophony was the raucous laughter of men and women, occasional shouts of unbridled male anger, women's frightened screams, and even a few pistol cracks.

It wasn't nine o'clock in the morning, but the two former train robbers would be damned if Frisco wasn't hopping like Abilene, Kansas, on a Saturday night, after a herd had been trailed up from the Panhandle.

They were halfway through the rustic, five-block town when a thundering boom, like that of a shotgun, sounded from the left side of the street, making not only Slash's and Pecos's horses lurch with starts but also most of the mounts passing by or hitched in the same area. A man gave an agonized bellow. Slash and Pecos jerked back on their mounts' reins and turned their heads as heavy boot thuds sounded from a small, unpainted clapboard, peak-roofed building over which a sign announced ALE 5 SENTS.

As the boot thuds grew louder, a big man with a tangled red

beard, a floppy leather hat, and clad in a grimy long-handles shirt and buckskin pants and hobnailed boots, stepped into the doorway. Holding his hands, one of which clenched an old conversion Remington revolver, over his bloody belly, he opened his mouth, forming a broad, dark O, and issued another loud wail that echoed off the false fronts on both sides of the street.

The wounded man staggered out across the small wooden front stoop and into the street, then swung around to face the open doorway of Ale 5 Sents. He raised the Remington in his right hand, clicked the hammer back, and shouted, "Creole Culpepper, you can go to hell for killin' me, you old ridge runner!"

He fired twice through the open doorway.

A small, dark man with a beard as ratty as the big man's—Creole Culpepper, perhaps?—stepped into the doorway, crouched over a double-bore shotgun, which blossomed smoke and flames as it sent another thunderous peal echoing around the town. The buckshot picked up the gut-shot man and hurled him straight back into the street, only a few feet behind and to the left of Slash and Pecos.

He lay on his back, staring up at Slash, who gazed back incredulously at the man over his Appy's left hip. The fast-dying man blinked his eyes, opened and closed his mouth several times, then broke wind, sighed, and lay still. His eyes instantly turned as opaque as those of a long-abandoned saloon in a ghost town in the middle of nowhere.

"You tugged on this ol' tiger's tail one too many times, Charley Dance!" shouted the short, grizzled, thickset man in the doorway, glaring over his smoking greener at the dead man. "I done told ya Cora was my gal. I even tattooed my name on her backside! Now start shovelin' coal for the devil! That's all you ever been good for, anyways, Charley!"

He spat a long stream of chaw into the street, wiped his mouth with the back of his hand, then turned to see a thickset, dark-haired, round-faced gal, not one bit pretty, standing just inside the grog shop behind him. She wore only a white cotton chemise and pantaloons. Her chubby feet were bare.

"Cora!" exclaimed Creole Culpepper.

Cora's chubby face blossomed into a smile. "Oh, Cully!" She wrapped her arms around his neck. "You *do* love me, after all!"

Cully hugged her back, chuckling, then Cully and his beloved strode hand in hand and none too steadily back into the murky bowels of Ale 5 Sents.

Meanwhile, the forlorn Charley Dance stared unseeing up at Slash.

Slash winced and turned to Pecos. "Now, that's true love, partner."

"Damn straight!" Pecos shook his head and booted his horse into motion.

As they followed a dogleg in the street, they angled toward a small log shack with a sign stretching into the street that announced in hand-painted red letters TOWN CONSTA-BLE BILLY EARLY. A man who appeared to be somewhere in his sixties sat in a chair on the cabin's raised front stoop, his back against the cabin's front wall, smoking a meerschaum pipe, one high-topped moccasin propped against a post of the railing before him.

He wore a cracked brown vest over a black-and-white plaid shirt, badly faded denims, and an old-model Colt holstered on his right hip, in a soft brown leather holster. He, too, wore a beard—as did most of the men Slash and Pecos had seen so far in Frisco—but this man's wasn't as thick and tangled and food peppered as the beards of Charley Dance and Creole Culpepper. His was dark brown streaked with gray, and while long, it was neatly combed beneath the sun-seasoned knobs of his leathery cheeks.

A seven-pointed star was pinned to his right snakeskin suspender.

Slash glanced back along the street, at where Charley

Dance lay sprawled in the middle of it, several boys and a dog gathered around him, one of the boys poking the body with a stick, the dog barking and wagging its tail. Slash and Pecos shared an incredulous look.

Slash turned to the man he assumed was the constable, Billy Early, and said, "Uh . . . did you happen to catch what happened over yonder?"

The constable puffed the meerschaum with a leisurely air and nodded. "Seen the whole thing."

Pecos said, "And you, uh, didn't feel the need to intervene?"

"Nah," the man grunted. "The key to working as a man of the law in a town as rowdy as Frisco is lettin' the citizenry police itself. Charley Dance an' Creole Culpepper have been fightin' over Cora Clark for years now, like two dogs over a bone. One of 'em was bound to buy a bullet, an' lockin' up Creole ain't gonna bring Charley back from the dead. Besides, the undertaker's gotta make a livin'," he said, switching his gaze to a buckboard wagon driven by a tall, lanky man in an Abe Lincoln hat and watching it swing onto the main drag from a side street and pull up beside the boys, the tail-wagging dog, and the lifeless Charley Dance.

"That's one way of lookin' at it," Pecos said with a wry chuckle, thumbing his hat brim up off his forehead. "You Constable Early?"

"I am."

"Can we go inside and palaver with you, Constable Early?" Slash said. "We're—"

"Slash Braddock an' the Pecos River Kid," said a tight, low, cautious voice behind Slash and Pecos. "As I live an' breathe!"

Slash and Pecos turned to see a skinny young man in an age-coppered suit coat two sizes too big for him and with an equally ill-fitting immigrant hat on his head walk toward them, crouched over the double-bore shotgun in his pale, long-fingered hands. A deputy town constable's star was pinned to his coat lapel.

He smiled shrewdly, narrowing his eyes, cheeks flushing with excitement. "Sure, sure, I know who you two are, ya ring-tailed devils!" He switched his gaze to Early but kept the shotgun aimed up at Slash and Pecos and said, "It's them, Uncle Billy! As I live an' breathe! I been studyin' them reward posters on the bulletin board in the office yonder, and it's them, sure enough! There's a one-thousand-dollar reward on each o' their ugly heads!"

"Hey, who's ugly?" Slash said, indignant. "And those dodgers must be older than Jehoshaphat's cat. Last time I checked, the rewards on our heads were north of two grand!"

Pecos turned to his partner, scowling. "You're not helping defuse the situation here, Slash!"

Slash pinched up one cheek and lamented, "Damn my vanity, anyway . . ."

The kid said, "I always wondered what it would be like, runnin' to ground a pair of owlhoots as famous as Slash Braddock and the Pecos River Kid!" He whistled and shook his head as he walked up beside Slash, aiming the greener at Slash's head. "It's a good feelin'. It purely is!" He shoved the shotgun's barrel to within two feet of Slash's face, squinting his eyes and hardening his jaws. "Climb down from there, you catamount! Can I put the bracelets on 'em, Uncle Billy? Can I? We can split the . . . *Hey, ow! Oh, you dirty dog!*"

The kid stumbled forward as Slash, who'd grabbed the shotgun's double bores in his left hand, jerked it out of the kid's grip. Holding the gun by its barrel, Slash rammed the butt against the kid's forehead, unseating his hat. The kid stumbled backward, clapping his hands to his forehead, where a red welt was already rising, and screamed again, "Oh, you dirty dog! Uncle Billy!"

"That's what you get for shovin' a double-bore into this

ring-tailed devil's face!" Slash said, breaking the shotgun open, removing both cartridges, and pocketing them. He tossed the shotgun into the street.

Uncle Billy Early pulled the meerschaum out of his mouth, tipped his head back, and laughed.

"Kenneth, why aren't you over at the opery house? You're supposed to be helpin' Boone McClory's bouncers tamp down the drunk miners fightin' over that actress gal and threatenin' to set the curtain on fire!"

Kenneth rubbed his sore forehead. "I was over there, Uncle Billy, but they're between shows. I headed for the mercantile for a sarsaparilla. That's when, glancing toward Main Street, who did I spy but—"

"Slash Braddock and the Pecos River Kid!" said the constable . . . laughing again.

"Sure as cow dung in a Texas windstorm!" agreed Kenneth.

"You take your shotgun, now, and get back over to the opry house. You got more shells in your pocket?"

"Yeah."

"All right, then. Them miners always make the most trouble when that purty little actress gal first steps onstage. They don't like it if she has too many clothes on." Turning to Slash and Pecos, Early added, "The miners are used to the showgirls around here takin' off their clothes and dancin' around with their you-know-whats jigglin', and kickin' their feet high and even kickin' off their red high heels to the howlin' crowd. But this gal, to the miners' everlastin' disappointment, only sheds her garments once every blue moon, just to keep the miners comin' back, hopin' she shed 'em again!" He laughed and shook his head.

Slash and Pecos shared a dubious glance. Both men wondered if the actress Constable Bill Early and his nephew had mentioned was the young showgirl Slash and Pecos had been sent here to fetch.

"All right, Uncle Billy," Kenneth said, scowling angrily and with deep frustration up at Slash and Pecos. "But don't turn your back on these two. They're likely here to kill the local law before they rob the consarned bank!"

"Run along now, Kenneth," admonished Early before sliding the meerschaum between his lips and puffing. "That actress gal needs you over there worse than I need you over here. If these two are Slash Braddock an' the Pecos River Kid, why, I reckon I can handle 'em. Hell, they look dang near as long in the tooth as I am."

Slash and Pecos swapped indignant glances.

"All right, Uncle Billy." Kenneth shouldered the shotgun and sulked away, casting indignant glances over his shoulder and nearly getting run over by a six-mule ore dray.

When Slash and Pecos turned their gazes back to the constable, he'd set his pipe on the railing beside him and filled his hand with his old Remington revolver. The barrel was aimed at Slash and Pecos.

"You two really Slash Braddock and the Pecos River Kid?"

Chapter 10

"We are," Slash said. "But you can put the hogleg away. Our horns have done been filed."

"What Slash is tryin' to say," Pecos said, "is we were given amnesties."

Early frowned. "Why in hell would anyone amnesty a couple of bank- and train-robbin' owlhoots?"

"We'd just as soon you kept this under your hat," Pecos said, "but we were given our freedom in exchange for workin' for Chief Marshal Luther T. Bledsoe, out of Denver."

"Doin' his dirtiest work," Slash said with a scowl. "Unofficially," he added. "That's why we'd just as soon you kept it under your hat." He tapped his left coat pocket. "We have the chief's orders right here. Includin' a letter of introduction from him of yours truly." He scowled. "Don't believe everything he says in it."

Pecos canted his head toward Slash. "That envelope explains why we're here. And what we need to talk to you about."

Early rose from his chair, rising to a full six feet, a lean man aside from a middle-aged paunch that stretched out his suspenders and drew his shoulders down. He stepped forward and, keeping the Remington aimed at his visitors, extended his left hand over the porch rail. "Let's see it. But go slow. Either one of you makes any sudden move . . ." He raised and lowered the gun in his hand.

"Yeah, we get it," Pecos said. "Give the man the envelope, Slash."

Slash gigged the Appy up closer to the stoop, slowly pulled the envelope out of his coat pocket, and extended it over the porch rail. Early took it. He backed up a step, gave Slash and Pecos a cautionary glance, then, keeping his gun aimed, plucked the papers out of the envelope, dropped the envelope; and as the envelope blew around the porch floor in the breeze, he opened the thrice-folded papers and held them out a ways to read them.

He gave only one page a quick scan, then lowered the pistol as well as the papers and said, "All right. Come on in." He turned, opened his office door, and went inside.

Slash and Pecos swung down from their mounts, tied them at the hitchrack, then mounted the stoop. Slash stepped on the envelope, held it down, then crouched to retrieve it. He followed Pecos into the office to find Early filling a chipped stone mug at the potbelly stove that stood back against the tiny office's rear wall.

He glanced at his guests and said, "Coffee?"

Slash glanced at Pecos, who shrugged. "Don't mind if we do," Slash said.

Early thrust the mug he'd just filled at Slash, who took it. He produced two more stone mugs, one black and one green, from a tomato crate that served as a cupboard on the wall above the stove, and filled each with smoking java. He shoved the green one at Pecos.

"Do train robbers take cream and sugar?"

"Nope," Slash said, blowing on the piping hot brew. "Train robbers take their mud hot and as black as their cold, cold hearts."

"Even *ex*–train robbers," Pecos said before blowing on his own brew. "This'll do just fine. We had a long night on the train."

"Heard about the holdup, er . . . attempted holdup, over the telegraph. I suppose I should wander over there and see what's what. No point in gettin' in a hurry, though." Early walked around behind his desk, slacked into a Windsor chair, and sipped his coffee. "Me? I'm semiretired."

Slash shot Pecos an ironic glance. The man had meant he was lazy, Slash silently opined. The little twitch that came to Pecos's mouth corners told Slash that his partner held the same opinion.

"I'd offer you fellas a chair, but I get few visitors except for the occasional prisoner. And I don't even get many of them since—"

"I know," Slash said, sipping his coffee, which he found surprisingly strong and good. "You're semiretired." Being semiretired, the man likely had plenty of time to brew coffee. He did a damn fine job of that, anyway.

"One of you can grab the chair from the stoop."

"That's all right," Slash said. "We'll get down to brass tacks and be on our way. We need to find a hotel and crawl under the quilts for a nap. Like you've pointed out, we ain't as young as we used to be."

"In a nutshell," Pecos said, leaning back against the wall beside the door, "we're here to fetch a young showgirl named Fannie Diamond. Gotta slap that subpoena on her and escort her back to Denver to testify in a murder trial one week from today."

"Ah, hell!" Early's forehead turned into a badly rutted washboard road, and he slapped the top of his desk with his open palm, making a rat or some other rodent squawk in one of the four jail cages flanking the room and run out through a hole in the base of the wall. "That's the purty little gal I was talkin' about. The one who the miners make such a fuss about, the one who won't take off her clothes or even just show her ... her ... well, her unmentionables but only once in a blue moon!"

"Ah, that's a shame," Pecos said.

"What is?" Slash said. "That we have to fetch her or that she won't take off her clothes but once in a blue moon?"

"Take your pick," Pecos said. "Likely, the miners in this camp ain't gonna be none too happy about us snatchin' their favorite showgirl."

"That's for sure. She's a looker, that one. A little like this"— Early tipped his nose up with his index finger and looked down at it, as though at lesser mortals—"but she's the best thing we've seen around here since old Max DeLaney and that mean old Ute squaw of his first found color on Lightning Peak and set up the first hogpen and suds shop in Frisco, even though it was a diseased perdition that caused many a man around here to howl themselves to sleep at night with the Cupid's itch. And I know every man in this camp is gonna keep patronizing her shows for as long as she's here, hopin' against hope she gives 'em a view of *something* on her pretty little person, anyway!"

"We got our orders," Slash said. "Bledsoe's a nasty old cuss. If we fail to get that girl down to Denver by the time the judge gavels that trial into session, he'll likely make sure we both stretch hemp." He gave Pecos a sidelong glance. "Besides, Pecos is havin' the time of his life."

Pecos grinned and hiked a shoulder. "Beats haulin' freight."

"That's 'cause you ain't hitched."

"Anyway," Pecos said loudly, changing the subject and turning to Early, "can you tell us where we'll find this gal, Constable? Say, around eight o'clock tomorrow mornin'? The train pulls out at nine, so we figure we'll hit her with the subpoena and give her an hour to pack a bag for the trip to Denver."

"She and her troupe are stayin' at the French Hotel, right next door to the opry house."

"Where's the opry house?" Slash asked.

"One block back the way you came, and hang a right. You can't miss it. Investors from Leadville built the place two years ago, and so far, it's been a mint printin' its own money." Early grinned. "Especially when a troupe rolls into town with a purty young actress in the lead. Especially one who takes her clothes off." He slapped the table and laughed. Then he sobered up and frowned. "Say, is it true she's the lady friend of that Texas outlaw Duke Winter?"

"So claims our boss," Pecos said. "He's gonna threaten her with jail time if she doesn't tell him where Winter's gang is holed up. Apparently, Winter's slipperier than the Hole-in-the-Wall Gang."

"And twice as deadly," Early said. "Real hard case, I hear. I wonder how such a purty li'l gal as Miss Diamond came to hook up with such a brigand."

"We'll ask her and let you know," Pecos said.

"I bet ol' Duke ain't gonna be none too pleased . . . even less than the miners . . . when he hears you two are haulin' his gal down to Denver."

"Has he been seen around here?" Slash asked, arching a brow with interest.

"Just last week. He was here to see his gal. Him an' his whole gang was here—a good dozen nasty cusses. They saw Miss Diamond's show, spent the night in the French Hotel, then slipped out of town early the next mornin'. I practically had to tie Kenneth down to keep him from tryin' to wave that greener in their faces. They'd have turned him inside out and toe down! As for me, well . . ."

"You're semiretired," Slash said, finishing for him.

"I alerted the sheriff over in Gunnison"—a wry smile quirked the constable's mouth corners inside his beard—"but I never heard back. Can't say as I blame him. No mortal man wants to pull the tail of a tiger like Duke Winter." He narrowed an eye in warning and dipped his chin. "You two best hope you don't run into him. He's set his hat for that gal, sure enough, and if he's anywhere close, he'll likely try to chase you down. Him an' all twelve of them coyotes of his. Gun-handy men, all."

Slash nodded and turned to Pecos. "We'll keep a finger on our triggers and one eye on our back trail." He finished his coffee, set the cup on a shelf by the potbelly stove. "Thanks for the information, Constable."

"And the coffee. I don't recollect ever tastin' any as good." Pecos pinched his hat brim to the man, and he and Slash left the office.

Their first stop after leaving the constable's office was to stable their horses. They'd brought them along because, having been chased around the West most of their lives, they never knew when they were going to need a fast horse. Livery nags were notoriously undependable. They hoped they wouldn't need their mounts, but better to be safe than sorry.

When they'd arranged to have their horses stabled and tended to, they heeled it over to the French Hotel, which, just as the constable had described, sat beside the Frisco Opera House. Both men stopped in front of the tiny theater to give it the slow, leisurely up and down.

Slash whistled his appreciation of the ornate building of red brick and sandstone. Large letters of black brick across the second story identified it as the Frisco Opera House. The building had a high domed roof of red tile, with turrets at each corner and a pedimented front portico supported by sandstone columns.

Stained glass adorned the windows of the broad oak front doors, which were closed. A two-sided placard standing on the portico announced PERFORMANCE IN SESSION and NEXT SHOW AT

4:00 PM. A mustached gent in a long, red velvet claw-hammer coat and black beaver hat was hawking tickets as he walked back and forth along the street fronting the impressive building. There were several eager takers, albeit ones attired far less grandly than the pitchman.

"Imagine something like that way out here in this backwater hellhole!" Slash exclaimed.

"You can say that again," Pecos agreed. "We might have to take in a show."

A canvas banner hanging in a U shape across the front of the building, over the doors, announced MADAME MARGUERITE: PORTRAIT OF A COURTESAN.

Slash frowned. "What's a courtesan? I didn't want to ask ol' Bleed-'Em-So, since he already thinks I'm as stupid as you."

Pecos gave him a cockeyed scowl. "Beats me."

"It's probably as boring as watching rocks bake in the sun," Slash said. "Besides, the constable said she keeps her clothes on between blue moons."

"Slash Braddock, you're a married man!"

"Bein' married don't mean a fella can't still appreciate a purty figure. But if you tell Jay I said so, I'll deny it and call you a bald-faced liar!"

Both men laughed.

"Come on," Pecos said, hiking his saddlebags higher on his shoulder while holding his rifle and war bag in his other hand. "Let's get a room. Me—I could use a couple hours of shut-eye."

"Me too."

The hotel, a three-story brick structure, wasn't as impressive as the opera house, but it had been built maybe fifty feet to the east of the grander building, and so it didn't overly contrast to it. They went inside and rented a room with two beds and ordered up a bath for each of them. They lingered for an hour in the steaming, soapy water, smoking and passing their bottle between them, then crawled into bed for a nap.

When they rose a couple of hours later, they took another sip from their bottle, then dressed and headed out for beer and sandwiches, which they found at a humble little hole-in-the-wall called Zhang Wei's, run by a fat Chinaman with one bad leg and his half-breed Indian wife, Leona, who sported a wandering left eye. The place specialized in pork, but the pork sandwiches probably would have been more palatable if they hadn't been accompanied by the stench from the Chinaman's hogpen, which sat directly behind the café.

When they'd finished their beers and paid for their meals, they headed outside and started back along the main drag, in the direction of the hotel. As they grew closer to the cross street that the hotel and opera house sat on, they noticed many men heading down the same cross street they were heading for. As they turned the corner, they saw several men in matching spruce-green three-piece suits and brown homburg hats barking, "Come one, come all! See the lovely and internationally renowned Miss Fannie Diamond in *Madame Marguerite: Portrait of a Courtesan*!"

"What the hell's a courte . . . whatever the hell you called her?" asked a burly gent, taking one of the handbills the barkers were passing out in the middle of the street.

The barker smiled, held a handbill over his mouth, and whispered.

The burly gent turned to several other men standing nearby and beckoned broadly. "It's about a whore, fellas! Come on. Let's see the show!"

As Slash and Pecos walked along the street, finding themselves amidst a small throng of men heading for the opera house, Pecos turned to Slash and said, "Hmm . . ."

"Wanna check it out?"

"It's still early. What else we gonna do for the rest of the evenin'?"

Chapter 11

The bullet slammed into a cedar with a loud thunk, but not before curling the air only inches from Jaycee's left cheek.

"Oh!" she said with a start as the rifle's crashing report reached her ears.

Her chestnut mare, Dorothy, reared suddenly with a shrill whinny, and Jay lost her hold on the reins and went tumbling off the mare's left hip. The ground came up fast and hard to beat her about her head and shoulders. As she struck the ground, her slitted riding skirt sailed up around her waist to expose her pantaloon-clad legs and black-booted feet.

She used both gloved hands to shove the skirt down. A second later, another bullet plumed dirt and dun grass to her left. Again, the rifle's crashing report followed. The echo of that report hadn't died before another bullet ripped into the ground a foot to the right of Jay's right shoulder, peppering her shoulder with dirt and bits of broken sage.

Again, the crashing report vaulted off the high, clay-colored ridges rising on either side of this deep, dramatically featured valley west of Camp Collins, on the west side of Horsetooth Rock. Jay rode her mare out here every chance she got, to relieve the stress of running her locally famous and growingly popular watering and gambling hole, the Thousand Delights.

At least, taking her mare out two or three times a week *usually* relieved her stress. But now, as Dorothy ran off, buck-kicking and shaking her head angrily, Jay rolled onto her belly and clawed and kneed her way along the ground, heading toward the cedar that had taken that first bullet. She clambered around behind the tree, put her back to it, then turned her head to look around it, casting her gaze in the direction from which the shots had come.

A haystack butte lay roughly a hundred yards away, its crown strewn with sandstone rocks, cedars, and ponderosa pines. She couldn't be sure, but the shooter must be up there. There was nowhere else to hide out here, for while rocks and trees stippled both valley ridges, the valley floor was relatively barren of trees. There was only bromegrass, wild mahogany, and mountain sage, and here and there a slender cedar, like the one offering Jay a modicum of cover now.

Now as Jay stared, her heart thudding wildly, sunlight glinted off something up near the crown of the haystack butte. Pale smoke puffed. Jay gasped and pulled her head back behind the cedar. A second later, a bullet slammed into the opposite side of the tree. Jay could feel the reverberations of the impact in her head, which she pressed anxiously against the cedar.

As that report echoed, Jay swung another look up the butte. Gray smoke wafted thinly just above the butte's highest point.

Jay's mind raced along with her heart. Who was trying to kill her?

All she could come up with was that maybe she'd accidentally trespassed on a range some rancher considered his own, even though she knew the range she was on belonged to the government. It was open range, not private. Ranchers were notorious, however, for claiming open range as their own. Maybe the rancher who'd claimed this stretch of graze was having rustling problems, and he'd ordered his men to shoot interlopers on sight.

Even a woman?

Whoever was shooting at her was close enough that he must have seen that she was a woman. While not a vain person, Jay was aware that her female attributes were easily recognizable by anyone but a blind man from a hundred yards away, even when she wore a man's black felt Stetson-like hat, which she'd been wearing before the tumble from her horse had ripped it off her head. Now her unmistakably feminine copper-red hair lay in messy tangles around her shoulders, peppered with bits of grass and weed seeds, glinting in the lens-clear high-country sun.

As she gazed up the haystack butte, she gasped again when a horse and rider came into sight, galloping up the valley's far ridge, rising up from behind the haystack butte from whose top the rifleman—*certainly that rider!*—had been shooting at her. Jay raised a hand to shade her eyes from the sun and scrutinized the rider carefully.

He was probably a quarter mile away now, but as his horse lunged up the ridge at a slant, she saw that he wore a low-crowned black hat, a black shirt under a brown vest, and a green, neck-knotted bandanna. The horse was a sleek dun.

Horse and rider neared the ridge crest, the horse pulling itself up with its front feet and pushing with its back legs, the muscles in its hips rippling, its sleek coat glinting brightly in the sunshine. As the horse pulled itself up and over the ridge crest, the rider cast a quick look behind him over his right shoulder, knotted green neckerchief whipping in the breeze. He turned his head forward again quickly, touched silver spurs to the dun's flanks, and galloped off away from the ridge and out of sight.

"Bastard!" Jay said and slammed the end of her right fist against the tree.

She drew a breath to calm her racing heart.

Who was out to kill her?

No. She amended her assumption. The rifleman could have killed her if he'd wanted to. Something told her he wasn't as bad a shot as he'd seemed. He hadn't been trying to kill her. He'd been trying to *frighten* her. He'd placed those shots right where he'd wanted them.

Why?

Immediately, her mind went to Grant Balldinger. She didn't want it to, but it did.

The other night, he'd tried so hard to convince her to sell the Thousand Delights to him. He hadn't been successful, of course. She could never sell, no matter how much work running the place was, or how much stress it often caused her. The Thousand Delights gave her purpose, and after nearly twenty years living in the remote San Juan Mountains, in an old outlaw cabin, the last five of them alone, she badly needed purpose and distraction. And good, hard, meaningful work.

Grant Balldinger had seemed deeply disappointed by her refusal. He'd left the Thousand Delights the other night seeming so frustrated and unsatisfied and downright un-understanding that Jay had come away from the conversation feeling a strange unease.

Apprehension.

She'd wanted to mention it to Slash, because that was what husbands were for, after all—to hear out the worries of their wives. But she hadn't wanted to worry him with her own worries, for he'd been heading out on another job for Chief Marshal Bledsoe the next morning.

She hadn't wanted her worries to distract him, for his work for Bledsoe was almost always dangerous, though it hadn't sounded as though this current job—escorting an actress to Denver to testify in a murder trial—would be. (In fact, she'd found herself feeling a twinge of jealousy at the prospect of his and Pecos's next job. If their charge was an actress, she was likely pretty. Maybe beautiful. Jay was relatively sure that

Slash's eye wouldn't stray from her, but still, it was one more worry, if only a small one.)

Anyway, she hadn't wanted to trouble him. She'd decided to tell him about her uncomfortable conversation with Balldinger after he returned to Camp Collins.

Now she rested her head back against the cedar and pondered the rifleman.

Could Balldinger have sent the man to put the fear of God into her as a roundabout way of coercing her into selling the Thousand Delights to him?

Of *threatening* her to sell?

No. She dismissed it out of hand.

She knew Grant Balldinger reasonably well. He wasn't capable of such strong-arm tactics. He was a friend, after all. True, he'd asked for Jay's hand, and she'd refused, and he'd seemed deeply disappointed and even angry about that. She'd written that behavior off to his being a stubborn man, a successful, powerful man not accustomed to or given to accepting defeat.

That didn't mean he'd threaten her life!

But if Balldinger hadn't sent that rifleman to frighten her, who had?

Jay heaved herself to her feet. She still felt shaky. She fingered debris from her hair and cleaned herself off and set her hat on her head. Then she tramped off to run down her mare, whom she found casually grazing only a couple of hundred feet away.

By the time she'd tightened the cinch and adjusted the bridle and swung up into the saddle, she'd decided that, while she doubted very much that Balldinger had not sent the rifleman for her, she would stop at his headquarters and have a visit with the man, just the same. The headquarters of Balldinger's Cheyenne Creek Ranch was on her way back to town, anyway. She was sure that a brief conversation with the rancher would set her mind at ease by convincing her once and for all that he had not sent the rifleman.

Maybe he'd even have an idea or two about who had. Maybe Jay had some enemies that she didn't know about but that others did. As a powerful businesswoman in northern Colorado, she likely had her share of enemies, though she couldn't think of any current ones offhand.

Maybe Grant would. . . .

She swung Dorothy east and batted her spurless heels against her beloved mare's flanks. A half hour later she rode through the portal of Balldinger's Cheyenne Creek Ranch headquarters. A moment's trepidation gripped her when she saw Grant Balldinger himself step out of his large two-story log house's broad front door and onto its wide wraparound porch, almost as though he'd been watching for her, expecting her?

The expression on the man's face—rather, the lack of expression on his face, and the dark chill in his eyes—also rocked Jaycee back on her proverbial heels. But then, as she pulled Dorothy up to the hitchrack at the base of the lodge's front steps, Balldinger's broad, weathered face blossomed into a bright, toothy smile.

"Well, well, Jaycee Breckenridge! What a sight for these sore eyes!" Clad in butterscotch whipcord trousers, a soft cream shirt beneath a butterscotch vest, a silver- and turquoise-trimmed bolo tie, and polished black, hand-tooled leather boots with his Cheyenne Creek brand stitched into each toe, the tall, gray-headed, rugged-looking rancher rubbed his big red hands together energetically. "To what or whom do I owe the honor?"

Jay's heart raced again. She read menace in the man's face, though she was sure it was just her imagination. He couldn't have smiled more broadly or welcomed her more heartily.

"Hello, Grant," she said, offering a stiff smile. "Do you mind if I alight?"

"Do I *mind*? Jay, I *insist*!" Balldinger raised his right hand high above his head as he cast his gaze toward the bunkhouse. "Garza! Come fetch the lady's horse! Water and grain her and give her a good—"

"No, no," Jay said, shaking her head as she swung down from her saddle. "I can stay only a minute or two. I came to speak with you about a rather pressing matter, I'm afraid, Grant."

"Just a minute or two, eh?" he said, beetling his brows at her disapprovingly. "Well, if you insist." He waved off Garza, who'd started striding toward the lodge. "Never mind, Rafael!"

The Mexican cowhand lifted his chin, nodded, and swung around to head back to the tack he was oiling on a bench fronting the bunkhouse.

Jay tied Dorothy's reins to the wrought-iron hitchrack, which also bore the rancher's brand at each end, then removed her hat and brushed dust from the crown.

Balldinger stood atop the porch steps, towering over her, smiling knowingly as he flicked his right index finger against the point of his chin. "A pressing matter, eh? I know what it is. You've come to your senses and rode out here to tell me you've accepted my more than generous offer for your wonderful saloon and gambling den!" He clapped those big hands together, and the loud crack made Jay jerk with a start, her heart rate increasing once again. "Wonderful! Get up here! We'll celebrate with a drink! I just got in a case of—"

"No, Grant," Jay said, standing at the base of the steps, smiling affably up at him. "That's not what I came to tell you."

Chapter 12

"It's not?" Balldinger's broad red face shaped an exaggeratedly pained expression. "It's not?"

"No," Jay said, climbing the steps and shaking her head. "It's not."

"Ah, *fudge*!" The rancher snapped his fingers in disappointment. "That's a shame!"

"I'm sorry." Jay came up to stand beside him, placed a hand on his arm. "Can we sit?"

"Of course, of course." Balldinger indicated two walnut rocking chairs separated by a low walnut table that sat to the right of the large timbered front door of the lodge. "I'll fetch us a drink."

He started for the front door, but Jay stopped him with, "No, please, Grant. I don't want a drink. I'll only be a minute."

"All right, all right. You'll only be a minute. I finally attract the most beautiful woman to my headquarters, and she keeps reminding me she'll only be a minute. All right, all right." Looking deeply disappointed again, he sat in the rocker nearest the door, while Jay slacked into the other one. "A pressing matter, eh?" He gave a foxy twist of his mouth. "You an' Slash get into a spat, and you need this fella's advice. Divorce him and marry me!" He threw his head back and laughed.

Jay feigned a smile but drew a deep breath, trying to calm her nerves. "That's not it, either, Grant. Not even close. I was ambushed out on the range about a half hour ago, as I was approaching the mouth of Redstone Canyon."

When she'd started that last sentence, Balldinger's head had still been tipped back on his shoulders as he'd laughed at his own so-called joke. Now he jerked his chin down sharply, sobering instantly, and widened his eyes in shock. "Did you say *ambushed*?"

His surprise seemed real, which comforted her slightly.

"Yes, ambushed! Someone took several shots at me. Dorothy reared, and I hit the ground, and the man continued firing to either side of me!"

"Good Lord, Jay. Are you all right?" The rancher reached over the table and wrapped his hand around her right forearm. He gazed at her with a concern she read as authentic.

"Yes, I think so. At least physically. I have to admit I'm still a bit shaken."

"Who do you think it was? Did you get a look at this scoundrel?"

"I saw him from a distance as he rode away. He wore a black hat, brown vest, and green neckerchief. He rode a sleek dun horse, likely an American."

"Who do you think he was? What were his motives . . . ?"

"I have no idea. I thought maybe you might know."

Balldinger looked suddenly offended, scowling at her curiously. "Why would I know?" His scowl grew more severe; his eyes more indignant. "Jay, you don't think I . . . ?"

"Sent that man?" Jay finished for him when he seemed to have trouble finishing the question for himself. She debated how honest she wanted to be, and decided to throw caution to the wind. What did she have to lose? She might as well hit him straight on with her suspicions. If he was offended, he was offended. She was offended, too. "I have to admit, Grant, that the thought crossed my mind."

There, that was about as much as she wanted to sugarcoat it.

Balldinger gazed back at her, his indignant scowl in place. His eyes had turned dark again. Dark and flat and menacing.

Jay's heartbeat increased once more.

"Grant, the other night, when you made me the offer on the Thousand Delights..." She paused, having trouble coming up with her own words now. "You...seemed awfully frustrated when I turned it down. You seemed...well...angry."

"I did, did I?" Unexpectedly, he smiled. It was as though her observation amused him.

"Yes, you did. Grant. I know you're a powerful man in this country. I know you're accustomed to getting your way."

"I am at that, Jay. I am, indeed. Why not sell?" ·

"What?" The question, the sudden change of subject, shocked her. "I told you, Grant—the Thousand Delights is my life. I wouldn't know what to do without it. I didn't come here to discuss..."

"Jay, my moneymen have told me I need to diversify my investments. Now, you have really built the Thousand Delights into a jewel here on the Front Range. With even more money—the kind of money I can put into it—it could be the jewel of Colorado!" Balldinger still had his hand on her arm. He squeezed her arm tighter, more insistently. "I really do want it. I need it. I don't want to stay out here and ranch forever. I'm alone. Aside from my son and my men, of course. I want to sell here eventually, move to town...find a good woman...run a good business. A *big* business. Be a man about town, if you will."

Again, he smiled, but his eyes were still flat and dark.

Jay studied him closely. Her pulse throbbed in her neck. Her hands were slick with sweat. "Grant," she said, hearing a tremor in her voice. "You didn't—"

"Send that man to frighten you into selling?" He smiled again, his tone too calm and flat and measured. Those hard, cold, dark eyes parried with her own. "No. Of course not. I can assure you, Jay, that if I'd sent him, you wouldn't be sitting here with me right now."

Again, she was rocked back on her proverbial heels.

She stared back at him, trying to decide if he was being serious.

Suddenly, he threw his head back on his shoulders and laughed as though at the funniest joke he'd ever heard. He slammed both big hands down on the arms of his chair and roared.

Jay found herself rising from her chair. She moved stiffly, for her legs were heavy.

Balldinger stopped laughing and, remaining in his chair, said, "Stay and have a drink with me, Jay. I sense your nerves could use a little greasing."

"No, thank you," she said, moving stiffly down the porch steps.

At the bottom, she turned and gazed back up at the rancher, who was still sitting in his chair, smiling at her, his eyes still cold and hard.

Jay's hands shook slightly, making difficult the simple procedure of untying Dorothy's reins from the hitchrack. When she did, she pulled herself unsteadily into the saddle.

"I'm going to add another five thousand to my offer, Jay!"

She swung her head back to the porch. Balldinger stood atop the steps now, gazing down at her, thumbs hooked in his front trouser pockets, his expression all business.

Jay gave a stiff half smile, shook her head. "I'm not selling, Grant."

"You will, Jay," he said, his tone now as cold and flat as his eyes. "Eventually, you will. You'll have to."

Feeling a stone drop in her belly, Jay swung Dorothy around and booted the horse across the yard and through the portal. She galloped out to the main trail and turned east, heading back to town. As she topped one of the several steep, rocky dikes that bisected the grassy ranching valleys west of town, she drew rein and gazed down and to the southwest.

From here, in the high-country light, she could clearly see a rider just then trot a dun horse into the yard of the Cheyenne Creek headquarters. The rider turned the horse toward the house. Balldinger was still standing atop the porch, at the edge of the steps.

The man riding toward him wore a black hat and a brown vest, the ends of his green neckerchief fluttering in the dry western breeze.

At roughly the same time in the rollicking mining town of Frisco, Slash and Pecos forked over ten cents apiece at the ticket window to an old, skinny gent in armbands, a green eyeshade, and a snoose-stained necktie.

They accepted the handbills an usher in a red coat and striped trousers gave them as they strode through the opera house's marble-floored lobby along with the laughing, smoking, unwashed crowd of townsmen, miners, mule skinners, and cowboys, most of whom smelled like a brewery and were in dire need of a bath.

Some of the men held the sudsy beer mugs they must have snuck out of saloons when the barkers had started announcing Miss Fannie Diamond's next show. A few even had chattering or giggling doxies on their arms. One of the girls wore not much more than hair feathers and a thrice-looped string of faux pearls and was attracting the lusty looks of nearly every man in the crowd.

Slash, Pecos, and the rest of the crowd, as spirited as schoolboys on a class picnic, passed through an arched doorway to each side of which was a stone statue of a naked young woman capped with a crown of flowers and holding a flambeau high in one hand, while using her other hand to cover her private lower stone parts with a large stone palm leaf.

This small sea of unwashed humanity hustled into the deep, dark, cave-like auditorium, over which a massive vaulted ceiling arched from the front end to the far end, where the black-painted stage rose, concealed by heavy red velvet, gold-tasseled curtains. A mural decorated the wall above the curtain, depicting buck-naked nymphs frolicking in a green glen surrounded by woods and cut through by a powder-blue stream.

Slash and Pecos took seats roughly in the middle of the auditorium. Not long after they and the rest of the crowd had been seated, an accordion wheezed out somber, grating Parisian strains for two long minutes. The curtain opened, and the show began with a pretty young lady in a sack dress hanging off one pale porcelain shoulder and with a head of golden curls dashing out of a cardboard facade of a building identified as a home for wayward girls to throw herself at the feet of the dapper gent passing in the street before the place, wielding a walking stick.

Immediately, Slash recognized the actress, Fannie Diamond, though in the picture Bledsoe had shown him and Pecos, her hair had been black.

The wayward girl wailed at the startled gent, beseeching him to save her from the evil nuns who ran the home and beat her mercilessly because they were jealous of how her beauty—which she could not help, she added humbly, or the way her body was filling out now, as she turned fourteen—turned the eyes of the priests. So, the gent picked her up and carried her away, and the rest of the show was hard to follow much less see through the haze of cigarette and cigar smoke hanging as dense as fog over a high-mountain lake on a warm autumn morning.

It didn't help that most of the other men were standing and hooting and hollering responses to the actors' lines as well as opining about the ripe blond beauty of the lead actress, who, according to the handbill, was indeed Miss Diamond herself.

Kicked back in their plush-covered seats, boots hiked on knees, hats tipped back on their heads, Slash and Pecos enjoyed the show just the same, if only to wonder, chuckling and elbowing each other, at Miss Diamond's hysterics.

Poor Miss Margueritte could be forgiven such hysterics, though. As far as Slash and Pecos could make out through the smoke and din, the show was the story of the orphan girl's journey from the horrific orphanage to marriage to the man with the walking stick, who dumps her for another woman. Alone and penniless again, what choice did Margueritte have but to become a whore on the seedy streets of Paris, where she became Madame Margueritte.

Margueritte was abused by one brute after another, tried suicide several times with pills and poison, without success, until finally a gentle, old, rotund fellow fell head over heels in love with her. He put her up in a big house in the French countryside, only to die a few years later, at which point Margueritte got turned out of the big house by the gentle, old, rotund fellow's slattern of a witch-faced wife!

Miss Diamond screamed and cried and shook as though she'd been struck by lightning, then tried to drown herself, only the cardboard stream was too shallow. So it was back to the brothel for poor Madame Margueritte, who, when she was proposed to again by another sweet elderly soul, was so jaded by life that she climbed into a bathtub—wearing a frilly red blouse and a skirt, to the deep disappointment of the crowd—and, singing a bittersweet song about how the Fates had been against her from the first, drank down an entire bottle of laudanum and passed out, dead.

The show did not end without hope, however.

Angels swooped down from a big golden cloud hanging over the stage. They picked the dead Margueritte up in their lace-clad arms, taffeta wings flapping, and carried her up, up, and up through the open roof of the Parisian brothel and to that hovering golden cloud as the ropes and pulleys that lifted them and the dearly departed Margueritte could be heard squawking even above the howling objections of the men in the audience to the fact that Miss Diamond never took her clothes off a single time!

"What the hell kind of show is this, anyway?" cried one of the men sitting not far behind Slash and Pecos, leaping to his feet. "The girl's supposed to be a *whore*!"

"When a man pays ten cents for a theater show, he deserves some skin, galldangit!" echoed another man, seated somewhere near the stage, which was being peppered with spitballs made from torn handbills.

Beefy men with bulging muscles in tight three-piece suits quickly ran to stand before the stage, lest any of the unhappy crowd stormed it. Young Deputy Kenneth was there with his greener, as well, looking a might on the nervous side.

The accordion player was standing on the stage, trying to play an ending theme, but after a beer bottle was hurtled at him, narrowly missing his head, he heeled it, cowering, back into the stage's bowels as the curtain was quickly closed.

"You know what, Slash?" Pecos asked as the raucous crowd was hurrying toward the exits and likely another saloon or brothel.

"What?" Slash said.

"I no longer feel so bad about hauling Miss Diamond down off this mountain against her wishes. Not even this unheeled crowd deserves a performance as bad as that one!"

Slash laughed as he finished rolling a quirley and gained his feet. "After that, I need a drink and a steak."

"Sounds fine as frog hair split four ways," Pecos announced, rising from his seat.

They had a big steak and a shot of whiskey at the Miners' Café, right across the street from the opera house, then headed up to the main drag to kill a couple of hours playing dice games, like high-low, chuck-a-luck, and grand hazard, and drinking beer. It was good and dark when they took a shortcut through an alley on their way back to the hotel.

They stopped when the silhouettes of three big men appeared at the end of the alley ahead of them, backlit by shimmering oil pots set out on the street behind the men. At the same time, quick footsteps rose behind Slash and Pecos. They turned to see three more big men closing on them fast—quick-moving shadows growing in the darkness.

"Uh-oh," Slash said, closing his hands over the grips of his .44s.

"Yeah," Pecos said, closing his own hands over the grips of his big Russian as he and Slash turned their heads back forward.

"We can involve guns or not," said a taut voice ahead of them. "It's up to you!"

Slash and Pecos stood frozen in confusion halfway up the alley, switching their gazes quickly between the two factions.

"You two are a real thorn in an important man's side!" said a deep voice behind them just as the three men behind them stopped and big hands quickly tore the pistols from Slash's and Pecos's holsters and tossed them away in the darkness.

"Hey!" Slash said, wheeling to see a clenched fist arc toward him so quickly he had no time to do anything but take the full blow against the nub of his right cheek.

He gave a grunt as the blow hurled him back against the side of one of the two buildings abutting the alley, stars bursting behind his eyes. A second later, Pecos was dealt a similar blow. He staggered backward and twisted around just as another fist was hammered deep into his solar plexus, punching the air out of his lungs on a loud, grunting sigh. He dropped to his knees and gasped, trying to fight precious air back into his lungs, which suddenly felt shriveled to the size of raisins.

Slash rose to his feet just as all six men now closed on him and his partner.

Rage flaring inside him, he threw a punch at one of the shadowy figures surrounding him but dealt the brute only a glancing blow across a temple before a roast-sized fist gave him as good as what Pecos had just received.

Slash gave an agonized grunt as he, too, dropped to his knees, gasping.

Funny how a single blow to the solar plexus could take all the fight out of a man.

Or men.

Both he and Pecos were immobilized just long enough that they found themselves at the mercy of the six brutes, who jerked them both to their feet to hammer their faces, ears, the sides and backs of their heads and necks, and their ribs for an agonized eternity, until all that both men were aware of was a world of big-time hurt as they each did a weird shuffling dance between the brutes delivering blows.

Finally, mercifully, they were allowed to fall and remain on the ground, groaning and gasping and gritting their teeth against the sundry aches and pains assaulting every joint, bone, muscle, and sinew.

A fist jerked Slash's head up by the collar of his torn shirt. A big round head, a single eyebrow mantling deep-set eyes, slid up close to Slash's face. The man was as bald as an egg, with thick, bushy muttonchops running down each side of his hard-planed face. He was wearing a dress shirt, vest, and foulard tie. The tie hung askew from the bulging muscles of his stout neck. That was the only thing that appeared disheveled about the gent.

He hardened his jaws at Slash and said in a thick Eastern accent, "Take some good advice, bucko. Forget the girl. Hop the train out of town tomorrow, just you and your partner. If you're still around at noon, you're dead men." He winked and gave a crooked smile. "Duke Winter is on his way. What happened here tonight won't be anything compared to what he'll give you."

He released Slash's collar, and Slash's head dropped to the ground with a thud.

He probably would have passed out then, but a woman's voice roused him with a slight interest in the world of consciousness, keeping him awake. "Is that them?"

He turned his head to see a silhouetted female figure move down the alley from the direction of the opera house. All Slash could see of her was piled-up blond curls and the feminine curves of her slender body, clad in what appeared to be a black cape. He could smell her perfume as she moved closer—the scent of sandalwood and cherries.

The bullet-headed man rose and turned to her. "Fannie, go back inside."

She continued walking toward the tough nuts standing around their fallen victims.

"Fannie . . . ," the man said again when the woman stopped between Slash and where Pecos lay at the base of the building on the opposite side of the alley from his partner.

In the stray light from the oil pots behind her, Slash saw the actress's oval-shaped face turn ugly with a bitter scowl. She narrowed her eyes, curled her lips, and flared her nostrils as she said, "Fools! How dare you try to subpoena *me*! You can go back to Denver and tell whoever sent you to go to *hell*!"

With that, she wheeled haughtily and strode forthrightly back the way she'd come.

Slash heard the men around him chuckling. Just as the girl's words had been, the chuckles were partly drowned out by the ringing in Slash's ears. Just the same, they and the venom with which she'd expressed them still echoed around inside his head, spreading his fury from the men who'd beaten him and Pecos nearly senseless to the cunning little bitch of a two-bit, haughty actress who'd just talked down to him and his partner as though they were dogs.

Then at long last he was granted the mercy of dark, warm, soothing unconsciousness, until a hand shook him and a man's voice said, "Hello there, partner. Hello there, partner. You still among the living?" The words had come on breath scented with the stench of whiskey and chewing tobacco.

Slash groaned.

The man shook him again, harder this time. "Come on. You two gotta git up. The coyotes come into town after midnight, and they'll mistake you for dead men an' pick your bones clean."

Chapter 13

Pecos's voice came to Slash then, saying, "Come on, Slash. Get your raggedy ass up."

Slash opened his eyes to see the elderly manager of the French Hotel kneeling beside him, staring down at him, eyes cast with concern behind his round steel-framed spectacles. Slash slid his gaze from the manager to Pecos, who was just then pressing his back against the side of the building on the other side of the alley and using it to help lever himself slowly, grunting and groaning, to his feet.

"If I can do it, you can, too," he told Slash.

Slash sat up, wincing against the pain in his head. Hell, not only in his head but all over his body, too. His left eye was swollen, and licking his lips, he detected the copper taste of fresh blood. He felt several nasty gashes on his cheeks and forehead, and one ear ached fiercely. Probably torn.

"Christ," he growled. "I do believe we got the stuffin' kicked out of both the north and south ends, partner."

"And various other directions," Pecos quipped, crouched there against the building, leaning forward, hands on his knees. He hacked, spat, and cursed.

"Come on, fella," said the hotel manager, whose name, Slash remembered, was Arnold Hano. He was the one who'd ordered the baths up to his and Pecos's room earlier that morning—a short, slender, but muscular fella with a craggy, sun-seasoned face sporting a trimmed gray mustache. "Let's get you inside before McClory changes his mind and returns to put bullets in you. They were talkin' about doin' that at first. I overheard 'em talkin' outside the opera house when I was smoking a cigar in front of the hotel. They decided to just send you a message to avoid more trouble, an' you'd best be damn grateful they did. Boone McClory is no man to cross, an' I reckon you crossed him purty good. What'd you do? Throw a beer bottle at Miss Diamond?"

Hano gave a wry snort.

Slash turned his head this way and that, trying to untangle the knots in his neck. "Who's Boone McClory?"

"Miss Diamond's manager. High roller in these parts. He takes it personal when men throw things at Miss Diamond while she's onstage."

"The bald fella with one eyebrow and the muttonchops?" asked Pecos.

"That's him, all right."

"Did you throw a beer bottle at Miss Diamond, Slash?"

"Nope." Slash shook his head. "Did you, Pecos?"

"Nope." Still bent forward, Pecos lifted his head and curled a devilish grin at his partner. "Good thing I didn't have one, or I'd have been tempted."

"Well, if you didn't assault Miss Diamond, how in blue blazes did you two get Boone McClory's neck in such a hump?" asked Hano, incredulous. "That's usually what does it. Not treatin' Miss Diamond with the respect he thinks she deserves, though it's common knowledge she can't act her way out of a paper sack and the fellas attend the shows only because they like how she looks in her skimpy outfits, though they sure wish she'd shed them a time or two!"

"We heard," Slash said with a dry chuckle, heaving himself

to his feet. He took a moment to take stock, investigating his weary, burning, aching, and throbbing carcass for broken or dislocated bones.

He didn't think there were any, but not for lack of those six brutes trying.

He spat blood from his lips and then joined Pecos in retrieving his guns and hat, grateful but surprised he hadn't left any teeth on the ground, as well.

When he and Pecos had their guns holstered and battered hats back on their equally battered heads, Hano led them out of the alley and back over to the hotel. Once inside the lobby, he said, "You two head up to your room. I'll have my boy haul you up water for a couple more baths."

"Thanks, partner," Slash said, leading Pecos wearily up the stairs. "Two baths is usually more than Pecos has in a whole year."

Pecos told him to do something physically impossible to himself.

He and Pecos were soaking in hot, soapy water once again, smoking and passing a bottle again, when a knock sounded on their door. Both men's reaction times had been considerably compromised by having the stuffing kicked out of them, but they still managed to pull their revolvers off nearby chairs, cock them, and aim them at the door as it came open.

They eased the tension in their trigger fingers when Hano poked his head through the door, smiling and raising a labeled bottle. "Thought you could use a little of the good stuff."

"Hell," Pecos said, depressing his gun hammer and returning the piece to the chair he'd pulled up beside his steaming tin tub, "I could use a whole lot of the good stuff."

"And a pair of good cigars?" Hano asked, closing the door and then producing three stogies in brown paper wrappers from inside his brown wool vest.

Slash and Pecos shared a skeptical glance.

"Don't worry," Hano said, popping the cork on the bottle and splashing brandy into one of the three water glasses on a table beside the room's charcoal brazier. "I have no dog in the fight. I just don't like seeing men—especially a pair of older fellas, though you're a good bit younger than me—ganged up on."

He poured whiskey into the third glass and looked at Slash and Pecos over his shoulder. "And I don't care one bit for Boone McClory. He's a bully. Not only does he manage Miss Diamond and several other so-called *actresses* runnin' with troupes in these mountains, but he also owns several saloons, gambling parlors, and mines throughout the central Rockies. He bullies other saloon and mine owners into selling to him for well below the market prices for their claims or businesses, and he's in cahoots with Miss Diamond's beau, Duke Winter."

Hano handed one of the filled glasses to Pecos and another to Slash, then gave each man a cigar. "He hires Winter to do his dirty work for him. His killin', I mean." While Slash and Pecos each lighted their cigars, he hitched up his broadcloth trousers, sat on the edge of one of the room's two beds, and sipped his brandy. "I just thought you oughta know about him. Us old outlaws gotta stick together, don't ya think?"

Slash and Pecos frowned in surprise at each other.

Turning back to the hotel manager, Slash said, "You're . . ."

"Chester Hannity." The man smiled shrewdly, his spectacles glinting in the light of a single lit lamp on the table behind him.

Wreathed in cigar smoke, Slash and Pecos looked at each other in even more surprise than before.

"*Chester Hannity*, the lone train robber that single-handedly robbed nearly every rail line from Missouri to California from the late sixties to the—" Slash said.

"Till about five years ago," Hannity said, chuckling and shaking his head. "Got a little too long in the tooth, I reckon. I figured I'd better change occupations before I ended up spending my old age in federal prison. Figured I wouldn't be so apt to be recognized way up here on this boil on the devil's backside." He raised his glass in salute to the mending of his ways and drank.

"I'll be damned!" Pecos intoned, staring at the small, compact, bespectacled man in shock. "No lawman or bounty hunter even got close to you!"

"You were even more slippery than we were!" Slash added.

Hannity only grinned as he fired a match to life on a bedpost and touched it to his stogie, which he turned as he lit it. When he had the cigar burning to his satisfaction, he waved out the match and frowned curiously through his own wafting smoke. "You never did tell me how you boys climbed Boone McClory's hump. I don't mean to pry. If you'd rather not say, well, from one former outlaw to two others . . ."

"It's the damnedest thing," Slash said. "Keep this under your hat, will you, Mr. Hannity?" He glanced at Pecos. "Though I reckon the cat's out of the bag . . ." He flexed his left shoulder, wincing.

"Please, call me Chester."

Slash chuckled and shook his head. "Oh, no. A man of your esteemed train-robbin' knowledge and practical experience is and will forever be called only *Mr. Hannity* by this raggedy-heeled amateur."

"This one, too!" Pecos said in agreement of Slash's estimation of the formidable old wolf of the iron rails.

Hannity gave a self-deprecating grunt and puffed his stogie.

"As I was sayin'," Slash continued, "this is . . . or was . . . a secret. Chief Marshal Bledsoe out of the Denver federal building—"

"Bleed-'Em-So himself," Hannity cut in.

"One and the same," Pecos said.

"He got us an amnesty from the president himself in return for us workin' for him as unofficial lawdogs," Slash said.

"Takin' on the jobs too nasty or *illegal* for bona fide bearers of the moon and star," Pecos said, tipping his head back and blowing smoke rings at the ceiling.

"You can say that again," Slash agreed.

Hannity whistled his surprise.

"So, we're here to serve Miss Diamond with a subpoena, and we're to escort her to the federal building in Denver in time for a murder trial that's supposed to get started next week. The fella on trial is Duke Winter's cousin, Chaz 'the Knife' Lutz. He killed an opera-house owner in Idaho Springs because the man refused to allow Miss Diamond to perform on his stage due to the way she worked up the crowd. Winter and Miss Diamond were present. An old swamper saw the killin' through a crack in the door and reported it to the local sheriff, who reported it to Bledsoe. Bledsoe sent several federals up that way to arrest both Lutz and Winter, but they could find only Lutz. He was whorin', as usual, and three sheets to the wind. Winter, the slipperiest of the pair, had returned to the gang's outlaw lair, wherever in hell that is."

"That's another thing Bledsoe wants out of the so-called actress," Pecos added. "The whereabouts of the gang's lair."

Again, Hannity whistled. "He saddled you with a tall order. Gettin' Miss Diamond away from Boone McClory ain't gonna be easy, as you both found out."

"Yeah," Slash said, wincing and shifting positions in the soapy water as he silently took inventory of his sundry miseries. "The chief said it was such an easy assignment he was embarrassed to send one of his bona fides!" He turned to Pecos. "Who do you suppose told McClory what we were up to here in town?"

Pecos shrugged. "Who else could it have been?"

"Sure enough," Slash said, nodding slowly and hardening his jaws. "Uncle Billy Early double-crossed us, that son of a bi—"

Pecos cut him off with, "Slash, do you think that old rapscallion Bleed-'Em-So was only blowin' smoke up our back-sides?"

"Sure as hell I do," Slash said, scowling as he studied the gray thumb of ash at the end of his quarter-smoked cigar. "He's tryin' to get us killed, sure enough. And Uncle Billy's givin' him one helluva helpin' hand. Damn his hide!"

Pecos winced and shook his head. "What the hell we gonna do? Ride down out of these mountains and tell him we failed?" He looked at the old robber, Hannity, and added, "That'd be a might embarrassin' for a pair of former cutthroats such as Slash and myself. To have to admit to that old polecat Bledsoe that we couldn't get a little actress—"

"*So-called* actress," Slash cut in with shrill sarcasm.

"Yeah, yeah," Pecos agreed. "That we couldn't get a little *so-called* actress who probably don't weigh much more than a hundred pounds drippin' wet to the federal courthouse in time to make sure that crazy killer, the Knife Lutz, stretches hemp . . ."

Hannity said, "After such an esteemed career as criminals, I can understand the potential humiliation of such a failure." He grimaced and shook his head.

"We can't let it happen," Slash said, staring into space, mulling the problem.

"We took a lot of money from banks and trains over the years," Pecos said, staring at the ceiling again and rolling the stogie from one side of his mouth to the other. "You'd think we'd be able to find some way of gettin' that so-called actress away from Boone McClory." He turned to Slash. "But you heard the man. Duke Winter's on his way."

"Yeah," Slash said with a grimace. "Likely with his whole damn gang!"

Again, Hannity whistled and slapped his knee. "Lock up the women and hide the children! Not even you two despera-does can hold off that bunch. They'll make what Boone

McClory did to you look like a pillow fight. You can't face them down alone, and I've turned right cowardly in my retirement."

"Ah, hell," Pecos said in defeat. "Bledsoe will likely hang us for such a failure. Leastways he might finally use that amnesty of ours to light his cigar."

"Savage man," Hannity said. "He was the one I feared the most."

"Yeah, well, he caught us," Slash said, his ears warming with chagrin. He turned to Pecos. "Maybe we ain't as good as we thought we were."

"Now, now, fellas," Hannity said, leaning forward and resting his elbows on his bony knees. "No long faces. Please. You're accomplished desperadoes, by God! You can't give up so easily."

"Any ideas?" Slash asked the older former outlaw.

Hannity stared at him, his eyes behind his spectacles cast with deep musing, the wrinkles at their outside corners deepening. Slowly, he nodded. He nodded some more, puffing smoke until Slash and Pecos could hardly see his face anymore. Then he looked at each man in turn through the roiling smoke cloud and said, "Yeah." He nodded again, drawing on the cigar. "Yeah, I think I just might!"

Chapter 14

"You ready, partner?" Slash asked Pecos the next night, around eleven o'clock, as they peered around the rear corner of the French Hotel, casting their cautious gazes toward the rear of the opera house next door.

"Hell, no."

"Yeah, me, neither." Slash glanced into the dark desert scrub flanking the hotel. "But Hannity and the horses are in place, so let's get a move on. Besides, it's almost time for Fannie to be swept up into that golden cloud."

Pecos grabbed Slash's arm. "Why do I feel the way I felt when Bledsoe had us standin' on that gallows with nooses around our necks? Remember? When he faked he was gonna hang us an' then faked our escape just to put the fear of God into us?"

Slash gave a caustic chuff. "He did a good job of it, too. How could I forget?"

"Well, that's how I feel. Like a trapdoor's about to open beneath my boots and I'm about to dance the midair two-step! Have we thought through this whole thing well enough? I don't know—seems awful risky to me! I mean, Duke Winter's right here in town, fer peein' into a rattlesnake nest!"

The previous night, Slash, Pecos, and the venerable old

train robber Chester Hannity had come up with a plan to nab Fannie Diamond out of the opera house at the end of her last performance, when, according to Hannity, she'd be the least guarded and the most vulnerable. All or most of Boone McClory's bouncers would be guarding the stage.

Hannity had admitted with some chagrin that out of sheer boredom he'd taken in several of Miss Diamond's performances. Also, he'd been in town when the place had been built. So he knew the building's layout well, and he knew the ins and outs of Miss Diamond's performance in *Madame Margueritte: Portrait of a Courtesan* well, too.

(Slash and Pecos both suspected the old bank robber even sort of fancied the gal, had a crush on her, so to speak. Why else would he or anyone endure more than one of her ghastly performances? Unless he, like all the other men around Frisco, were just hoping to get a glimpse of her forbidden flesh. Oh, well, just because a man knew how to rob a train like no one else, even Slash and Pecos themselves, it didn't mean such a rare talent would necessarily translate into good taste in women.)

Once they had come up with a plan and had had a night's healing sleep, even though neither Slash nor Pecos had gotten much sleep with all the pain they were in, they had made a big show of riding out of town the next morning in apparent obeyance of Boone McClory's warning. In fact, as soon as they were a half a mile beyond Frisco, they'd left the trail and set up camp along a creek.

They'd spent the day out there, drinking coffee laced with medicinal whiskey and lounging around, letting their bodies heal as much as they could over the next eight hours. As soon as the sun had gone down, they'd stolen quietly back into town, taking a roundabout way so they wouldn't be seen by either Early, the town constable who'd betrayed them, or McClory. They'd met Chester Hannity in the dark shadows at the rear of the French Hotel, intending to follow through with their plans.

Hannity had informed them that he'd spied Duke Winter and several gang members in a saloon earlier that day. That information had caused the short hairs to stand straight up on the backs of Slash's and Pecos's necks, but they'd decided to follow through with their plan to kidnap the actress, anyway. Neither former owlhoot was so much afraid of Bledsoe as they were piss burned about their rude treatment the previous night. They weren't about to let the thuggish manager of Miss Diamond send them down the mountains with their proverbial tails between their legs.

No, when they rode down out of these mountains, they'd do so with the nasty little viper of a so-called actress, Miss Fannie Diamond, tied belly down across a saddle!

Now both men were silently reconsidering their plan even as they stepped out from around the hotel's rear corner and headed down the alley toward the rear of the opera house. According to Hannity, there were two back doors at the building's rear. Three, actually, but the third was sort of like the hayloft doors of a barn, meant for the use of winches and pulleys in hauling up premade sets or set building materials from a freight wagon.

One of the other two doors was at ground level. The second of the other two doors gave entrance to the balcony above the stage. It was onto this balcony that Miss Diamond was swept up by the two lace and taffeta "angels," for the balcony hovered over the golden cloud. Here Slash and Pecos should be able to grab the actress while the two "angels" were still trussed up in the harnesses that, with a rope being manipulated by a couple of brawny gents and a pulley in a side wing of the stage below, would be the most vulnerable.

To be sure, Hannity had allowed that there would be someone—likely a stage manager or manager's assistant—on the balcony, waiting to pull her up out of the "angels'" arms and onto the balcony, but a stage manager or two shouldn't be too hard "for a pair of owlhoots of Slash and Pecos's caliber to overcome!"

Hannity had cackled a delighted laugh and rubbed his hands together eagerly. The old outlaw seemed to have gotten bored in the years after he'd given up haunting the western rails, and this kidnapping scheme seemed to give him no end of devilish joy.

Slash and Pecos were glad not to find anyone lurking around behind the opera house. There was the lingering odor of cigarette smoke, as a stagehand or two must have slipped out during the play for a smoke, then gone back inside, apparently. Slash and Pecos made their way in the dense darkness behind the hulking building to the metal stairs that rose to the door about a hundred feet up from the ground.

Now they had to hope the door wouldn't be locked, but Hannity had doubted it would be, for it was often used for the comings and goings of the stagehands who worked on the balcony during the play's first half.

There would be no reason to lock it. Unless, of course, you were worried that two former owlhoots had been sent by a devilish federal marshal to kidnap the show's starring actress. And who would be worried about that? Slash and Pecos had made sure to ride past Constable Early while he sat outside his small jailhouse as they'd hoofed it out of town earlier that morning. They'd each given the man indignant looks, which they had not had to feign.

Early had grinned and touched two fingers to his hat brim, apparently thoroughly satisfied with himself and believing the two men working unofficially on federal business were gone to stay.

Slash and Pecos made their way up the stairs in the darkness. They could hear the roar of the crowd now, which meant the show was likely nearly over. Judging by the anger they heard in Fannie Diamond's mostly male audience, she had not taken her clothes off again tonight. Walking ahead of Pecos on the outside stairway, Slash glanced back at him and snickered.

"I gotta feelin' she loves drivin' 'em all mad," Slash said.

"We'd best hurry, Slash. She'll be headin' for that golden cloud soon!"

"All right, all right. I'm tryin' not to break my neck in the darkness."

They gained the top of the stairs. Slash gave Pecos a nervous glance, raised his hand to the door handle, curled his fingers through it, and, stretching his lips back from his teeth, pulled.

It didn't come open.

"Ah, hell!" Pecos said.

"Wait, maybe it's just stuck."

Slash pulled again.

Sure enough, it had only been stuck. The door balked a bit, but then, scraping its frame, it opened. Slash held it open a foot and peered inside. The roar of the crowd assaulted him on a thick wave of hot air rife with the smell of man sweat, cheap perfume, and tobacco smoke.

"Boo! Boo! Boo!" came the thundering roar.

Slash could feel the reverberations of the din in the metal door handle.

He peered into the balcony, lit by only a couple of hurricane lamps hanging from wires from the slanted ceiling. The lamps rocked from the crowd's roar, shunting thick shadows this way and that, their flames guttering in the draft from the door.

There were so many sets and parts of sets that Slash couldn't see much of anything else. He glanced at Pecos and then moved through the thick shadows, meandering around false wooden store facades and pieces of furniture of every shape and size. He shouldered past ropes and nets dangling from the ceiling. When he and Pecos had walked maybe thirty feet, Slash stepped out around a buckboard wagon, which had likely been used in one production or another, and stopped suddenly.

Twenty feet beyond, and just beyond a railing, the balcony gave way to open air and a view of the stage below. The crowd's roar rose even louder, and blinking against the sting of the tobacco smoke, Slash felt his gut tighten when he saw a man standing at the edge of the balcony only a few feet beyond, where there was no balcony rail.

That was likely where the actress, being hoisted off to heaven, would mount the rail with the help of her "angels."

The man standing there was big. Easily as big as Pecos. Wavy blond hair hung to his shoulders, tumbling down from a high-crowned black Stetson. He wore a natty gray jacket and black trousers with decorative white stitches running down the outside of the legs, and he had two silver-chased Colts holstered on his hips.

Slash's heart thudded. This was no stagehand or even a stage manager or stage manager's assistant. It wasn't Boone McClory, either.

Pecos cast a peek out around Slash and then looked at Slash, frowning curiously.

Slash gave him a blank stare. Then, as Slash heard the screech of the pulleys beneath the crowd's roar, which meant the poor, dead Margueritte was being lofted toward the golden cloud, he returned his gaze to the big man standing about two feet back from the edge of the balcony. The man was staying just far enough back that he probably couldn't be seen from below—by anyone but the angels and the actress, that was.

Slash could see the man's right profile, and something about the way he stood there, a blond-headed but darkly shaded specter, told Slash he was up to something. Something not good, for a devilish smile curved his thickly mustached mouth.

Not only that. But Slash, lowering his gaze, saw that the man held a long-bladed knife in his right hand.

Pecos turned to Slash and said in his usual tone, because he couldn't be heard above the crowd's enraged roar by anyone but Slash, "Know who that is?"

Bledsoe had placed a wanted circular in the envelope he'd given to Slash and Pecos. The circular bore the penciled likeness of the notorious cutthroat Duke Winter. The man standing before Slash and Pecos bore the same likeness as the man depicted on the circular.

Pecos's eyes widened in recognition. He gave his chin a dark dip. "Damn."

"Yeah."

"What the hell's he doin' with that knife?" Pecos asked.

Just then, the devilish smile grew on Winter's face, lifting his thick blond mustache, and he raised the knife.

"Let's find out." Slash hurried forward, palming one of his two Colts.

He'd taken two steps when Fannie Diamond's gold-blond head appeared between the heads of the two bewinged "angels," whose own gold-blond wigs and heavily painted faces, Slash saw now, were meant to conceal the fact that they were men.

Two beefy men. Likely two of McClory's men.

Who else would he trust to hoist his most prized actress to heaven?

Winter raised the knife higher and slid it toward the rope angling above him, toward an unseen pulley in the ceiling.

"Holy shit," Pecos wheezed to Slash. "He's gonna kill her!"

Slash raised his pistol as he closed on Winter.

He was four feet away from the man when Winter turned his big, broad face toward Slash and his close-set eyes widened and glinted his astonishment and sudden anger. Slash took one more step forward, then smashed the barrel of his Colt down hard on Winter's head, badly denting the crown of the outlaw's crisp Stetson.

The big man grunted and dropped to his knees, his hat tumbling from his head.

Slash slammed the Colt's barrel down hard on the man's head again, in the same place as before. Winter's eyes closed. He toppled to one side and lay still.

To Slash's right, a woman screamed.

"Here she is!" Pecos bellowed, reaching over the edge of the balcony to grab the actress out of the ridiculous-looking "angels'" brawny lace- and cotton-clad arms.

"Hey!" both "angels" barked as Pecos lifted the actress, who was kicking and screaming and peering in horror down at her unconscious beau.

Pecos drew the kicking and screaming Fannie Diamond over his right shoulder and wheeled toward the door. "Come on, Slash!"

"I'm right behind you," Slash said, turning to the two trussed-up "angels," who were struggling to gain the balcony. Even in their ridiculous costumes and wearing wigs of tight golden curls above their broad, savage faces, Slash recognized both men from the alley the previous night. "But first I need to get somethin' off my chest."

He stepped forward and slammed his right knee into the ugly face of the angel to his left, turning the man's wedge-shaped nose sideways and causing it to ooze blood. The man screamed and grabbed his nose as his harness swung out away from the balcony.

"Hey, what's goin' on up there!" a man shouted from below, though Slash could just barely hear him above the continuing unsatisfied din of the crowd, even though the curtain had been closed.

Slash slammed that same knee against the face of the other angel, giving the same bloody treatment to that man's wedge-shaped nose. That angel grabbed his own ruined nose as he flew back, gossamer wings still beating, away from the balcony.

"There!" Slash said, wincing against the hitch in his knee. "Now I feel better!"

Slash ran back through the debris cluttering the balcony and gained the door just as Pecos was trying to step through it with the girl on his shoulder. What made it a particularly difficult maneuver was that the screaming girl was grabbing the doorframe with her hands, trying desperately to keep herself from being carried through it.

"Damn you, big ugly brigand!" she screamed at Pecos. "Damn you to hell! What do you . . . what do you think you're *doing*?"

"We're gonna get you to the courthouse on time, princess!" Slash said, trying to restrain the girls' hands.

Pecos glanced over his shoulder at Slash and said, "I got her, partner! It ain't gonna be purty, but . . ."

He swung the girl hard to one side. She saw the doorframe flying toward her and widened her eyes and screamed even louder.

Thunk!

Her head struck the frame.

Her eyes closed, and she flopped down against Pecos's back and hung there like a wet sheet.

"Sorry, honey!" Pecos said and hurried down the night-dark outer stairs.

Slash followed Pecos and the girl, running both hands along the rails to either side of him. "Partner, I believe you enjoyed that."

"After last night," Pecos said, breathless, "I gotta admit to a certain satisfaction."

Chester Hannity was waiting at the bottom of the steps with the two horses.

The old train robber chuckled delightedly and said, "How'd it go?"

"We found a little hair in the butter," Pecos said.

"In the form of Duke Winter," Slash told Hannity.

The old train robber sucked a sharp breath through his teeth.

As Pecos slung the girl over his saddle, Slash accepted his horse's reins from Hannity and said, "You know what, Mr. Hannity? I do think the man was gonna cut the harness rope and send her and them two guardian angels tumbling back down to earth!"

Hannity whistled as Slash swung up into his saddle and Pecos swung up behind the girl on his buckskin. "He must've figured," the old train robber said, thoughtfully rubbing his chin, "that ol' Bleed-'Em-So would get his claws into her sooner or later and make her testify against Lutz and even spill the beans about where he and his gang hole up between jobs. So . . ." The old man showed the white line of his teeth in the darkness and ran his index finger from right to left across his throat.

"Now, that there is true love!" Slash said. "Thanks for your help, Mr. Hannity. It's been a pleasure. But you'd best haul your freight. I gotta a feelin' it's only a matter of time before—"

A man's enraged wail cut through the relative silence behind the hulking opera house. "*Fan-nieee!*"

Slash turned to see a man-shaped shadow crouched in the doorway atop the outside stairs. "See?" Slash said. "I done told you!"

"Good luck, fellas!" the old man wheezed before he hurried off in the direction of the hotel.

A gun barked, flashing in the darkness atop the stairs. Slash and Pecos put the steel to their mounts' flanks and galloped off down the alley, in the opposite direction of the hotel.

Bang-bang-bang! spoke Duke Winter's Colt, flashing behind the fleeing riders. The bullets whistled through the air around their heads and thumped into the ground around them.

"Slash," Pecos yelled as he and his partner galloped side by side, "why in the hell didn't you shoot him when you had the chance?"

"Oh, shut up!" Slash returned, crouched low in his saddle as the Colt crashed again. "In retrospect I suppose I should have, but you know what they say about hindsight!"

"Don't tell me to shut up!"

"Shut up!"

"Slash, if we somehow make it out of this whipsaw, I'm gonna whup your scrawny ass!"

Slash laughed as the Colt thundered again. "Partner, I don't think I have a damn thing to worry about!"

Chapter 15

Slash and Pecos knew they were liable to kill their horses on the curving mountain trail they'd taken at Chester Hannity's recommendation after leaving Frisco with haste, Duke Winter yelling with a shrillness surprising for such a big, masculine-looking hombre, and emptying his Colt's cylinder with an equally high degree of frustration and rage.

Yep, Pecos is right, Slash thought. *I should have put a bullet in the mustachioed tough nut's head when I had him sprawled out like a big sack of potatoes at my feet.* He hadn't done it, because he wasn't accustomed to shooting unconscious men. There was something way too cold-blooded about that. Downright cowardly. He'd never shot a man in the back—at least not intentionally. His bullet that had crippled Bleed-'Em-So had been a ricochet. And he'd never shot a man when he was down and defenseless.

Still, he should have done it. He wouldn't flog himself about it, though. He was sure his partner would flog him plenty.

Fortunately, a three-quarter moon revealed itself through a notch in one of the toothy ridges jutting blackly to each side of the trail, offering a modicum of light for the horses to avoid the mining road's most perilous chuckholes and wheel ruts.

Still, they didn't gallop far before slowing their mounts to trots and then to walks, pricking their ears for the hoof thuds of pursuing riders. The night was so quiet amongst the towering, dark crags around them, without a breath of wind, that Slash and Pecos figured if Winter gave chase—which he surely would do, given the level of the man's acrimony back at the opera house—they'd hear him and his men coming from a good half mile back.

They passed several abandoned mines showing their black portals in the ridge to their left, then turned off on a side trail to the right and reined up in a hollow amongst the rocks and ponderosa pines. A valley dropped away to the south. They could see through the columnar pines and firs a creek or river glistening snakelike at the valley's bottom in the moonlight.

Owls hooted and wolves howled from distant crags.

Slash turned to Pecos and the girl lying slack across the saddle before the big man, who rode behind the cantle and atop his soogan. "Has she moved or said anything since we left Frisco?" Slash asked.

Pecos looked down at her hanging there like another sack of potatoes, this one smaller and bagged in a costume—low-cut red blouse and pleated purple skirt—from the last scene of *Madame Margueritte: Portrait of a Courtesan.* "Nope."

"Jesus, I hope you didn't kill her."

"Damn, I never thought of that!" Pecos nudged the girl's shoulder. "Hey, you, Miss Diamond. You alive?"

Slash snorted. "'Hey, you, Miss Diamond. You alive?'" he mocked his partner as he swung down from the Appaloosa's back.

Pecos glowered at him. "What the hell am I supposed to ask her? You *dead*?"

"You big dummy. Let me check it out." Slash reached up and pulled the slack actress down from Pecos's saddle.

Pecos glared down at him. "You take that back, dammit, Slash. I'm tired of your insults!"

Slash swung an admonishing look at the big man, who just then slid up over his cantle and into his saddle, then used the left stirrup to dismount. "Keep your damn voice down, dummy. Winter is likely behind us!"

Shaking his head, Slash carried the slack actress down to where a blowdown pine lay amongst rocks. He set the girl on the log and let her rest back against a large white boulder. He doffed his hat and lowered his head to her chest clad in the torn, puffy-sleeved red blouse that was low cut enough to offer a good view of creamy cleavage, which was what got the miners stirred up every day and night in Frisco.

Slash turned an ear to her chest and then listened.

"Hear anything?"

"Not with your caterwauling!"

"Slash, if we weren't in such a sour pickle of a situation, I'd kick your scrawny ass seven ways from sundown! But I know you're just feelin' stupid for not pumpin' a coupla pills into Duke Winter when you had the chance—which, I might add, you have every right to feel stupid about, because you *were*!— so I'm gonna spare you the misery."

"Oh, shut up!" Slash raised his head and donned his black topper. "Can't hear nothin'."

"Damn," Pecos said, worried suddenly. "What if I killed her?"

"Not good, partner. Not good at all."

Slash thought, hesitated, then pinched her nostrils closed.

Almost immediately she jerked to life, opening her eyes and flinging her hand against his arm to remove his fingers from her nose.

"She's still kickin'!" Slash laughed in his relief.

"Thank heavens! I woulda swung for sure less'n I coulda convinced ol' Bleed-'Em-So you did it, which I surely would've done, by the way. An' he woulda believed me. Killin' the very actress—and I use that term loosely—you were supposed to haul safely down out of the mountains is way more like somethin' *you'd* do. Not me!"

"*Will you shut up?*"

"Oh, my God!"

They both jerked their heads toward the girl, from whom the exclamation had been ejected on an agonized wail. She flicked her hand through the air again, though Slash had lowered his arm.

Her eyes stopped fluttering, and she gazed at Pecos and then at Slash in shock. "Oh, my God! Who are you? What have you *done* to me? Is it *rape*? Have you *raped* me, you savages? Just like you've done with your *eyes* every day and night in Frisco! Oh, my God. *Rape*! I ache all over! What am I *doing* here?"

She opened her mouth with a loud rasping gasp. "Oh, my God. It's *you two*! The brigands from Denver! You've kidnapped me—taken me literally out of the hands of my true love—after you so savagely hit him over the head!" She was staring at Slash now, eyes wide, lower jaw hanging. "Did you *kill* him? Is Duke dead!"

"Keep your damn voice down, lady, or I'm going to have my partner blow out your candle again!"

"It was him. He did that," Pecos said, canting his head toward Slash.

Again, she gasped, eyes and mouth widening even more, as she glared at Slash. "How dare you speak to me with such venom, *brig*!"

Slash lunged toward her, closed one hand over the back of her neck, the other over her mouth, cutting off the scream, which continued to echo around the ridges.

Through gritted teeth, he said, "Listen, lady, we're gonna haul you down out of these mountains to that murder trial in Denver, an' that's bond. You can either make the trip riding the normal way, *sitting up*, or you can make the whole rest of it just how you came here—*belly down*. You'll be bound an' gagged, lady! If that's how you want it, just scream out again!"

Slash glanced at Pecos, who shrugged. Slash removed his

hand from her mouth and the other hand from the back of her neck. He lowered them slowly, studying her cautiously.

She glared at him, but he didn't think she was going to scream again, until she threw her head back and did just that.

Slash lunged toward her again, closed his hand over her mouth, pinching off the scream. He turned to Pecos. "All right, dammit, get a rope and somethin' to gag her with!"

"You got it!"

Before Pecos could take more than one step toward their horses, which were standing in the shadows nearby, reins dangling, a bullet spanged loudly off a rock just inches from where Miss Diamond sat on the log. Her scream was half drowned by the shrill screech of a rifle.

"Ah, hell!" Slash grabbed the girl and dropped to his side, the girl on top of him. He rolled on top of her and dragged her to the cover of a large boulder, against which another bullet ricocheted loudly.

At the same time, Pecos threw himself behind another rock, drew his .44, and sent a round streaking toward where he'd seen an orange flash in the rocks above him and to the north, along his and Slash's back trail.

"Damn, Slash, I do think they done caught up to us!"

"What was your first clue?"

"I didn't hear a thing. Did you?"

"No, but we're gettin' on up in years, partner," Slash said as he held the screaming, wailing girl down against the ground while he snapped off two of his own shots at where he'd just seen a second gun flash. "I reckon our hearing ain't what it used to be!"

Miss Diamond lifted her head and gazed up into the rocks from which the bullets were coming hot and furious at the moment—too hot and furious for Slash and Pecos to return fire or do anything but keep their heads down. "Duke!" the actress screeched, throwing up her arms. "Duke, it's Fannie! Oh, Duke, help me! These brigands—"

Slash shoved her down and put more weight on her. "Lady, keep your fool head down, or you're gonna get it blown off!"

"Duke wouldn't shoot me! He's trying to shoot you and that big ape over there!"

"Hey!" Pecos objected to the insult.

The shots tapered off. In the sudden silence, a man called from high in the dark rocks, "Dave, get on your hoss an' fetch Duke an' the others. We'll keep these fools pinned down till Duke gets here!"

"You got it!" came the shouted reply, which echoed around the ridges.

Silence.

Hooves thudded; the sound dwindled quickly.

"Hey, you two down there!" shouted the man in the rocks who'd told Dave to fetch Duke. "Why don't you send out Miss Diamond, and we'll let you walk away without a severe case of lead poisoning!"

The girl wriggled half of her supple body out from under Slash and lifted her head again. "Charlie!" she called. "Charlie Wade, is that you?"

"It's me, darlin'!"

"Oh, Charlie, help me, please! These men want me to testify against Chaz!"

"I know they do, princess." A slight pause, and then, his voice pitched darkly, Charlie added, "We ain't gonna let that happen, Fannie. I guarantee you that!"

From another spot among the dark rocks, another man chuckled.

Slash and Pecos shared a look, and then Slash yelled, "You want us to send her out so you can put a bullet in her because ol' Duke wasn't able to cut the rope hauling her and them two beefy angels up to the golden cloud!"

"What?" the girl cried, swinging her shocked look to Slash.

"That ain't true, princess!" Charlie called from the rocks. "We're here to take you back to Duke. Duke loves you—you know that. Why, Duke wouldn't harm a hair on your pretty lit-tle head!"

"Oh, you dirty, rotten liar!" the actress snapped at Slash.

"It's true," Pecos said, hunkered down fifteen feet away from her and his partner. "He was gonna cut the rope lifting you an' them angels, prob'ly make it look like an accident."

"You too!" she screeched at Pecos. "Dirty, rotten, low-down, bald-faced liar!"

"Don't listen to them, Fannie!" Charlie called. "You got it right. They're liars. They were sent by the U.S. marshal in Denver. Everybody knows a no more duplicitous man has ever lived or worn a badge!"

Slash and Pecos shared an incredulous look. In the light of the moon, which was nearly directly overhead now, they could see each other mouth, *"Duplicitous?"*

An educated bushwhacker. Imagine that!

Slash chuckled and turned to the dark rocks rising before him and in which, having counted the rifle flashes earlier, at least three shooters were forted up. "Hey, you, Charlie Outlaw with the good vocabulary, why don't you tell her the truth?" He looked at the actress. "We're not lyin', princess. Duke was about to cut that rope. If I hadn't smashed my gun barrel down on his head when I did, you an' them angels would be nothin' but blood puddles on the opry-house stage."

He'd said it loudly for the outlaws to overhear in the quiet mountain night.

"Don't believe him!" Charlie called loudly.

Maybe a little too loudly. The actress's face acquired a skeptical cast. She slid her gaze to Slash, wrinkling the skin of her fine little nose. Then she shook her head. "No. No . . . I don't believe it. Duke loves me. He lives for me, in fact. He just told me so yesterday!" Her voice had a tremor in it.

"All right, then." Slash slid off her. He jerked his head to-ward the rocks. "Go on. Go to Charlie an' good ol' Duke."

He was taking a chance, but something told him—the wary cast far back in her eyes—that she wouldn't accept his challenge.

She stared at him, eyes wide, lips parted.

"Go ahead," he said again, this time looking at Pecos, who sent him a dubious look.

"Come on, princess!" Charlie called. "Let's get you back to town an' to Duke. He's plumb *worried* about you. He sent us out here to fetch you back to him! He would've come himself, but he's got a headache, thanks to them two fools down there!"

Again, the girl slid her uncertain gaze from the dark rocks to Slash.

Chapter 16

Earlier that day, Jaycee had walked with purpose along the boardwalks on the south side of Camp Collins's bustling main street, a feathered picture hat on her head, a knit brown shawl draped over her otherwise bare shoulders, and a beaded reticule, the same burnt-orange color of her day dress, dangling by a white chord from her wrist.

She also wore an uncharacteristically dark, downcast, and brooding expression on her green-eyed face, one framed by her rich copper-red hair, which she'd chosen to wear down today. Deep in thought, it took her a while to realize that beneath the afternoon din of the town around her, she was hearing a familiar female voice pitched with scolding.

The voice was coming from ahead of her. She looked up now to see her young friend Myra Thompson, dressed in her customary plaid work shirt, sleeves rolled up to her elbows, her long brown hair tied back in a long queue, step toward the large wheel of the freight wagon parked in front of her.

She swung her right arm back, then forward and rammed a stout hammer against the wheel with a loud ringing clang!

"There. See how easy the rim comes off!" she fairly bellowed at the gray-bearded, middle-aged wheelwright and farrier, Herman Beckett.

Beckett's deep-lined, weathered face colored with exasperation. He pointed the stem of his smoldering corncob pipe at the wheel. "Well, it wouldn't come off if you didn't pound it with a consarned *hammer*! Listen here, little girl, you just—"

"Don't 'little girl' me, you old hornswoggler," Myra shrilled, eyes narrowed feistily. She pointed the hammer at the man. "You didn't put the rim on tight enough in the first place, and you didn't fix the crack in the axle. And the hub you put on the wheel isn't new, like Slash and Pecos—er, I mean *Mr. Braddock and Mr. Baker*—ordered! You put a secondhand hub on there, and it's not gonna last, just like the rest of your shoddy work isn't gonna last until you do it *right*!"

Beckett turned to see Jay stop a few feet away from where he and Myra, Slash, and Pecos's freight wagon sat in front of Herman Beckett's Front Range Livery & Feed Barn. His gaze turned imploringly; then he threw up his hands in defeat. "I say, Miss Jay, help me with this mulish child, won't you? She accuses me of not knowing my work—work that I have been performing for over thirty years, little miss!" he added, turning back to the angry-eyed Myra, who was standing before him with her fists on her hips.

Jay chuckled and crossed her arms on her chest. "I think she's accusing you of cutting corners, Herman, which, I say with some regret, you are known to do. And in Miss Thompson here"—she stepped forward and wrapped both her arms around the young woman's right arm, brushing her forehead warmly against Myra's shoulder—"I think you've met your match!"

Beckett threw up his hands again with a sigh, shoved his pipe into a front pocket of his wash-worn bib-front overalls, then dropped to a knee beside the wheel and his wooden toolbox, which was overflowing with the implements of a longtime wheelwright. He cursed in German, shaking his head—or at least what Jay took to be German.

Myra turned to Jay with chagrin. "I'm sorry you had to see that, Jay. I'm afraid I wasn't acting very ladylike."

"There are times and places for acting like a lady, young lady," Jay said, reaching up and sliding a lock of brown hair back from the girl's still anger-flushed left cheek. "And there are times and places for turning your she-wolf loose. Take it from me, who's been around a whole lot longer than you! And who, I might add, knows Mr. Beckett's, um, *questionable* business tactics!"

She'd added that last part loudly enough for Beckett to hear. The stout German merely sighed and shook his head as he used a large wrench to remove the freight wagon's wheel hub.

Both women laughed, and then Jay gave Myra an affectionate kiss on the cheek.

She'd felt a motherly affection for the young woman since she'd first met her in the mountains of southwestern Colorado, back when she had furtively followed Slash and Pecos on their first assignment for Chief Marshal Bledsoe. Myra had thrown in with Slash and Pecos's old gang, the Snake River Marauders, whom Bledsoe had assigned Slash and Pecos to hunt down and kill because they'd killed Bledsoe's young granddaughter in a bank robbery. The gang had turned savage after they'd gotten shed of Slash and Pecos, who as senior leaders had managed to keep the younger men in the gang on short leashes.

Myra had turned outlaw, but after the gang had been turned toe down during an attempted train robbery that Slash and Pecos had foiled, it hadn't been hard for Jay and Slash and Pecos to see the innate good in the girl and turn her back to the straight and narrow trail. Myra had turned to the dark side only because as a young girl who'd suddenly found herself an orphan in the Colorado high country, and who'd been exploited by men, she'd had few other options.

Now she was like a daughter to Jay and the two roguish former outlaws. Slash and Pecos often said they couldn't run their freighting business without Myra's help. Jay had just seen, as she'd seen many times before, that they weren't exaggerating. Myra might have been young—she was still only in her early twenties—and pretty, to boot, even in the masculine work garb she wore around the freight yard. But she'd been raised in rough country, and she still had the bark on, much like the former Jaycee Breckenridge herself. Neither woman was afraid to prove it when necessary.

Jay admired the young woman as much as she genuinely loved her, as she would her own daughter.

To the grunting and muttering Beckett, Myra said, "Let me know when you're finished, Mr. Beckett. You can find me back at the freight yard." She turned to Jay with a sidelong look. "Slash and Pecos were keeping the books last month—when I took the train down to Pueblo to see my aunt—and no matter how sharp I get my pencil, the figures do not add up."

Jay laughed. "I don't doubt it a bit, poor child. You're too good for those two rapscallions." She squeezed the girl's hand. "I'll see you later, dear. I have business to tend to."

"Where you headed?"

"To the courthouse. I have to talk to your beau's favorite uncle—the sheriff."

"I'll walk with you," Myra said.

Jay smiled. "Hoping to have a few words with Deputy Thayer?"

"Possibly." Myra hooked her arm through Jay's as they headed on down the street together, leaving Herman Beckett grunting and muttering behind them.

"You're really taken with the lad, aren't you?" Jay asked as they strolled.

"I must say I am. He's tall and bucktoothed and not very smart, but the only man alive I know who's sweeter and gentler is none other than the Pecos River Kid himself. And he thinks he's too old for me, so . . ." Myra rolled her eyes.

"He is sweet, isn't he?" Jay said, smiling bemusedly. "I mean Pecos. Delbert Thayer is, too, but Pecos has always had a heart of gold, which, I might add, he wears pinned to his coat sleeve—right out in the open for all to see."

Myra smiled and turned to the older woman. "Jay, don't take this wrong, but . . . but . . . have you ever wondered . . ." She paused, as if not sure how to continue with what she was asking.

"Do I ever wonder why I chose Slash over Pecos? Is that what you're trying to ask?"

"Please, don't take offense! I love Slash as much as Pecos. Truly I do!" Myra turned her head forward, frowning. "It's just that it took me so much longer to get to know Slash than it did Pecos. Slash—he's . . ."

"Not as talkative?"

"Yeah."

"He's also darker and more cynical, given to brooding," Jay added, smiling foxily at the younger gal walking beside her.

Myra frowned, nodding. "Exactly. I mean, he has a big heart, too. Maybe even as big as Pecos's. It's just that . . ." Again, she let her voice trail off, searching for words.

"It takes a lot longer to find that out about him than it does with Pecos," Jay said, finishing for her.

"Exactly."

"Don't get me wrong—I love Pecos. As a brother. But I think I fell in love with Slash long, long ago . . . even when I was in love with another man, the larger-than-life Pistol Pete Johnson, leader of the Snake River Marauders. You can love two men at the same time, though. I used to feel guilty, though I never acted on the feeling. But it was real, and there was no denying it. I knew right away that Slash and I were kindred spirits."

Jay smiled with fond remembering. "I remember him and me stealing glances at each other across a fire or across that old cabin Pete and I lived in up high in the San Juans. Sometimes Slash and Pecos holed up with us for a month or two at a time, when they and Pete were waiting for the gang's trail to cool after some job they'd pulled. There was just a feeling between us, Slash an' me, right off that I don't think either one of us could make heads or tails of. It was just there, a pull toward each other, and we both knew it, though neither one said anything about it until . . ."

She gave a throaty laugh. "Until only a few months ago, when the shy, tight-lipped son of a gun finally asked me to hitch my star to his wagon!"

"Took him long enough, didn't it?"

Jay was still chuckling. "Seven years after Pete passed."

"Maybe he was trying to be respectful of Pete's memory."

"No." Jay shook her head. "He's just shy. Around women. Men not so much. But he's shy, and deep down, I think he feels vulnerable. Deep down, I think he was worried I might have rejected him." She drew a deep, long breath and then turned to the mountains rising in the southwest. "I sure wish the old scalawag was here right now. I could really use his help . . . his reassurance in a certain matter."

"What matter is that?"

"The matter I'm here to talk to the sheriff about. Here we are at the courthouse. I'll tell you after I've talked with Sheriff McGuire."

"Jay, is it serious?" Myra asked with concern as she and Jay entered the courthouse, which flanked the old town marshal's office and jail.

"Don't worry, dear. I'll be fine. At least I'll feel better after I've talked to the sheriff."

She and Myra stopped in front of a door about halfway down the building's shadowy main hall. The door's upper glass panel was adorned with gold-leaf lettering announcing MATTHEW H. MCGUIRE, COUNTY SHERIFF. Jay and Myra gazed through the beveled glass of the door and into the main office, which was outfitted with a big, wagon-sized desk at the room's rear and three smaller desks to the right and left of it. Only the big, wagon-sized desk—the desk of the sheriff himself—was occupied.

It was not occupied by Sheriff McGuire, however.

Jay and Myra shared an incredulous glance after they saw that the man behind the desk, kicking back in the sheriff's swivel chair, spurred boots crossed on the edge of the desk before him, was none other than Myra's tall, lanky, bucktoothed sweetheart, Delbert Thayer.

Young Thayer had his nose buried in a thin book with a yellow pasteboard cover bearing the title *The San Antonio Kid Fogs the Border Sage!* At the moment, as Myra peered through the beveled glass once more, the string bean pulled a cigarette from between his lips and leaned forward coughing, blowing a thick smoke cloud into the air before him.

"What on earth?" Myra said, some of the same shrillness with which she had addressed the German wheelwright a few minutes ago entering her voice. Her cheeks flushed as she stared at Jay. "Del doesn't smoke!"

Jay arched her brows and gave a crooked smile. "It appears he does now . . . or is giving it his best shot, anyway."

Hardening her jaws, Myra pushed the door open and stomped into the office, snapping, "Delbert Eugene Thayer, you take that cigarette out of your mouth this instant, or I'm telling your mother!"

Young Thayer swung his head toward his chosen gal, gave a startled, strangled yell. He let the poorly rolled quirley drop onto his uncle's desk.

"Myra!" he croaked. "Jay! What're you two doin' here?"

He leaped out of his chair, dropping the dime novel he'd been reading, while coughing his lungs out and waving both hands at the smoke, as though to hide it.

Chapter 17

Myra said, "A little bird told us you were over here, sitting at your uncle's desk, reading a dirty book, and smoking his tobacco."

"A little bird told you that?" Del said skeptically.

"I had such a hard time believing that little bird," Myra said, scolding, "because I've always known you to be such an upstanding young man that I couldn't believe you'd be reading a dirty book or smoking cigarettes!"

"It was my first one!" the deputy indignantly insisted.

"Which? The dirty book or the cigarette?"

"Both!" he insisted, gazing in flush-faced terror at the angry young lady staring up at him, her nostrils flaring. "I mean, it ain't a dirty book. It's a true story about the San Antonio kid runnin' hog wild down in Mexico with a senorita named—"

"Oh, a senorita's in it, too, huh?" Myra crossed her arms on her chest, cocked a hip, and slid one booted foot forward, then tapped the toe on the floor impatiently. "I bet she takes her clothes off every other page! And what do you think you're doing smokin', Del? I told you I can't stand the smell of a tobacco on *any* man's breath and on *my* man's breath most of all!"

The string bean smiled suddenly, his blue eyes softening, his narrow, tanned cheeks dimpling. "Ah, heck, honey." He placed his hands on her arms, beaming down at her. "I just love it when you call me *your* man, Myra. Makes me feel all funny inside, even when you're hotheaded about it."

Myra glowered up at him but took the razor's edge out of her voice. "We'll discuss this matter later. Where's the sheriff? Jay has an important matter to discuss with him."

"Oh!" Del turned to Jay, who was standing with an amused expression just inside the office's open doorway. "I plumb forgot you was there, Jay!"

Jay smiled. "I don't doubt it a bit, Del. All will be forgiven if you can point me in the direction of the sheriff." She frowned suddenly with concern. "He is in town, I hope."

"Nope." Del shook his head. "Uncle—er, I mean *Sheriff* McGuire done left town early this mornin' for Denver. Gonna be there for the next five days. All the county sheriffs in the whole territory are gathered at the Larimer Hotel for some kind of sheriffs' shindig. A convention is what he called it. They all gathered there at the same time last year."

"He sure does leave town a lot," Jay said, scowling her disappointment.

"You can say that again. Them sheriffs, I tell you, they always seem to find some reason or another to gather up in a hotel somewhere and, uh, make policy. That's what Uncle— ah, *damn!*—I mean that's what *Sheriff* McGuire calls it." Del chuckled.

"Makin' policy, right," Myra said, sharing a doubtful glance with Jay. "They probably mostly just gather at the opera house to watch girls dance with little on."

"It's all right with me, though," Del said, ignoring Myra's last remark. "Since the sheriff promoted me last year, after you an' me, Myra, helped Jay get out of that tight spot with Cisco Reeves, he always puts me in charge when he leaves town. The other three deputies are out in the county, tendin' to this an' that—I won't bore you with the official partic'lars of what they're doin'—so I'm here holdin' down the fort, so to speak."

He glanced at the half-smoked quirley on the sheriff's desk and then at the dime novel on the floor at his boots and blushed.

"Yeah," Myra said, looking at same. Then she added with sarcasm, "'Holding down the fort, so to speak.'"

Del's flush grew redder.

"Damn!" Jay said, stomping one foot down hard on the floor. "I really wanted to talk to your uncle, Del."

"What's the problem, Jay?" Del asked. "You can tell me. I'm in charge now." As if to prove it, he hitched his cartridge belt and holstered .44 higher on his skinny hips and brushed his fist across the badge on his chest, as if to buff it.

"Have a seat, Jay," Myra said, indicating a chair.

"Yeah." The string bean deputy pulled up the leather-seated wooden chair fronting the sheriff's desk. "Have a seat and tell me what the trouble is. You can count on me." He grinned. "Didn't I solve your, uh, problem last year?"

"With help," Myra reminded him.

"Yeah, with help," Del allowed, shrugging a shoulder.

"I'll stand. I'm too nervous to sit." Jay leaned back against the sheriff's desk and crossed her arms. She cast her serious, worried gaze from Myra to Del and said, "When I was riding Dorothy west of town yesterday, I was bushwhacked."

"*Bushwhacked*?" Del and Myra said at the same time.

"By who?" Myra asked.

"I'm pretty sure Grant Balldinger sent one of his men to do the dirty deed. I didn't get hit, obviously. And I'm fine, if a little sore from my tumble from the saddle. Mostly, I'm scared. And worried what he'll do next."

"Hold on, here, Jay," Del said, lifting a boot onto the chair he'd pulled up for Jay and leaning his arm on it. "Why on earth would Mr. Balldinger send a man out to shoot you? As far as I know . . . or ever heard . . . he's a fine, upstandin' man. One of the most respected in the county. Heck, he's good friends with the sheriff! I thought you an' him was friends, too!"

"Good Lord. Your grammar, Del," Myra put in. " 'I thought you and he were friends, too!' "

"That's what I said, honey," Del said.

Myra rolled her eyes, then turned to Jay. "Do you really think it was one of Balldinger's men, Jay?"

"I do."

"How do you know?" Del asked. "And why in tarnation would he want to do such a low-down dirty rotten thing as shoot *you*, of all people?"

"To answer your second question first—because I refused his offer to sell the Thousand Delights to him. To answer your first question, because I got a look at the man who fired at me, as he rode away. I saw him later, after I left the Balldinger ranch. I rode there to talk to Grant himself. When I was leaving and topping that first rimrock to the east, I looked down into the Balldinger compound and saw the bushwhacker I'd seen earlier riding into the yard and up to the house."

"Holy cow!" Del said. "So it *was* Balldinger!"

"When I talked to him at his house, he seemed weird. Weirdly menacing, while saying all the right things."

"Oh, Jay, I'm so sorry!" Myra threw her arms around Jay and hugged her affectionately. "How frightened you must be." She hardened her pretty jaws. "And mad!"

"Exactly. It's as maddening as it is frightening."

Myra turned to Del, her cheeks flushed with anger once more. "What're you going to do about this, Del?"

"I'll tell you exactly what I'm gonna do about it, honey." The young deputy unsheathed his old Remington revolver and opened the loading gate. As he pinched a cartridge from his shell belt and thumbed it into the open wheel, he said, "I'm gonna have me a ride out to Cheyenne Creek right now. Me an' ol' Balldinger are gonna have us a powwow!"

"No!" Jay said, stepping forward and shoving the young

deputy's gun down. "That's exactly the wrong thing to do. I wasn't sure when I came over here what I expected the sheriff to do about the matter, but now I know that nothing can be done until I have more evidence that Balldinger is trying to coerce me into selling to him."

"Ah, heck, Jay," Del said. "I can at least ride out there and warn him that we're onto his devious exploits an' that if he tries to throw down on you again, tryin' to ramrod you into sellin' when you don't wanna sell, well, then he's gonna have a whole heap of trouble rain down all over him. Yessir, lettin' him know we're onto his blackhearted deviltry may just save your life!"

Myra stared dubiously up at the young string bean. "'Devious exploits'? 'Blackhearted deviltry'?" She picked the dime novel up off the floor and dropped it into a trash can. "No more Deadeye Dick for you!"

Jay said, "I appreciate your wanting to help, Del, but Grant Balldinger is not a man to scare easily. Or to change direction. For some reason, he has made up his mind that the Thousand Delights is going to be his. I have a strong feeling he's going to do everything in his power to make it so."

She glanced darkly at Myra and then turned to the young deputy again. "I'm going to wait him out. He'll try something again. I know he will. I could see it in his eyes yesterday afternoon. He's angry at me for turning down his wedding proposal, and taking my business is his way of getting back at me for humiliating him. That's not the only reason he wants my business, but it's a big one. The biggest one is his ego. He wants to own the largest business in this part of the Front Range, and he won't take no for an answer."

She nodded darkly, pursing her lips. "He'll try something again to frighten me into selling. And when he does, I'm going to be ready for him. I'll get the evidence I need to have him arrested."

"All right." Del sighed his disappointment at the undramatic strategy and dropped his Remington back into its holster. "If you insist, Jay. But don't you worry—I'll be shadowin' you close. *Close as the bark on a tree.* That kinda close! If and when the old ranny tries anything, rest assured that Deputy Delbert Thayer is gonna be there to throw the bracelets on him or fill him with so much lead he'll rattle when he walks!"

Jay and Myra shared a skeptical glance.

"Yep," Myra said, returning her gaze to her beau and slowly shaking her head. "No more dime novels for Deputy Thayer."

Del blushed, then turned to Jay. "I'll walk you back over to the Thousand Delights, keep a close eye on you."

Jay smiled and shook her head. "I appreciate the sentiment, but that's too close. I don't want him to know we're onto him." She stepped forward, rose onto her toes, and planted a kiss on the deputy's cheek. She squeezed his wrist. "Thank you, Delbert. I do feel safer knowing you'll be close enough to hear me scream."

"Let's just hope it doesn't come to that!" Myra said. "Anyway, I'll walk you back to the saloon, Jay. Nothing odd about that."

"Thank you, dear," Jay said, kissing Myra's cheek now, too, and placing her hands on her shoulders. "I'd like to walk back alone. I don't think he'll try anything in town in broad daylight. Besides, I'd like to do some thinking."

Actually, she wanted time alone to pine for her new husband, Slash. She sure wished the old outlaw was here, so she could cry on his shoulder. Also, she had a feeling that Slash would know exactly what to do about her situation.

On the other hand, knowing Slash, he'd probably ride out to Cheyenne Creek Ranch and fill Balldinger so full of lead he'd rattle when he walked!

Chapter 18

"Come on, princess!" Charlie called again from the dark rocks above Slash, Pecos, and Fannie. "Let's get you back to town an' to Duke. He's plumb worried about you!"

The actress, on her knees and hunkered behind the same boulder as Slash was, looked at the former outlaw, a miniature three-quarter moon reflected in the dark brown pool of each wide-open eye.

"You heard the man," Slash said with irony. "Duke's plumb worried about you."

Her eyes suddenly narrowed in spite. "Go to hell, you . . . you . . . *scalawag*!" She lowered her head and bowed her shoulders, as though in prayer. Only she did not pray. She sobbed, saying in a pinched voice, "I don't know what to do! I don't know what to do!"

"You stay here and keep your head down, or I promise you, you're gonna get it blown off!" Slash looked at Pecos, crouched fifteen feet away to his right, and then at the dark rocks towering over him.

He looked at Pecos again and then pointed with his left index finger toward the east before tracing an arc in the air with the same finger.

Understanding, Pecos nodded, then rose to his feet and,

keeping low, strode off to the east along the embankment of piled boulders. When the darkness had absorbed him, Slash rose and tramped off in the opposite direction, intending to steal up into those dark rocks, flank Charlie and the two others he believed to be hunkered down up there, and kick them out with cold shovels.

In a manner of speaking.

He had no intention of burying men who would kill him. The carrion eaters needed meat, too.

When he'd moved fifty feet west of where he'd left the girl, he swung right and began climbing up into the piled rocks and boulders. He half expected Fannie to have a change of heart and to call out to her would-be saviors, warning them of Slash and Pecos's ploy. He probably should have tied and gagged the girl, but there wasn't time. Besides, his and Pecos's horses had run off when the first shots were fired, taking both men's ropes along for the ride.

Bleed-'Em-So's words ran through his head: *The job I have for you is embarrassingly simple. Should take you a week at the most. It's so simple and easy that I would send one of my junior deputies, but I have all of them chasing counterfeiters out Utah way. So, I am sending you and the dancing bear over here.*

Slash laughed under his breath as he hoisted himself up one boulder and then around the side of another, steering by the pearl moonlight, which cast as many shadows as light, making for a perilous climb, not to mention a difficult one for a man who smoked and drank too much and who'd had the stuffing kicked out of both ends just the previous evening.

"That lyin' SOB. When I see that cripple again, I'm gonna—"

"What's that?" a man's voice interrupted him.

He stopped suddenly, gloved left hand on the edge of a rock, his right hand wrapped around his Winchester's stock.

"What cripple?" the man asked in the darkness just ahead

and to Slash's left. He must be on the other side of the rock Slash had his hand on. A brief silence and then the man said tentatively, "Blade, that you?"

"Yep," Slash said, keeping his voice low and a little garbled. He hurried forward, his right boot on one boulder, his left boot on the ledge of the larger boulder on his left. "Just came to bum a smoke!"

"Wait," the man said, his voice rising skeptically. "You don't smoke!"

Slash stepped around the front corner of the boulder on his left, saw the man-shaped shadow ahead and to his left, capped with a cream hat, the crown of which was limned by the milky moonlight.

"Oh, that's right. Never mind, then!" Slash said, the "then" drowned out by the loud bark of his Winchester.

The man grunted and tossed his own rifle high as he flew back in the moonlight and shadows, and the rifle clattered to the ground a few seconds later.

"Damn, that was careless!" Slash scolded himself. He hadn't realized he'd been talking out loud to himself.

A gun stabbed orange flames to his left, and the thundering report reached his ears just after the bullet carved a hot line across the nub of his left cheek.

"Galldarnit," he wheezed out, gritting his teeth against the burn and turning sharply to his right. "I just did it again!"

He aimed and triggered, but another rifle had spoken an eye blink ahead of his own and knocked the man-shaped shadow in the darkness above him backward and out of the path of Slash's own round. Pecos's Colt's revolving rifle spoke again, shrilly, and the man above Slash rocked back again, turning toward Slash, moonlight reflecting off the Yellowboy's barrel.

Slash shot the man two more times. The man cursed and flew back, to be swallowed by the moonlight and shadows.

"Hey, now! Hey, now! Hey, now!" a man screamed in the darkness to Slash's right.

Slash recognized Charlie's voice, and he smiled as Pecos's revolving rifle sang twice of Charlie's demise.

Silence fell over the rocks.

Slash's ears rang from the rifle fire. His cheeks burned against his carelessness.

"Am I gettin' so damn old I don't know enough to keep my damn mouth shut when I'm talkin' to myself?"

"What'd you say, Slash?" Pecos asked in the shadows above him.

Boots clacked on rock. Slash looked up to see his partner's tall silhouette step between two rectangular boulders above him, roughly twenty feet away. The moonlight pooled on the broad brim of the tall man's brown Stetson and on the long barrel of the Colt's rifle he held in both gloved hands.

"Did I say that out loud, too?" Slash wheezed into the darkness toward his partner.

Pecos stopped, leaned against the side of a rock, and chuckled dryly. "What the hell? Are you talkin' to yourself up here, you old scudder?"

"I do believe I was, an' damn near got drilled a third eye for my foolishness!"

"You know what they say about fellas who talk out loud to themselves?"

"What's that?"

"Time to put a bullet in 'em." Pecos continued forward and then grunted as he took a long step down toward Slash. "Leastways that's what we used to say as outlaws. Yessir, when a man gets so old he starts talkin' out loud to himself an' don't even know it, it's time for a bullet. Put him out of his misery."

"Don't even think about it," Slash growled as Pecos approached.

"Don't you worry," Pecos said, stopping before his partner

and shaping a grin in the moonlight. "You ain't even worth a bullet, ya ornery old cuss."

"Thanks."

"Don't mention it."

"Best get back to the girl and haul our freight outta here. Lead the way."

"All right but we gotta take it slow. It ain't an easy climb comin' up. It's gonna be even harder goin'—"

The girl's shrill, agonized scream cut him off.

"What the *hell*?" Slash and Pecos said at the same time.

Slash stumbled forward, running his right hand along the boulder on his right for balance. He dropped down into a corridor between two more boulders, then, Pecos wheezing close behind him, boots clacking on the rocks, followed a dogleg down to his left.

The girl screamed again, but the scream came from farther away this time.

"*Damn*!" the two former owlhoots said at the same time.

A minute earlier, Fannie had sat fuming in the darkness, leaning back against the stone embankment, frightened and badly confused.

Had the two men who'd so unceremoniously kidnapped her out of the opera house, after one had smashed his gun down on Duke's head, been honest with her? Had Duke really meant to cut the rope supporting her and the two "angels," sending all three of them to their deaths on the stage below?

No, of course he hadn't! Why had she even given it a moment's consideration?

She drew a breath, swallowed, splayed her right hand over her heart, as though to quell the organ's frenetic fluttering.

She had considered the possibility, though, hadn't she?

Yes. She had. Why?

What would ever lead her to believe even for a moment that Duke would kill her?

He loved her as she loved him.

Still, as she probed her own fluttering heart, she discovered that doubt lingered.

In the rocks above and behind her, guns barked loudly. With a horrified gasp, she turned around, rose onto her knees, and gazed up into the darkness to the west and saw the brief orange flashes of the crashing guns.

A man screamed.

"Oh, my God!" Fannie gasped. She should have warned Charlie!

The thought had just winded through her brain when a man's breathless voice said tightly behind her, "*Grab her! Grab her!*"

Fannie leaped with a start as a scream vaulted out of her.

She'd just begun to turn when she saw two horseback riders ride up on her fast. Too shocked and terrified to move, Fannie found herself frozen in place on her knees.

"Come here, you little polecat!" the lead rider said, reaching down to grab her arm and then to pull her up onto the saddle before him.

She groaned as the saddle horn bit into her painfully.

"I got her," the man who'd grabbed her said. "Let's go, George!"

"Right behind you, Pete!"

"No," Fannie groaned as she hung down across the man's cantering horse like a sack of oats, her long hair trailing down nearly to the ground. "Oh, God . . . help . . . help me . . . ," she cried, too weakly to be heard by anyone but the man Pete, who'd grabbed her.

Again, she'd been kidnapped!

Twice in one night!

"Oh, God! Oh, God!" she cried as the saddle horn bit into her side as painfully as the toothy jaws of an angry dog.

"Stop your caterwaulin'!" Pete scolded.

"Please!" Fannie sobbed. "Let me sit up!"

"Oh, hell!"

Pete checked his horse down. Brusquely, he wrapped his right hand around her waist and drew her up into a sitting position before him. The position still wasn't comfortable, but it was better than having that savage horn grinding into her.

"There. How's that?" Pete said, keeping his arm around her, touching her in a most ungentlemanly fashion, and pressing his moist lips up against her left ear.

He spurred his horse forward and along a stream that glittered in the light of the high-kiting moon. "Feel better, Miss Diamond?" he asked, his breath hot against her ear and reeking of whiskey. "We wouldn't want to hurt you, now, would we? Uh-uh. Best not damage Duke Winter's prized goods—the showgirl herself, Miss Fannie Diamond!"

He squeezed her, pawing her, nuzzling her neck. "Sure, sure. We know who you are. We heard them two old owlhoots—Slash Braddock an' the Pecos River Kid no less—who done nabbed you say your name. George and me—we was dry camped in them rocks back there when you three rode up!" He chuckled devilishly. "Call it your lucky night!"

Pete lifted his mouth to her ear again. "I wonder how much ol' Duke thinks you're worth? Wonder what he'd pay to get you back! Not that we need the money." He reached behind to pat a bulging saddlebag pouch. "Hah! Hah! We're flush!"

"Yeah, that bank in Conifer sure paid out! How much do you think we hauled out of there, Pete?"

"More'n I expected—that's for sure! Must be twenty, thirty thousand dollars!" Pete shook his head. "An unexpected surprise. I reckon it's our day for surprises." He squeezed Fannie again where he shouldn't have. "A coupla hours later who do we find out here in the high 'n' rocky but the showgirl of all Rocky Mountain showgirls herself—Miss Fannie Diamond!"

"Hey, now, Pete!" George said, riding a cream horse just behind Pete and Fannie. "Don't pinch all the lovin' out of her before we even reach the cabin. Save some fer me!"

"I don't know if I can, George!" Pete yelled. "She's right temptin'. The purty li'l showgirl who rarely takes her clothes off but only now an' then to keep the poor suckers comin' back for more!"

Again, he pawed her, nuzzled her neck.

"Oh, God," she cried, leaning away from the savage man and twisting her mouth distastefully. *"Oh, God! Oh, God! Oh, God!"*

The old saw "Out of the frying pan and into the fire" came to her, and she found herself sobbing openly while the uncouth Pete pawed her as though she were the cheapest of whores.

She, the actress Fannie Diamond, being treated like the cheapest of whores!

Chapter 19

"Ah, hell!" Pecos said when he and Slash had reached the spot at the base of the stone embankment where they'd left the so-called actress Fannie Diamond. "She's gone!"

"I can see that, but what I wanna know is, who in the hell took her?"

"Beats me!" Slash was walking around, staring at the ground and angrily kicking rocks. "Looks like two horseback riders came in fast. Musta just grabbed her an'..." He turned to stare south, along the secondary trail ribboning off into the darkness, climbing gently through pines. "Rode off with her."

Pecos looked at him. "Men from Winter's bunch?"

"No idea. Hard to believe there'd be two other men skulking around out here in the dark, waiting for a purty actress to come along so they could nab her and ride away with her!"

"What the hell's wrong with us, Slash? How'd we let this happen?"

"Don't ask me. I'm so damn old I don't even know enough to keep my mouth shut when I'm talkin' to myself!"

"We'd best get our horses an' get after 'em." Pecos bit off a glove, stuck two fingers between his teeth, and whistled. "If we don't get her safely back to Denver, Bleed-'Em-So is likely gonna throw one hell of a big party of the necktie variety."

"Yeah, I know. In our honor," Slash said as he heard the thuds of two trotting horses rising in the direction of the main trail, which they'd pulled off of before getting ambushed by one faction of Duke Winter's bunch, most of whom now lay dead in the high, dark rocks.

Earlier, when the shooting had started, Slash had glimpsed both his and Pecos's mounts hightailing it back out toward the main trail. Now they swung off the main trail and came trotting up to their riders, snorting, reins trailing.

"Let's get after it!" Slash said and stepped up into the leather.

"I just hope we catch up to the so-called actress before Duke Winter catches up to us!" Pecos said as they both touched spurs to their mounts' flanks. As they rode up the curving rise in the moonlight-dappled darkness, Pecos turned to Slash. "I just hope if you get Winter in your sights again, you'll have sense enough to pull the trigger!"

"Oh, shut up!"

"Dammit, Slash. Don't tell me to shut up!"

"Shut up!"

Dawn pearled the eastern horizon between jagged mountain peaks silhouetted against it by the time Fannie and her most recent captors rode through some of the starkest, baldest country Fannie had ever seen. They turned into a sage-carpeted valley between two forested ridges. On one side of the valley sat an age-silvered log cabin, at the edge of the pine forest spilling down the side of the mountain.

Fannie didn't know which side, direction-wise, the cabin was on. She had no sense of direction even when she hadn't been hauled on horseback for half the night on up and down mountains and across several valleys, turning this way and that, and that way and this, until her head fairly spun. She had no idea where she was or what was going to happen to her up here at the hands of these two goat-ugly outlaws, who'd plucked her out of the frying pan, so to speak, and into the fire.

As the dawn light had grown, she'd gotten a good look at both her captors, and to say that they were goat ugly was an insult to goats. They were ugly, and they smelled bad, and their denim jeans and buckskin shirts and shapeless hats appeared to be rags.

She had a very good idea what was going to happen to her, after all.

She was going to be used up by these two goatish, smelly, stupid men—used up and tossed away like so much trash, no doubt. When they were finished having their fun with her, they'd likely cut her throat and toss her into the nearest ravine.

"Here we are, Miss Diamond. Your new home," Pete said before placing his wet, leathery lips to her cheek and kissing her.

She gave a half groan, half wail of revulsion and tried to slam her right elbow into the man. However, she was so sore and weary from the long ride, she lost her balance and went tumbling backward off Pete's horse. She screamed as the ground came up behind her fast.

The ground clipped off the scream as it crashed into her, making stars burst behind her eyes. Her skirts flew up into her face. Sobbing, her head and the back of her neck throbbing from their unceremonious introduction to the ground, she swept her skirts back down her legs with her arms, aware that she was likely exposing way too much of herself to these goatish fiends.

When she sat up, sobbing, she saw them both sitting on their horses, staring down at her in mute fascination. She frowned curiously. She lowered her head to follow their gazes and saw that the right strap of her low-cut red blouse, which was part of her costume from *Madame Margueritte*'s last scene, her suicide scene, had slipped down her shoulder to expose almost the entirety of her right bosom.

She gasped and quickly pulled the strap back up her arm.

"Damn," Pete said, staring.

"Yeah," George said thickly from the saddle of his cream horse. "Damn." He turned to Pete, his expression suddenly a little hesitant, maybe even wary. "What'd we get our hands on?"

Fannie sat on the ground, glaring back at them, aching and wanting to continue sobbing, but then she saw the bulging saddlebags hanging over the back of Pete's chestnut gelding. Her heart fluttered a little, hopefully.

She looked at each man in turn. Yes, to say they were goat faced was an insult to goats, but there was something in their eyes that gave her sudden hope. No, not something that was in their eyes. It was the something *lacking* in their eyes that gave her hope.

That thing both men were lacking was intelligence. She had a strong feeling that these two were maybe as smart as a smart dog, but no more.

What *was* in their eyes, though, was goatish male need. They wanted her. They wanted her very badly. But the fact that they hadn't thrown themselves on her by now, even after the strap of her blouse had come down to give them a very nice view, meant that they were a little afraid of her, too. Or that maybe they were smitten by her just enough that they wanted her to see them as more than simple savage rapists.

She was an actress. A famous one. At least locally, though it was a well-known fact at least in thespian circles that she had a rare talent that would likely one day take her to New York and San Francisco—if she could get out from under Boone

McClory's thumb before she got too old, that was!—and these two men respected that about her.

She wasn't just some simple prospector's daughter or a cheap whore they'd picked up in a gold camp.

No, by the light of day they could see that she was more than that. For lack of a better word, they were a little afraid of her. Afraid of her beauty, maybe. Or afraid of Duke Winter, whose woman she was. At least they were afraid enough that they wouldn't just throw her down and cover her like dogs and be done with her.

Maybe she had a little time to use their dim-wittedness to her advantage.

She glanced at the bulging saddlebags again. Again, her heart fluttered.

That money might just be her escape from Duke Winter and Boone McClory. . . .

Pete swung down from his saddle. He was a small, bandy-legged man with a patch beard and dull yellow eyes set too close together beneath the ragged brim of his shapeless hat. He squatted down before Fannie and stared simplemindedly at her.

"I'll be hanged if you ain't cuter'n a speckled pup!" Pete grinned, a bashful flush rising in his hollow, pitted cheeks.

Fannie sniffed, smiled fleetingly, and glanced away as though with embarrassment. "Why, thank you, Pete."

George stepped down from the cream horse and tossed his reins on the ground beside his partner. "Pete, you tend the horses. I'll show Miss Diamond around the premises. She'd probably . . . probably . . . I bet she wouldn't mind havin' a bath." A flush rose behind George's thick, tangled black beard and his voice quavered and his left eye twitched as he said, "Ain't that right, Miss Diamond?"

Her face tightened as her exasperation rose. Wouldn't these two lowly dogs just love to watch her bathe. Hah! As if she'd give them the satisfaction of seeing her in anything less than what she had on right now. Which, she had to admit, wasn't much. It was cool at night in the mountains, but she'd been so afraid that she hadn't even noticed.

"What I really wouldn't mind right now, Pete and George," she said, looking at each man in turn, feigning shyness but also unable to keep from glancing at the bulging saddlebags again, as well, "is something to eat. If . . . if that wouldn't be too much trouble . . . ?"

Pete glanced at George and said, "You tend the horses, George." He anxiously ran his hands up and down the thighs of his faded, dirty denims and smiled down at Fannie. "As for grub—that can wait until after Miss Fannie and me have gotten to know each other a little better . . ." His eyes glinted lustfully.

"Now, now," Fannie said, pushing herself to her feet and trying to keep her rage in check. "George, a girl can't feel very romantic on an empty stomach, now, can she?"

Pete and George shared a shocked, delighted look before returning their gazes to the actress.

"You, uh . . . you think you can, uh, feel *romantic* to, uh, me an' George?" Pete asked.

Fannie shrugged. "To be honest with you, during the ride to your cabin here, I sort of thought over my situation. For several years now, I've felt sort of enslaved by my manager, Boone McClory, and by my beau, Duke Winter. My life and career just have not been my own. Then those two scalawags, Slash and Pecos, come along and kidnap me! Do you know what they were trying to do to me? Why, they were trying to haul me down out of these mountains—against my will, no less—to testify at the murder trial of Duke's cousin! I can't testify against Duke's cousin. He's Duke's *cousin!*"

"Whoa!" George said.

Pete whistled, duly impressed by the information.

"So." Again, Fannie shrugged. "I reckon I have you two men to thank for getting me out of *that* dangerous situation. Now, if you think you can protect me up here, keep me from falling back into either Duke's and Boone's hands or the hands of those two scalawags working for the U.S. marshal in Denver . . . well . . . I reckon we can probably come to some, um, business agreement . . ."

Her stomach churned with revulsion. She covered it by feigning a flirtatious smile, crossing her arms beneath her breasts, shoving them up a little, cocking one hip, and shoving one foot forward. "First, however, I'll be needing something to eat."

Pete and George looked at each other, eyes wide and round and glinting eagerly.

"Sure, sure," George said. "I'll get you some grub." He took Fannie's arm and began leading her toward the decidedly humble cabin with its sagging front stoop. "Pete, you tend the hosses an' I'll pad out Miss Diamond's—"

"Like hell," Pete said, hurrying to catch up to George and Fannie. "The hosses can wait. I'm gonna make sure Miss Diamond's belly is done well padded out, so she'll be in the mood fer a little romance!" He chuckled lustily.

Again, Fannie's stomach churned and her skin crawled.

At least, however, the two fools seemed to have fallen for her story. Now, how was she going to cut through the invisible bonds binding her to them? And then, after she'd managed that tricky maneuver, how was she going to get herself as well as the two outlaws' loot out of these mountains and away from the men who were trailing her?

With these two idiots' loot, she had a good chance of eluding Duke and Boone and the two scalawags, Slash and Pecos, and making her way east to New York, and proving herself on the largest stages in the world! It was high time she left the lowly Rocky Mountain gold camps behind and gave to the rest of the world the gift of her talents!

When she had been escorted inside the cabin by Pete and George, however, and saw what a filthy mess it was, she was visited by another round of revulsion. My God, did they ever clean or organize *anything*?

"Uh," Pete said, apparently having read the expression on her face, "it ain't in the best shape right now. George an' me have been right busy of late, but don't you worry. We got plenty of airtight tins of good, clean food, an' if you'll just give me a min—"

"No, no, I'll do it."

Kicking debris out of his way, Pete had been scrambling over to a counter at the back of the cabin, above which several shelves sagged beneath the weight of burlap food pouches and a dozen or so cans of vegetables, pinto beans, and meat. But now he stopped and turned to the young woman in surprise.

"What's that, Miss Diamond?"

"Call me Fannie, Pete."

Pete and George shared another surprised glance.

"All right," Pete said, rubbing his hands on his grimy buckskin shirt. "Fannie it is . . ."

"Please," Fannie said, forcing another smile that she thought would break her jaws, "allow me. You men have been on the trail longer than I have. And you were good enough to free me from those two craven captors of mine and to give me an all too longed for hope that I had thought was lost. Let me fix you men a meal. All you have to do is build a fire in the stove for me."

George and Pete had argued briefly about who would bring in wood from outside and build a fire, and Pete had lost after they'd flipped a coin. As the stove ticked and groaned while heating, blue smoke slithering out from around the ill-fitting door, Fannie walked over to the eating table. It, too, was burdened with clutter, including plates heaped with rotting food scraps.

From the debris, she picked up an uncorked brown bottle, which she discovered to be half full. She grabbed a couple of tin cups from the table—two of the cleanest ones she could find, which didn't mean they were clean at all—and splashed whiskey into each.

"Here," she said, handing one cup to Pete and the second cup to George. "You fellows sit down and take a load off. Enjoy a before dinner drink while I fix you a meal you won't soon forget. All right? How would that be? Would you do that for Fannie as my way of saying thank you?"

She was a little afraid she was laying it on too thick, something that Boone McClory had often warned her about regarding her stage performances, but she didn't think such a thing were possible. Not in the Rocky Mountain gold camps and not up here with these two dunderheads, either!

The uncouth fools didn't even mind the dirty cups she'd nearly filled with whiskey. They smiled at her like they'd just died and gone to heaven. Imagine their luck. They had kidnapped a beautiful, famous actress—*locally* famous, anyway—and had hauled her up to their remote mountain cabin, only to learn that she wanted them to sit and drink whiskey while she cooked them a meal!

Sure enough, the fools had swallowed her charade hook, line, and sinker!

But, then again, her acting skills were second to none, though she rarely got the credit she was due even from Duke and Boone.

"Well, hell," George said, grinning at Pete and sipping his whiskey. He kicked out a chair and sagged into it.

When Pete had taken a seat at the filthy, cluttered table, as well, Fannie made her way around the table to the shelves at the cabin's rear. As she did, she cast her gaze around the cabin. What she needed now was a weapon. Yes, she knew how to shoot a gun. Even a rifle. She'd never shot a man before, but given her beauty, she'd had to fend a few men off before with guns. Even a knife once.

She could shoot a man if she needed to. And she needed to shoot two of them now. . . .

Chapter 20

If only she could find a gun in this disgusting mess, Fannie thought as she cast her gaze around the fetid little hovel once more.

There must be a dead rat somewhere, she thought. But then she decided that the smell was coming from her two captors sitting at the cluttered table, grinning at her, ogling her with eyes that grew glassier with each sip of their rotgut swill. Their stench hadn't been as strong before, because they'd been outside in the fresh air. But now that they were inside the cabin, with the doors and windows closed against the chill morning, Fannie was getting hit with the full force of their fetor.

They stank, and their cabin stank! How was she going to cook them a meal without fainting?

Fannie was a gal who when she put her mind to a task, she fulfilled that task. That was how she got through the countless performances she gave each week to howling drunks in saloons and opera houses scattered throughout the Colorado Rockies.

Of course, she was using the meal to buy her time. Time away from the goatish hands and other sundry goatish parts of these two hoopleheads, time to figure out a way to incapacitate them and to get their loot. If she could do that, and take one of their horses, she could start her journey out of this savage country.

She picked out some tins with which to throw a stew together and then realized she'd need a knife to open them.

A knife!

She saw the wooden handle of a knife lying amongst the debris on the table. Her heart thudding, she reached for it. She'd no sooner got her hand around it than a big, fat, thick-fingered, dirty-nailed hand closed over hers. She followed the arm of the hand to where Pete sat gazing at her, one brow arched with suspicion.

"I need to open these tins, Pete," she said innocently.

Pete glanced at George. Then, turning back to Fannie, he said, "You let me do that, pretty lady. Wouldn't want you to cut your purty little fingers." He winked.

Crestfallen, Fannie smiled another phonily cheerful smile and said, "Thank you, kind sir!"

She turned away, noting that George had been slurring his words. She'd also noted that the level of the whiskey in the bottle had gone down considerably since she had poured both men a liberal portion, which meant they'd had more. Quite a bit more. Their eyes were even glassier than before, and they were no longer even trying to cover the fact that they were both staring at her most boldly.

Staring at certain curvaceous parts of her most boldly!

That they were both getting drunk was good in that she could more easily subdue them. It was bad in that her time before being thrown onto one of the cabin's two grubby cots and being taken against her will was likely running out.

Somehow, she had to find a gun or another knife!

She glanced furtively around the cabin once more.

Her gaze landed on a square brown bottle on a shelf near the one from which she'd plucked the airtight tins. The bottle poked up from behind a bag of Arbuckles coffee. Only the top half of the label on the bottle was showing above the coffee bag.

RAT.

The rest of the label probably had the word *poison* on it!

RAT POISON.

In other words, arsenic, which was both odorless and taste-less!

Fannie had seized upon her weapon.

Oh, joy!

She glanced over her shoulder. George and Pete were star-ing at her behind. She had to admit it was a nice behind, but she really, truly did get tired of men staring at it. She was more than her physical parts, nice as they admittedly were. What could she do to get George and Pete to stop staring at her rump, specifically, and at the rest of her in general . . . ?

Her thoughts landed on an obvious choice.

"Fellas," she said, casting a plaintive smile over her shoul-der, "would one of you please fetch a little more wood for the stove?"

"What I brought in ain't enough?" Pete grumbled.

"No, it must have been a little green or damp. The stove doesn't seem to be heating up fast enough."

Pete turned to George. "Your turn!"

"Go to hell!"

"Dammit, George. I done fetched the first batch," Pete countered, slamming his fist down on the table.

George slammed his own fist down on the table, and a short but passionate verbal tempest followed, during which Fannie reached up and plucked the square brown bottle from behind the sack of Arbuckles on the shelf on the wall before her. She'd dumped the contents of several airtight tins into a cast-iron skillet; and now, her heart racing and her hands shaking, she plucked the stopper from the bottle, which was indeed—

oh, hallelujah!—labeled RAT POISON, and dumped a goodly portion into the tomatoes, pinto beans, and beef she'd mixed together in the skillet.

She quickly returned the stopper to the bottle, and because the tempest was over—George having slammed his fist down on the table once more before slogging outside to the woodpile, yelling, "Next time she can fetch it her own damn self! I don't care if she is a big hoity-toity or whose woman she is!"—she hid the bottle in the clutter on the counter before her, praying they wouldn't see it or see that it was missing from the shelf on the wall before her.

She doubted they'd notice much of anything except her, as she had them so captivated. They were quickly becoming three sheets to the wind.

Still, her heart raced as she stirred the makeshift stew she'd thrown together. When it was bubbling hot, she found a couple of tin bowls, blew the dust, cobwebs, mouse droppings, and dead flies out of them, and filled each with the steaming stew.

"Here we are!" she trilled, her heart hammering her breastbone painfully, as she turned and set a bowl in front of each man.

George leered at her through the steam rising from his bowl. "Hell, I ain't even hungry. Leastways not for food." His eyes roamed brazenly, widening, lights of goatish lust flickering in them.

"Oh, come on, George," Fannie said, breathless. "I went to the trouble of cooking it, so you can at least give me the satisfaction of eating it." She gave her version of a lusty leer. "We have all day—you, me, an' Pete—for the other."

She winked at him.

George sucked a sharp breath through his teeth. Pete chuckled throatily.

George picked up the spoon she'd set on the table beside the bowl. Fannie stared down at him, feeling faint with anxiety, her palms sweating, knees quaking. George looked up at her and frowned.

"Ain't you eatin'? You're the one who was so gallblasted hungry!" The scowl cut the lines deeper across his leathery, wart-stippled forehead. "Or is you just playin' games?" He pounded the fist holding his spoon down on the table.

"Oh, no, no, no!" Fannie trilled a nervous laugh. "I was just waiting to hear how you fellas liked it. I'm gonna fill a bowl right now."

She wheeled, grabbed another tin bowl off a dusty shelf, and blew the crud out of it.

As she ladled stew into her own bowl, she glanced over her shoulder. George was staring at her suspiciously. That made her heart race even faster, her knees quake even more severely. Then, still staring at her, he sank his spoon into his stew, lifted the spoon to his lips, stuck it into his mouth, and chewed, some of the stew clinging revoltingly to his untrimmed mustache.

Hallelujah! rang out between Fannie's ears.

"How is it?" asked Pete, who had not yet taken a bite.

George only shrugged. But he dipped his spoon into his bowl again, and that was the important thing.

To Fannie's horror, instead of dipping his own spoon into the poisoned stew, Pete slid his chair back from the table, rose a little unsteadily, kicking the chair, and swung to the door, saying, "Before I can eat, I gotta see a man about a horse."

George chuckled as he shoved another spoonful of the poisoned stew into his mouth.

Fannie gasped as Pete opened the door and went out, leaving the door partway open behind him.

"What the hell's the matter with you?" George said, glowering up at her again. He was obviously a man who shouldn't imbibe, as the liquor did nothing to improve his manners. "He's just goin' out to, uh . . . you know"—he leered at her again, wrinkling his mouth inside his poisoned stew–stained beard and mustache—"shake the dew from his—"

He lowered his gaze to the bowl, a terrified expression suddenly washing over his face. He dropped his spoon loudly onto the table, then looked up at Fannie. His face had turned nearly as pale as flour. Beads of sweat glistened across his forehead. He opened his mouth to speak but made only a strangling sound. He opened his mouth again . . . and again . . . resembling a landed fish gasping for a breath.

Still, he made only strangling sounds.

He pushed himself to his feet, kicking his chair out, the legs barking loudly across the floor. Eyes bulging, he glared across the table at Fannie, who was still standing at the cluttered counter, anxiously wringing her hands.

George's face turned a shade even whiter, but his neck turned a weird red and purple color. He raised both hands to his neck, his terror-stricken, agonized eyes pinned to Fannie.

"What . . . ?" he croaked out, taking two stumbling steps backward, ramming himself back against the front wall and knocking a yellow rain slicker from a wall peg and kicking over some boots lined up on the floor at the base of the wall. "What . . . did . . . you . . . ?"

Fannie stared back in horror at him.

"What the hell's goin' on in there?" Pete yelled from outside.

Fannie could see him standing on the grassless area fronting the cabin, crudely making water, hands on his hips, sort of leaning back so he could peer into the cabin through the window to the door's left.

Lower jaw hanging, heart tattooing her breastbone without surcease, Fannie stared back at him through the window. Meanwhile, George pushed himself off the back wall. He rammed into the table, knocking over the whiskey bottle. Keeping his horrified and enraged gaze on Fannie, he turned to his left, rammed the table again, and then walked out from around it. He walked heavily, dragging his boot toes, his mouth open now, his shoulders and chest muscles spasming, the muscles resembling snakes writhing inside his filthy buckskin shirt!

"Oh, God," Fannie couldn't help saying aloud. "Oh, God! Oh, God!"

As George stumbled toward her, Fannie stepped to her left, knocking the skillet of poisoned stew off the range. It crashed loudly onto the floor.

"What the *hell* . . . ?" Pete said again, leaning back on his hips to peer through the window, his expression deeply puzzled.

George ran into the counter where Fannie had prepared the poisoned stew. He looked up at the shelf on which she'd found the rat poison. He swept his hands up toward the bottle. They shook violently as he swept them around on the shelf, knocking the bag of Arbuckles onto the counter, and then he turned to Fannie again, his eyes even wider than before.

"*You . . . !*" he croaked out. "*You . . . !*"

He turned to the counter, swung his head from right to left and back again. He stopped when his eyes landed on the bottle. He shoved his right hand to the bottle, raised it in his trembling fingers, his furiously accusing gaze pinned to Fannie, who was backing away from the crazed, poisoned man in horror, both hands closed over her mouth.

I'm going to die now! I'm going to die now! The words drummed in her head.

George stepped toward her. He took only one long, halting step before he dropped to his knees with a heavy thud. He rolled onto his side on the floor, foam oozing from his mouth, every muscle quivering, as though he'd been struck by lightning.

The door jerked open, and Pete stepped into the cabin. "What in blue blazes is . . . ?"

He looked from Fannie to his partner on the floor.

"What happened to him?" he yelled.

He ran around the table and stared down in hang-jawed horror at the quivering, writhing George, who stared up at him, eyes bulging from their sockets. Foam continued flowing up out of his mouth and oozing down his bearded cheeks. George flopped his violently shaking right hand at where the bottle of rat poison lay on the floor beside him, half under the range.

The label could be seen clearly.

RAT POISON.

Pete snapped his enraged eyes at Fannie. "*Poisoned* him!" He moved toward her, his ugly face flushed with rage. "Poisoned the *stew*!"

"*No*!" Fannie screamed and backed toward the door, wanting to run, but her feet were like lead.

Pete ran toward her. Just before he reached her, Fannie saw the wooden-handled knife on the table to her left. She closed her hand over it, lifted it off the table, and thrust it straight out in front of her belly, blade forward. Pete closed the distance between them, reaching up to wrap his hands around her neck.

They only brushed her throat before his eyes bulged suddenly and he sagged before her, closing his hands over her shoulders. He dug his fingers deeply into her flesh as he put more and more of his weight on her, trying to use her to prop himself upright.

For a moment, Fannie wasn't sure what had happened.

Then she felt the warmth and molasses-like consistency of the man's blood bathing her hands. She couldn't see the knife down between them, but she could feel her knuckles pressing against Pete's bulging belly quickly growing wetter and warmer with the flowing of the man's blood from his guts.

His mouth wide, his shocked and anguished eyes stared into hers.

"Bi—! Bi—!" he tried to say.

Then his eyes rolled back into his head, and he fell forward.

Fannie screamed as his weight knocked her backward, and she fell to the floor with Pete on top of her, bleeding out against her. He quivered as he died, making her shake, too.

She lay gasping beneath the dead man's weight, hearing hoof thuds grow louder outside the cabin. Horseback riders were approaching.

"Oh, God, no!" she sobbed.

She wanted so desperately to fetch the money from the floor by the door and leave.

She realized that wasn't going to happen, however, when she saw those two scalawags and former outlaws leap down from their blowing horses and run through the cabin door, the shorter, darker man, Slash, wielding two revolvers, while the taller man with long gray-blond hair, Pecos, held a sawed-off, double-barreled shotgun, which hung from his neck and shoulder, straight out in front of him.

They stared into the cabin, eyes slowly widening as they got the lay of the land.

They turned their heads to regard each other skeptically.

Fannie slammed the ends of her fists against the floor and bawled.

Chapter 21

"Those two fellas sure grabbed a tiger by the tail," Slash said.

"They sure did," Pecos said.

"What a way to go. Rat poison and a knife to the guts."

"What a way to go," Pecos agreed.

He sipped the coffee he and Slash had brewed after they'd dragged the two men, whose names the girl had said were Pete and George, out into the yard in front of the cabin. Now they stood over the bodies, which they'd covered with the men's own saddle blankets, tin cups of coffee in hand. The girl remained in the cabin, changing into more comfortable riding gear than what she'd been wearing.

Besides, her blouse and skirt had been soaked with Pete's blood. When they'd pulled the man off her, it had looked as though he'd practically bled out on her. It had been a horrific scene, even for two men who'd seen much bloodshed over their fifty-plus years on the western frontier. What had made it especially horrific was seeing a pretty blonde so covered in blood, and so wild-eyed, and the foam that had still been issuing from George's open mouth even in death.

Pecos looked at Slash. "Which would you choose?"

"Hell, neither!" Slash said.

"Yeah. Me too." Pecos sipped his coffee, then looked at Slash again. "I think we mighta grabbed a tiger by the tail our ownselves."

"A job so damn easy old Bleed-'Em-So was embarrassed to put us on it."

"My tailbone!"

Slash swirled the coffee in his cup, staring down at it. "Just don't turn your back on her."

The door latch clicked, and Slash looked up to see the cabin door slowly open, hinges groaning. He felt his right hand slide toward the Colt holstered on his right thigh. Neither he nor Pecos had very thoroughly checked the cabin for guns, other than the revolvers that George and Pete had been wearing when they'd dragged them outside. The cabin had been too much of a mess to give it a good going-over. Fannie might have found one in there.

Slash half expected her to come out shooting. A girl who'd feed one man rat poison and stick a knife in the other one's guts was capable of anything. Hell, coming out shooting would be tame for her!

Slash closed his hand over the Colt's grips and was about to free the thong from over the hammer but left it where it was when he saw the girl standing in the half-open doorway, looking down guiltily. She almost looked like a boy standing there in her oversized plaid flannel shirt and baggy denim jeans, held up on her slender but femininely curved hips by rawhide suspenders. She'd knotted a rope around her waist, helping out the suspenders a little. She must have rolled the cuff of each leg a half dozen times, and they still hung down over her stockmen's boots, which were so worn they resembled Indian moccasins.

She wore a floppy brimmed black hat. She'd brushed her curly blond locks so they shone in the morning sunlight as they tumbled prettily down her shoulders. In the crook of her right arm, she held a blanket-coat, as the mountains got cold at night, even in the summer. Slash and Pecos intended to hurry down out of them before Duke Winter caught up to them, but they'd likely have to camp a night or two in the high country before arriving at the railroad line.

They'd hop a train wherever they could find one. The truth was, George and Pete had led them on such a serpentine trail in the dark, they had no idea where they were. Until they got their bearings or found some prospector or some such who would give them directions, they'd be steering by instinct, mostly just heading east and down out of the mountains, hoping that one trail or another would lead them to a railroad line. Taking a train would be faster than riding, especially with the girl, whom Slash and Pecos figured wasn't much accustomed to riding horseback. They couldn't be tracked on a train, either.

The girl lifted her chin. Her eyes slid to where Slash was just then removing his hand from his gun.

She glanced at the blanket-covered bodies on the ground to her left, wrinkled her nose at Slash and Pecos, and snapped, "They had it coming!"

"You'll get no argument from us," Pecos said, then grinned. "But if it's all the same to you, we'll do the cookin'."

"And if you need anything cut or chopped," Slash said, "just give either one of us a whistle."

She gave an angry groan, flushing. She drew a deep breath and said, "I'll make a deal with you."

Slash and Pecos shared a skeptical look.

The girl opened the door a little wider, then reached inside. Again, Slash's hand went to his gun, but he removed it again when she dragged a pair of saddlebags over the threshold and into the yard. She toed one of the bulging pouches.

"Know what's in there?"

Pecos glanced quickly at Slash, a sudden anxiety flashing in his eyes. "We don't wanna know!"

"What's in 'em?" Slash asked the girl, ignoring his partner.

"Slash," Pecos insisted, "we don't wanna know what's in them pouches. We don't need to know that. Let's just say there's rock samples in there. Sure, sure. Pete an' George had been prospectin' when they grabbed the girl. Sure, sure. That's what's in them bags. Probably mostly worthless rock samples." He beckoned quickly to the girl. "Come on, come on, Miss Diamond. We're burnin' daylight! Ol' Duke an' his rowdy horde could be here at any old time, and I will guaran-damn-tee you, you don't want nothin' . . ."

He let his voice trail off when he saw the girl and Slash staring at each other. The girl was smiling crookedly, devilishly. Slash stared back at her with much the same expression.

"Hey, Slash," the girl said, toeing a bulging pouch of the bags once more, keeping her almost coquettish gaze on the former bank and train robber. "Wanna know what's in the bags?"

"No, he don't!" Pecos said, holding up his hands, palms out. "Now, like I said—"

"Stolen cash," the girl said to Slash, narrowing one eye and spreading her lips a little wider, showing her teeth.

"How much?" Slash said.

"Ah, hell!" Pecos said. "Don't tell him. You see, little lady, we got us a weakness, we do, and it ain't . . ."

"Almost thirty-four thousand dollars in cash," the girl said to Slash with that come-hither smile. "I just counted it. I don't think Pete and George even knew how much loot they'd stolen out of that bank in Conifer. They didn't have a chance to count it. But I just did. Thirty-four thousand is a good bit of money . . ."

"Ah, hell," Pecos said again, scowling anxiously at Slash.

Slash turned to him and said very softly and quietly, a shrewd smile twisting his own lips, narrowing his own devilishly twinkling eyes, "Thirty-four thousand could get us out of Bleed-'Em-So's leg trap."

"Well, we'd have to split it," the girl said. "We'd each get a third. Eleven thousand is all I need. Just enough to get me to

New York City. After that, I'll be just fine . . . once I flounce out onto one of those fancy New York stages . . . on the arm of James Cavendish . . ."

"Who's James Cavendish?" Pecos asked her.

She turned to him, wrinkling the skin above the bridge of her nose, which she lifted to stare down it at the philistine before her. "Only the most famous thespian now performing in New York City and London. He has a home in Italy, I've heard! *Italy*!"

"Italy, eh?" Slash said sarcastically. "Let's see the loot."

"No!" Pecos thrust his hand out to the girl and stomped over to Slash. "We can't take that money, Slash, an' you know it!"

"Like I said, that money—"

"Wouldn't get us anywhere, because there's no getting us out of Bleed-'Em-So's leg trap. Besides, you know very good and well why we can't take it."

"Why?" both Slash and Fannie Diamond asked at the same time.

Keeping his hard-edged gaze on his partner, Pecos said, "Because we didn't steal it. You know the rules as well as I do, Slash. We don't take money we didn't steal!"

"Hah!" the girl laughed. "That's quite the code of honor you two old owlhoots have!"

"Every profession has it's code, and that's ours," Pecos told her.

Slash studied him, scowling. "Ah, hell," he said finally, lifting his hat and tossing his longish hair straight back over his head. "I reckon you're right, partner. Besides, I can't run off to Mexico. I can't leave Jay, an' she wouldn't leave the Thousand Delights."

Fannie frowned. "Who's Jay, an' what's the Thousand Delights?"

"Jay's Slash's wife," Pecos said. "The Thousand Delights is Jay's saloon in Camp Collins."

"You're married?" Fannie said.

"Why so surprised?" Slash said.

"Poor long-suffering woman!"

"Yeah, I don't deserve her, but she saw fit to hitch her star to my wagon, so I reckon my partner's right." Slash picked up the saddlebags, opened the cabin door, and tossed them inside. "The money stays here."

Fannie glowered up at him, her fists on her hips. For several seconds, she was speechless. Then: "How in holy blazes can you two old owlhoots pass up that kind of money?"

"Will you please stop callin' us old, Miss Diamond?" Slash said, genuinely indignant. "You're startin' to make me *feel* old. I can do that all by myself just fine, thank you!" He grabbed her by the arm and led her over to where their own two horses stood, as well as a coyote dun that had belonged to either the dearly departed George or Pete. They'd unsaddled and bridled the other mount and turned it loose. "Now, climb up on the dun, so we can get out ahead of that kill-crazy beau of yours."

"Oh, go to hell!" Fannie tried to pull away from Slash, then gave an indignant yelp as he flung her up onto the dun's back. She crossed her arms on her chest defiantly and glared down at him, slit eyed. "How dare you manhandle me so, you brute! I want you to know I don't believe one word you said about Duke wanting me dead. The man is purely gone for me. You are both blackhearted liars. Duke wouldn't hurt a hair on my head!"

Just then a buzzing sounded; it grew quickly louder.

There was a dull thud. The girl's saddle gave a violent jerk. She screamed and reached for the horn, then screamed again and looked down at the horn. Slash and Pecos looked at it, too. The leather was shredded.

The bark of the rifle that had sent the slug into the saddle horn of the girl's horse resounded shrilly.

"*What the hell?*" Pecos bellowed.

Slash pulled his Winchester from his saddle boot and peered off in the direction the bullet had come from. "I think Miss Diamond's true love, who wouldn't harm a hair on her head, just tried to blow it *off*! Grab her reins and take the girl up the ridge behind the cabin. I'll buy you some time!"

Slash dropped to a knee as he saw the morning light flash in the branches of a fir roughly a hundred yards away and at the very edge of the forest curving down from the top of the ridge, to the north. He aimed quickly, sent three bullets flying into the fir, and watched them hammer bark from the branches.

He watched in satisfaction as a man tumbled from one of those branches, losing his high-crowned cream hat and rifle in the process. His bellowing wail reached Slash's ears a second or so after the son of a buck had struck the ground.

That was Winter himself. Slash recognized the hat and the man's big, rawboned body.

Slash sent another couple of rounds after Winter, but the sage was so deep that Slash couldn't see him clearly. Wisely, the bushwhacker was keeping his head down.

More men ran out of the pines to the right of where Winter lay mostly concealed. There had to be a good dozen of them, all wielding rifles, which they raised to their shoulders now as they dropped to their knees in the grass.

"Come on, Slash!" Pecos said as he mounted his buckskin and led the girl's horse around the far side of the cabin.

Fannie rode crouched over the shredded horn of her saddle, head turned to stare in wide-eyed terror at the smoke puffing from where the dozen would-be killers were hurling lead at her and Slash and Pecos. Slash's Appaloosa was running in circles as bullets buzzed around him and thudded into the short grass and sage, way too close to the mount for either its or Slash's comfort.

Slash sure as hell didn't need to be set afoot out here!

He ran toward the gelding, scissoring his arms and legs. "Hold on, boy! Hold on, boy! *Easy!*"

The horse looked at him sharply, as though to say, "Hold this, you old fart!"

It was just about to wheel out toward the open valley when Slash managed to stomp down on its reins. The horse tugged the reins out from under Slash's boots. It was like having a rug pulled out from under him. He gave a yelp as the reins jerked him off his feet.

After striking the ground on his back, he flung his left hand out and managed to grab one of the reins, which had gotten twisted around a sage shrub. Squeezing his rifle in his right hand and wincing as more lead thudded into the ground around him, he let the horse jerk him to his feet. He pulled back on the single rein. Before the screaming horse could swing around again, Slash stooped to grab the other rein.

He hauled back on both reins. The horse whinnied, violently shying from the continuing barrage. Slash ran to the side of the horse, but just as he flung his left hand toward the saddle horn, a bullet tore his hat from his head. He felt the icy burn of the bullet's kiss at the crown of his skull.

"Damn!"

"Slash!" Pecos bellowed from the forested ridge rising behind the cabin, "get your butt on your horse and *come on* before they fill you so full of *lead*, we'll need an ore dray to haul you to potter's field!"

"What the hell do you think I'm tryin' to do?" Slash bellowed back.

He crouched to pluck his hat off the ground—a man was nothing without his hat—and set it on his head. As he flung his left hand toward the horn again, he turned his head to see all dozen men now on horseback and galloping toward him, slinging lead as they did, the smoke from their thundering rifles sending out a pale blue fog into the crisp morning air around them.

Bullets screeched around him, one smashing into the Appy's saddle, two more grazing Slash's left arm and lower right leg.

Slash skip-hopped with the sidestepping horse and finally managed to gain the leather. He swung the horse around sharply and put the steel to it. Horse and rider soon had the cabin between them and the oncoming riders. And then he and the horse thundered past the small log stable flanking the cabin and into the forest and up the ridge, weaving around pines and firs and occasional aspens, leaping blowdown and deadfall.

Hearing Winter's men whooping and hollering behind him, closing on him like wolves on the blood scent, Slash put his head down and said, "It's times like these this old sinner becomes a prayin' man. 'Our Father, who art in heaven . . .'"

Chapter 22

Slash thundered to the top of the ridge and was about to start down into the valley on the other side.

"*Slash*!" Pecos shouted.

Slash reined up, curveting his horse. He looked to where his partner was hunkered behind a boulder to Slash's right. The girl sat a ways off from him, her back to him, but also behind the boulder. She sat with her spread legs stretched out in front of her and was gazing down into the opposite valley with a stricken expression.

"I say we slow 'em down a little!" Pecos said.

His and the girl's horses stood several yards down the slope, grazing.

"It's about time you come up with a good idea!" Slash put his horse a few yards down the slope, swung down, and pulled his Winchester from the saddle boot.

"I come up with plenty!"

"Oh, shut up!" Slash dropped belly down behind the lip of the slope, about fifteen feet from the girl and Pecos, and started thumbing shells from his cartridge belt into the Yellowboy's loading gate. "Here they come!"

"I see 'em," Pecos said, stretching his lips back from his teeth as he gazed back down through the forest at where kill-crazy Duke Winter's bunch was galloping up the slope hell for leather, weaving around trees. A few were still slinging lead. Pecos thought he could make out Duke Winter—the big man with a big cream hat and a big blond mustache riding a tall black horse near the right in the middle of the pack. He held a carbine in his left hand and was holding his reins lightly with the other, letting the black pick its own way.

Pecos glanced at Slash. "And don't tell me to shut up!"

"Shut up!"

"If we live through this, I'm gonna kick your scrawny ass!"

"Like I said before—"

"Yeah, I know, I know. It doesn't look like you have much to worry about!" Pecos clicked back the hammer of his Colt's rifle and snugged his cheek up against the walnut neck. "I'm gonna shoot Winter—cut off the snake's damn head!"

"No!" The girl rose to her feet and threw herself at Pecos, tried to wrestle the rifle away from him.

"Christ!" Slash said. "How many times do you need to let him shoot you before you finally believe . . ."

He let the query dwindle on his lips while Pecos struggled with the girl. She was all over him, losing her hat, Pecos losing his hat, her hair dancing around her shoulders. Slash could see now that the gang was within fifty yards and closing fast.

He lined up his sights on the forehead of the man he'd picked out as Duke Winter, just beneath the wide brim of the man's high-crowned cream Stetson. He drew a breath, let it out slow, and tightened the tension on the Winchester's trigger.

He held his breath, planted the sights on his target, just above the man's wide, long nose, and gently increased the tension in his finger.

The rifle boomed.

At the same time, Winter's big black horse jerked left to avoid something on the ground in front of it. Instead of cork-ing Winter, Slash watched his bullet plant a dark kiss on the left cheek of the man who'd been riding directly behind Winter—a beefy hombre in a high-crowned black sombrero and wearing a long gray mustache and a billowy red neckerchief.

Without so much as a grunt—at least not with one that Slash could hear above the drumming of the horses' hooves—the man threw up his hands, tossed his rifle away like a hot potato, and flopped straight back against his bedroll and saddlebags. As his horse swerved to avoid whatever Winter's horse had swerved to avoid, the Mex flew sharply off his big gray's right hip. The man's head struck a birch trunk with a thud loud enough that Slash could hear it—it was like a single smack of a drum—and dropped like a fifty-pound bag of parched corn.

"Hold up! Hold up!" Winter yelled, stopping his black horse abruptly and leaping out of the saddle. "They've set a trap at the top of the ridge!"

As the others did likewise, Slash emptied his Winchester at them but mostly hit only trees, for it was too dark in the sun-dappled forest and his targets were moving around too much, their horses obscuring them, for accurate shooting. It would have helped if he'd had help, but a glance over his left shoulder told him that Pecos was still wrestling the girl.

"Pecos, dammit. Thanks for the help!"

Pecos paused in the foofaraw to look at him, taking his eyes off the girl. She'd been slapping and punching him, but he'd been deflecting her blows with his arms until now, when Slash had distracted him.

Crack!

She laid a nice tattoo across his left cheek, which instantly turned apple red.

"Ouch! Dammit, Slash. Can't you see I got my hands full over here!"

"Subdue that crazy catamount!" By now, Winter's crew was forted up behind trees and flinging lead at him and Pecos—

and at the fool girl, too—so Slash was hunkered low beneath the lip of the ridge. Bullets plowed into the ground just above him, spraying him with tufts of grass and dirt.

"Never mind!" Slash crabbed down the slope. Then, when he was low enough that he wouldn't get his head shot off, he rose and ran down to where his horse grazed with the other two. "Mount up!"

"What about her?"

"Duke!" she screamed and scrambled away from Pecos, crawling on hands and knees toward the lip of the ridge.

Slash glanced back at her. "I'd say let her get her fool head blown off, but Bledsoe has other ideas!"

"Hold on, you little polecat!" Pecos grabbed one of her ankles and pulled her, screaming, down the slope toward him.

Meanwhile, bullets continued to throw dirt, gravel, and bits of broken grass over the lip of the ridge.

"Duke!" she screamed. "Duke, it's me, Fannie. *Help*!"

Pecos grabbed her around the waist and ran with her down the slope toward the horses, all three of which were watching the warring middle-aged man and the young actress, twitching their ears dubiously. She kicked and flailed her fists at him, trying to punch him.

Slash ran over to Pecos and the girl. "Here, let me handle this, fer chrissakes!"

"What're you gonna—"

Smack!

Slash's right fist connected with Fannie's left cheek. She sagged back in Pecos's arms, eyes rolling back in their sockets, lights out.

Pecos gasped. "Jesus, Slash!"

"What? You're the one that taught me that little trick! Put her on your horse and lead hers!" Slash turned and ran back to his own mount, which was edging off down the slope, frightened by the gunfire, which, Slash suddenly noticed, was tapering off. Winter's bunch had probably realized that their quarry was about to flee again after their trap had yielded only one dead son of a gun.

"Why do I always get stuck with her?"

"It's your fate to get beat up by hundred-pound showgirls!"

Slash gave an amused snort as he swung up into the saddle. He pointed his mount downhill and touched spurs to its flanks. Again, he and Pecos and the girl were on the run—this time downhill. This time with the girl again riding unconscious, but sitting up this time in front of Pecos, while Pecos led the girl's horse by its bridle reins.

They rode down into the valley and then followed the river bisecting the valley downstream, riding roughly northeast. Forest pushed in close to the three riders—two conscious, one unconscious—from both sides. The stream chugged in its rock-lined banks, stitched with white-water river. They rode for maybe a half hour without seeing or hearing their pursuers behind them.

But then, as they rounded a bend in the trail hugging the stream, Pecos yelled from where he and the girl rode behind Slash, "We got company, partner!"

Slash hipped around in his saddle. He could see Winter's gang, led by Winter himself and a big man in a brown suit and bowler hat riding very straight-backed in his saddle, through the trees on the other side of the bend that Slash and Pecos had just rounded. Slash thought the bowler-hatted gent might be Boone McClory.

He cursed and turned his head forward. Immediately, he saw the mouth of a side canyon cut into the ridge wall maybe sixty yards ahead and on his right.

He turned and yelled back over his shoulder at Pecos, "Follow me, partner!"

Slash reined his Appaloosa into the forest right of the river and urged it up the slope, angling his route toward the canyon mouth. As he approached the yawning break in the ridge wall,

Pecos galloping close behind him, he saw that the canyon was a dry riverbed. At least it was dry this time of the year, midsummer. It was likely a raging torrent in the spring, when the snow was melting in the higher reaches. Bleached wood and rocks and boulders of all shapes and sizes had been washed down out of the canyon to litter the forested slope all the way to the stream into which this side canyon's spring floods emptied.

"Careful!" Slash called over his shoulder to his partner. "Lots of rocks!"

"I see that. Holy Jehoshaphat!"

"Yeah."

"You sure this is a good idea, Slash?" Pecos asked, following Slash through the rocks and boulders and onto the rocky floor of the riverbed. He cast a quick, cautious look behind him and was glad not to see their shadowers.

Not yet, anyway.

"Too late to change course now!" Slash kept his head forward, eyes down, watching for obstacles. "Winter will have a harder time tracking us in here. These boulders will make good cover if we need to fort up and hold 'em off till dark, then make our way up the canyon under cover of darkness."

"All right," Pecos said, not sounding any too convinced. "If you say so . . ."

"How's the actress?"

"Startin' to come around. If she starts fightin' me again, I'm gonna throw her to those wolves back there. She can pack a punch, and she don't quit!"

Slash chuckled as his horse picked its own way through the debris littering the canyon, which was cut deep, with nearly sheer stone walls on both sides, spread about two hundred feet apart. The ridge crests towered another two hundred feet over the narrow cut, the eastern wall shading the wash nearly to its center.

"I don't know, Slash," Pecos said, his voice echoing off the stone walls. "Pretty slow travel . . ."

"Slow for Winter's men, too."

"Just hope it ain't a box."

"Oh, shut up about that!"

"I wasn't meanin' that, Slash!" Pecos meant he wasn't referring to the box canyon to which Slash had inadvertently led their old gang, the Snake River Marauders, when they'd been running from a posse comprised of Pinkertons and deputy U.S. marshals the night that Jay's longtime beau, Pistol Pete Johnson, had been drilled by a .44 slug and killed. "You know I wouldn't bring that up, you sour old devil! Leastways I wasn't blamin' you for Pete's death!"

"Oh, shut up!"

"Slash, I am going to pull you off that horse and kick your scrawny ass!"

Just then a bullet ricocheted off a rock to their left. It crossed the narrow cut to clip a branch from a cedar tree spidering out from a crack in the opposite ridge wall.

"Like I said," Slash said, shaking his head at the broken cedar branch. "I ain't worried!"

"They're closin' on us," Pecos yelled.

Slash glanced behind him through the gaps in the rocks and boulders littering the canyon floor to see Winter's men strung out in a long serpentine line behind them. Winter was down on one knee, holding a smoking repeater straight out from his shoulder. He was the one who'd fired that shot.

"All right, that tears it!" Slash stopped his Appy abruptly, swung his right leg over the horn, and dropped straight down the left stirrup to the canyon floor. As Pecos rode up to him, the girl now awake and glaring at him through the screen of her long, disheveled blond hair, Slash tossed his reins up to Pecos. "Keep goin'! I'm gonna buy us some more time!"

"You SOB!" the girl screamed at Slash, rubbing the welt on her right cheek.

Slash chuckled as he spanked the rump of Pecos's buckskin and said, "Honey, don't think you're the first woman whoever called me that!"

He pumped a round into his Winchester's breech.

"And she likely ain't gonna be the last, neither!" Pecos added.

Despite the direness of their situation . . . or maybe because of it . . . he and Slash tipped their heads back and roared. Their laughter echoed bizarrely off the canyon's steep stone walls.

Chapter 23

Slash shouldered up against a boulder on the canyon's right side as he gazed down toward where Winter's men, having seen him dismount, now hurried to cover on both sides of the canyon. One man released his horse's reins to scamper down behind a wagon-sized, flat-topped boulder in the ravine's dead center, which likely churned up a good bit of white water during the spring snowmelt floods.

Winter had given Slash an idea.

Now he grinned as he fired three shots off the ravine's wall to his left, down around where Winter's men had scurried to ground, their horses retreating back down the ravine toward the river. Slash's rifle's screeching reports echoed raucously.

Grinning, he fired three more rounds off the canyon's right wall and grinned even more broadly when he heard one of Winter's men give a painful yelp.

One of the devils had apparently been at least nicked by a ricochet.

Winter poked his mustached mouth and cream-hatted head out from behind a boulder maybe fifty feet back down the ravine and on its left side and shouted, "Braddock, you SOB!"

Slash saw the man cock and level his rifle.

Slash popped a cap toward him, but in his haste, his bullet only puffed rock dust off the side of the boulder behind which Winter was partially concealed, only the very front of his hat brim showing. Winter cursed again, bunching his mouth with an enraged grimace, and extended his rifle toward Slash.

Slash drew back behind his own covering boulder as Winter sent three rounds hammering the boulder's far side. Then the others followed suit, and Slash could feel the reverberations of the men's bullets through the rock against which he pressed his back. As he stared up the canyon, he just then saw Pecos and the girl and the girl's and Slash's horses disappear around a bend in the canyon wall, Slash's Appaloosa giving an angry swish of its tail, not happy with the gunfire erupting behind it.

Slash didn't blame it. He didn't much care for it himself, since each and every one of those bullets hammering the backside of his boulder was meant for him. More than a few ricocheted off the walls to either side of him, nearly giving him as good as what he'd given the man who'd yelped only a minute ago.

Slash waited for a lull in the gunfire.

When it came, he drew a breath and started to snake his rifle around the boulder's right side, intending to send a little more lead of his own ricocheting at Winter's bunch. He forestalled the rifle's slide when a low rumbling sounded. Through the soles of his boots, he could feel a trembling.

He'd be damned if it wasn't the ground that was trembling!

That trembling grew as the rumbling grew louder. Both sensations felt and sounded as though a train were approaching. But Slash was not standing on a cobbled train platform, dammit.

What the hell . . . ?

One of Winter's men shouted, "*Look!*"

Slash slid his right eye around the side of his covering boulder. One of Winter's men, half-visible where he was crouched behind a rock on the canyon's left side, was pointing up at the ridge wall to Slash's right. Slash followed the man's pointing finger to roughly two-thirds of the way up the ridge wall from the canyon floor.

Slash gave a shudder as he felt the devil's cold finger reach up from hell's bowels to tickle his feet. Several thumbs and knobs of rock jutting out from the ridge were shaking, quivering, blurred with movement. Smaller rocks were breaking away from around the sides of those thumbs and knobs and tumbling down toward the canyon floor, bouncing off the ridge wall as they did.

One of those rocks was tumbling nearly straight down toward Slash, doubling in size with each fast-passing second!

Others were tumbling down toward Winter's men and the canyon floor behind them.

One of them cursed loudly.

"Rockslide!" another shouted.

"Fall back! Fall back!" That sounded like Winter himself, though the rumbling had grown so loud now that Slash barely heard him.

As more and more rock broke away from those apparently disintegrating thumbs and nobs, Slash shared the man's sentiment.

Wheezing out a curse of his own, he pushed off the boulder and started hotfooting it up the canyon. As he did, a wagon-sized shadow flicked across the ground to his left. A half second later, a great explosion rose behind, deafening him, the force of the impact hurling him forward and down, and then he was rolling along the canyon floor, pelted and enshrouded by rocks and dust.

He rolled onto his chest and looked back toward where he'd been standing a few seconds before. He blinked against the dust-laden air only to see that the boulder he'd taken cover behind a moment ago had been struck with one that had fallen from above, so that in the billowing dust and the jumbled pieces of broken rock, he couldn't even see "his" boulder anymore.

There was only a much larger pile of broken rock!

A quick glance upward made his insides writhe like cold snakes.

The ridge wall a third of the way up from the canyon floor was literally crumbling and dropping, individual chunks of rocks of all shapes and sizes pushing away from the ridge itself and crashing into each other as they tumbled into the canyon.

Slash yelled a curse and heaved himself to his feet. Suddenly feeling as light in his boots as a twenty-year-old, he ran as fast as he'd ever run before in his life, hurling rocks toward where Pecos and the girl and the horses had disappeared around the bend in the canyon wall.

As he did, quickly breathless, eyes wide and jaw hanging, sucking dust-laden air into his lungs, more explosions erupted behind him until they all became one giant, near-deafening roar. Winter's men's screams and howls were quickly drowned out. The ground slid around beneath Slash's boots so that several times he nearly lost his balance and fell before he actually did fall, feeling as though the very earth had been pulled out from beneath his boots.

He struck the rocky ground and rolled. When he came to a stop, he looked behind him and felt his jaw drop nearly to his chest.

"Holy . . . ," he said, shocked to see the upper half of the entire western ridge collapsing into the canyon.

At least that was what it appeared was happening. All he could see was a large mushroom cloud of roiling dust. Inside that cloud, he could see the vague shapes of boulders falling toward the canyon floor. The cloud was swelling, rushing toward him, as more of the ridge over him joined in the obliteration of itself.

Grunting his desperation, Slash pushed to his feet and continued running while the concussive explosions resounded behind him. They were so loud that his ears ached and rang.

He followed the canyon floor up and around the bend in the canyon wall.

He kept running, even when the concussive explosions became less loud, though the ground was still reverberating beneath his boots. He was so exhausted by the seemingly endless climb that he was dragging his boot toes.

Finally, realizing he'd climbed to the top of the canyon, he dropped to his hands and knees in mountain sage, sucking great draughts of air into his lungs, which ached from the long run and the rock dust that seemed to have filled his chest, making each breath painful, as though he had inhaled pepper.

A shadow flicked along the sage ahead of him. Pecos said beneath the ringing in Slash's ears, "Slash, what in the hell did you *do*?"

Panting, Slash looked up to see his partner crouched over him, gazing down at him in horror, his rifle in his right gloved hand. The girl stood behind Pecos, gazing with an expression much like that of Pecos into the canyon, which now lay to Slash's right.

Turning to peer into the chasm himself, Slash saw that it was hidden by that roiling mushroom cloud of rock dust. Likely sealed up tight as a mausoleum.

Slash spat grit from his lips, then turned to his partner and said, "Partner, I think I just broke the world!"

Pecos turned to stare into the canyon. Into the mushroom cloud hovering over it, concealing it, rather. He shook his head in disbelief. "Leave it to you!"

Fannie Diamond dropped to her knees and sobbed as she gazed miserably at the roiling cloud. "Duke!" she cried. "Oh, God. *Duke!*" She tugged at the sage.

Slash turned to Pecos again. "Those two have a complicated relationship."

"That's one way of puttin' it."

After Slash had rested and regained his wind, as well as drained his canteen, drinking the water as well as bathing his face and eyes with it, he and Pecos and the girl mounted up and headed east. They rode slowly, saving their horses. Besides, there was a good chance the entire gang of Winter's cutthroats was nothing more than jelly beneath that broken ridge wall. Slash and Pecos headed east mainly because Denver lay in that direction, though they really had no idea where they were or where, in the short term, they were going.

They didn't even talk about it. There was no point until they figured out where in hell they were or found someone who could tell them. Looking around, though, they saw no sign of another soul. Not even any trails that might lead to mine shacks or old fur trapper cabins.

There was one more matter. Pecos brought it up as they rode along at a slow walk through the high mountain valley they now found themselves in. He kept his voice low so that the actress, now riding her own horse, though Pecos was leading it, wouldn't overhear.

"Slash, you think there's any way in hell Winter's bunch might have survived that . . . that . . . whatever you call it . . . ?"

"Yeah. I know what you mean," Slash said, hipping around in his saddle to gaze back at the still roiling cloud of rock dust behind them. "I don't know what you'd call it. Rockslide? That's too tame. More like an earthquake." He turned his head back forward and wagged it. "Never seen such a thing. A whole canyon tumbling in on itself." He glanced at Pecos. "Musta been the rifle fire and a weakness in the ridge."

"I reckon." Pecos narrowed an eye at him. "Back to my question . . ."

"Yeah, yeah. I don't know." Again, Slash glanced behind him. "I doubt it. They'd have had to run pretty damn fast to avoid those rocks, because it was that whole end of the canyon that caved in on itself. Winter's bunch was right smack-dab in the middle of it."

"If so," Pecos said, smiling, forgetting to keep his voice down, "I reckon we done took down Duke an' his whole dang gang. Won't ol' Bleed-'Em-So be impressed!"

"Shhh!" Slash chastised his partner. "Let sleeping dogs lie!" He canted his head at the girl.

Too late. Fannie had overheard. Riding behind Pecos, looking pale and distraught, she cast her castigating gaze between the two men, her otherwise pale cheeks flushing angrily. "Duke's alive. I know he is. He'll hunt you down and kill you both!"

Slash glanced back at her, deep lines of mystification cutting across his sun-bronzed forehead. "You better hope he don't. He damn near killed you earlier. You think that shot that hit your saddle horn was meant for either of *us*?" He canted his head at Pecos.

"Yes, I most certainly do!" she exclaimed, suddenly defensive.

Somehow, her heart didn't seem to be fully in on the explanation, however. There was something in her eyes—an uncertainty—Slash thought. Maybe she was smarter than she was acting.

Slash chuckled dryly. "Well, then, he's sure a bad shot."

"How do you know it was him who fired that shot?" she asked hopefully. "He was a good distance away."

Slash said, "He was a ways off, but the man who fell out of that tree was big, blond, with a blond mustache, and he wore a big cream Stetson."

Fannie pondered that, glancing down at the split leather of her saddle horn, then cast another narrow-eyed, wrinkle-nosed glare at her captors. "You two fools can believe whatever you want to believe. But I know the truth!"

"Don't be a fool, Fannie!" Slash snapped back at her. He was still on edge from nearly being turned to mush by the rocks dropping into that canyon, and the so-called actress was getting on his nerves.

An easy job, his butt . . .

They rode along for a time in silence. The shadows grew long as the sun angled down in the west. The girl spoke again, this time with sarcasm. "You don't really think you two cretins can get me to Denver, do you?"

Pecos glanced at Slash, who was riding beside him. "Slash, what's a cretin?"

"I don't know, but I got a feelin' we ain't just been complimented."

"Thank you for proving my point," she said in the same snotty tone.

"Cretins or not," Slash said, keeping his eyes straight ahead, "we're gonna get you to Denver, all right. Mark my words, lady."

"Not gonna happen."

"It'll happen," Slash assured her.

"Nope. Do you know why?"

Slash said, "I got a feelin' you're gonna tell us."

"Because I'm smarter than the both of you put together. And I'm shrewd. Nope, you'll never do it. Mark my words, cretins!"

Slash only sighed, then glanced at his partner. "We'd best

look for a place to hole up. We only have a coupla hours of good light left, and after that little foofaraw in the canyon, I'd like to have a few mouthfuls of whiskey an' turn in early." He shook his head. "It takes it out of a man, nearly bein' crushed to bug juice. I don't mind sayin' I got the nerves of a June bride the night before her weddin'!"

"Yeah, I'm tired, too. Didn't get much sleep last night."

Pecos glanced back at the girl, who smiled saucily and said, "It's not my fault I'm hard to resist. That I can get a man's blood up even in the dark, when he can barely see me." She fluttered her eyelids at him haughtily.

"Yeah, well, you won't get these two fellas' blood up," Pecos said. "We seen what you done to ol' Pete an' George." He chuckled.

"May their souls rest in peace," Slash added with irony. He glanced over his shoulder at Fannie again. "Are all actresses as full of themselves as you, Miss Diamond? And spiteful?"

"Go to hell!"

Slash turned his head back forward with a sigh.

A half hour later, he glanced off the left side of the horse trail they were following and saw a small stream curving into the valley from the north. Pines and aspens lined it.

"Good water over there," he told Pecos. "Enough trees to hide a cook fire."

"I'm game."

They swung off the trail and into the trees, then found a good spot sheltered by rocks as well as large spruces and tamaracks. The two men tended their and the girl's horses, both keeping a close eye on their charge lest she should run off and get herself lost.

She only sat on a log and glared at them as they toiled on her behalf, gathering wood, building a fire, and hanging a coffeepot, which Pecos filled at the stream, from an iron tripod. Slash boiled some pinto beans, and they and the girl sat around the fire, washing the beans down with the coffee.

When they'd finished their meal, Slash washed the dishes in the stream while Pecos remained at the camp, keeping an eye on Fannie. It was not yet dark, the setting sun showing a painter's palette of bright colors between hulking western ridges, when both men and their saucy charge rested back against their saddles.

Slash and Pecos rolled smokes and sipped whiskey.

The girl watched them closely, arms crossed on her chest. She had a strange little smile on her pert mouth, and cunning in her amber eyes. Slash didn't like it. He didn't like it one bit. Like Pecos had said, they'd both seen what she'd done to Pete and George. Not that they hadn't had it coming, but still, Slash and Pecos had had firsthand looks at what she was capable of.

Slash studied her curiously, apprehensively, as he drew in another lungful of tobacco smoke.

"What have you got on your mind?" he asked her finally, pitching his voice low with suspicion.

"Who? Me?"

"Yeah," Pecos said. He'd been studying her, too. "You . . ."

Fannie smiled another one of her shrewd smiles, then climbed to her feet. "What I have on my mind is a bath." She cast a quick glance through the trees flanking Slash and Pecos, the firelight dancing in her eyes. "That stream over there has been calling my name all evening!"

She shrugged out of her oversized coat and tossed it on the ground.

Keeping her challenging gaze on both men, who were gazing up at her incredulously, she began unbuttoning her man's plaid flannel shirt, also too big for her.

"Hold on, now," Slash objected, scowling at her. "What the hell you think you're doin', you silly thing?"

She didn't stop but kept right on unbuttoning that damn shirt, exposing more and more ripe, creamy flesh, until both Slash and Pecos felt their tonsils had swelled to the size of billiard balls.

She removed the shirt, held it out to one side with a flourish, and dropped it.

Her amber eyes glinted devilishly in the firelight. "Anyone care to join me?"

Chapter 24

A red-throated trout leaped from the sliding water of the Poudre River north of Camp Collins, near the mouth of the Poudre Canyon. The long fish bent itself into the shape of an eyelash, flashing green and yellow and salmon in the light of the sun setting behind the high, forest-carpeted canyon walls to the west, then dropped back into the glistening water with a plop!

The silver splash quickly changed back to green and yellow and salmon as the fish's dark shadow dashed out away from it and down, down, down and gone.

"Hey, did you see that?" exclaimed Myra Thompson, pointing.

Delbert Thayer ripped meat from the chicken leg he'd just bitten into and, chewing, said drolly, "Yeah, when they're jumpin', they ain't eatin'."

He turned glumly to where his cane pole rested against a log just ahead of where he and Myra sat on the bank of the river, on a large red wool quilt. Myra's open picnic basket sat between them. It had recently been stuffed with all kinds of goodies, including a chicken she'd fried earlier that afternoon, as well as the potato salad and deviled eggs she'd prepared, a jar of her own bread-and-butter pickles, a wheel of cheese, a loaf of bread, and two big slices of the rhubarb pie she'd baked.

Myra followed Del's gaze to the pole. There was no tightening of the line angling from the end of it into the placid backwater pool at the edge of the river.

"Sorry, Del," Myra said. "Skunked again, eh?"

"Not much of an angler, I reckon," the sheriff's deputy said, chucking the chicken bone into the river and dropping his napkin into the basket, which now contained the leavings of the meal he and Myra had enjoyed. "That's all right," he added. "That's not what I wanted us to come out here for, anyways. Leastways not tonight."

"Oh?" Myra smiled. "Just wanted to enjoy a good meal . . . alone . . . with your favorite gal?"

The long-faced, loose-limbed, bucktoothed young man flushed one of his trademark flushes and shrugged. "I reckon."

"I find that downright endearing." Myra leaned over the basket to wrap her arms around the young man's neck and pecked his cheek. She rubbed the kiss into his cheek with her finger, then gave his chin a playful nudge. "After a long, hard day of running owlhoots to ground, no less!"

"A man's gotta make a livin' some dang way!" Del turned to his gal and grinned. "But, um . . ." He looked a little constipated, which he often did when he was trying to say something that made him uncomfortable. Or bashful. Yes, he was a bashful boy, was Myra's young man. It was one of the things she liked most about him. She herself was only twenty years old, but she'd known quite a few young men, most of them not bashful at all.

In fact, most had been quite bold. She'd once thought she preferred boldness in a man. Now, after settling down to a good, regular, upstanding life here in Camp Collins, she realized that wasn't what she preferred. She didn't even need her young man to be dashing or handsome. While far from ugly,

Del was neither of these. He was good and he was sweet and he was as honest as the day was long. Hardworking, too. And his was honest work, which also made him stand out from most of the other young men she'd known.

"But, um, what?" Myra reached up to slide a wing of his sandy hair from his left eye.

"Here. I'll show ya." Del set his brown Stetson on his head, unfolded his long, thin legs, and gained his feet.

Myra frowned. "Where you going, Del?"

"Stay right there, honey. I'll be right back." He got a spur caught in the edge of the blanket and tripped. "Oh, shucks!" he said, glancing annoyingly down at the blanket.

Myra smiled fondly, tucking her lower lip under her upper teeth.

Awkward was the boy. He'd grow less awkward, though, with manhood. Well, maybe not. It was hard to tell with Del. He was a couple of years older than she but not nearly as experienced, even though he'd been his uncle's deputy for two years now.

No, she'd be just fine with him keeping his boyish awkwardness, she decided now, as she watched him tramp through the grass and sage to where their two horses stood hobbled several yards upstream, idly grazing and swishing their tails at flies. Del cast his vaguely sheepish gaze over his left shoulder at Myra, grinned his bashful grin, then stepped up to his sorrel gelding, which he'd named after his older brother, Roy, who'd enlisted in the army a couple of years ago.

He opened a saddlebag pouch, and glancing over his shoulder at Myra again, he grinned. This grin was a little devilish.

Myra frowned. "What're you up to, young man? You don't have a frog in there, do you? You're not gonna try to drop a frog down my blouse, are you?" she asked with mock sauciness. "And you better not be haulin' out a bag of Bull Durham, either!"

Del laughed as he let the flap of the pouch drop back into place and turned to walk back toward her. He held something clenched in his right hand. He looked down at that hand as he walked, then stopped suddenly. He winced, placed a hand to his belly.

"What is it, Del?" Myra said, suddenly concerned.

"Just a little stomachache is all." He continued toward her.

"Well, I hope I didn't poison you!" she said, kneeling and gazing toward him with growing concern.

He shook his head as he stepped back onto the blanket and dropped to his knees. "Nah, I'm just a little nervous. I never done nothin' like this before. I been thinkin' about it plenty over the past month or so, an' every time I do, my stomach starts actin' up."

Oh, my God! Myra thought suddenly, heart leaping. *He's going to . . . He's going to ask me to marry him!*

She gazed at him, suddenly speechless, and splayed her right hand over her heart.

Del opened his hand. It held a small pasteboard ring box. "This here," he said, his voice sort of quaking now, as he stared at the box. "This here . . . Well . . . it's my favorite aunt's engagement ring, God rest her soul. She was my ma's twin sister, never had kids of her own. Before she died, she told me she wanted me to have this ring, Aunt Loretta did. She said it wasn't gonna do her no good after she was gone. She wanted me to have it . . . to give to the right gal." He gave another bashful smile as he lifted his boyish blue eyes finally from the ring box to Myra. "When the right gal came along . . ."

Myra's lower jaw fell in astonishment. "Del," she said just above a whisper, "are you . . . saying . . . I'm the *right gal*?"

Del smiled, showing his two protruding front teeth. He'd chipped the corner of the left one not long ago, when he tripped on a boardwalk, having gotten a spur caught between the cracks, and it made his smile all the more endearing.

Slowly, he opened the small ring box. Inside, nestled on a bed of cream burlap, was a gold band set with three amber stones and two green stones, one on each side of the amber ones.

Two of the amber stones were heart shaped.

"Aunt Loretta said the amber stones are garnets. The two small green ones are emeralds. It came from England. Just like Aunt Loretta. She an' Ma an' my pa came from England, too. All three came over here together right after Aunt Loretta's husband died from a sickness."

Del plucked the ring out of the box and held it up between his thumb and index finger. "I reckon . . ." He paused to swallow. His fair-skinned, suntanned cheeks were mottled red. "I reckon . . . I reckon I'm askin' . . . if you'd do me the, the, uh . . . the, uh . . . *honor* of bein' my bride, Miss Myra."

"You are, Del?" She studied him closely, shaking her head. She hadn't seen this coming. At least she'd thought that if Del asked her to marry him, he'd have waited another six months to a year. "You'd really want to marry me, Del?"

He grinned and dipped his chin, keeping his bashful eyes on hers. "I purely do." Suddenly, he frowned. "You seem surprised, Myra."

"Del, honey," she said, placing her hand on his wrist, "you know . . . you know that I'm . . . well, that my past is a little checkered, don't you?"

"I know that when your pa died when you an' him were livin' in the mountains—that's when you met up with Slash an' Pecos an' Miss Jaycee—you were alone for a coupla years. I know it ain't easy bein' a girl alone in the mountains. Or anywhere, for that matter."

"Del, I'm not as innocent as you." Of course, they'd never talked about it openly, but she believed him to be a virgin. She was not. Not by a long shot.

"Yes, you are, honey," Del said, his bashful grin in place, giving his chin another endearing dip. "In your heart you are. And that's where it really counts, don't it?"

She gasped, her heart swelling so that she thought it would explode.

Choking back tears, she said, "But, Del . . . I'm so stubborn . . . and bossy. Why, I'm . . . I'm downright *nasty*! There, I said it. You know it's true!" She was laughing and sobbing at the same time now.

"That is maybe what I like most about you, believe it or not, honey."

She couldn't speak just now, so she threw her arms around the young man's neck, sobs racking her. She just realized that she'd never really felt loved before. Her mother had died when she was too small to have known her, or even to have felt loved by her. As for her father, most of the time, she believed, he'd found her a mere annoyance.

Then, after he died, the boys she'd taken up with hadn't even pretended to love her. It hadn't been a conscious thought, but she'd believed in her heart of hearts that she would never in this world and throughout her life know love. Maybe that was why feistiness—no, downright anger—crept into her character now and then.

Until now, she hadn't realized—not really realized deep in her heart and soul—that this awkward but charming young man really did love her. And that she loved him.

"Myra, Myra . . . ," Del said, patting her back a little uneasily, confused by her reaction to his question. "I don't understand, honey."

Finally, she sniffed, trying to compose herself. She pulled her chin up and stared into his eyes, tears still raining down her cheeks. "Mr. Delbert Thayer," she said, practically strangling on the words, "I would be right honored to be your wife!"

It was young Thayer's turn to be surprised. "Whew!" he said, smiling his relief. "I was sure hopin' that'd be the answer I'd—"

One of the horses whinnied, cutting him off.

He and Myra turned to stare at their two mounts. Both horses stood looking back over their shoulders toward the trail that paralleled the river about fifty yards away. Myra's roan swished its tail apprehensively. Both horses bent their ears and worked their noses, sniffing the breeze.

"I wonder what startled them," Myra said, scrubbing tears from her cheeks with her hands as she composed herself, staring toward the trail, which was screened by a ragged line of ponderosa pines, firs, and aspens. The fading light played among the branches of the trees, which were mostly in the shadow of the western ridge rising beyond them.

"I don't know," Del said, climbing to his feet. Casting his puzzled gaze toward the trees, he called, "Anyone there?"

The only reply was the murmur of the breeze and the sucking and rippling sounds of the river.

Myra turned to Del. "Maybe it's just a deer."

As if in reply, a man said loudly from the other side of the trees, "Hy-yahh!"

Hooves thudded fast and hard, then dwindled quickly to silence, save for the breeze and the river.

Myra felt a cold hand splay chill fingers against the small of her back.

She turned to Del, frowning. "I'm frightened, Del."

"You wait here, honey," he said. "I'll check it out."

The young man walked over to his horse, tightened the cinch, slipped the bit into the horse's mouth, and mounted up. Shucking his rifle from his saddle boot, he swung the horse around and trotted off across the clearing, which grew darker with each passing minute, and into the trees.

Myra stared at the darkening trees, their branches nudged now and then by the evening breeze angling down from Elephant Rock to the west.

Del was gone for a long time. At least it seemed a long time to Myra, whose apprehension grew.

"Del?" she called at last, hearing the tremor in her voice.

When there was no response, she stiffly gained her feet and continued gazing toward the dark line of trees. "Del?" She walked forward, frowning. "Del, are you . . . ?"

She let her voice trail off when she saw movement in the trees and heard the thudding of horse hooves. Ambient light played across the lanky figure of her mounted beau, and Myra felt her heart lighten.

"Oh, Del," she said, "you frightened me!"

"Whoever it was," Del said as he approached, "he's gone now. He headed up canyon. I'm thinkin' it was some fella who wanted access to the river. Prob'ly saw us here and decided to try farther upstream."

"I see," Myra said, feeling a genuine relief, though she could not deny a certain lingering fear. It was probably just because of how dark it seemed to have become so suddenly, which it always did in the mountains. Especially in a mountain canyon as narrow and deep as Poudre.

"Don't be afraid, honey," Del said, dismounting, seeing the lingering fear in her eyes. "Whoever it was, he's gone now." He grinned. "Besides, you got this uncompromisin' lawdog to protect you." His grin broadened. "For the whole rest of your life."

"Uncompromising lawdog, eh?" She smiled foxily up at him. "Is that what the dime novels call them?"

He chuckled and wrapped his arms around her.

"Oh, Del!" She threw her arms around him, hugging him tightly.

He really did love her. She was loved. And she loved him.

She felt wonderful about that. More wonderful than she'd ever felt in her life about anything. Still, her apprehension lingered.

She pulled away from him, looked up at him. "I think we'd better start back to town now, Mr. Uncompromisin' Lawdog. It'll be good dark soon."

"You got it, honey."

As he walked over to tighten her horse's cinch, she cast her dubious gaze again to the dark line of trees.

They headed back to town, riding side by side, often holding hands.

Quickly, Myra forgot about her fear caused by the mysterious horse and rider. It had only been the darkness. That was what had frightened her. She'd always been a little afraid of the dark, despite having been raised in the mountains, where the night always settled quickly.

But now as they followed the trail back into Camp Collins, she and Del chatted about their future together, and love and joy filled her heart.

They pulled into the dark freight yard. She had decided to spend the night at Slash and Pecos's freighting company headquarters to oversee the place while the two men were away, and so she could get a quick start at deciphering the account books first thing in the morning.

Riding up to the main office building, where she'd once lived with Slash and Pecos, Del said, "I'll see you inside, honey."

"No, that's all right, Del. I left a lamp burning on the table." She glanced at the curtained, lamplit window right of the door. "I'll be fine."

"Well, I'll put your horse up, then."

"No, I'll take care of that, too. I don't want you gettin' any ideas you married some hothouse flower." She leaned over, flicked a finger against his hat brim, and kissed him.

They shared a long, deep kiss and a hug before gradually parting with effort.

When Del had ridden off into town and toward the house he shared with his mother, Myra put her horse up in the barn after feeding, watering, and currying the mount.

She closed the barn door, paused to appreciate the starry night and the great feeling of love and companionship that was fairly bursting inside her heart, and then crossed the yard and stepped up onto the main office porch. She unlocked and opened the door and went inside.

She'd just crossed the threshold when the lamp suddenly went out, enshrouding her in darkness.

She smelled the sweat and horse stench of the man a second before he grabbed her roughly, suddenly, coming up on her from her left, and wrapped his arm around her neck. She felt the cold, hard end of a gun barrel pressed against the underside of her chin.

A deep, uncompromising male voice rumbled into her ear, "Call out, and I'll blow your brains out, little girl!"

Chapter 25

"Care to *join* you?" Pecos said. "In the *stream*? In case you ain't noticed, it ain't only dark, but it's *cold*!"

"That's all right. I like it cold. Very refreshing!"

To Slash's horror, having removed her shirt, she now wore only a thin chemise that clung to her like a second skin.

Smiling at him defiantly, she lowered her hands toward the bottom of the chemise.

"Hold on! Hold on!" Slash said, holding his hands up, as though in supplication. Or possibly he was trying to restrain her without touching her . . . ? He didn't know. He just sure as hell didn't want her to take off that damned chemise. If she did that, there was no telling what might happen, and he was a married man!

But then she did just that, crossing her arms, lowering them, grabbing the bottom edge of the spindly garment, and lifting it up and over her head.

"Ah, Jesus. Close your eyes, Pecos! Close your eyes, for Pete's sakes! She's tryin' to *torture* us is what she's doin'!"

"Besides," the girl said, continuing to undress, though Slash was squeezing his eyes closed and willing himself to have strength enough to *keep* them closed, "I find a mountain stream at night wonderfully mysterious. Don't you, gentlemen? All those *stars*! *So romantic*!"

"Oh, Lordy," Pecos said. "I do believe you're right, Slash. That's exactly what she's doin'. First, Pete an' George, and now us. Only it's gonna be slower for us!"

Slash heard a boot plop onto the ground, then another.

"Ah, hell," he said miserably.

Slash turned to Pecos and opened his eyes to slits. "Don't look at her, you big fool!"

Pecos squeezed his eyes closed and lowered his head. "I got 'em closed! I got 'em closed!"

"You were peekin'!"

"Well, hell, I can't help it. Jesus, Slash, she's . . . she's . . ."

"Shut up! Don't say it! Just keep your eyes closed, but make sure she don't grab our guns. Now that she's got us right where she wants us, she's liable to *gut shoot* us!"

"There's a thought," Fannie said in a devilishly bewitching as well as taunting tone. Hearing her move around a tad breathlessly, Slash could tell she was still disrobing. "Now, why didn't I think of that?"

"Don't be crazy, lady," Slash said. "I don't know what you're up to, but it's not gonna work."

"Oh, I think it's already working."

"She's right, Slash," Pecos said miserably. "It's already working!"

"Keep your eyes closed. One look at that, and we're liable to go blind or worse—lose our minds and agree to let her go or some such!"

"Slash, you're a married man!" Pecos accused.

"There. See how bad she is? She made me *forget*!"

"Gentlemen, gentlemen," Fannie said. "Why do this to yourselves? Do you know how many men pay good money every night just to catch a *glimpse* of me? If you'd open your eyes now, you'd see *all* of me . . . in my raving, otherworldly glory!"

"Otherworldly glory?" Slash said.

"A scribbler from Denver called me that, and he hadn't even seen all of me . . . not like you two could right here tonight, if you'd only open your eyes." She tittered a mocking laugh.

Slash kept his head down, but somehow his eyes opened just enough that looking down, he could see her two little pink, pretty bare feet on the ground just in front of his worn, scuffed leather boots. "Oh, God," he moaned. "If you're gonna kill us, get it over with. I'm ready to let her go, Pecos. I'm a married man. I don't need this sort of thing. An easy job, my scrawny ass!"

"Open your eyes, Slash," she said softly but throatily, taunting him.

His eyes slitted again. She was still standing right in front of him. He thought he could smell her. She smelled like cherry blossoms with a hint of sage. How in the hell could any woman smell like that after riding all day on a horse, all her loveliness trundled up in a man's grimy trail clothes?

"Come on, Slash." She lifted one of those pretty bare feet and nudged his knee with it. "Live a little. Take a peek. We're dead a long time, you know."

"Go away! Go away!"

Chuckling softly, very pleased with herself, Miss Fannie Diamond turned from Slash to walk over to where Pecos sat against the woolen underside of his own saddle, head down, hat pulled down over his eyes.

"Look out, Pecos. She's comin' for you!"

"Oh, hell. Leave me alone, purty miss!" Pecos said, keeping his eyes squeezed shut, his head down.

Slash couldn't help watching as she lifted a bare leg and nudged Pecos's own upraised knee with her pretty foot.

"Hey, there, big fella. Sure you don't want a look?"

"In exchange for what?" Pecos said, keeping his head down, eyes covered by his hat.

She raised her voice suddenly, sharply, shrilly—angrily.

"My satisfaction at knowing how I so thoroughly frustrated and tortured you two old kidnapping train robbers, who don't even have the good sense to take hard, cold, albeit *stolen* cash shoved right in your faces! No, no, you feel some sort of allegiance. Or is it *yellow-livered, chickenhearted fear* of that old, crotchety, pencil-pushing civil servant in an off-the-rack three-piece suit who sent you up here to kidnap me—me, *hardworking and big time–headed actress Fannie Diamond*—and make me testify at a trial when he likely knows full good and well that doing so would likely land me in jail for perjury or get my throat cut by the only man I've ever loved in this whole scheming, two-faced, cruddy world. *Duke Winter!*"

"Ah, hell!" Pecos said.

"And you don't even have the good sense to open your eyes and enjoy the sight of a beautiful naked actress out here in this canker on the devil's ass. *Cowards!*"

"That tears it," Slash said.

He opened his eyes. He opened them wide and heaved himself to his feet. She swung to face him as he walked up to her, glared down at her in all her pale, lovely nakedness. "I thought you were going for a swim."

Her mouth corners crooked a devilish grin; in her eyes, starlight glinted devilishly. "I thought you were going to keep your eyes closed. Here I am. Too bad you can't have me. Just try to sleep now, after having seen me." She threw her head back and laughed devilishly.

"Like I said," Slash said, suddenly crouching and picking her up in his arms. "I thought you were going for a swim. Maybe I can help . . ."

The girl screamed and threw her arms around his neck. "Oh, my God. Put me down this instant!"

"It was your idea! You're goin' for a swim!"

"Slash, what're you doin'?" Pecos yelled behind him as

Slash swung around and tramped through the trees toward the water glinting in the star- and moonlight.

She kicked and wriggled in his arms, trying desperately to free herself. "Unhand me, vermin!"

"You know, Miss Diamond?"

"Get your grubby hands off me this instant!"

Striding toward the bank, Slash said, "You're the worst actress I've ever seen. You couldn't act your way out of a Christmas pageant made up of four-year-olds and a burro." Slash stepped up onto the stream's rocky bank and held her out over the oily-dark water. "And now that I've gotten a look at you, I see why you so rarely take your clothes off onstage."

Slash dropped her.

She screamed just before she hit the water with a loud splash.

"Because," he added, shouting so she could hear him under the water, "since you ain't even all that much to look at, you'd likely lose your audience to the high-kicking, buck-naked showgirls in the hole-in-the-wall saloon on the other side of the tracks!"

"Slash, what the hell did you do?" Pecos scolded him, coming up behind him through the trees.

"I just thought she needed a little cooling off's all," Slash said, staring down at the dark water.

Pecos stopped beside him, looking down. "Where is she?"

"She'll likely come back up in a second or two."

Pecos turned to Slash. "Slash, she ain't comin' back up!"

Slash frowned. He'd be damned if his partner wasn't right. She wasn't coming back up.

"Fannie," he said as he stepped down off the bank and onto the sandy, gravelly strip of the water's edge. "Fannie, where the hell are you?"

He looked around. Nothing but dark water, upon which the starlight winked. The stream slid on past him and Pecos, gurgling. From somewhere on the stream's far side, seventy yards away, a night bird screeched.

Pecos hurried down the bank to stand beside Slash. "Slash, you cork-headed fool! If you drowned her, Bledsoe's gonna hang us for sure. And hangin' would be too good for you!"

"Oh, shut up!" Slash kicked out of a boot.

"Don't tell me to shut up!"

"Shut up!" Slash kicked out of another boot and then ripped off his shirt and peeled off his pants.

"Slash, dammit. Don't tell me to—"

Pecos's voice was drowned by the stream, into which Slash dove, straight out away from the shore. He then angled downstream. and kept his eyes open, though he couldn't see much in the murk. The water around him was a dark fog. He thrust his hands out, swimming, hoping one or both of those hands would find the girl.

He lifted his head above the surface. Just as he did, he spotted something floating ahead of him and a little farther out, near the middle of the stream. It was either driftwood or . . . A ray of moonlight flashed on her blond head.

It was her! She was being carried downstream roughly twenty feet ahead of him and to the left, bobbing and swaying with the current.

"Hold on—I'm comin'!" Slash yelled and picked up his pace, thrusting one arm forward and then back, the other forward and then back, pulling at the near-black water and thrusting it back behind him.

Her head turned. Moonlight flashed in her eyes.

"Leave me alone!" she sobbed. She turned her head forward. "Just leave me alone!" she cried again, her voice less loud this time because she was facing downstream. She sounded genuinely despondent.

"Ah, hell!" Slash increased his pace, pulling the water back behind him with his arms, propelling with his legs. Gradually, he closed on her, the distance between him and her narrowing to fifteen feet . . . to ten.

She glanced behind her. Again, the moonlight glinted in her eyes.

"I said leave me alone!" she wailed. "Just leave me alone!"

Slash grunted as he swam. "If I leave you alone, you're gonna die out here, you fool polecat!"

"That's what I *want*! I want to *die*!"

"Oh, you don't, neither," he said, approaching her, reaching forward and grabbing her arm.

"Unhand me!" she cried, though she did not try to pull her arm out of his grip. She sobbed.

"Come on." Slash wrapped his left arm around her waist, just beneath her breasts, and swam toward shore. She did not fight him but sort of hung off his left side, sobbing. He could feel her bare foot occasionally touching his own.

"Won't you please just leave me to drown?" she said through her sobs. "I want to die!"

"No, you don't."

"I do! I really do! You were right!"

"No, I wasn't."

"I can't act! And I'm nothing much to look at! You were right! That's why I keep my clothes on!"

Slash's toes raked the bottom. He continued swimming until he could walk. He kept his left arm around the girl's waist, leading her forward, the water dripping down their bodies, and then he led her up onto the bank. She did not fight him but walked slowly along beside him, sobbing. He could feel her body trembling against the frigid water, against her own despair.

Nice going, Slash, he scolded himself. *Really nice going. You insult her, and then you damn near drown her. Now she wants to die! Really nice going, Slash! Give the man a cigar!*

"Leave me here!" she cried, suddenly stopping after they'd

stepped up onto the grassy bank. "Just leave me here! I want to be alone!"

"Too cold." Slash crouched and picked her up in his arms and began tramping back upstream, following a gradual bend in the narrow strip of sand and gravel.

A man-shaped figure appeared just ahead, stepping through a wild berry thicket. It was Pecos. He held the girl's blankets. "Here!" he said, stopping before Slash and draping the blankets over her dripping, naked body.

"Oh, go away—both of you!" she cried, turning her head away in defiance.

Slash paused to wrap the blankets around her. Pecos cast him a disgusted look. Slash cursed and continued forward, wincing against the rocks and pebbles nipping at the soles of his bare feet. He followed the stream's bend, keeping to the edge, and headed for the orange flames of their campfire maybe a hundred yards ahead and to his left.

When he reached the fire, he laid the girl down by her saddle, then tossed more wood on the fire.

She lay shivering inside her blankets, mumbling, "Damn you, damn you, damn you . . ."

"Yeah, I know," Slash said with a sigh, tossing one more small branch on the fire. "Damn me."

"Yes," Pecos said, just then entering the camp, "damn you. That was the nastiest thing I ever seen you do, an' that's sayin' somethin'!"

"Oh, go to hell!"

Slash tramped back through the trees to gather the clothes he'd left on the shore. He brought them back into the camp and tossed them down by his saddle. Pecos was down on one knee, offering Fannie his whiskey bottle.

"Here, have you a tug on that, darlin'," he told her. "It'll warm your insides."

She lay on her side in a tight ball, holding her blankets tightly around her, shivering. "No!"

"Oh, come on. Take a pull." He glared at Slash, who was peeling out of his soaked and freezing long handles. "Slash is sorry, ain't you, Slash?"

Slash muttered under his breath as he tossed the underwear over a rock to dry by the fire.

"What's that, Slash?" Pecos said, hardening his glare at his contrary partner.

"Ah, hell," Slash said, wrapping his shivering self in his own blankets and sitting back against his saddle. "Yeah, yeah, I'm sorry."

"What's more," Pecos added, still kneeling by the girl, holding out the uncorked bottle, "he didn't mean it. Did you, Slash?"

"No, I didn't mean it. I already done told her that."

"He did, too, mean it!" she said.

"No, he didn't, did you, Slash?"

"No, dammit. I didn't mean it!" Slash pulled his hide-wrapped traveling flask from a saddlebag pouch beside him and unscrewed the cap.

"He did, too! And he was right!"

"Pshaw!" Pecos said, chuckling. "No, he wasn't. Not by a long shot. Slash is hardly ever right about anything. But I'm here to tell you, little lady, he was most definitely wrong about that. About your looks, anyway. And the acting, too. You're a damn good actress. You sure held my interest!"

He cast another castigating glance over at Slash, who was stifling a wry snort by taking a quick pull from the flask.

She lifted her head to look up at Pecos through the blankets. In a thin, suddenly bashful voice, she said, "Did you see the show?"

Pecos smiled. "Sure did." He shook his head. "Just plumb

amazin'. Why, I never seen such as that ever before in my life!"

Again, Slash stifled a snort with a quick pull from the flask.

"What about," she asked, suddenly timid, maybe even shy, "the other . . . ?"

"The other?" Pecos asked.

"Yeah. You know. How I look, you know . . ."

"Without your clothes on?" Pecos asked.

Chapter 26

"I wouldn't know about that," Pecos said. Slash could see him blushing in the firelight. "I didn't look."

"The hell you didn't," the girl said, chuckling caustically, sitting up, and grabbing the bottle out of his hand. She could go from a monsoon squall to clear skies at the drop of a hat. She took a quick pull and then another, her eyes watering and cheeks coloring against the burn.

She pointed the bottle accusingly at Pecos, narrowed one eye, and said, "You peeked! I saw you. Several times you peeked!"

"I seen him!" Slash sided with her.

Pecos chuckled as he watched the girl take another pull from the bottle, then lower it and gaze up at him, another devilish smile on her lips as she awaited his response.

"All right, all right," Pecos said, chuckling incredulously as he sat back against a log on the girl's side of the fire. "You caught me in a fib. I did look. Couldn't help myself."

"And . . . ?" Fannie said, still waiting.

Pecos smiled at her, slitting his soft, kind blue eyes. "That there was an image that's gonna plague this old outlaw for the rest of my misspent life. Likely the last thing I'll see on my deathbed. Likely several times over!"

Again, he smiled.

"You're not just saying that?" she prodded skeptically, narrowing her other eye.

"No, I'm purely not, darlin'."

She pooched out her lips, smiling at him. Her cheeks turned red. So did her ears. "I sorta like how you call me darlin'." She winked at him, making him blush once more.

Holding the bottle by its neck, she turned to Slash. "What about you, you actress-drowning reprobate?" she asked with half-feigned disgust and anger.

Slash took another pull from his flask, lowered it, and sighed. He smiled across the fire at her. "Biggest lie I ever told." He winked at her.

She flushed even redder.

At least regarding her looks, he added silently to himself. *Not about her acting skills or lack of such . . .*

"All right." She took another pull from the bottle, then handed it back to Pecos. "All is forgiven." She glanced at Slash. "I reckon I had that swim coming, anyways. Prodding you two the way I was. Using my body to tempt you just to get even with you for kidnapping me."

Slash glowered as he gazed off into the darkness beyond the fire. "That's not what riled me."

"Oh?" Slash and Fannie said at the same time, brows arched.

"Truth be told," Slash said, his tone droll, "what riled me was realizing you were right." He looked at Pecos. "About our boss an' why he sent us here."

Pecos frowned. "Ol' Bleed-'Em-So?"

Slash nodded, hooked a shrewd half smile. "That old devil didn't think this was gonna be an easy job. I'd bet gold nuggets to horse apples he knew we'd have a devil of a time gettin' Miss Fannie out of Frisco, her bein' so popular an' all with the menfolk. Especially with Duke Winter."

Pecos's eyes widened with sudden understanding. He nodded slowly. "You think he knew we'd be facing Ol' Duke himself?"

"I do." Slash glanced at the actress. "She's a whole lot smarter than we are, partner. She figured it out. We should have, too. He didn't just send us up here to get *her*. He sent us up here to kill Winter. Or die tryin'.'"

"Or die tryin'," Pecos said, nodding again slowly, fingering his chin whiskers. "The old devil . . ."

Fannie frowned, perplexed. "Your boss would like to see you dead?"

"He wouldn't mind it one bit," Pecos said.

"Sending us out on dangerous missions is a source of amusement for him," Slash added.

Pecos sipped from the bottle. "You see, years ago, Slash put a bullet in his back. Crippled him."

"I didn't mean to," Slash said. "It was a ricochet."

"No, what he was really tryin' to do was *kill* him."

"Only 'cause he was tryin' to kill *me*!"

Fannie frowned even more deeply as she cast her gaze between them. "And . . . now . . . you're working for him . . ." It wasn't a question but a perplexing statement.

"Long story," Slash said. "But, yeah, that's how it stacks up, I'm afraid."

"So, essentially," she said, trying to puzzle it all out, "I'm the bait meant to attract Duke Winter. So you could kill Duke." She put a little salt in her voice, frowning, when she added, "Which you likely did . . . back in that canyon."

"Hope so," Slash said.

She looked into the fire's flames, a sheen of emotion entering her eyes once more.

Pecos cast Slash another admonishing look. "Do you have to be so damned honest? Can't you see Miss Diamond here still has feelin's for the man?"

"Oh, *hell*!" She extended her hand for Pecos's bottle, which he put into it. "I don't know what I feel anymore. Or what to believe! Duke an' Boone gave me a great opportunity up here, and yet they smothered me. I loved Duke, truly I did, and yet I wanted to go East, to New York, to the *big time*. Yet . . ." Her face crumpled again with sorrow. "I may . . . I may not be . . . well . . . *good enough* for the big time . . ."

Slash and Pecos glanced at each other but said nothing, keeping their own counsel on the matter of Fannie's lack of acting talent.

She took a deep pull from the bottle and then one more. It was plain to both Slash and Pecos, who shared quick, amused glances, that she'd obviously sampled the who-hit-John a few times in the past. She wiped her mouth with the back of the hand holding the bottle, sniffed, and said, "It's just that I know I'm not really as good . . . you know . . . of an *actress* . . . as I sometimes think I am. Duke and Boone don't really think I'm much good, I'm afraid, and it's always burned me! They think I'm only good enough for the gold camps."

She turned to Slash and added in a plaintive voice, "That's why I need Duke and Boone so badly. Without them, I'd likely have no work at all. No protection from the kind of men who flock to my shows in the hopes of seeing my . . . my . . . you-know-whats!"

She spat that last out like a lemon seed, making a sour expression.

"Duke protects me . . . loves me," she continued. "At least I thought he did. Still *hope* he does . . ." She turned to Pecos and said in the same plaintive voice as before, "Because I have no one else. Except for Boone, that is. Boone sees me only as a meal ticket."

She took another drink from the bottle, then handed it back to Pecos.

"Oh, Lordy," she said, leaning back against her saddle and

crossing her arms over her breasts beneath the blankets. She tilted her head toward the stars and added, "I'm sooo alone."

"No, you're not," Pecos said. "Hell, for now you got us!"

She scowled at him. "Yes, I have you . . ." She shuttled her gaze to Slash. "*You*, who will drag me into a Denver courtroom and force me to testify against Chaz 'the Knife' Lutz!"

Slash shrugged. "If Winter's dead, what have you got to worry about?"

"The Knife himself will have me killed . . . *after* I've testified. He may go to prison or hang, but before he does either, he'll send someone to cut my throat."

"We'll make sure you got protection until he hangs," Pecos said.

She shook her head, having none of it. "He has family. A brother just as nasty as him. Ed Lutz will see to it I'm killed."

Slash and Pecos shared a conferring glance. Pecos's brows were ridged, troubled. Slash shrugged.

"Oh, well," the girl said, rolling onto her side and resting her head against the woolen underside of her saddle. "It hasn't been much of a life, anyways. I'd just as soon be dead. So . . . I'll go back to Denver with you two." She cast Slash and then Pecos a direct, sincere look and added, "I won't be any more trouble. I promise. I'll go back to Denver, walk into that courtroom, sit down in the witness chair, and spill my guts. The Knife will hang, and I will have my throat cut, and that's just fine with me!"

With that, she snuggled down deeper into the saddle as well as the blankets and closed her eyes.

Pecos looked at Slash.

Slash didn't say anything. He just took another sip from his flask and tossed another log on the fire.

Pecos rose from where he'd been sitting on the girl's side of the fire and returned to his bedroll and saddle near Slash. He sat down, doffed his hat, set it down beside him, and crossed his long legs at the ankles.

He turned to Slash. "What do you think, partner?" he asked quietly so as not to disturb the girl, who appeared to have already fallen asleep, her chest and shoulders rising and falling heavily, regularly.

"Ah, hell, I don't know." Slash took another pull from the flask, then reached over to pull his makings sack from the front pocket of his shirt. "We're between a rock and a hard place. If we don't get her back to Denver, we'll likely stretch hemp. Or go to the federal hoosegow in Michigan. I'd rather die than spend the damn winters in a federal pen in Michigan for the rest of my life."

"But if we do take her back to Denver, and she testifies against the Knife," Pecos said, "*she'll* likely die."

Slash dribbled chopped tobacco onto the wheat paper troughed between his thumb and index finger. "But if we don't take her back to Denver, what do we do with her?"

"Take her back to Frisco. That's where she belongs. Hell, she does have a job. And a manager—that fella named McClory."

Slash scratched a match to life on his saddle and held it up to the quirley protruding from his mouth but did not light it. "I think McClory's with Winter. In that canyon. Which means he, like ol' Duke, is probably nothin' but a grease stain under a very large rock."

He lit the quirley. Puffing smoke, he said, "You and I both know that if we don't get her down to Denver, Bleed-'Em-So will only send someone else to fetch her to Denver. He'll be doubly piss burned because the trial will have to be delayed. You know how impatient the old son of Satan is."

"Ah, hell." Pecos tipped his bottle back, then returned it to its previous resting place on his thigh. "I miss the old days,

Slash," he said, looking longingly out into the darkness beyond the fire.

"We're too old for the old days." Slash drew on the quirley, dragging the smoke deep into his lungs, and exhaled it before adding, "You gotta be young to be a bank robber. We got old, Pecos."

"Ah, hell, you're just happy 'cause you got Jay. All I got is you and ol' Bledsoe, who gets a kick out of feedin' us to the wolves every few months. That's just what he's done here. Fed us to the wolves—Winter's bunch."

"Winter's bunch is likely dead."

"We don't know that."

"If he is somehow alive, he had to find another way around that canyon. So he's likely hours behind us."

"It's a damn mess, though, ain't it?"

"What? Havin' to haul her back to Denver against her will?"

"Yeah."

Slash sighed, nodded. "It ain't the sorta thing I thought I'd be doin' once I retired from robbin' banks and trains. We don't have much choice, though. No point in squawkin' about it."

"Yeah, I reckon."

Pecos sipped from his bottle, then gazed moodily into the darkness. From somewhere a long way out in the starlit mountain night, a pair of wolves took turns howling from separate ridges—one to the south, one to the north.

Pecos turned to Slash. "Hear them wolves?"

Slash nodded.

"They're free."

"And we're not?"

"Not by a long shot."

Slash took another drag from his cigarette and glanced at Pecos. "What you need is a woman."

Pecos gave a wry snort. "You done took the best around."

Slash chuckled.

"You miss her?" Pecos asked him.

Slash hiked a shoulder, flushed a little.

"Oh, come on, Slash—you can admit missin' your wife. How could a man not miss the former Jaycee Breckenridge curlin' his toes for him of a night?" Pecos smiled dreamily.

Slash glanced at him again, crooked an ironic half smile. "Yep. You need you a woman. I'm gonna have to help you look into that just as soon as we get Fannie back to Denver."

He glanced over at the sleeping girl.

She wasn't really asleep, however.

No, Miss Fannie Diamond had only feigned sleep.

She'd been listening to the two old scalawags' conversation, hoping to hear that, feeling sorry for leading her off to the proverbial cemetery—yes, for her that Denver courtroom would be a cemetery, make no mistake!—they'd changed their minds and decided to let her go.

But no! The cowardly fools were going to force her back to Denver.

Unschooled cretins!

After the one had fairly tried to drown her!

That was all right. She was glad Slash had thrown her in that river. It would make what she would have to do tomorrow—bright and early, right after she saw the dawn's first blush—so much easier.

She felt a little guilty, though, she had to admit. Both men had sort of grown on her, though why, she had no idea. To her they meant certain death.

Still . . .

Oh, never mind, Fannie. You have to do just what you've always done to survive out here in the man's frontier West.

Exactly what you've been forced to do!

With that, she nodded off. She didn't slip into a very deep

sleep, however. How could she with the two old scalawags sawing logs so loudly that Fannie thought if there were rocks on the ridges like those that might or might not have killed Duke and his gang, these two would surely bring them down on top of themselves and her!

That was all right, though, under the circumstances. She didn't want to sleep too deeply and possibly *over*sleep. She couldn't oversleep. She had to wake up before the two old scalawags did.

Finally, when the first smudge of the false dawn came, she opened her eyes.

She looked at the two old owlhoots lying on the other side of the fire from her. Both were sawing logs as before, Slash snoring into his pillow, Pecos lying back against his saddle, hat pulled down over his eyes. His mouth was wide open, and the loud, raking snores fairly vaulted out of him, making Fannie's eardrums rattle.

Lordy, she couldn't wait to get away from these two. . . .

With that thought in mind, she rose very slowly. Naked beneath her blankets, which were still damp, she tried not to shiver. Breathing shallowly, afraid to awaken her captors, she walked slowly toward Pecos. He lay nearest her, so she would go to him first.

She looked at the holstered gun lying to his right, the shell belt coiled around it. She stared at the walnut handle jutting up above the sheath. She looked at the man himself, mouth open as he snored, lips fluttering a little with each wailing exhalation.

With such a din, how can they not wake each other up?

Fannie looked at Slash. He lay on his left side, face turned into the woolly underside of his saddle. His two guns also lay on the ground to his right, shell belt coiled around them.

Her heart fluttered as she took one step at a time, silently willing each man to remain asleep. She put her bare right foot down on a sharp stone and stretched her lips back from her teeth in a grimace, pausing until the pain subsided.

Then she continued walking toward Pecos, holding the blankets up tight about her body.

She drew within six feet of Pecos. Within four feet.

Three . . .

Two.

She looked at his face, the upper half of which was concealed by his brown hat. Beneath the hat, his mouth was wide open, letting loose a snore, drawing a raking breath, then loosing another god-awful snore.

She grunted caustically to herself. *Go ahead and see if you can find a woman who'd put up with that kind of racket every night!*

She slid her bare feet up to within a few inches of his holstered revolver.

She glanced at him once more, heart quickening, nervously licking her lips.

Then she crouched, reached down with her right hand. She lowered it to within two inches of the handle of the gun when suddenly both feet were kicked out from beneath her.

She gave a shocked cry as the dawn world went topsy-turvy, and suddenly she found herself lying on the ground, stars bursting behind her eyes.

"What the hell's goin' on?" Slash yelled beneath the ringing in her ears.

Sitting straight up now, Pecos looked from the girl on the ground before him to his partner, who was also sitting up, both of Slash's pretty Colt .44s in his fists.

"The little devil was goin' for my gun!" Pecos said. "Prob'ly gonna drill us both third eyes, partner!"

"Oh!" Fannie said, sobbing and holding her hands to her head. She lay there, the blankets in disarray, revealing more than they hid.

"Don't 'oh' me, you little polecat!" Pecos groused. He glanced at Slash. "I reckon we should have learned a lesson from ol' Pete an' George an' tied her up."

"Don't worry," Slash said, lowering his Colts. "Tomorrow night we won't be so careless."

"There ain't gonna be no tomorrow night!" a man shouted from out in the dawn murk somewhere. "Not for her an' you two, leastways!"

Chapter 27

Jay stood before her mirror in her and Slash's suite on the second floor of the Thousand Delights, running a wood-handled brush through her thick red hair. As she did, she slid her gaze to the rumpled bed behind her. She smiled, remembering how Slash enjoyed leaning back against his pillow, watching her brush her hair in the mirror in the mornings.

In the mirror, Jay watched her smile fade.

That empty, rumpled bed gave her a pang of lonesomeness. Worry too. She hoped that everything was all right up in the mountains and that Slash and Pecos hadn't run into trouble guiding that actress down from the mining town of Frisco to Denver. If their assignment went according to plan, Jay should see them again in a few days and be back in the arms of her new husband.

And Slash would be back in the big canopied four-poster bed again, smiling as he sipped his morning coffee and watched his wife brush her hair in the mirror.

That thought returned the wan half smile to Jay's freshly red-painted lips.

Finished brushing her hair to its usual morning shine, Jay set down the brush and glanced at the clock on the wall by the door. It was nearly seven o'clock. She had to get downstairs and see to the kitchen staff, to make sure everything was ready to start serving breakfast. She was already dressed in a metallic green pleated gown and a white shirtwaist with a low-cut, ruffled front and puffy sleeves, trimmed with a gold-washed neck chain strung with pearls, so now she grabbed a light shawl from her armoire and wrapped it around her shoulders to fend off the usual morning chill. She went to the door, opened it, and started to step into the hall, then stopped when she noticed something hanging from the outside knob.

It was a small manila envelope, hanging from the knob by a string.

Frowning curiously, Jay removed the sealed envelope. Nothing was written on the outside of it. Frowning even more curiously, she used her thumbnail to slice it open. From the envelope she pulled a single sheet of trifolded notepaper. She unfolded the paper and sucked a sharp, startled breath when she saw a long lock of light brown hair fall from the bottom fold to the hall's carpeted floor.

She stared down at the hair. The lock was roughly ten inches long, curling slightly at one end.

A chill touched her as she slid her gaze from the lock of hair to the paper she held in her right hand. On it was written in blue-black ink a note in a large looping, but masculine hand.

Come and get her. Bring the deed. Tell anyone, show this note to anyone, and your friend will disappear after knowing much pain. I'll be waiting at the Elkhorn cabin in Redstone Canyon. You know where it is. I met you there for a picnic two springs ago.

Jay gasped as she lowered the note and looked down at the lock of hair on the carpeted floor between her feet. She crouched, picked up the hair, and held it up before her.

"Myra . . ." She gazed off into space, her heart quickening. Her racing thoughts were slow to cohere.

When they did, when they finally clarified the improbable notion that Grant Balldinger had taken Myra . . . was holding the girl hostage in return for Jay handing over the deed to the Thousand Delights, she stumbled back against the doorframe in disbelief.

"The man's an animal," she heard herself breathe. "A monster."

Breathless with fear and rage, Jay looked at the note once more.

Tell anyone, show this note to anyone, and your friend will disappear after knowing much pain.

"Miss Jay? You all right, Miss Jay?"

Jay gasped, just then realizing that beneath her loud and racing thoughts, she'd been aware of footsteps on the stairs down the hall on her right. Now she turned to see Delbert Thayer walking toward her, frowning curiously, concernedly.

"Miss Jay?"

Jay placed her hand on her chest, as though to quell her racing heart. "Oh . . . Del!"

Myra's young man!

Jay glanced down at the note in her hand, feeling heat rise in her cheeks. Even her ears were burning. She stared at the rangy young deputy who stopped before her, studying her closely.

"I'll be hanged, Miss Jay, if you don't look like you seen a ghost!"

"Oh, it's nothing, Del. Nothing at all." Jay feigned a laugh. She wanted so much to show the note to the young deputy, but good sense held her back. He would no doubt fork a saddle pronto and ride out to Redstone Canyon and get both himself and Myra killed!

No, Jay couldn't do it. Something very deep down inside

her, maybe her memory of the coldness of Balldinger's eyes the other day on the porch of his ranch house, told her that what he'd warned her of in the note was not an idle threat. If she told anyone that he'd kidnapped Myra, the girl would disappear. He would likely kill her or have her killed and tossed into a canyon, never to be seen or heard from again. Yes, Jay would have Balldinger's ransom note to show the sheriff, but that wasn't going to do Myra any good if she was dead.

Besides, Balldinger was a powerful man in Colorado. He could, likely would, deny that he'd had anything to do with the penning of the ransom note.

Jay chuckled again, though she was well aware of how phony it sounded. "I'm just a little weak with hunger is all. I didn't have much time for supper last night . . ."

Del crouched before her. "Here," he said. "You dropped somethin'."

Jay glanced down, horrified to see that the ransom note was not in her hand. It was on the floor in front of her, just now being scooped up by young Deputy Thayer! She must have dropped it when he'd startled her.

"Here, I'll take that!" Jay said a little too shrilly.

She was about to grab the note when the deputy suddenly lowered the hand holding it, as well as his head, and looked back down at the carpeted floor. Jay couldn't see his expression beneath the brim of his hat, but she could tell by the slow way he moved that he was pondering something very thoroughly.

Then she saw what that something was, and her heart leaped.

She'd also dropped Myra's lock of hair. It was on the carpeted floor to her left. She'd just started to reach for it herself when young Thayer plucked it up off the floor and held it in front of his face, staring at it in silence.

Down on one knee, staring at the lock of hair, Del said

softly and with an air of deep bewilderment, "I was over at the freight yard, looking for Myra. Couldn't find her anywhere. The front door was open."

Jay couldn't see his face concealed beneath the brim of his hat.

Now young Thayer tipped his head up, lifting his gaze to hers. His eyes brightened with a growing anxiety. "I came over here to see if you seen her . . ."

He lowered his head again, held the ransom note in front of his face.

"Here, Deputy. Give me that, please!" Jay reached for the note, but he drew it back away from her, then gazed down at it, sort of holding Jay back away from him with his other arm, the lock of hair pinched between his thumb and index finger. "Del, no!"

She reached for it again. Del pulled it away so quickly that he lost his balance and fell onto his right hip and smacked his back and the back of his head against the wall with a hard thud. If it hurt, he didn't show it. No reacting to losing his hat, which had tumbled down his chest to the floor, he kept his eyes glued on the note he now held in both hands in front of his face, the lock of Myra's hair dangling from the thumb and index finger of his left hand.

"Del, please . . ."

He raised his eyes to hers. "This is Balldinger, ain't it?" He gave the note a little shake. "And by 'your friend,' he means Myra." He held up the lock of hair dangling down along the side of his hand. His eyes were wide and hard and serious in a way that Jay had never seen before.

Jay drew a deep, calming breath and shook her head. "Del, before you go off half-cocked, you saw the note. His warning. You can't know about this!"

She realized she'd spoken too loudly, and looked around anxiously, but all the doors around her were closed. All her percentage girls were likely still asleep and would be until around three or so, when they'd awaken for baths and their first meals of the day before starting work at five.

Del bunched his anger-flushed face, hardening his jaws, pushed off the wall behind him, and rose. "But I do know about it, Miss Jay!"

Jay raised two fingers to her lips. "Shhh!"

Del glanced around, then continued a little sheepishly and more quietly, "I do know. He's got Myra, but he ain't gonna have her for long!"

He'd started to turn away, but Jay grabbed his arm. "No! Del, you wait!" When he turned back to face her, she said, "If you go riding out there, he'll kill her."

"He's bluffin'." Del shook his head. "He's gotta be bluffin'. A lotta water flows Balldinger's way around here, but he's never been . . ."

He let the words die on his lips, unable to finish the unspeakable thought.

Jay glanced around again cautiously, then squeezed the young man's arm with more urgency, keeping her voice very low, almost a whisper. "I think he is. I saw it in his eyes the other day. I think he's fully capable of murder if he doesn't get his way. I think Grant Balldinger has been a wolf in sheep's clothing, and my refusal to sell the Thousand Delights to him has made him shed that phony wool."

Del stared back at her, his eyes gravely thoughtful, deep lines carving ladder rungs across his broad forehead, which never tanned properly but merely turned red and peeled. "Uncle Matt once told me Balldinger has ordered his men to shoot rustlers on sight an' bury 'em. He told me it wasn't worth gettin' crossways with Balldinger over much of anything. That's all he said. I never knew what he meant. But now I know. The way he said it." Del ran two fingers across his face, indicating his eyes. "He had such a dark look. I think . . . I think Uncle Matt's afraid of Balldinger. Never figured Uncle Matt to be afraid of anyone, but . . ."

"He's afraid of Balldinger," Jay finished for the young deputy. She nodded, thoughtful. "I've heard bits and pieces of stories, as well. Usually told in hushed voices by cowboys bellied up to the bar downstairs. About how Balldinger has never had to worry much about land or business disputes, like other ranchers and businessmen have. I've never heard it explained, but judging just by the tones those clipped tales are usually told in, other ranchers and farmers give him a wide berth, because they're afraid of him. And their fears are no doubt based on solid evidence."

Jay shook her head again, perplexed. "Funny, how it never thoroughly registered in my brain. I just thought I was hearing bits and pieces of idle rumors told by sour men with bones to pick with Grant."

"Now he's got Myra," Del said, his voice hushed with awe and desperation. "What're we gonna do about it? The sheriff won't get back till Sunday!"

"Shhh!"

"Oh, sorry!" Del covered his mouth, grimacing and glancing around. "I reckon I'd better not tell Big Hans or the other deputies, huh?"

"No!" Jay exclaimed in a whisper. "You need to stay in town while I ride out there and turn my deed over to that madman." She shook her head slowly. "I see no other choice."

"I can't just sit in that office over there, Miss Jay, while you—"

She squeezed his arm again. "You have to!" She paused. "If Slash and Pecos were here, they might have a better idea."

"I'm a deputy sheriff, Miss Jay," Del said in frustration. "And they have my girl! Myra's gonna be my wife!"

Chapter 28

Slash jerked both of his .44s up with a start, looking for the source of the man's shout.

Two bullets whined in and tore up ground in front of him, kicking dirt up over the blanket still covering him. Pecos had just reached for his own Russian but stopped the movement when the shooter shouted, "Lower the hoglegs, or meet your Maker, you two old cutthroat devils! We're deputy U.S. marshals Vince Quarles and Ed Thomas, an' we'd love nothin' more than to trim your wicks!"

Slash and Pecos shared an incredulous look.

Having drawn her own blankets around her to cover her nakedness, Fannie had pushed up onto her knees and was staring off toward the source of the shouts as well as the gunfire, looking even more crestfallen than when her plan to snatch Pecos's Russian from its holster had failed, the old former train robber being savvier—or at least a lighter sleeper—than she'd suspected.

"Quarles and Thomas?" Slash mouthed to Pecos.

Brows ridged, Pecos said, "Two from Bleed-'Em-So's stable of bona fides. Remember, we seen 'em both in the old man's office right after we started workin' off the books for the old ridge runner."

Slash nodded. "Ahh. Now I remember. They looked down their noses at us, as I recall."

"Thomas blew smoke in my face on his way out of the office," Pecos added bitterly.

"That was just plain rude," Slash said.

"We're ridin' in!" the man shouted. "Keep those guns down. We're not lookin' for a fight. The old man sent us!"

Slash kept his Colts down but sat up straight and shouted, "Shootin' at a man is a funny way to not be lookin' for a fight!"

From nearly straight out through the trees, toward the valley center, a man chuckled, then hacked phlegm and spat. Then two riders appeared, moving their horses out from behind two stout firs, coming together, then turning their horses toward Slash and Pecos and booting the mounts into fast walks. Both men were tall and dressed in three-piece suits— one brown, one black. Slash recognized the man in the black suit, who rode a steel-dust gelding, as Vince Quarles. He was hawk faced and mustached, while the man in the brown suit, Ed Thomas, was heavier and fairer skinned, a bushy redblond mustache adorning and hiding his upper lip.

Thomas rode his beefy sorrel toward Slash and Pecos, grinning, blue eyes flashing with wicked amusement. Quarles was the darker, leaner, more taciturn of the two.

As they approached Slash, Pecos, and the girl, Fannie glanced worriedly at both her captors, then, holding her blankets tightly around her, scuttled backward on her butt, pushing herself toward her saddle with her bare pink feet and showing a good bit of both creamy bare legs as she did.

Quarles and Thomas looked at the girl from beneath their hat brims, both men frowning incredulously.

"Well, well, well," said Thomas, switching his ironic gaze to Slash and Pecos. "You three been havin' yourself a party out here?"

Frowning indignantly at both newcomers, Fannie sat back

against her saddle, raised her bare knees and carefully covered them with her blankets, and pulled her bare feet inside the blankets, as well, though most of her toes peeked out from beneath them.

"It's not what it looks like," Pecos said, also indignant. He held his Russian down low against his right thigh.

Quarles looked at the girl, his dark brown brows beetled, a vaguely ironic smile quirking his own mouth corners. "Young lady, you don't have a stitch on under them blankets. Why?" He glanced at Slash and Pecos. "These two old owlhoots been pesterin' you, have they?"

She glanced at Slash, curling her upper lip with anger. "That one threw me in the river!"

"Threw her in the river, eh?" Thomas said, glancing at Slash and giving a wry snort. "You tryin' to drown ol' Bleed-'Em-So's star witness?"

"It's a long story," Slash said with some chagrin. "Suppose you two tell us what you're doin' out here? That mean old man in Denver told us all his bona fides were tied up over in Utah."

"You can't believe everything the old man says," Thomas said. "You oughta know that by now, Braddock."

"We're here to take her off your hands," Quarles said, glancing at Fannie. Slash noted a vague cast of lust in the man's dark brown eyes, which slid up and down the girl's blanket-wrapped body, from her plump red lips to the tips of her toes peeking out from beneath the wrappings.

"What're you talkin' about?" Pecos said. "We were sent to fetch her."

"No." Thomas shook his head, grinning like the cat that ate the canary. "You were sent to nab her . . ."

"And draw Winter out in the open," Quarles said. "So we could shoot him and as many of the rest of the gang as we could get!"

"Back shoot 'em," Thomas said, "while they were chasin' you."

Slash and Pecos shared another angry look.

"You mean that nasty old man sent us up here as *bait*?" Slash asked, feeling his ears burn with fury.

Angry now, too, Fannie turned sharply to Slash and Pecos. "I told you I was bait! Hah! And you two cork-headed fools were bait, too!"

Slash didn't look at her. He kept shuttling his own furious gaze between the two bona fides sitting their horses before him. "That crazy old man sent you two because he didn't think we'd *make* it?" He'd figured he and Pecos had been sent to draw out Winter. But he hadn't suspected that he and his partner had been used as *bait* so other, *real* lawmen could finish the job Bledsoe didn't think they could finish!

"Just covering his bets, I reckon." Smiling, Quarles shrugged his shoulders. "Probably figured there was a chance you wouldn't—what with the whole gang likely on your trail." He chuckled. "He didn't figure on that canyon falling in on 'em, wiping them all out in one fell swoop. He wasn't sure the girl would make it, either, but in case she did, he wanted us to come in and swoop her up and take her on down to Denver to testify against the Knife."

"Well, I'll be jiggered," Pecos said to Slash. "Partner, we been whipsawed!"

"How long have you two been following us?" Slash asked.

Thomas said, "We came up the next day from Leadville. We were finishing up another job when we got the orders over the telegraph wires from Bledsoe. He told us to shadow you and watch for Winter. When Winter started shadowin' you, we were supposed to shadow him and his gang. When they were good and distracted by you, we were supposed to throw the lead to the whole gang." He chuckled devilishly.

"We were about to do that very thing in the canyon back

yonder," Quarles said, hooking his gloved right thumb over his shoulder, smiling broadly. "But when that whole ridge started disintegrating, we realized we weren't gonna have to waste a single round." He grinned over at his partner. "That was a piece of work, wasn't it, Ed?"

"Sure enough was." Thomas looked at Slash and Pecos and narrowed one eye shrewdly. "Tell the truth, now. Was that an accident, or did you have that planned?"

Pecos started to answer honestly, but Slash cut him off with, "Planned the whole damn thing!" He narrowed his own eye shrewdly. "How'd you know we made it out of there?"

Thomas said, "We rode up another canyon and over to the rim of the one you two *broke* and picked up your tracks."

"We figured it had to be you," Quarles added, "since you three were ahead of the others."

"Duke didn't make it?" Fannie asked in a pinched little girl's voice, her eyes large and round and touched with sadness.

"Duke's bug paste, Miss Diamond," Quarles said flatly. "Couldn't have happened to a nastier SOB, either."

"Our condolences for your loss," added Thomas ironically, doffing his hat and holding it over his heart, revealing the bald dome of his head. "Now, why don't you grab them clothes and get dressed so we can get on the trail? We're taking you to Denver."

"Why are you taking her?" Pecos asked. When he remembered how she'd intended to shoot him and Slash with their own guns, he added quickly, "I mean, not that we give a fiddle!"

"Sure as hell not," Slash said. "Just curious is all."

Quarles hiked a shoulder. "I don't know. You two are supposed to be dead. Leastways the old man figured there was a good chance you'd be dead. He told us to grab the girl if she still had some life in her an' take her on down to Denver."

He glanced at Thomas. Each man shrugged in turn.

"As you can see, they're still alive," Fannie said, indignant again. "They can take me to Denver!"

"Hold on, hold on!" Slash protested.

Quarles and Thomas shared another conferring glance, and Thomas said, "I don't give a rat's tail end who takes her to Denver. But since we're out here . . ."

"You can take her to Denver," Slash said.

He wanted nothing more to do with the cold-blooded little she-cat. If these two were sent to take her to Denver, they could do just that. Even if Slash and Pecos had somehow managed to keep their ghosts. Besides, he'd love to see the smug looks wiped off these two tinhorn law bringers' faces, which would no doubt happen before they were a mile on down the trail, when Fannie either started caterwauling or trying to brain them both with a rock.

"Like you said, since you're out here with nothin' else to do, she's all yours," Slash added.

"She's all yours," Pecos said, holding both hands up, palms out, in supplication and casting an indignant glare at the girl, who'd been about to drill him a third eye with his own weapon.

"No," Fannie protested, glaring at Slash and Pecos now. "I started with you two, I will continue with you two!"

"No, you won't," Slash said, leaning over to blow on the charred and smoking end of the log in the fire. "They'll take you."

He blew up a little spark and added some tinder in the form of bits of bark and dead leaves.

"Why are you two in such a hurry to get rid of her?" Thomas said, narrowing a curious eye. He looked at the girl, and a little lust entered his gaze, as well. "She's right easy on the eyes . . ."

Slash chuckled, then blew up a small flame and glanced over his shoulder at Pecos, who returned the look.

"No reason in particular," Pecos lied to the bona fides. "We was just thinkin' that since we're up here, we might do a little, uh . . . fishin'."

"Yeah, that's it," Slash added, feeding the small flame some more bark and crushed leaves. "We're gonna do some fishin'." He smiled up at the two mounted lawmen. "We are semiretired, don't ya know?"

The bona fides studied him and Pecos skeptically.

Slash glanced at Fannie to find her regarding the newcomers with an entirely different expression from the one she'd been wearing a minute ago. This time she studied them closely, pondering deviously. Slash thought he could see the dark rocks of deception rolling around behind her eyes.

Fresh meat, she was thinking. These two lawmen were babes in the woods when it came to the cunning and deadly little she-cat known as Miss Fannie Diamond.

Slash's suspicions were validated when she suddenly tossed her blankets aside, revealing her naked little well-curved and filled-out self, saying with feigned resignation, "Oh, all right! If you insist on taking me down the mountains to Denver, why protest? It appears that *someone* is going to get me to Denver whether I want to go or not!"

She rose in all her glorious nudity and tramped barefoot over to where she'd dropped her men's duds the previous night, when she'd been torturing Slash and Pecos. Slash stifled a laugh and glanced at the two bona fides.

Both men's eyes widened, and their lower jaws sagged.

Slash glanced at Pecos, who smiled back at him crookedly.

"Looks like you're going to Denver," Fannie said, stumbling around beautifully as she lifted each bare leg to stuff it down in a leg of the worn denims. "Whether you like it or not. Why protest? Just a waste of darn time!"

She took her time with the pants, and when she was done, she took her time with her socks and boots, again dancing around and jiggling, until both Slash and Pecos thought the two bona fides were going to strangle themselves on their own tongues. The color rose in their faces and crawled quickly to the tips of their ears.

They sat their horses, riveted.

Still talking to herself, as though oblivious of the bona fides' awestruck stares, Fannie shook out her men's flannel shirt and then stuffed each arm slowly into a sleeve, giving the two newcomers the performance of a lifetime—one that Slash could tell they fully appreciated.

Slash quickly dressed himself and, chuckling, said, "I'll saddle her horse."

He glanced at both lawmen once more as he tramped over to where he and Pecos had picketed the horses. He doubted either man had heard him. Their attention was elsewhere at the moment, as they were watching the pretty little well-turned actress button her shirt with painstaking slowness while she muttered her feigned resignations.

Slash glanced back at Pecos.

They chuckled and shook their heads.

They chuckled again and shook their heads when, ten minutes later, they watched the two bona fides ride off, with the actress following on her dun.

As the trio rode through the trees, heading for the middle of the valley, Fannie turned her head, shook her golden locks back from her face, and cast her former two captors a devious wink over her shoulder.

Pecos glanced at Slash. "Think she'll even mark their graves?"

"What?" Slash said with a laugh. "You think she'll even *bury* 'em?"

Both men, feeling giddy with their newfound freedom, threw their heads back and roared.

Chapter 29

Feeling a cold wind push against her from behind, blowing her hair forward and across her saddle horn, Jay reined her mare to a halt.

She looked up and winced. Low clouds the color of dirty rags slid across the sky from the east. The wind was shepherding the smell of rain, as well. And now she heard the kettle-drum of thunder as she gave a more pronounced wince.

A monsoon was brewing.

Silently, she cursed, then curveted Dorothy on the trail west of Camp Collins and cast her gaze behind her, along her back trail. Nothing back there but the tawny valley hemmed in on both sides by cedar-stippled ridges. If someone was back there, he or they were doing a good job of keeping out of sight. No one appeared to be following her, but Jay had an uneasy feeling—a crawling sensation between her shoulder blades—that she was, indeed, being shadowed.

As the first drops of rain blew against her, ticking against her coat and hat and chilling her cheeks, she reached behind for the oilskin she'd wrapped around her bedroll in the event a monsoon would strike again today, as they'd been doing every afternoon and early evening for the past week or so. It was that time of year, but she could really do without rain today. She had enough on her mind.

Namely, getting Myra back from the abominable Grant Balldinger, as well as the prospect of her losing her beloved business, which she'd worked so hard over the past three years to build into something she was proud of.

But the Thousand Delights was just a business whose value dwindled to nothing when set against the life of her young friend Myra Thompson.

As she shrugged into the oilskin, Jay glanced at the saddle-bags draped over Dorothy's hindquarters. The deed was in the left pouch, tucked into a manila envelope. She would turn it over to Balldinger. She had to in order to save Myra's life. But she would report the extortion to the sheriff as soon as he returned from Denver.

Balldinger would not get away with taking Jay's business. She didn't care how powerful, corrupt, and downright evil he was. . . .

That determination foremost in her mind—well, behind Myra, that was—she buttoned the oilskin to her throat, glanced at her back trail once more, then once more at the sky, from which the rain was coming down harder and at a hard angle from the east, and put Dorothy up the trail.

After another twenty minutes' hard ride she turned the mare into a canyon opening in the ridge wall to her right. She followed the narrow, winding horse trail up the canyon, abutted on both sides by sheer red sandstone ridges that were taller in some places than others and less sheer, as well. Horse-tooth Rock, looking like nothing more than the three side-by-side horse teeth of its name, reared ahead in the east, beyond and above the canyon's right wall, the formation's very top obscured by the dirty clouds.

After another fifteen minutes' ride, Jay turned the mare into yet another side canyon, this one opening on her left. She remembered the route to the Balldinger cabin when she'd been foolish enough to let Balldinger spark her, they'd met here for a picnic. She was eminently glad she had not fallen for the man, even then having the vague sense that something was not totally right with him.

Now horse and rider climbed a steep, low ridge into ponderosa pines. Beneath the rush of the rain, which came down steadily, thunder rumbling and lightning stitching the mass of clouds hanging over the canyon, hooves thudded behind Jay.

At least two riders were coming fast.

Fear gripped Jay. Just as she reined in the mare and turned to peer behind her, one rider and then another rider came around a curve in the trail, their horses climbing hard and fast, kicking up mud behind them. As the first rider came to within twenty feet of Jay, she recognized the face of Grant Balldinger's son, Todd, beneath the brim of the young man's dripping black hat. He wore a yellow oilskin just like the one Jay was wearing. It shone with beaded rain. Todd looked at Jay without expression as he passed her.

The man behind him was the cold-eyed and tight-lipped foreman, Ace Calloway, who rode past Jay on the opposite side from Todd, not looking at her.

As Todd pulled ahead of Jay and angled back onto the narrow trail, he hipped around in his saddle, locked eyes with Jay, and said, "Come along, Miss Jay. Pa's waitin' on ya!"

He hooked a crooked grin, glanced at Calloway, who was angling onto the trail behind him, then turned his head forward. Both men continued to put their horses up the trail and then disappeared around another bend maybe forty feet beyond where Jay sat staring dreadfully after them.

So, she had been followed. . . .

She drew a deep, calming breath, then booted Dorothy up the trail, which soon leveled out in a copse of firs and aspens. Todd Balldinger and Ace Calloway were just then trotting their horses up to a log shack that sat amidst the rain-lashed trees at the base of a lumpy granite ridge. Three other men in range gear and rain slickers milled on the cabin's front stoop, smoking, turning their Stetson-hatted heads toward where Jay rode her mare up behind the boss's son and the foreman.

The cabin's front door was open. Watery amber lamplight shone within. Through the door, Todd Balldinger called, "She's here, Pa. She wasn't followed out from town. We made sure!"

"Send her in," returned Grant Balldinger's deep voice from inside the cabin.

As Jay reined her mare to a stop, she saw Balldinger sitting at a crude table just inside the cabin. He sat on the side of the table opposite the door, his big, red, granitelike, clean-shaved face staring out. He wasn't wearing his hat. It sat crown down on the table ahead of him and to his left. He gazed out at Jay, blinked once, brought a cigar to his lips, and took several smoky puffs, exhaling the smoke through his nostrils.

Ace Calloway swung down from his buckskin ahead and to Jay's right. He turned to Jay, frowning, sandy brows ridged over his cold gray eyes, and said, "Well, what're you waitin' for? Christmas?"

Jay drew another deep, calming breath—only it wasn't so calming—then stepped down from Dorothy's back. She dropped the reins. Dorothy would remain with the reins even when she was nervous, which Jay could tell she was now. Jay could feel the horse's muscles expanding and contracting beneath the saddle, could feel the hard pumping of her heart.

The horse's heart beat almost as fast and as hard as her own. The mare didn't like these hard-eyed men any more than Jay did. Jay wondered if she felt as repulsed by the man staring out through the open door from the other side of the table while calmly, expressionlessly smoking his cigar as Jay did.

She pulled her saddlebags off Dorothy's back and strode forward between Todd, who was still forking his saddle on her left, and Ace Calloway on her right, the foreman's face as stony as Balldinger's. Todd stared down at her, a crooked smile on his mouth, jeering in his eyes.

Jay mounted the porch and felt the other three men's eyes on her. There was a goatishness about their gazes, which she felt was particularly distasteful, especially given the fact that the youngest of them was a good twelve or even fifteen years younger than she. She did not look back at them but strode across the porch and stopped in the open doorway, ten feet from where Balldinger sat on the other side of the table.

She shuttled her gaze to her right and gasped. "Oh, God, no!"

She rushed into the cabin but stopped when Balldinger said, "Hold it right there, Jay, or I'll kick the chair out from under her boots!"

Jay stood frozen, heart really racing now, and clamped a hand over her mouth as though to quell a scream. She stared in mute horror at Myra, who was standing on a chair at the table's far end, clad in a plaid work shirt, denims, and men's boy-sized stockmen's boots. Balldinger had looped a riata around her neck. He'd tied the other end of the riata around a ceiling beam three feet above Myra's head.

Myra's hands were behind her, apparently tied.

Myra stood gazing down at Jay, ashen faced, terror in her eyes, tears rolling down her cheeks. She was shifting her weight from one foot to the other atop the chair, which betrayed its ricketiness by creaking and groaning beneath the girl's weight.

Jay lowered her hand and switched her gaze to Balldinger, who sat slightly angled toward Myra, resting one boot on the edge of the chair she stood on, threatening to kick it out from under the girl.

"Grant, you bastard, I brought the deed!" Jay shouted. "Cut her down!"

The man's eyes lit up with a devilishness similar to that of his son. "Did you tell anyone?"

Jay shook her head. "No one." Except Delbert Thayer, of course. She'd made him promise to remain in town. She hoped against hope he would. Why, oh why had she had to go and drop that damn note in front of him? The note and Myra's lock of hair.

"You weren't followed?"

"No," Jay said.

"We made sure, boss," Calloway said from outside.

"Just wanted to hear it from the horse's mouth."

"Cut her down before that chair crumbles beneath her! Damn you, Grant!"

Balldinger's mouth corners rose, and his flat brown eyes glinted. "Sit down. Have a drink with me."

He had a labeled bottle on the table, as well as two cut glass goblets, which looked as out of place in this rustic line shack as would a bouquet of bloodred roses in a Grecian vase.

"Cut her down!"

The smile left Balldinger's lips. Threat darkened his eyes. "Have a drink with me, Jay." He turned his head and looked at the boot he held up against the edge of Myra's chair.

"You devil!" Jay pulled a nearby chair out from the table. She gave Myra a worried glance.

"Don't do it, Jay," the girl said, her voice firm. She was composing herself, hardening herself against the horror of what was happening. She was tough, and she wanted to be tough to help set Jay at ease, God bless her heart. "Don't turn over the deed to this madman. Not for me!"

"It's just a piece of paper, Myra. It's just a business. I'll buy another one."

"No, Jay . . . please . . . ," the girl said in a pinched voice.

Jay swung the saddlebags off her shoulder and onto the table. "The deed's in that pouch," she said, glancing at the pouch nearest the obviously mad rancher. "It's all yours. Now, cut Myra down!"

Balldinger had poured whiskey into the second glass on the table. Now he slid the glass over to Jay's side of the table, smiling at her, looking quite satisfied with himself, the light of insanity glinting far back in his eyes.

No, not so far back. It was there near the surface now. Jay wondered how she hadn't seen it clearly before, though her suspicions had been rekindled the other day on the porch of his house at the Cheyenne Creek Ranch headquarters.

Jay lifted the glass to her lips, threw back the entire shot, and slammed the glass back down on the table. "Cut her down." She slid her eyes toward Myra. "I'll take my money for the Thousand Delights, and Myra and I will leave."

Balldinger sipped his own drink, swallowed, and studied Jay shrewdly. "What will you tell your husband?" He hiked one heavy shoulder inside his cream oilskin and corduroy jacket. "About selling."

"Don't worry. I won't implicate you." The hell she wouldn't!

The dark smile that spread his mouth again told her he wasn't buying it.

"I'm sorry, Jay."

Dread pooled like rattlesnake venom in her belly.

"I can't let you go back to town." Balldinger slid his eyes to Myra, who was still anxiously, desperately shifting her weight on the creaking, crackling chair. The girl stared down at him, her eyes wide and cast with disbelief. "Or her."

Enraged, Jay slammed her fist down on the table hard, leaning forward in her chair. "I fulfilled my end of the bargain, you son of Satan!"

"I know—it's a bleeding shame. You can't trust me as far as you could throw me." Again, Balldinger smiled. "You're a fighter, Jay. That's one of the things that attracted me to you, in fact. You'll make a fuss. You'll try to bring the sheriff into it, lawyers into it. I doubt anyone would believe your word against mine—being a former outlaw woman and the wife of a former, very notorious train robber. Yes, Jay, you might be respected for your business prowess, for the way you run your saloon and hurdy-gurdy house, but your reputation is less than stellar."

The mad rancher—yes, he really was deeply insane, wasn't

he?—drew a deep breath, puffing out his chest. "Still, your caterwauling over our business arrangement would be an unwanted distraction for me. No, my story is this. You sold to me. You kept your intentions a secret to Slash. You wanted to surprise him. Now you two can go away together, start fresh. You'll be together more without the distraction of running a successful business—both of you. You want him to sell the freighting business, as well. I mean, neither one of you is getting any younger.

"I paid you good money for the Thousand Delights"—he glanced at the valise sitting on the chair to his right, at the end of the table opposite where Myra stood with the rope around her neck—"but on your way to town this stormy afternoon, the Fates intervened the way the Fates often do. Sadly. Poor dear, in the storm you rode your prized mare off a cliff and into a canyon."

"*No!*" Myra screamed.

Balldinger ignored the girl. Keeping his taunting gaze on Jay, he said, "As for her, she will simply disappear. Who knows what happened to her? Given her own less than honorable past, she might have just decided that the young deputy Delbert Thayer wasn't man enough for her. In fact, I believe someone in town is going to say they saw her riding off with a handsome gambler." He peered around Jay to call out through the open front door. "Don't I have that right, Todd . . . Ace?"

"That's right, boss," Ace Calloway called from the stoop.

"You got it, Pa. We paid good money for that story, an' the fella owes you a favor to boot. That's what he'll say, all right. The girl and the gambler rode off in a buggy, arm in arm. Oh, she's a two-timin' little—"

"All right, that's enough, Todd. Thank you!" Balldinger gave a dry laugh and glanced up at Myra. More tears were streaking the poor girl's cheeks. She couldn't control them anymore.

Jay gazed across the table at the rancher, heart thudding,

terror a galloping horse inside her. She shook her head slowly. "You'll never get away with it. You'll never get away with it!" She glanced at her saddlebags. "Besides, the deed can't just be—"

"Don't worry," Balldinger said, cutting her off. "My attorneys will go over the deed, and by the time they're done, there will be no question—none at all—that I am the rightful, legal owner of the Thousand Delights. Your husband will be bereaved, of course. I'm sure that grief will be assuaged at least somewhat by the pile of money he'll find in those saddlebags, though, of course, he'll have to find lodging elsewhere. That money will also prove the legality of our transaction here today, which, of course, *actually* occurred in my office at the Cheyenne Creek headquarters." He lifted his head to call through the door. "Didn't it, boys?"

"Sure did, boss!" one of the men on the stoop called. The others agreed, chuckling.

"Why?" Jay said, shaking her head slowly, truly puzzled. "Why are you doing this to me?" She glanced at Myra. "To us . . . ?"

"I have nothing against the girl. Her only mistake was being your friend. She means only leverage to me. She is how I got you out here with that deed. As for you—you should have married me. Instead, you married that outlaw Braddock." He hardened his jaws and spat through clenched teeth. "You humiliated me, Jay. Now I have your business. And you . . ." He smiled and looked over Jay's head at someone whom she had just spied in the corner of her eye as he stepped into the open doorway behind her.

She turned to see the man in the brown vest over a black shirt, the green neckerchief, and black hat—the devil who'd bushwhacked her!—filling the doorway behind her. She hadn't looked at the men on the stoop carefully enough to have picked him out. He wore black gloves. He had the fingers of both black-gloved hands entwined over his belly. He smiled, as though eager to use those black-gloved hands.

"And you," Balldinger repeated, returning his evil gaze to Jay. "Will have gotten your just deserts." Keeping his eyes on Jay, he said, "Conklin, kindly break the lady's neck."

"You got it, boss," Conklin said beneath Myra's shrill scream.

Jay's heart turned a double somersault in her chest as she heard a boot thud behind her, saw a shadow move across the table on her left.

The cabin's rear door, directly behind Balldinger, exploded inward, latch and bolt crashing onto the floor, along with large slivers of wood from the frame. The tall, lean figure in the doorway snapped a rifle to his shoulder and aimed the barrel over Jay's head.

The rifle crashed raucously, the sudden cacophony sounding like an exploding keg of dynamite. It made Jay leap in her chair with a start as orange flames stabbed from the rifle's maw.

The man behind Jay grunted as the bullet threw him backward out the door to land on the stoop with a loud thump!

Jay and Myra stared in shock at the thin, bucktoothed young man standing just inside the rear doorway now, holding the door back with one foot.

Smoke curled from the Winchester's barrel as the young man cocked it, ejecting the spent casing over his shoulder. The casing clattered to the floor with a ping.

Jay was too flabbergasted to say anything, but Myra screamed, "*Del*!"

Chapter 30

"Nature stop!" Fannie called out.

Both deputy U.S. marshals, Vince Quarles and Ed Thomas, stopped their horses and looked back at her, scowling. "What're you talkin' about?" Quarles snapped. "You had a nature stop not fifteen minutes ago! We got a train to catch in Sundown, an' we're not gonna catch it if we have to stop to let you make water every fifteen minutes."

"It's the coffee," Fannie called, feigning an endearing smile with her ripe mouth, batting her eyelashes a little. "Goes right *through* me!"

She swung down from her saddle, handed her reins up to Thomas, giving the husky deputy an ingratiating smile, then flounced off into the brush along the trail, making her golden locks bounce on her shoulders.

Behind her, she heard Quarles say to Thomas, "You know what I think? I think she's tryin' to play us."

"Play us how?" asked Thomas.

"Beats me. I just got a notion I been played, that's all. Maybe we shoulda asked those two old train robbers more about her."

Thomas said something back to Quarles, but now Fannie was too far away to clearly overhear the two lawmen's conversation. She snickered to herself as she continued to move through the brush and pine trees, glancing back over her shoulder, making sure they couldn't see her.

Babes in the woods, those two. If they hadn't realized when she'd pranced around in front of them naked that she was playing them, well, then they likely never would. She'd done that to catch them off guard, to get them to think about something more than their jobs. If they were thinking about how she'd looked in her birthday suit rather than keeping a close, suspicious eye on her, maybe she could take advantage of their goatish male lust and make her break for freedom.

Or . . .

Looking around on the ground, she found what she was looking for. She stopped, crouched, and wrapped her hand around the rock. She held it up in front of her face. It was roughly the size of a billiard ball and nearly as round.

She tossed it up, caught it, tossed it up, caught it again. Smiled shrewdly.

Now she looked around for a good hiding place.

A boulder lay just a few feet away, evergreen shrubs climbing up along both sides. A crow sat atop the boulder. It looked down at her with its beady, little coal-black eyes and cawed.

"Oh, hush!" Fannie said, scowling up at the bird.

The crow gave several raucous cries, then spread its large black wings and took flight, its continued caws dwindling quickly beneath the rustling of the afternoon breeze.

"What the hell's goin' on over there?" Quarles called from where she'd left them with the horses.

Fannie stepped behind the boulder, edged a look around it toward the deputies, and said nothing. She tucked her upper lip under her bottom teeth and hefted the rock in her hand, testing its weight.

"Hey, Miss Diamond!" Thomas called, his voice a little resonant and friendlier than that of the more serious Quarles. "Don't wander too far. Don't want a bear to get ya!"

She could hear the two men chuckle. She narrowed her eyes and flared a nostril as she gazed back in their direction.

A minute passed. Thomas called again. He sounded concerned.

Roughly thirty seconds passed, and then Quarles called again. He sounded annoyed.

She could hear the two men conversing in peeved tones, but she couldn't make out what they were saying. Then silence.

A minute later, footsteps sounded from the direction in which she'd left both badge-toting fools.

She pulled her head back behind the boulder, then stepped a little away from it. Holding the rock in her right hand, she untied her rope belt and dropped her trousers down around her knees.

The footsteps grew louder.

She turned her head to peer around the boulder. A shadow moved on the ground maybe fifteen feet away from her.

With her pants down around her knees, she squatted and turned her head forward, as though oblivious of the approaching federal and the fact that he was about to catch her tending nature, which, of course, was exactly what she wanted.

To distract him again.

In the corner of her left eye, she saw Deputy Thomas step out from behind a fir tree only a few feet away from her. She whipped her head toward him, feigning shock, and screamed, "Don't look, you scoundrel! Oh, you're depraved! How dare you stalk me out here!"

Thomas stopped abruptly, his cheeks instantly coloring.

"Oh, hell!" the man said, slow to cover his eyes with his hand, taking a good couple of seconds to appreciate what lay before him. "I wasn't stalking you! We were wondering what the hell happened to you! Besides, it ain't like we ain't both seen a whole lot more of you than that!"

He chuckled.

"Cretin!" she cried, pulling her men's denims back up on her hips. "Turn away this instant! A gentleman would avert his gaze!"

He seemed reluctant to do so. Fannie didn't blame him.

"Oh, hell, all right!" Thomas rolled his eyes, shook his head, glanced at her once more, his eyes glazing the way men's eyes did when taking in her admittedly fine features, then turned around, giving her his back.

Inwardly, she laughed. The damned fool deserved what he was about to get.

Fannie stepped forward, raised the rock high, then gave a grunt as she slammed it down against the back of the man's head, crushing his hat crown. The rock connected with a solid thud. Thomas grunted and dropped like a fifty-pound sack of horse feed, out like a light.

Moving quickly, Fannie dropped the rock and pulled the revolver from the holster thonged on the lawman's right thigh. She searched his slack body for more weapons and found a folding barlow knife and a pearl-gripped derringer. She tossed away the barlow knife and pocketed the derringer, which might come in handy later. From the left pocket of the deputy's broadcloth coat, she produced a set of handcuffs.

Oh, joy! Exactly what she'd been hoping to find!

She pulled each of the man's arms behind his back and secured each cuff to each wrist.

"Ed!" Quarles called. "Now, where in the hell did *you* go?"

With a devious glint in her eye and tucking her upper lip under her bottom teeth, Fannie straightened. Holding the walnut-butted revolver down in front of her in both hands, Fannie strolled back in the direction from which she'd come.

"Slash, I haven't felt so light an' carefree in a month of Sundays!" Pecos said.

"I know, partner," Slash said as they followed a downward-slanting valley floor between high, rocky ridges. "Getting that so-called actress off our backs has made me feel a hundred pounds lighter."

"Ain't it the truth?"

"I feel like I been given a new lease on life," Slash said. "I feel like I did when them Pinkertons saved us from Bledsoe's gallows. Yessir, a new lease on life." Slash laughed and slapped his thigh. "Them two so-called *bona fides* can have that nasty little so-called actress, an' give the devil the hindmost!"

Pecos chuckled as, his long right leg hooked leisurely over his saddle horn, he took his time building a quirley. They were headed generally northeast, having run into a prospector, who'd given them directions to the nearest narrow-gauge rail-head, which lay in the little town of Sundown, another eight or so miles beyond.

Now they were following a well-worn two-track trail likely cut by ore drays. They had passed several mines after leaving the prospector and had entered better-settled country, including ranch country with cattle grazing along streams and in grassy valleys, than what they'd traversed before in the higher country.

"What a polecat!" Slash exclaimed, wagging his head and chuckling dryly.

"Polecat, hell!" Pecos said. "That there was a dyed-in-the-wool wildcat of the nastiest stripe imaginable. Never known a girl that nasty. Do you realize she was actually gonna *shoot* us?"

"Certain sure she was." Slash wagged his head once more.

"Here, I was just startin' to feel sorry for her, leadin' her to Denver against her will, an' with her bein' afraid one of the Knife's friends or family would cut her throat for her."

"Don't believe it. She's a trickster, that one. The way she disrobed right in front of us. What a way to treat a pair of ol' . . . er, well . . . slightly older but still very handsome gentlemen!"

"Temptin' us that way was almost as nasty as poisoning

poor ol' Pete an' George." Pecos licked his quirley closed and turned to Slash with a big grin on his face. "Somethin' to look at, though, wasn't she?"

"I wouldn't know. I didn't look. Remember, I'm a married man!"

"Your loss, then, my friend, because she truly was beautiful in her birthday suit!" Pecos threw his head back and gave a wolflike howl. "Just glad to be rid of her. If we'd had to continue hauling her nasty little behind down to Denver, we'd have had to take turns staying awake all night for the rest of the trip."

"Hell, we'd have tied her up. Trussed her up like a damn calf for the brandin'!"

"Sure enough!"

Again, Slash chuckled. "Just glad to be rid of her. Don't want to ever lay eyes on that gnarly li'l tiger ever again. Not even naked!"

"I thought you didn't look!"

Slash narrowed an ironic eye at his partner. "A married man is still a man, by God. Besides, I'm the one who threw her in the river! Hah!" Slash frowned, sobering, as he stared straight ahead over his Appy's ears. "You know, I almost feel sorry for Quarles and Thomas."

"The hell? After how they treated us? Like we was no better'n dog plop on the front porch?"

"In light of that so-called actress's rabidness, I do." Pecos lit his quirley and, exhaling smoke, turned to his partner. "They're liable to have their throats cut or get shot with their own guns!"

As if to validate the notion, a pistol popped from somewhere ahead, and the hollow report echoed off the forested ridges.

Slash and Pecos shared a curious look.

They looked ahead again when a man yelled from that direction and another gun pop echoed.

Again, the man yelled.

Slash and Pecos rose in their stirrups to gaze ahead along the valley. Maybe a quarter mile away they could make out what looked like a man running around in the sage and rocks near the stream that bisected the valley to the left of the trail. What looked like another man, this one smaller than the other one, was walking slowly, deliberately, toward the running man, aiming what appeared to be a pistol at him as he looked around desperately for adequate cover.

Pop!

Pale smoke burst from the gun's barrel.

The man yelped and threw himself behind a gnarled cedar.

Another man yelled. The little man with the gun turned toward yet a second man running around in the sage, brush, and rocks. This man appeared to have his hands tied behind his back, which made his fleeing the little man with the gun an awkward maneuver, indeed.

Pop!

The man with his hands behind his back yelped and threw himself down behind a rock much too small for adequate cover.

Slash turned to Pecos, lower jaw hanging in deep, dark dread. "Oh, no! Could it be . . . ?"

He and Pecos turned toward the trio ahead of them.

Sure enough, the "little man" with the gun had a thick head of golden curls tumbling about "his" slender shoulders.

"Just our luck!" Pecos cried. "Of course, they'd be heading for the railhead, too! Dammit, Slash. Let's pretend we didn't see 'em!"

Slash turned his crestfallen gaze on his partner and said, "She's gonna kill 'em fer certain sure. We're their only chance, though they admittedly don't deserve us. You wanna take that to your grave?"

Pecos started to rein his buckskin around. *"Yes!"*

"Don't ask me how come I suddenly grew a heart," Slash said, booting his Appaloosa straight ahead. "But I can't!"

Slash whipped the Appy's right hip with his rein ends, and the horse lunged into a hard gallop. The girl triggered another shot at the federal man nearest the stream, then, apparently hearing Slash thundering toward her, whipped around to face him. She cursed and raised the pistol, aiming in his direction.

Slash jerked the Appy hard right as smoke and red flames blossomed from the barrel of the gun in the girl's hands. He dragged out the .44 holstered for the crossdraw on his left hip, aimed over the Appaloosa's head, let fly three quick rounds, and watched in satisfaction as the bullets tore up dirt and grass and bits of sage in front of the girl, within inches of her men's boots.

She screamed, covered her head with her arms, stumbled backward, and tripped over a sage shrub and dropped to her butt.

Slash approached her at a hard gallop, then reined in suddenly.

The girl had rolled onto her belly and was reaching for the walnut-butted hogleg she'd dropped when she'd fallen.

Slash triggered another round into the ground near her flailing hand.

"Leave it where it is, you little she-cat, or the next one's going into your pretty little head!"

She turned to glare up at him, eyes squeezed to slits, cheeks red with raw fury. "Damn you! Go away! This is none of your affair!"

Pecos reined up his buckskin to Slash's left and a little behind him. "You know, Slash, she's got a point!"

"Good God!" came a man's wail from over near the stream. "You coulda told us we had a tiger by the tail!"

Deputy Vince Quarles looked cautiously, fearfully, out from behind the rock he'd taken cover behind. He'd lost his hat, and his hair hung in his eyes. His suit was peppered with dirt, grass, and pine needles. "She's plumb loco! You got both guns? She had two of 'em!"

Slash dismounted and reached down to grab the Colt she'd been reaching for up off the ground. He stuck it behind his cartridge belt, then saw a second gun wedged behind the girl's own belt, at the small of her back. He reached down just as she went for the second weapon. He slapped her hand away and grabbed the second gun.

"Damn you!" she cried with bitter fury.

Still seated on his buckskin, Pecos glanced at Quarles. "How'd she get your guns?"

"Trickery! Pure trickery!" shrieked Deputy Ed Thomas, who was now walking toward Slash, Pecos, and the girl from where he'd been cowering behind his own cover. His hands were cuffed behind his back. "She knocked me over the head. Knocked me plumb *out*! Took my gun and used it to take Quarles's!"

"She was gonna shoot us both!" Quarles said in red-faced exasperation. "I turned over my gun, and when I saw she was gonna shoot me, anyway, I just started runnin'." As he approached Slash, Pecos, and the girl, he glared down at her.

"Fortunately, she's a damned lousy aim, or we'd both be dead!" added Thomas, also glaring down at Fannie. "I heard the gunfire an' came runnin', an' then she started shootin' at *me*! Crazy catamount!" He turned around, showing his cuffed hands behind his back. "Quarles, get these cuffs off me, dammit."

"Hold on." Quarles moved toward his partner, walking wide around the girl, as though she were a coiled diamondback. He pointed an enraged finger at Fannie with one hand while retrieving a ring of small keys from his left coat pocket with the other hand. "You just stay down there! Don't try nothin' funny!" He looked at Slash and Pecos. "Hard to believe somethin' so easy on the eyes can be so deadly!"

"Ain't it, though?" Pecos agreed.

"You mighta warned us about her!" Thomas said, glaring indignantly at Slash and Pecos.

"What?" Slash said, grinning deviously. "And have you miss out on all the fun?"

"Besides," Pecos added as Quarles removed the cuffs from his partner's wrists, "*we* had to find out about her firsthand. Why shouldn't *you*?"

Quarles gave the cuffs to Thomas, then held his hand out for the gun wedged behind Slash's cartridge belt. "Yeah, well, she's all yours!"

"Wait," Slash said, frowning, as he turned the long-barreled Smith & Wesson over to the angry deputy. "What're you talkin' about? She's in your custody."

"Not anymore she's not," Thomas said, snatching the other pistol out of Slash's hand.

"Hold on, now," Pecos said, swinging down from his buckskin's back. "You took her off our hands, remember? You can't just give her back!"

"The old man sent you two for her. She's all yours!" Thomas holstered his pistol, swung around, and walked several feet away to retrieve his hat. He repaired the dent in the topper's crown, donned it, and strode over to where his and Quarles's mounts stood idly grazing with Fannie's dun.

Quarles holstered his own pistol, glanced at Fannie once more, then curled his upper lip jeeringly at the two befuddled, indignant former train robbers. "Have a good time! Hell, you might even make it!"

He swung around to retrieve his own hat, adding over his shoulder to Slash and Pecos, "I wouldn't bet on it!" He picked up his hat, dusted it off, reshaped it, and tramped over to his own horse and mounted up.

"In fact," added Thomas, neck-reining his horse around, turning it east, "I'm betting you *won't*!"

He cast another glare at the girl, then shook his head in disbelief.

Slash and Pecos watched in mute exasperation as both lawmen put spurs to horse flesh and galloped away.

Slash and Pecos looked down at Fannie.

She smiled up at them. It was the smile of the devil when seeing fresh coal shovelers walk through the smoking iron gates. "So," she said, flaring a nostril at the crestfallen pair, "we meet again . . ."

Pecos turned to Slash. "Why'd you have to go and grow a conscience all of a sudden?"

"I know." Slash looked down at the girl. "At such an inopportune time . . ."

Fannie kept smiling up at both men, devilishly.

Chapter 31

"Have your men stand down, Balldinger, or the next bullet's goin' into the back of your head, you black-hearted, fork-tailed varmint of the first stripe!" warned Deputy Delbert Thayer.

Balldinger had risen half out of his chair and was twisting around at the waist, gazing back at where the string-bean deputy stood just inside the cabin's back door. Del had his Winchester snugged up taut against his shoulder and was aiming the barrel at the rancher's head.

"I mean it!" the young man shouted as all four of the remaining men on the stoop were aiming their drawn revolvers through the open front door behind Jay. They were bunched up together like cattle in a loading chute, standing over the dead man, who lay several feet beyond the threshold, showing a puckered blue hole in his forehead.

"Stand down, boys! Stand down!" Balldinger held his exasperated gaze on the deputy, slowly raising both hands to his shoulders, palms out. "Easy now, there, Deputy Thayer. What's this all about?"

"You know what it's about." Del slid his gaze to Myra, who was staring at him with wide-eyed, tearful beseeching. "Hold on, honey," he said softly, but with his voice quavering anxiously. "We're gonna get you cut down from there in just a minute."

"Oh, Del," Myra sobbed.

Del turned to Jay as he reached into his pocket and pulled out a folding barlow knife. Jay rose quickly from her chair and held her hands out for the knife. Del tossed it to her. She caught it, grabbed her chair, dragged it over beside Myra's chair, and stepped up onto it. Biting her lip, she sawed through the hemp. When the rope fell free, Jay sighed with relief, then took Myra's hand and helped her down from the creaking, crackling chair. She took the girl in her arms and hugged her, rocking her gently.

Del looked at Balldinger, who stood now, hands raised, facing the deputy.

"Put that rifle down, young man. How dare you bare down on me!"

Del slid his cheek up taut against his rifle's stock and narrowed one eye, aiming down the barrel at the rancher's broad forehead. "Have your men toss those guns off the stoop, out into the yard."

"What're you talking about . . . ?" Balldinger was acting as though there'd been some misunderstanding.

Del said, "I know what you were doin'. I seen, heard through the window. I know all about it. I seen the note you sent Miss Jay. Seen the lock of Myra's hair." He raised his voice on that last, hardening his jaws in fury, glancing at his terrified betrothed, who was for the moment safely ensconced in Jay's arms.

Myra looked back at him, tears still glazing her eyes.

Balldinger turned his head to cast Jay a castigating look. Jay hardened her jaws and narrowed an eye at the man.

"Sorry, boss," came Calloway's contrite voice through the front door, where he stood with the others gathered around him, all aiming their revolvers at Del. "We really checked our back trail."

"Figured you would," Del said. "I took a different route." He glanced at Jay. "Sorry, Miss Jay. I . . . I had to . . ."

Jay gave a crooked, knowing smile.

Del turned back to Ballldinger and slid his eyes quickly to the men in the doorway. "I want those guns gone now, Balldinger. By the time I count to three, or . . ." Again, he snugged his cheek up taut against his Winchester's stock, threateningly.

Jay grabbed her saddlebags off the table, slung them over her shoulder, then walked around the table toward Balldinger. She pulled the man's ivory-gripped Colt .44 from the black holster on his right hip and stepped back, aiming at Balldinger's belly. "Better do what he says, Grant." She gave a hard, threatening smile and clicked the Colt's hammer back. "You'll get one to the head and one to the belly."

Balldinger glared at her. "You'll never make it out of here that way."

"Neither will you."

Balldinger turned to the four men clustered in the open doorway, the storm flashing behind them, the rain a billowing gray curtain behind them, as well. "Do it."

"You sure, Pa?" Todd Balldinger asked.

"Toss 'em into the yard, boys!" Balldinger said, glancing at his own cocked Colt aimed at his belly. Then he added, "Pronto!"

Jay smiled her satisfaction at the man's fear. She doubted he'd ever known what it felt like. Now he did.

"I'm watchin'!" Del told the men on the stoop. "Give 'em a good toss. Anybody holds out on me, the boss here gets a pill he can't digest!"

Keeping the Colt aimed at Balldinger's belly, Jay peered around the man. The men on the porch looked at their boss, then turned and, one by one, tossed their revolvers underhand out into the storm.

"Todd, you'll need to toss the second one out there, too!" Del yelled.

Todd Balldinger turned to him, wrinkling his nose distastefully. He was the only one wearing two holsters. The younger Balldinger removed his second, pretty Colt Peacemaker, which he fancied himself handy with, and looking at the gun in his hand as though it was a precious diamond he did not want to part with—apparently, he'd figured he could keep it and maybe even use it, but no, Del was too smart for him—he gave it an underhanded toss out into the rain.

Jay heard it land with a thud on the wet ground.

Del glanced at Myra. "Honey, come over and stand by me, will you?"

Myra glanced at Jay and then hurried around the table, stepping around Jay and the rancher, as well. When she'd sidled up to Del, he looked at the men on the stoop peering into the cabin again through the door and gave his head a little toss. "Get in here. All of you." He canted his head to the left. "That side of the cabin."

"What're you gonna do?" Balldinger asked suspiciously.

Del ignored the question. He watched the four ranch hands file into the cabin, looking hard-eyed at the young deputy. Single file, because there was no room to do otherwise, they walked around to the far end of the cabin, just beyond where Myra had been standing on the chair.

When they were all standing there, glaring at Del but also looking edgy, as though wondering what he was going to do next, Del turned to Jay. "Miss Jay, would you go on outside, now, please? You, too, honey. Mount up and ride away."

Jay turned to him, frowning with concern. "What are you going to do?"

"I'll be right behind you." Del looked at the rancher. "With Mr. Balldinger here."

"The hell you are!" Balldinger protested.

Del looked at him hard. "I'm gonna marry this gal you was gonna hang. If you don't think I'll shoot you, you best think again. 'Cause I will. I'll kill you, and I'll kill you for keeps." He nodded his head slowly. "You're comin' with me."

"Pa, what do you want us to do?" asked Todd Balldinger, looking very frustrated and furious, keeping his eyes on the deputy.

Balldinger looked at the rifle and then at the pistol Jay held on him as she and Myra walked around the table toward the door. Keeping his eyes on Del, the rancher said tightly, barely opening his mouth, "Nothing."

When Jay and Myra were outside, Jay turned around to see Del motion Balldinger toward the door. Reluctantly, the rancher complied, slowly lowering his hands. Del kept the rifle leveled on him as he followed him to the door, but he kept his head turned toward the right side of the cabin, where through a window Jay could see the four hands bunched in front of the brick fireplace.

When he reached the door, Del stopped. "If I see any one of you behind us, he gets a bullet in the back."

"Pa?" Todd called to his father, rage in his voice.

"Do as he says, boys," Balldinger said as he moved to the edge of the stoop and stopped. Del stepped out and drew the door closed behind him.

"Get mounted up," Del told Balldinger, motioning toward the two saddled horses standing close nearby.

Thunder rumbled.

Lightning flashed sporadically.

The rain came down in a steady stream. The ground rippled and glistened.

Jay turned to Del. "Should we gather up their guns?"

"Yeah, hurry!"

While Del shoved Balldinger toward a horse, Jay and Myra crouched to retrieve the ranch hands' guns.

A gun roared. In the corner of her eye, Jay saw Del stumble forward against Balldinger, saying, "Oh, *crap!*"

"Del!" Myra screamed.

Jay swung around to see a man aiming a rifle from the cabin's left front corner. It was Todd Balldinger, who, racking a fresh round, yelled, "I got him, Pa!"

There must have been a rifle in the cabin. Likely the rancher's saddle gun!

Balldinger swung around and reached for the carbine in Del's hands. Del pulled it away from him, rammed the butt into the man's belly. Balldinger stumbled backward and dropped to a knee, cursing.

"Stop right there, Thayer, or I'll drill you another one!" Todd shouted.

Jay had picked up one revolver. Now she dropped to a knee, aimed quickly, and fired. Todd yelped and spun around behind the corner of the cabin, triggering his rifle into the air. The cabin door opened, and a man started to step out.

Jay triggered the Colt in her hands, and the man stumbled back inside, yelling and slamming the door.

Myra ran to where Del stood holding his rifle over his upper left arm, where Todd must have shot him. "Del, honey, are you all right?"

"I'm all right. Mount up, honey! Let's get outta here!" Del said, ushering her quickly over to Todd Balldinger's horse. "We'll have to ride double! I left my mount on the rim!"

Jay ran to her own horse and slung her saddlebags over Dorothy's rump. Del climbed awkwardly into the saddle of Todd Balldinger's horse. Myra mounted behind him. Jay turned to see Grant Balldinger run heavily toward where the pistols lay on the ground fronting the stoop.

She hurled a round at him, but in her haste and nervousness, the bullet flew wide. Balldinger ducked and then scrambled to cover behind a pine tree. He returned fire from around the side of the tree, and Jay felt the sting of the bullet across the nub of her left cheek.

She fired again, but Dorothy was jostling around nervously, and her bullet didn't come close to its target.

"Let's get out of here!" Jay cried, brushing at the blood on her cheek, then leaning forward and ramming her heels into Dorothy's flanks.

"Don't have to tell me twice!" Del grunted out.

Behind them and beneath the roar of the storm, Jay heard Balldinger shout, "Come on, boys. Let's get after 'em! All three of them are dead, do you hear?" He raised his voice to a womanish screech, bellowing, "Do you hear, Jay? You're *dead*!"

Chapter 32

"I wasn't trying to shoot those two federal men, you know," Fannie said as she rode behind Slash and Pecos aboard her sorrel.

Slash was leading her horse. Pecos had tied her hands to her saddle horn. They weren't taking any chances.

Slash glanced back at her. "Could've fooled me."

"Me too," Pecos said.

"I wanted to, but I couldn't do it."

"Because your aim is bad," Pecos said with a snort. "That's why them federals are still on this side of the sod."

"Not true," Fannie said. "I mean, I'm rusty with a gun. It's been a long time since I fired one. My father taught me how to shoot. But he's been dead a long time, and I haven't had the chance to shoot a gun in many a year." She looked off, pensive, wistful. "Still, though, I missed on purpose."

"You didn't miss Pete an' George on purpose."

"Oh, no," Fannie said. "Those two brigands had it comin'. They would have mauled me to death and left me to the carrion eaters!" She drew a breath, swallowed. "The federal men were just doing their jobs. That's why I couldn't shoot them. I'm not a cold-blooded killer. I was just trying to frighten them, buy myself some time to get away."

Slash glanced back at her. Maybe she was, maybe she wasn't a cold-blooded killer. He did not blame her for what she'd done to Pete and George. She was right—they would have raped her. They deserved the punishment they'd received. Still, the poison was a shocking way to kill a man. On the other hand, what had been her options?

Maybe she was, maybe she wasn't a killer. Still, he wasn't taking any chances. His and Pecos's job was to get her down to Denver, and that was what they intended to do.

Slash frowned curiously at her over his right shoulder. "You said your pa taught you to shoot? Who was your pa? Where'd you grow up?"

He was just curious. Besides, they had another couple of miles to go before they reached Sundown, which, the prospector had said, lay dead ahead in a grassy basin of this broad, fawn-colored mountain park they were riding through and on a hillside east of the Middle Fork of the South Platte River. A giant gray spine of snow-tipped peaks reared back behind them and to the north, hazy in the midday sunshine.

"My father was Rutherford Leadbetter."

Pecos glanced at her over his left shoulder, one brow arched. "The mining magnate?"

"One and the same."

"Well, hell, you're rich," Slash said, chuckling ironically and regarding her skeptically. "What're you doing caterwauling in opry houses, in front of the unwashed masses?"

Fannie flared a nostril at him. "I am *caterwauling in opry houses, in front of the unwashed masses*, as you so unflatteringly put it," Fannie said in a snit, "because my father went broke and hanged himself. My mother had died two years before from influenza. My father had sent me to the Froghman Academy of Dramatic Arts in Boston, where I was taught by none other that Melvin Tulane Sargent himself, who, I might add," she added saucily, making a face at Slash and flipping her hair back over her shoulder, "told me I showed an *enormous amount of promise* after only my first year. After my father died indigent, and with a mountain of debt I had known nothing about, it was no longer possible for me to continue my studies.

"Mr. Sargent, however, knew a man back in Denver who hired actresses to perform in stage performances in the Rocky Mountains. He said such work was a great way for a *talented, young actress* to cut her teeth in lieu of the academy. So, he wrote me a letter of introduction to the man in Denver . . . who wrote me an introduction to Boone McClory, who headed his own theater troupe out of Leadville. And the rest, as they say onstage just before the drop curtain falls, is history."

"Well, I'll be hanged," Slash said. He looked over his shoulder at her again. "Sorry for the run of bad luck. And, uh . . ." He gave a contrite smile. "For the caterwaulin' remark."

Fannie smiled back at him. "You're forgiven, Slash."

Slash turned his head back forward.

Behind him, Fannie said after a few minutes of silent riding, "I wouldn't have shot you two, either, you know."

Slash and Pecos shared a skeptical glance.

"Nah," she said with a wistful air. "You two old scalawags have kind of grown on me. When I was with the real federals, I rather sort of missed your company."

"Oh?" Pecos said skeptically.

"They were stuffed shirts. Especially Quarles. Thomas rather ogled me. You two are kind of rough around the edges . . . and genuine. I like that in a man. Authenticity, no matter how crude. Even in a man who tried to drown me."

"Ain't gonna happen," Slash said.

"What *ain't gonna happen*?" Fannie asked, her tone suddenly miffed.

Pecos smiled knowingly over his shoulder at her. "What ain't gonna happen is we ain't gonna stop and untie your hands from around that saddle horn." He winked at her.

"Oh, and by the way," Slash said, reaching into the right pocket of his broadcloth jacket. He held up the over-and-under, pearl-gripped derringer she'd taken off Ed Thomas. "If you're thinkin' you're gonna bring this into play, well, you got another think comin'!"

Fannie gasped in shock. Then: "*Oh, go to hell!*"

Miffed at her captors again, Fannie didn't say anything for the rest of the twenty minutes it took them to reach the little mining and ranching town of Sundown, which had a narrow-gauge railroad, the Pikes Peak & Pueblo Line, running down the center of its broad main street. The little log depot building sat right smack-dab in the heart of the town, which was bustling with trade this time of the day.

She said nothing to Slash while Pecos went into the depot and purchased three tickets for the next train headed east, which, it turned out to both men's delight, would arrive from the west in only a half hour. She said nothing while they ate the hot pork burritos Slash purchased from a Mexican street vendor, and she said nothing as they boarded the train after it had rumbled into the station. She said nothing but looked angry and morose as they took seats in the combination's only passenger coach, which quickly filled with wayfarers of all shapes, colors, ages, and sizes—mostly miners and drummers in cheap suits, but also three cavalry soldiers, who, judging by the brightness of their eyes and the easiness of their ways, had awaited the train in a Sundown grog house.

The train was a good half hour east of Sundown, trundling along through a deep canyon through which the Arkansas River churned its white water over rocks and boulders hugging the canyon's southern ridge, when Fannie rose suddenly from her seat between Slash and Pecos, turned to the three soldiers, and said loudly above the clicking of the train's iron wheels and the squealing of a baby, "Gentlemen, please help me! I am the actress Fannie Diamond, and these two *cut-throats* have kidnapped me for their own carnal pleasure!" She looked down at Pecos, sitting before her on the outside seat, and then turned stiffly to regard Slash, who was sitting next to the window. "If you free me from these, my craven tormentors, I promise you will be aptly rewarded!"

The three soldiers—in fact, everyone in the coach—swung their heads around to regard Fannie in brow-furled incredulity. As though to prove her story, or at least that she was who she said she was, she reached up and removed her man's round gray hat. She shook her hair out luxuriously, making all those lovely curls tumble down her shoulders and back. They glistened in the high-country light streaming in through the soot-streaked windows.

"Sit down!" Slash said, giving her left arm a hard tug.

"Unhand me, you cur!" she squealed, jerking her arm out of Slash's grasp.

When she'd shaken out her hair, a low rumble of appreciation had lifted from the mostly male crowd of passengers around her. Eyes had widened; unshaven lower jaws had dropped.

The smallest of the three soldiers slapped the back of the seat in front of him and said, "See now, didn't I tell you fellas that little fella looked *just like* that actress from up in the mining camp opry houses!"

Pecos glared up at Fannie, biting out through gritted teeth, "Dammit, Fannie. Sit your tailbone down before I take you over my damn *knee*!"

"Another beating, is it?" she intoned, planting a fist on one admittedly well-turned hip. She looked at the soldiers, then swung her head around to include in her castigation of her captors the entire coach of mostly unwashed males. "The other night they came damn close to *drowning* me!"

The little soldier climbed up from his seat between the two others and climbed over the knees of the man beside him, saying, "Don't you worry, Miss Diamond. I'll save you from those nasty old coyotes!"

"Hey, who's old?" Slash said, glaring over his shoulder at the young man and rising from his seat. "Sit down, there, Corporal! We're takin' her back to Denver to test—"

"Turn her loose, you devils!" sounded a deep, raspy voice almost directly behind Slash.

As Slash heard the heavy clicks of two hammers being cocked, he swung his head around in dread to see a bearded man in his sixties, clad in a grimy work shirt, suspenders, and a battered green canvas hat, aiming a long-barreled shotgun straight out from his right shoulder—straight at Slash's head from maybe eight feet away!

"Ah, hell!" Slash said, switching his glare to Fannie. "You got no idea what you're gettin' yourself into here, you little polecat!"

The small soldier with a dark charcoal smudge of a mustache under his pale pug nose, and a bad complexion, hurried up the aisle, swaying with the motion of the train, to stop beside Pecos and extend his hand to Fannie. "Come on, Miss Diamond. You can come over and sit with us. We'll make sure these two old fools don't hurt you ever again!"

"Thank you, kind sir!" Fannie said, thrusting her hand into the soldier's hand.

"Oh, no, you don't!" Rising, Pecos pulled her hand back out of the soldier's grasp and shoved her back toward Slash. "Listen here, sonny," he said, poking his right index finger into the little soldier's skinny chest, clad in the traditional blue tunic and yellow suspenders of a frontier soldier, "this little polecat of a so-called actress is trouble in capital letters. She's jerkin' your chain, see? Me an' my partner got official orders to . . . *ohh, ahhh*!" Pecos cried, raising both hands to his nose, to which the hostile little pinch-faced soldier had just delivered a surprisingly powerful left jab up from his left shoulder.

Slash had just started toward Pecos to render aid when suddenly two big arms wrapped around his neck from behind, the bearer of those arms shouting, "Grab 'em both! Let's throw these lowly kidnappers off the *consarned train*!"

"Yeah!" another man shouted, this one up ahead of Slash somewhere, though Slash was being pulled so far back over his seat back that he couldn't see the man or much else but the coach's domed, pressed-tin ceiling.

"Get 'em!"

"Grab 'em!"

"Get outta my way!"

"You get outta *my* way!"

There was a smacking sound and a yelp.

In the corner of his right eye, Slash saw three, then four men converge on Pecos, pull the big man off his feet, and drag him down the aisle toward the rear door. Like Pecos was doing, Slash tried to free himself from the grip of the big man behind him, but there was no doing that. Just as he dug his fingers between the man's stout arm and his neck, another man—then two more men!—joined in the fun, grabbing Slash's legs. They pushed and pulled him over two seat backs and then into the aisle.

All the while, Slash cursed and tried to fight, to no avail. He managed to evoke a yelp or two when he kicked one hombre in the knee and another elsewhere, but he got only a fist to the face for his trouble. He couldn't stop fighting, however, trying desperately to get the big arms from around his neck, because they were pinching off his wind. His vision was dimming and he was about to pass out before they wrestled him out onto the coach car's rear vestibule and dropped him.

Bang!

He hit the platform's steel floor hard with his head and

shoulders. Little birds tweeted in his ears above the rushing of the wind. He tried to heave himself to his feet, but a good half dozen hands were reaching for him, grabbing at him, pulling him up and then to one side. They got him halfway to his feet before a boot was slammed against his rear end.

He bellowed as he suddenly found himself thrust into the wind and the stench of coal smoke from the locomotive . . . suddenly without benefit of the platform beneath him . . . suddenly without *anything* beneath him but air and a long, wide stretch of lime-green grass and sagebrush.

He struck the side of the railbed and rolled . . . rolled . . . rolled some more, then stopped on the shore of the river hugging the railbed.

He opened his eyes. Atop the bed, the train was trundling past him . . . the little dining car . . . the parlor car . . . and then the stock car followed up the little red caboose. The passenger coach from which he'd been thrown was already several car lengths down the track and beginning to curve around a southward bend.

Slash lay with the top of his head near the lapping water, his boots facing up the railroad bed. His mussed hair hung over one eye. He gritted his teeth against his sundry aches and pains, finding himself once again taking stock of his physical condition.

Anything broken? Dislocated? Poking through his hide? Sprained?

Crushed?

To his right a man cursed hoarsely.

Slash turned to see Pecos lying belly down, mostly parallel to the river, one leg hung up on a white rock. He had his head up, and he was groaning and cursing a blue streak. Slash didn't think he'd ever heard the man curse with as much venom as he was unleashing now, or with the words he was using. Slash had to admit feeling, beneath his own pain and rage and exasperation, admiration at his partner's extensive vocabulary of epithets. The otherwise gentle giant must have had even more restraint than Slash had given him credit for, not to have ever uttered such colorful oaths before. At least not within Slash's hearing . . .

Pecos turned to look over his shoulder, one eye shut, at Slash, his face red with fury.

"You still kickin', partner?"

Slash spit grit from his lips and said, "I don't think I'll kick anything again for a long time. I think both my legs are broken, kneecaps dislocated."

"Really?"

"No. But I ache like hell. And my pride aches worse of all!" Slash hammered the end of his fist against the ground beside him.

"I thought we was gonna stop doin' that sort of thing," Pecos said. "Jumpin' from movin' trains."

"I tried to explain that to the bruisers givin' me the bum's rush, but do you think they'd stop an' listen to reason?"

"Hell, no!" Pecos said, cursing again. "They had visions of that so-called actress dancin' through their pea-sized brains!"

Slash turned to gaze up the track to his left. He could still hear the rumble of the train, but it was growing fainter and fainter now. No sign of the coal smoke lingered but a faint stench in the air.

Slash turned to Pecos. "What the hell was she thinkin'?"

"I don't think she thinks," Pecos said. "I think she just opens her mouth and lets it run!"

"If she thinks we were bad, wait till them soldiers get their paws on her!"

"Hell, they probably already have!"

A rumbling sounded from somewhere up the tracks. It was followed by a distance-muffled screeching sound.

Again, Slash turned to Pecos. "What the hell was that?"

Pecos frowned as he looked up the raised railroad bed and up the tracks, in the direction in which the train had disappeared around a bend to the south, following the canyon.

Faint pops sounded. Men shouted, and then a woman screamed.

"No . . . no," Slash said, his voice pitched with awe. "No way . . . can't be . . ."

Pecos's eyes widened as he turned his gaze to Slash. "Yessir, I think it can, sure enough." He rolled onto his side, then shoved up on his knees, staring up the tracks in astonishment. "I think the train is bein' *held up!*"

Chapter 33

Thunder crashed like cymbals and lightning danced along the top of the ridge high above and to Jay's left as she galloped back down Redstone Canyon in the direction in which she'd come a half hour ago.

Riding behind her on Todd Balldinger's horse, behind Delbert Thayer, Myra yelled, "Jay! We have to stop! Del's bleeding! I mean, he's really *bleeding*!"

Jay checked Dorothy down and turned to look at Del and Myra galloping toward her, Del crouched low in the saddle and turned to favor his left arm. He shook his head as the hammering rain sluiced off his hat brim. He checked the cream duster down before Jay and shook his head again.

"No, we gotta keep goin'. You heard 'em. Those fellas mean business!"

He had just started to boot his mount up the trail but stopped when Jay grabbed his left wrist. "Let me see!"

She sidled Dorothy up close to Del to inspect his arm. Blood ran pink in the rain streaming down his arm clad in a cream canvas duster, from the ragged hole roughly halfway between his elbow and his shoulder.

"It's not that bad!" Del said, casting a quick look behind. "We gotta keep goin'. They're likely all saddled up by now!"

Jay looked at Myra, who stared back at her, miserable with fear and worry, then turned Dorothy forward again and yelled, "Follow me!"

She rammed her heels into the mare's loins, and the horse bounded up the sodden, muddy trail. When she'd ridden a couple of hundred yards back down toward the main canyon, she swerved quickly to the right, glancing behind at her compatriots and yelling, "This way!"

She forded a swollen creek, the swirling, clay-colored water rising to nearly her stirrups, but the sure-footed mare handled it well, after four or five strides lunging up the opposite bank. She glanced behind to see Del steering his mount into the rushing creek and up the near bank. He scowled at Jay through the rain sluicing down the middle crease in his hat brim and said, "Where we goin'?"

"I know a cabin. It's up that side canyon."

"We could be trapped in there, Miss Jay!" Again, Del cast an anxious look behind, though now the primary trail was hidden by brush, cedars, and rocks stippling the opposite side of the creek.

Jay shook her head. "It's not a box canyon, if that's what you mean." Fleetingly, she remembered the box canyon that Slash had inadvertently led the Marauders into and in which her former lover, Pistol Pete Johnson, was killed by Bledsoe's deputy U.S. marshals, an event that Slash to this day blamed himself for. "Besides, Balldinger won't be able to follow us. The rain has likely already washed away our sign. Also, the cabin is high—a good place to hole up and tend that arm of yours and hold Balldinger off if he comes!"

She swung Dorothy around and booted the horse into the narrow canyon just ahead, between two sheer red stone walls. "This way!"

The canyon floor was a veritable river, but the canyon narrowed not far beyond its mouth, and here the water ran considerably shallower. The canyon rose gradually, and after a twenty-minute ride, Jay put Dorothy up a steep bank roughly a hundred feet high, then reined up in front of a mud-brick, earthen-roofed cabin flanked by the dark oval of an old mine chiseled out of the canyon's red sandstone wall.

"I'll be hanged," Del exclaimed, reining his cream down beside Jay. He stared in surprise at the cabin and the cavern behind it. There was a stone stable back there, as well. "I didn't know this was here!"

"I wouldn't either if I hadn't gotten lost out here one day while Dorothy and I were stretching our legs." Jay dropped her reins and dismounted, then walked over to the left side of Del and Myra's horse. "The weather was much like it is now. I came from the western ridge, where the canyon rises to merge with the bench. I was looking for a place to hole up out of the rain and stumbled onto this place. It's been abandoned for years, and I don't think anyone else knows about it. A hermit lived here, I think—well off the beaten path."

As Myra leaped fleetly straight back off the horse's rump, Jay placed her hand on Del's lower left arm. "Let me help you, son."

"Nah, I got it." Del rose in his saddle, swung his right leg over the horse's rump. He'd just gotten that foot over the horse's tail when he gave a ragged sigh, dropped his head and chest down against his saddle. When his right leg hit the ground, his upper torso dropped toward it, sliding down the stirrup fender.

"Del!" Myra cried as she and Jay lunged toward him.

They both snaked their arms around his waist and, grunting with the effort, got him back upright. At least partly upright. He seemed only half-conscious, sagging and grinding his boots into the wet sand and gravel, grunting and sighing as he tried to gain purchase.

"He's weak from blood loss, probably in shock!" Jay told

Myra. "We have to get him into the cabin and tend that wound!"

"Come on, Del honey!" Myra said, looking worried as hell, Jay could see.

"I'm all . . . I'm all . . . right . . . ," Del said as they turned him and then, Jay on one side, Myra on the other side, began leading him toward the humble cabin hunched before them, obscured by the wavering gray curtain of rain.

When they reached the cabin, Jay tripped the metal latch by its dangling bits of hemp, likely unbraided from a rope, and opened the door. They were greeted by a sudden screech, and Jay saw something scuttle along the floor to her left, then disappear into the cabin's dense shadows.

Myra gasped.

"Just a rat," Jay said. "Probably the only one who calls this home anymore. There's a cot against the back wall over there," Jay said, nodding toward the homemade cot constructed of pine branches that lay along the back wall and behind a small sheet-iron stove, atop which sat a cast-iron skillet.

"How do you know a hermit lived here?" Myra asked Jay as they half led, half carried Del across the hard-packed earthen floor.

"I assume he was a hermit," Jay said, her voice tight from the effort of trying to keep the wounded deputy on his feet. "I found his bones in the mine back yonder. Since nobody buried him—at least I'm *assuming* it was him, as the skeleton was dressed like a prospector and there was even a pick and shovel among the remains—I assume no one had known about him."

Myra made a face as she and Jay eased the half-conscious and muttering deputy down on the cot. "Sorry I asked."

Jay chuckled, but her nerves were shot. She was as concerned for Deputy Thayer as Myra was. Against her strict orders, he'd saved their lives—hers and the girl's. She still couldn't believe that Grant Balldinger had actually intended to murder them both, but there it was. There was no denying the man's vileness now. There seemed no bottom to it. She owed the deputy her life.

She and Myra got him stretched out on the mattress, which was several pieces of sewn-together burlap filled with hay and was covered by a couple of sour-smelling trade blankets and one wildcat skin. Myra hooked Del's hat on a wall peg above the cot.

"Let's get him out of that duster," Jay said.

When she and Myra had fairly wrestled the groaning young man out of the sodden garment, Jay removed the bandanna she had knotted around her neck, and wrapped it tightly around the wound. Del groaned louder as she knotted it.

"That should stop the bleeding for now," Jay said, turning to Myra. She placed her hand on the girl's shoulder. "Why don't you heat some water and look around for a sewing kit? The place might have been empty for several years, but the hermit had it amazingly well stocked before he died. I have a feeling you'll find one. Try those shelves over there."

"All right," Myra said, nodding, as she stared down in concern at her beau, whose eyelids fluttered as he fell in and out of sleep.

Jay patted her hand reassuringly. "He'll be all right, Myra. I promise."

Jay strode toward the door. "I'll be right back."

Myra turned to her quickly. "Where are you going, Jay?"

Jay stopped and turned back to her, hearing the fear in the girl's voice. Myra had been through a lot herself, and now the young man who'd asked her to marry him only the day before lay half-conscious before her with a bullet in his arm.

"I'm going to stable the horses and grab Del's carbine and the rifle from Todd's horse. With those and this six-shooter"— she patted the bone-gripped Colt jutting up from the waistband of her dark blue denim trousers—"we should have enough firepower to defend ourselves. But first, I have to get those horses out of sight." She offered a reassuring smile. "I won't be long."

Myra returned the smile with a half-hearted one of her own.

As Jay went out into the continuing rain, Myra turned to Del, lying on the cot before her. She took his hand in her own, squeezed. "Del, you stay with me, now, you hear?"

The young man's eyelids fluttered, opened. It was as though his eyes took a minute to focus. Then he smiled and said, "Oh, I ain't goin' anywhere, honey."

Myra choked back a sob, then gave a dry laugh through another strangled sob and squeezed his hand. Pitching her voice with feigned reproof, she said, "You're *not* goin' anywhere. Good Lord, Del. Your grammar!"

"Aww," the young man said, smiling fondly up at his girl. "I was so worried I wouldn't have you around anymore to scold me for my English an' my dime novel readin' and smokin' an' such . . ."

"Once we're out of this, Delbert Thayer, you can read all the dime novels you want. The smoking I won't abide, but you can read any damn thing you want, including Deadeye Dick!"

"Oh, well—heck, then," he said, chuckling softly. "I need to get shot more often, so my girl lengthens my leash for me . . ."

"Oh, Del, I love you so much!" Myra choked on another sob and pressed her lips to his.

When she pulled her head back from his, he said, squinting up at her, "You . . . you really *do* . . . a bucktoothed fool like me? I messed up bad back there. Shoulda"—he stopped, swallowed, licked his lips—"shoulda made sure I didn't leave a dang rifle in the cabin with them killers. Hell, I deserve what I got!" He glanced at his arm.

Myra sandwiched his long face in her hands and pressed her forehead to his. "Delbert Thayer, I'd likely be hanging from that ceiling beam right now if it wasn't for you. In the nick of time, you kicked that door in and shot the devil who was about to break Jay's neck. Deadeye Dick couldn't have written it better himself. 'Have your men stand down, Balldinger, or the next bullet's goin' into the back of your head, you blackhearted, fork-tailed varmint of the first stripe!'"

Myra sobbed and ground her forehead against his. "I've never been prouder of anyone before in my life!"

"Ah, heck . . ." Del smiled, his eyelids appearing heavy again.

Myra kissed him again and straightened, composing herself. "Oh, dear, look at me, sobbing and carrying on when I'm supposed to be heating water to clean your wound!"

With that, she began scrambling around the cabin until she found a good-sized kettle, then set it just outside the door to fill it with water streaming off the roof. She found dry wood in a wooden bin by the door, and soon she had a fire burning in the stove.

Outside, Jay stabled and unsaddled the two horses.

She pulled Del's Winchester carbine from its boot, and then she pulled Todd Balldinger's rifle from its sheath, as well. She was glad to see that Balldinger's long gun was a sixteen-shot Henry .44, and that its loading tube running beneath the barrel was fully loaded. With two rifles, one being the Henry, and two pistols—the one she had and the one Del had in his holster—they should be able to give a good account of themselves if Balldinger and the man's cutthroats came calling.

In the very least, they would not go down without a fight.

She closed the stable doors, and with her Colt jutting up from behind her black leather belt, and a rifle resting on each shoulder, Jay made her way back around to the front of the cabin. As she approached the door, hoof thuds sounded from the canyon floor below the shelf the cabin was on.

Jay stopped dead in her tracks, heart thudding.

The hoof thuds grew louder. Someone was coming, and they were coming fast.

"Damn!"

Jay leaned Del's carbine against the front of the cabin. She pumped a live round into the Winchester's breech, dropped to a knee, and raised the Henry to her shoulder. Her gloved index finger caressed the trigger as she waited for the rider or riders to show themselves.

Chapter 34

Grunting against the aches in his battered and beaten old carcass, Slash pushed himself to his feet. He glanced at Pecos, who did likewise, cursing and spitting grit from his lips. "We're too old for this crap!"

"You can say that again." Pecos limped over to where his battered hat lay and set it on his head. Then he climbed the bank a few feet to retrieve his Russian .44, which had been ripped out of its holster during his unceremonious descent from the railbed.

Slash retrieved his own hat. Somehow, his pistol had remained in its holster. He and Pecos grunted and groaned as they climbed the bank, heading for the rails. As they climbed it, the bank seemed even steeper than when they'd rolled down it, tossed off the train like ticketless freeloaders or cheating gamblers.

When they reached the rails, they peered off in the direction the train had gone. It was out of sight around the bend, the rocky southern cliff blocking it from view. But they could hear men whooping and hollering victoriously, some shouting angrily, a horse whinnying shrilly, and pistols barking.

Again, a girl's scream vaulted above the rest of the din.

Pecos turned to Slash. "Could that be her?"

"Sure sounded like her."

"Ah, hell!"

"We'd best get a move on," Slash said, tramping on up the rails, taking annoyingly mincing steps on the ties, his feet, knees, and hips barking with every step.

"What're we supposed to do about a train holdup?" Pecos complained, falling into step beside Slash. "Our rifles and my sawed-off are still on the train. We can't take on a gang of train robbers with just our pistols."

"What're we supposed to do?" Slash said, picking up his pace and wincing with each painful step. "Sit down here and wait for the next flier?"

"That's not a bad idea! Yeah, I like that one!" But Pecos increased his pace, as well.

Soon, they rounded the bend, and stopped.

The train lay a couple of hundred yards beyond, idle on the rails. Horseback riders were just then galloping up along the right side of the rails beyond it, to the south, the dust of the riders' horses obscuring them, so that neither Slash nor Pecos could see how many there were. A couple of the robbers triggered pistols into the air above their heads, the flashes showing inside the billowing dust cloud. They whooped and hollered and quickly diminished in size until they were gone.

"I'll be damned," Slash said, crestfallen. "If it wasn't for bad luck, we'd have no luck at all."

"So easy ol' Bleed-'Em-So was embarrassed to send us— like hell!" Pecos barked as he and Slash continued tramping up the rails in the direction of the robbed train. He glanced at Slash. "Suppose there's anything left of her?"

"I hope not."

"Yeah." Pecos gave a wry snort. "Me too. I'm done with that little polecat of a she-cat!"

As they approached the train, the conductor, a brakeman, and several passengers, including a few who'd thrown Slash and Pecos off the train, walked down off the passenger coach's two vestibules, front and back, and onto the railbed, then peered up the rails after the robbers. They moved wearily, warily, muttering amongst themselves. One angrily kicked a rock, then cursed the pain the kick had evoked in his foot.

Slash thought he recognized a couple of the men who'd thrown him and Pecos off the train. He slid his Colt from its holster, just in case they wanted to try something like that again, or maybe just to get even. He'd love nothing more than to make every last one of them dance, but he had bigger fish to fry.

Namely, the girl . . .

One man must have heard Slash and Pecos coming, because he turned toward them, widened his eyes in surprise, then turned his head slightly to speak to one of the other men gathered around him. The others turned to Slash and Pecos then, too, and a couple of the armed men slid their hands to their holstered revolvers.

Slash barked, "Leave 'em where they are, or I'll blow your damn heads off!"

That forestalled the hands that had been drifting toward leathered iron.

"Where's the girl?" Pecos asked them, also aiming his Russian at the wary-looking passengers before him.

Inside the coach car, a baby was screaming.

"The robbers took her!" said one of the men standing farther up the rails. He was a husky gent with a long salt-and-pepper beard and the look of a miner. He was red-faced indignant at having been robbed. He pointed angrily up the tracks. "They took the girl and every damn thing I own, includin' my poke!"

Slash and Pecos shared a look of weary exasperation.

Wincing, crestfallen, Pecos looked at the man. "You're sure they took her?"

"Certain sure!"

"One of 'em recognized her as the actress from up Frisco way," said a man in a three-piece business suit, whom Slash did not think had been among those who'd detrained him and his partner. The pockets of his broadcloth trousers were literally turned inside out and hanging off his hips like miniature white tongues.

Slash and Pecos shared another weary look. Then Slash said, "I'll fetch the horses. You fetch our long guns."

As Slash turned and strode back in the direction of the stock car, a man yelled behind him, "You two must really want her bad to go after that bunch. Why, that's the Talon Renfro gang!"

Slash looked back at the coach car. The man who'd spoken was one of the soldiers who'd started the melee earlier—the largest of the three. For now, in light of the actress's kidnapping, Slash decided to let bygones be bygones. "Who's the Talon Renfro gang?"

The beefy, round-faced soldier narrowed a warning eye at him. "You'll find out if you go after 'em! I know she was special an' all. We was just startin' to get acquainted when them robbers blew the rails up yonder"—he hooked a thumb out the window, indicating south—"but, hell, you'll find more showgirls in the gold camps. Not like her," he said with a lewd grin. He turned his head to stare longingly up the rails to the south. "No, prob'ly not like her . . ."

Slash and Pecos rolled their eyes at each other, and then Slash continued his trek to the stock car to retrieve their horses, and Pecos headed into the passenger coach for their long guns and his sawed-off twelve-gauge.

Armed and mounted, they galloped on up past the blown rails and the train crew inspecting the damage while muttering lamentations and sadly wagging their heads.

"Slash, why are we doin' this?" Pecos said, keeping his buckskin in stride with Slash's Appaloosa. "That girl damn near got us killed back there! It's a wonder she didn't!"

Slash reined his Appy to a halt and curveted the mount toward his partner, who was following suit. "Well . . . I don't know," he said, shoving his hat up onto his forehead to scratch the back of his head with his gloved right index finger. He looked off, pondering, then returned his gaze to Pecos. "Can we *not* do it?"

Pecos shrugged. He looked off then, also pondering, before shuttling his gaze to his partner. "Why couldn't we *not* do it?"

"Well, we're supposed to get her down to ol' Bleed-'Em-So," Slash said.

Pecos shrugged again. "So, we failed. Have we ever failed before? What we did do—leastways *you* did it while dang near breaking the world—was wipe out the entire Duke Winter bunch. Hell, that mean old man'll probably pin a medal on our chest for that! The old skinflint might even give us a raise!"

"Yeah," Slash said, nodding slowly, grinning. "I did take down the Winter bunch, didn't I? Though, truth be known, they sorta took themselves down—you know, with all the gunfire."

Pecos grinned devilishly. "Bleed-'Em-So will hear only what we tell him! You give me half the credit, let's leave that nasty girl to them devils that took her, an' let's shake on it!" He spit in his gloved right hand and extended it to Slash.

Slash looked off again, scowling.

Again, he pondered the situation, then shook his head slowly. "No." Again, he shook his head, then turned his incredulous gaze back to his partner. "I don't want to do it. And she's certainly given us good enough reason not to do it. Still, I can't *not* do it. Know what I mean?"

Pecos sighed deeply. "Yeah." Slowly, the bigger man nodded. "In the back of my mind, I keep wonderin' what she might be goin' through right now." It was his turn to scowl incredulously. "Why do I care?"

"I know. It don't make sense. But . . . I'll be damned if I ain't worried about her, too." Slash chuckled without mirth. "Imagine . . ."

"You know what you've gone and done, partner?"

"No. What's that, partner?"

"You've gone an' grown a heart. I think yours is even bigger than mine now."

"Pshaw!"

"No, no, I think it is."

"You think so?"

"I do. Marriage musta done it," Pecos said, frowning at his partner, as though trying to solve a riddle more formidable than the meaning of life or the origin of God. "Imagine that. Slash Braddock, the cutthroat train robber and notoriously heartless devil who waited to fall in love on the downslope of fifty, went and got hitched an' grew a heart!"

Slash slapped his thigh. "I'll be damned if I didn't!" He laughed. "Come on, partner. I got a wife to get home to. Let's go fetch that so-called actress back from Talon Renfro!"

"Ah, hell—all right,'" Pecos said grudgingly and put the steel to Buck.

At the same time but several miles ahead, Fannie giggled and said, "Talon, you stop that, now, you devil. That tickles, an' what would Duke say?"

"Oh, come on, honey," Talon Renfro said, continuing to lick and nuzzle the pretty young actress's long, pale neck. "Duke ain't here. It's just you an' me an' the boys." He chuckled and looked at the other six gang members riding their sweat-lathered horses around him.

The hard-faced train robbers regarded the outlaw leader with no little pique in their expressions. They were openly envious of Renfro's good luck. Imagine robbing a train way out here in the middle of nowhere and finding none other than your long-lost friend, the famous opry house actress Fannie Diamond! And then not only riding off with her in the saddle before you, after she'd come not only willingly but eagerly, but with you snugged up taut against her, too, pawing her through her shirt and nuzzling her neck without surcease!

And her not even making a good show of *not* enjoying it!

Not easy for a man to take way out here on this canker on the devil's forked tail!

"Tell me, honey," Renfro said, turning his attention from his men and sniffing her hair, then poking his nose into her left ear, "How'd you end up on that train, anyways? What're you doin' way out here? I heard you were puttin' on a show in Frisco, an' what a show it was, too!"

Again, Fannie giggled. Imagine her own luck! She had to admit she'd been a little impetuous, siccing the other dogs in the passenger coach on Slash and Pecos. She had to admit she hadn't thought it out all that well. What had she expected to happen to her after Slash and Pecos were gone?

It turned out that what had been about to happen was, she'd been about to be fought over by the soldiers and the other men in the passenger coach and then likely mauled to within an inch of her life before being cast away much as Slash and Pecos had been cast away—like flotsam! (Though they'd deserved what they'd got, the scalawags!) But then the rails had been blown, saving Fannie's life. The train had come to a screeching halt, throwing nearly everyone in the passenger coach over the seat ahead of them.

And then who was the first outlaw to board the coach?

None other than her former lover before Duke, the handsome rake and former gambler Talon Renfro.

Renfro recognized Fannie immediately. Of course, it was easy to pick a gal with Fannie's looks out of the clutter of unwashed humanity aboard that car, and he did it right away, eyes glazing in shock at his good luck. (She'd been the one to break it off with him a few years ago, breaking his heart, the poor man. But she hadn't been able to abide his wandering eye.)

"Oh, Talon! Talon! Talon!" she cried, running up the aisle and into the handsome cutthroat's arms. "What a sight for these sore old eyes!"

"Took the words right out of my mouth, honey!"

While Talon's gang defanged the conductor and the rest of the crew and robbed the passengers, Talon and Fannie smooched and made calf eyes, like the long-lost lovers they were. . . .

Now Fannie said, "How'd I end up on that car, ensconced in unwashed humanity, surrounded by brigands of the nastiest variety . . . ?" She sighed and wagged her head. "It's a long story, Talon. Can I tell you after a long hot bath and over a big steak and a bottle of good wine . . . ?"

He'd told her they were heading for Saguache, a town of some size and boasting the locally famous San Juan Hotel.

Talon threw his head back and whooped.

His men glared at him.

Chapter 35

Jay held the Henry rifle taut against her cheek as she aimed down into the canyon, the clomps of the approaching horse growing louder.

The rain continued to come down but not as hard as before. The storm seemed now to have settled into a steady rain, the thunder and lightning part of it having moved out.

The horse appeared, trotting around a bend in the ridge of the canyon below, just south of Jay's position. Jay tensed, began squeezing the Henry's trigger, aiming just above the saddle, expecting to see a man. She eased up, frowning curiously.

There was no man in the saddle.

The horse, a leggy sorrel, had a saddle but no rider. Its leather reins trailed along the ground, leaping when the horse stepped on them, which it did several times until the rain-silvered mount suddenly stopped dead in its tracks, looking around, twitching its ears, sniffing the air.

Jay's heart quickened. *A horse but no rider . . . ?*

A trap!

No!

She recognized the bay. It was Delbert Thayer's horse. The bay must have seen its rider from where Del had left it atop the ridge, ripped its reins free, and come dogging the deputy's heels. Relief started to ease the tension between Jay's shoulder blades. Then her shoulders tightened once more. The horse had followed her, Del, and Myra. It had been far enough behind them that there was likely a chance that Balldinger's men might have seen the horse and followed it up this side canyon.

Jay lowered the Henry, off cocked the hammer, and rose. She stepped forward, casting her cautious gaze behind the sorrel. Seeing no movement that would indicate the mount had been followed, she whistled softly. The horse whickered, startled, then swung around and raised its head, its brown eyes meeting Jay's.

"Come!" Jay said, beckoning urgently.

The horse whickered and put its head down as it turned and began climbing the shelf, heading toward Jay and the cabin. It gained the top of the shelf and trotted toward Jay, shaking and bobbing its head in friendly greeting. It hadn't wanted to remain on that ridge in the storm, and it was happy to finally see a human.

"Come on, boy!" Jay grabbed the reins, and casting another cautious glance behind her, into the canyon, she led the horse around behind the cabin to the stable, opened the stable door, and led the horse inside with the other two.

She quickly unsaddled the horse, then went out, closed the door, and hurried around to the front of the cabin. When she'd peered into the canyon again and seen nothing suspicious down there—at least not yet—she grabbed both the Henry and Del's rifle, tripped the latch on the cabin's front door, and stepped inside.

Myra sat on the edge of the cot Del was stretched out on, and was just then ringing out a cloth in the porcelain basin filled with water that sat on a hide-bottom chair she'd pulled up beside her. Glancing at Jay, the younger woman said, "I think he's running a fever. He's flushed, and he feels clammy."

"Well, then, you're doing the right thing." Jay set both rifles on the table.

Myra had lit the stove and set a small pan of water on it. The water steamed now as it heated, a few bubbles rising to the surface. As she looked around for a bottle of whiskey on the cabin's well-stocked shelves—what prospector didn't stock some who-hit-John, if only for medicinal purposes?—Jay told Myra about Del's horse and her worry that Balldinger might have seen it. She didn't tell Myra that last part to worry her but to keep her on her toes.

They both needed to keep their eyes skinned on the canyon and their ears pricked for the approach of riders or the stealthy tread of a man or men stealing up to the cabin.

"Found it!" Jay said, finding a half-filled brown bottle that even had an Old Kentucky label on it on a shelf cluttered with airtight tins and small burlap sacks of dry goods.

She wiped the dust, stove soot, and spiderwebs from the bottle, popped the cork, and sniffed. "Hmm, not bad." She found a semi-clean rag, then used the rag to lift the pan of water off the stove. She set the pan, rag, and the bottle on the chair near Myra and fished from her trouser pocket a knife she'd taken from her saddlebags—a thin-bladed folding knife in a black leather sheath—and set it on the chair, as well. The knife she would use to dig the bullet out of Del's arm.

She pulled up another hide-bottom chair from the table, positioned it to the left of the first one, sat down, and looked at Myra. "While I get started, why don't you look around for a wide-bladed knife? A bowie knife would be perfect. I think I saw one on those low shelves over there by the door. Add a little more wood to the stove and set the knife on the edge.

Myra frowned at her, puzzled.

"For cauterizing the wound," Jay explained.

Myra nodded. "Right." She looked down at Del, who seemed to be sleeping uneasily, muttering and fluttering his eyelids. Myra's cheeks were flushed with worry; she seemed reluctant to leave his side.

"He's going to be all right, honey," Jay said, squeezing the girl's arm.

Myra turned to her, tears in her eyes.

Jay smiled and put some ironic steel in her voice, wrinkling her brows. "Not to worry! This outlaw gal lived with the old owlhoot Pistol Pete Johnson for a good many years, and sometimes with Slash Braddock and the Pecos River Kid, to boot, holed up in an outlaw shack in the San Juan Mountains, where sometimes all the Snake River Marauders would gather after a job. You can bet I've tended more than my fair share of bullet wounds, young lady!"

She winked and nudged Myra's chin with her right index finger.

That seemed to cheer the girl, whose eyes brightened. Myra rose and began looking around for a knife.

As she did, Jay removed her bandanna from Del's arm, then cut the shirtsleeve away from the bloody wound, some of the dried blood the texture of jam. She cleaned the blood away gently with the warm water and the rag. Myra found a large-bladed knife, set it on the stove, and then sat down on the edge of the cot again and watched Jay work very slowly and methodically.

"Good news," Jay told the girl.

"What is it?" Myra asked hopefully.

"There's an exit wound. The bullet went all the way through. I can't feel any of it in there. Sometimes they break up. Flesh wound. I won't have to dig around for a bullet, so he'll heal faster. So far, I don't think the bullet struck the bone. That's good, too."

Myra blinked slowly as she nodded and sighed with relief. "That's good news."

Still wiping the blood away from both wounds, the entrance and the exit wound, Jay glanced at Myra and smiled. "You really love him, don't you?"

Myra smiled, nodded. "He's a good man." She leaned forward to place her hand on his knee and squeezed. "A good, sweet man."

"And a brave one," Jay said. "I made him promise not to follow me. But he did, anyway. He loves you, too, honey. Very much."

"I know." A single tear ran down Myra's left cheek.

"No matter how long you're together, never take it for granted. That's wisdom gained from experience." Jay shook her head slowly, sadly. "Sometimes they ride away and don't come back."

Myra sniffed as she stared down at her semiconscious beau, who groaned and mumbled as Jay tended his arm. "No . . . I never will . . ." She looked at Jay. "Do you . . . still love Pete?"

"Of course."

Myra frowned, curious.

"I have enough love in my heart for two men. Don't worry—Slash knows. We haven't talked about it, but he knows. Pete—he was my first. My first true love. Slash . . ." Jay smiled as she continued cleaning the wounds. "He'll be my last."

"How do you know?"

"You just do, honey."

Myra watched Jay gently clean Del's arm, then turned to the older woman suddenly, her eyes grave. "I don't deserve him."

Jay rang the bloody rag out in the basin and soaked it again in the small pan of now barely steaming water. "Yes, you do. You know how I know?"

"How?"

"Because you love him back. That's all you need to do to deserve a man. Any man. Just love him back as much as he loves you. Now, after today, you know how much he loves you, don't you, child?"

Myra nodded, blinking tears from her eyes. She used her index finger to brush one away from the corner of her right eye.

"Now you know how much to love him back," Jay said in a soft, almost singsong voice as she finished cleaning the young man's arm.

Again, Myra nodded. She studied Jay for a time, again curiously, then said, "Has Slash ever saved your life?"

"Well, not like this, no."

"Then . . . how do you know how much he loves you? How much you need to love him back?"

"Easy," Jay said. "I can see it in his eyes . . . feel it in his hands when he caresses me." She smiled warmly as her gaze again went to Myra. "You know . . . when we're together in that special place only two people who truly love each other can be . . . in that special way."

Myra shook her head as she gazed down at her beau, sadness touching her eyes. "I've been with men . . . but never to that place."

"You will be." Jay gazed down at the young deputy. "Very soon. Just don't rush it. Savor it, enjoy it, and you'll remember it forever."

Myra smiled again and leaned over to plant a kiss on the older woman's cheek; then sniffing, she brushed her own cheek across Jay's shoulder with great affection.

"All right," Jay said, dropping the rag in the basin and rising from the chair. "Time to cauterize the wounds."

Jay walked over to the stove and used a swatch of leather to pick the knife up off the stove. The blade glowed as bright as coals in a blacksmith's forge and was smoking.

"Oh, dear," Myra said, sucking a breath through gritted teeth. "It's going to hurt him terribly, isn't it?"

"I'm afraid so. Honey, go up to the head of the cot and press down on his shoulders with your hands. He's going to wake up and buck hard, and I have two wounds to close."

Myra rose, but instead of walking up to the head of the cot, she stood facing Jay. "I'll do it."

"What? Why?"

"One, you're stronger than I am. You'll be able to hold him down better. Two, I love him. I should be the one to hurt him." She glanced down at him. "To save his life."

Jay arched her brows in surprise. Pride welled in her. She loved this girl like a daughter, and she couldn't have been prouder of her if she'd been born of her own flesh. *The girl will do*, Jay thought. *She most certain will do.*

She carefully handed the glowing knife to Myra, who gazed at the blade, the red glow reflecting in her wide, soulful brown eyes.

Jay looked down at Del as she moved to the head of the cot, leaned down, and placed her hands on his shoulders. "Master Thayer, congratulations. You've wrangled you a keeper." She looked up at Myra. "Whenever you're ready."

Myra looked down at the arm, just a little blood now leaking from both wounds.

"Wipe the blood off," Jay said. "Then do it. First one and then the other. Hold the blade to each wound for two seconds, and then quickly do the other."

Myra licked her lips and trembled a little. "Oh, Lord . . ."

"No second thoughts," Jay said. "Don't hesitate. Just do it."

Myra wiped the blood from each wound, dropped the rag on the floor and, drawing a quick, deep breath, pressed the glowing blade to the wound on the back of Del's arm.

It hissed and smoked, sending the foul smell of scorched flesh into the air over the cot.

Del yowled and bucked up on the cot. Jay struggled to hold him down, her hair tumbling down over her right breast.

"Again!" Jay said. "Hurry!"

"Del, honey, forgive me!" Myra screeched and placed the blade over the second wound.

Again, the young man bucked, screaming.

Jay fought him back down and held him, but she didn't have to hold him for long. He gave a long, ragged, fluttering sigh, his eyes rolled back in their sockets, and he lay still, out like a blown lamp.

Myra dropped the knife, threw herself down on the cot, wrapped her arms around the young man's neck, sobbing, convulsing, and curled her body against his.

Flushed, Jay straightened, blew a lock of her hair from her eye. She gazed down at the lovers before her. "Yessir, Master Thayer," she said, slowly shaking her head. "You wrangled yourself a keeper."

Chapter 36

Slash and Pecos rode into the town of Saguache around six o'clock that evening, halted their horses at the edge of the business district, and looked around.

Pecos said, "Suppose they're still here? Maybe they switched horses and rode on."

"I got a feelin' they're still here."

Slash poked his hat up off his forehead and stared down the wide, dusty main street before him. There wasn't much traffic, but there were plenty of men—cowboys and miners, mostly—gathered on boardwalks fronting the five or six saloons that Slash and Pecos could see from their vantage.

"They probably don't think they were followed, since they struck the train well between stations," he added. "Since there's no telegraph along that line, they know the conductor couldn't wire ahead and sic a posse on 'em."

"Maybe stompin' with their tails up, you figure?"

"That's what we'd be doin', wouldn't we?"

"Certain sure." Pecos snorted a laugh. "Shouldn't be too hard to find 'em. Seven men ridin' into town with a pretty girl in oversized men's garb would stand out. Someone saw 'em."

"Yep," Slash said, raking a gloved thumb along his jawline. "And someone knows where they are." He booted his horse ahead. "Come on."

"Where we goin'?"

"Where they went first thing, most like."

"Livery barn."

"I swear, partner, sometimes your thinker box impresses me!" Slash chuckled.

Pecos scowled at him.

Winthrop's Livery & Feed lay just ahead and on the trail's right side—a big, sprawling place with a weathered wooden fence encircling its yard. There appeared to be a blacksmith shop flanking it, near a chicken coop around which barred rocks and leghorns strutted, pecking at the ground and quarreling with each other. Black coal smoke unfurled from a tin chimney pipe in the smithy's roof, and the regular clanks of a hammer on an anvil rang out from the small square wooden building's open front door.

The doors of the much larger barn were open as Slash and Pecos swung their horses into the straw-strewn yard. A tall, rawboned, unshaven gent was just then plowing a large hill of hay, straw, and manure out the front doors with a grain shovel, then hefting part of it with a grunt into a large wooden wheelbarrow. He paused when he saw the two newcomers approach and squinted his good eye—his left one. The right one rolled, unmoored, in its socket.

"Help you, gents?" he asked, removing a smoldering brown worm of a cigar stub from the left corner of his mouth, dropping it, stepping on it, then picking it back up and tossing it into the wheelbarrow. "Best prices in southern Colorado!"

"Not sure yet," Slash said. "We're lookin' for friends of ours." He gave a dry chuckle and jerked his thumb at Pecos. "My partner and I can't come to an agreement on just where it was we was supposed to meet. I say it's right here in Saguache. My partner seems to think it was Crested Butte, farther on down the trail."

"Ah, I see," said the big rawboned liveryman, turning his head slightly to one side and squinting his good eye suspiciously. "Well, if they rode into town, they likely stabled their hosses here. My place is the biggest barn in town, everybody knows about it, and I have a right stellar reputation. A hump-backed half-breed named Tangen has a smaller place, but he scrimps on feed an' drinks on the job. Typical damn Injun. Yessir, if they pulled into Saguache, their horses are here, all right."

"There's seven of 'em," Pecos said. "And a girl in a man's work duds."

"Purty little thing," Slash added with a twinkle in his eye.

The big man flushed. Suspicion flashed darkly in both eyes now, and he slid his scrutinizing, downright paranoid gaze from Slash to Pecos and back again. "Friends of yourn, eh?"

"That's right," Pecos said. "Friends of ourn."

Again, the big man's good eye and his wobbling fish eye slid between the two men sitting their horses before him. Suddenly, he lowered his head and returned to work with the shovel on the pile of hay, straw, and manure. "Nope. Sorry. I ain't seen no seven men an' a girl. No, sir. Check with that mangy rock worshipper. Little fallin' down place on the far side of town. They mighta put up there."

"You sure?" Slash asked, shaping a crooked, skeptical smile.

Holding up a shovelful of hay, straw, and manure, the man scowled at Slash. "Said so, didn't I?" With a grunt, he tossed the hay, straw, and manure into the wheelbarrow.

"I don't know," Slash said. "Seems like you might—"

The man jerked his head toward Slash, heavy brown brows beetling angrily. "Mister, you callin' me a liar?"

"All right, then," Pecos said with a heavy sigh, pinching his hat brim to the gent. "Thanks, anyway, pard."

He and Slash started to rein their horses around but stopped when the man said, "Hey, I know you!"

Slash and Pecos looked back at the man, frowning curiously.

"You do?" Pecos said.

The big man smiled shrewdly, his unmoored eye rolling slowly from the outside of its socket to the inside and then dropping, as though to stare at the large blunt tip of the big man's sun-leathered nose. "Sure, sure! Why, you're Slash Braddock an' the Pecos River Kid!"

Slash and Pecos shared a skeptical glance, hands automatically sliding toward their holstered hoglegs.

Slash said, "You have us at a disadvantage, friend."

"A. J. Winthrop." Grinning, showing a more or less full set of tobacco-rimmed teeth, he leaned on the shovel. "I was in Hayes, Kansas, when you robbed the bank and trust. Joined the posse. You boys led us into the Rattlesnake Butte and had us riding in so many circles we was all dizzy for a month! Then your trail just disappeared!" He snapped his fingers. "Just like that—like you never was even ahead of us, but we all just imagined it. I tell you, the sheriff, Bill Watley, he was so mad at bein' hornswoggled by the Snake River Marauders, he wouldn't come out of his jailhouse for two weeks. Just sat in there and drained one whiskey bottle after another!"

A. J. Winthrop slapped his thigh and roared.

Suddenly, he wrinkled his brows again, curiously, then held up a hand to the side of his mouth and said very quietly, so that Slash and Pecos could barely hear him above the pattering of a piano that had kicked in from somewhere on the main drag a couple of minutes ago, "You boys ain't runnin' with Talon Renfro, now, are ya?"

He dropped his hand and looked around sharply, warily

then. Reassured no one was eavesdropping, he returned his curious gaze to Slash and Pecos.

"So, Renfro's here?" Pecos said.

Suspicion again entered the man's gaze. He smiled, but the smile did not ameliorate the suspicion. "Nah . . . you ain't ridin' with Talon Renfro. What happened? Did your boys get crossways with Talon's bunch?" Winthrop's smile broadened; both his good and unmoored eye glittered merrily. "Things about to come to a head between you?" He clapped his big hands together and rubbed them like a kid just waking up and remembering it was Christmas morning. "I do love me a good dustup between outlaws!"

He looked back in the direction from which Slash and Pecos had come. "Where's the Marauders? They keepin' out of sight?" He dropped his chin as well as his voice, smiling shrewdly, and said, "Maybe settin' up a *bushwhack*?"

Slash chuckled. "Nah, nah. Nothin' like that."

He looked at Pecos, and both men laughed.

"Nah, ya see . . . actually . . . we did throw in with Talon. Ya see, we got crossways with our own gang. Truth be told, we got a little long in the tooth for them younger fellas, so they went their ways and we went ours. Yessir, we ride with Talon now. He's here, then, I take it?"

"Ah, that's a shame," Winthrop said, now looking like the boy whom Santa did not visit. "We get such little entertainment here in town. An' the whores are overpriced. Yeah, yeah, Renfro's bunch rode in about an hour ago. Talon himself an' the girl weren't with 'em. I heard the others talkin', an' they mentioned that Talon an' some girl headed to the hotel straightaway, and the others led Talon's horse here. I got all seven corralled out back."

He chuckled, shaking his head. "Them fellas were sure piss burned. Apparently, Talon's hogging that gal all for hisself, an' it sounds like she was quite the looker, too!"

Slash and Pecos shared a quick glance; then Slash jerked his head back to the liveryman. "Which hotel?"

"The best an' biggest one in town. Nothin' but the best fer Talon Renfro, I reckon. The San Juan. Just up the street and on the left. Can't miss it."

"Obliged, pard," Slash said, reining his Appy around.

"Hey!" Winthrop yelled behind him. "You is friends of Talon's now, ain't ya?"

When neither Slash nor Pecos bothered to reply but trotted their horses back out of the yard and then swung right onto the main street, Winthrop yelled, "Well, if'n you ain't, you didn't hear about him from me, *all right?*"

He yelled something else, but by this time the piano and the general din of the street drowned it out.

The San Juan Hotel was right where the liveryman had said it would be and easily the largest building in Saguache's business district, with its name splashed across the top of the third story. It was a big three-story clapboard affair with two front doors. Painted on signs over each door were the words SALOON and FINE DINING. A dozen or so saddled horses were tied out in front of the place, and a couple of fancy leather buggies, as well.

"They gonna let us in, Slash?" Pecos swung down from his own horse and then brushed at the trail dust clinging to his broadcloth coat and trousers. They tied their horses to the hitchrack.

"If they let that mangy Talon Renfro's bunch in, they'll let us in." Slash shucked his Yellowboy from its saddle sheath and racked a round into the chamber.

Pecos grabbed his arm. "Hold on, hold on, you old coon dog you. What're you fixin' to do? Just waltz in there an' start shootin'?"

"Why the hell not?"

"Well, first, we don't know what any of the gang looks like."

"We'll know 'em when we see 'em. We were train robbers once, too. They likely look like us, only not as handsome as me." Slash pulled his arm out of Pecos's grip and walked toward the steps rising to the door labeled SALOON.

Pecos hurried up behind him, grabbed his arm again, and pulled him back. "Slash, now . . . I know you're worried about Fannie. I am, too."

Slash looked up at the second- and third-story windows. "God only knows what they're doin' to her up there. I know she damn near got our wicks trimmed, and I'll likely never walk right again after being thrown off that train, but she doesn't deserve what they're likely doin' to her."

"How're we gonna find her?"

Slash shrugged. "I don't know. I figure it'll come to me while I'm pumping rounds through all seven of those train-robbin' devils!" He frowned at his taller partner. "Are you comin', or you gonna stand out here, twistin' your bloomers?"

"I don't consider a little careful plannin' twistin' my bloomers!"

"You know me, pard. I plan as I go!"

"Ah, hell." Pecos sighed and wagged his head. He grabbed his twelve- double-bore gauge hanging from his saddle horn and looped the leather lanyard over his head and right shoulder.

Following Slash up the steps, their spurs ringing, he said, "Just don't do nothin' hasty, now, Slash. We could get her killed, you know?"

"Let's go in and get the lay of the land."

"Ah, hell. Why do I bother?"

Slash pushed through the big double doors, and Pecos followed him inside. Out of long habit, Slash stepped to his left, Pecos to his right, to prevent the door from backlighting them.

They stood looking around the large, oval-shaped, smoky, sunken-floored saloon, with what appeared to be nearly a block-long mahogany bar with an ornate and mirrored backbar stretched across the rear wall, over which several grizzly and elk and moose trophies kept their silent, dour, dull-eyed counsel. What they thought of the horde of boisterous humanity—men of all shapes, colors, sizes, and styles of dress mingling with each other and a whole bevy of colorfully albeit scantily clad percentage gals—milling and conversing and laughing and gambling and smoking and drinking beneath their noses was anyone's guess.

A staircase rose to the left of the bar, the burgundy-carpeted risers disappearing into the second story. A man in a miner's blue dungarees and hobnailed boots was just then climbing the stairs with a brown-haired, olive-skinned parlor girl decked out in a metallic blue corset and bustier and blue high-heeled shoes, and with matching blue feathers in her hair. The miner, big and bearded and wearing a black immigrant hat, held her hand up high, helping the girl negotiate the steps in those dangerously high-heeled stilettos, the man talking loudly and the girl tittering, though seeming a little nervous about the stairs, given her shoes.

"She's up there," Slash said. "She sure ain't down here. They got her upstairs, poor girl. Somehow, we gotta get up there."

"Oh, oh."

"What is it?"

"Look there—straight across the room."

Slash followed Pecos's gaze to a man staring at him and Pecos curiously in the backbar mirror. The man was tall and dark.

Five other men stood beside him, all wearing dusters, all bellied up to the bar. The tall, dark man was the only one staring at Slash and Pecos with mute but definite—suspicious?—interest.

Until he nudged the men standing to his left.

Then Slash and Pecos had two of Talon Renfro's men giving them the woolly eyeball.

Chapter 37

Jay stood in the cabin's open doorway, gazing out across the shelf toward the canyon below. She couldn't see the trail from here, but if riders came, she'd hear them.

The rain had lightened even more than before. Now it was a gentle mist. In the sky to the west, it looked as though the clouds were breaking up. She could see glimpses of blue sky between a few of them.

She held the Henry repeating rifle in her right hand. She held a tin cup of whiskey in her other hand. Now, as she raised the cup to her lips and took a soothing sip, she heard Myra walk up behind her, felt the girl's hand on her shoulder.

"Now what do we do?" the girl asked, her eyes swollen from crying, her cheeks pale and puffy from emotion on the lee side of having cauterized Delbert Thayer's arm wounds.

"Now we wait until he can ride. We'll spend the night here, keep your young man warm and comfortable, see if we can get him to eat something for supper. Maybe in the morning he'll be well enough to fork a saddle. I'll fashion a sling for his arm."

"I don't suppose there's much else we can do."

Jay gave a gentle smile, shook her head. "We'll get through it, Myra. You and me."

"What if Balldinger comes?"

Jay raised the Henry. "Together, we'll hold them off. You can shoot, can't you?"

Myra nodded. "Pa taught me to hunt with a rifle, but it's been a while."

"Believe me, it'll come back to you when you need it to."

Just then a horse whinnied from somewhere down in the canyon.

Myra gasped. Jay stiffened.

Turning to Myra, she said quietly, "Quick. Del's rifle. It's on the table."

As Myra swung around toward the table, Jay stepped outside, moved slowly, crouching slightly to keep from being seen from below, toward the lip of the shelf. As she moved forward, she brought more and more of the narrow canyon below into view.

Now she could hear the slow clomp of horse hooves. They grew steadily louder.

A man said something, his resonant voice echoing around the narrow corridor to Jay's left.

Her heart thudded. She'd recognized Grant Balldinger's voice.

As she approached several large rocks peppering the lip of the shelf, to the left of where the prospector's old trail dropped down the shelf into the canyon, Jay dropped to a knee behind one such rock and peered around the rock's right side, into the canyon. As she did, a rider came riding around the bend in the cliff wall.

Jay's heart increased its pace. The man was Balldinger. He was followed closely by another. Then two more men, riding single file, as well, came out from around the bend in the wall. Balldinger leaned slightly out over his palomino's right wither, scrutinizing the ground, the horse walking slowly forward.

"You're sure that sorrel came this way, Dempsey?"

"Pretty dang sure, boss," said the third rider in the four-man string.

Jay squeezed the Henry in her hands. She started to raise it when, for some reason, a footstep behind her caught her off guard, and she gasped as she whipped her head around to see Myra, holding Del's old-model Winchester carbine, take another step forward, then drop to a knee.

"Sorry . . . ," Myra said, glancing with concern at Jay.

Jay whipped her head back around to stare into the canyon just as Balldinger said, "What was that?"

The rancher turned his head and looked up toward Jay, the brim of his high-crowned Stetson rising to reveal his broad red face. His jaws hardened and his eyes narrowed as he said, "There they are!"

He took the rifle he was holding in both hands, sat up straight in the saddle, glaring up the shelf at Jay and Myra, and bellowed, "You killed my son, you wild she-cat! You killed my son! *Todd's dead*!"

Jay snarled as she pumped a round into the Henry's action and raised the rifle to her shoulder, "And so are you!"

Balldinger started to raise his own rifle.

Jay steadied the Henry's sights on the man's forehead and squeezed the trigger. But just then the palomino started, lunging forward and to one side. Jay's bullet caromed inches behind the rancher's head to blow a slender limb off a cedar. Balldinger fired his own rifle just as the palomino reared, giving a shrill whinny.

As Balldinger's bullet crashed into the face of Jay's covering rock, kicking up a shrill ringing in Jay's ears, the rancher bellowed an indignant cry as, throwing his left arm out wide, he went tumbling off his pitching mount's right hip.

"Oh, Christ!" he wailed as he struck the muddy trail with a wet thump.

"Damn!" Jay said, ejecting the spent cartridge and seating a fresh one in the Henry's breech.

She lined up the sights again on Balldinger as one of the men hastily dismounting behind him yelled, "Boss, you all right?"

Balldinger pushed himself up quickly to glare up the shelf at Jay. He was now hatless, his right cheek streaked with mud. Good thing for him he rose right then, or Jay's next bullet would have carved a hole through his weathered forehead. Instead, it plumed mud and rainwater where his head had been half an eyewink before.

Balldinger heaved himself to his feet, calling the lady with the Henry repeater a most ungentlemanly name, and skedaddled off the trail and into the rocks on the trail's far side just as Jay's next bullet slammed into a rock just right of her intended target.

Again, Jay cursed, then drew her head back behind the rock as Balldinger's three hands began triggering lead at her.

Myra crouched behind another rock a few feet to Jay's right, wincing as the ranch hands' bullets hammered the rocks she and Jay were crouched behind. She looked at Jay apologetically and yelled above the fusillade's din, "I'm sorry I didn't help. They sort of caught me by surprise!"

"That's all right," Jay yelled, also wincing as the bullets crashed into hers and Myra's covering rocks. "I wasn't much help, either!" She paused, then yelled, "Just let them pop all the caps they want. Maybe they'll run out of bullets!"

When the shooting tapered off, both Jay and Myra snaked their own rifles through the gap between their rocks. Jay set her sights on the left cheek of a man poking his head out between a rock and a short, stout cedar and fired. The man screamed as his head jerked back so sharply that his hat fell forward. He slammed back against the ground, clutching that cheek with his gloved right hand, and writhed there.

Jay shot him again, this time in the chest, just before the other three opened up on her and Myra again.

Myra had just fired an errant round and now, pulling her head back behind her own rock, looked at Jay as Jay said with curt satisfaction, "That's more like it! Culled the herd a little!"

When the three men's shooting tapered off again, Balldinger poked his head out from behind his own covering boulder to the right of the other two men and bellowed, "You're going to die slow here today, Jay. Should have done it my way. Would have been so much quicker. You're gonna die slow, like my boy died, *gut shot*!"

The man's stentorian wail echoed eerily around the ridges.

Myra glanced at Jay. "He means business!"

"So do I." Jay pumped another round into the Henry's action, quickly snaked the rifle through the gap between her and Myra's rocks, drew a bead on Balldinger's half-exposed face, and fired.

Seeing the rifle aimed at him, Balldinger widened his one exposed eye in fear and jerked his head back behind his boulder.

Jay's bullet caromed through the air where his eye had just been to spang shrilly off a rock several feet behind the rancher's position.

The others threw several more bullets at Jay and Myra.

Then silence.

Jay glanced at Myra. "This is getting us nowhere."

Myra said, "They could keep us pinned down up here till after dark, then work in around us. We'd be sitting ducks in that cabin."

"Hmm." Jay pondered the notion. "Thank you, honey. You just gave me an idea."

Myra looked at her, brown eyes wide with the gravity of their situation. "I did?"

Jay nodded. "I'm gonna see if I can work around behind them, catch them by surprise. Back shoot the devils," she added with a curled upper lip. "Better than what they deserve!"

"Oh, Jay . . ."

"It's our only chance. Like you said, we don't want to be in this position after dark."

"No, I suppose not, but . . . what do you want me to do?"

"Stay here. Trigger a round at them every now and then, make them believe we're both up here. I'll hurry, try to get around them before they become suspicious."

Myra drew a deep breath, looking wary. She jerked with a start as a rifle spoke from below and a bullet sizzled through the air of the gap between her and Jay's rocks. The bullet tore up sand and gravel a few feet beyond the gap. "Please be careful, Jay!"

"You too. Keep your head down. Don't take any chances."

Myra drew her mouth corners down and nodded once.

Jay snaked the Henry through the gap, triggered a shot, then swung around and crawled along the lip of the gap to her left, in the direction from which she and Balldinger's men had entered the canyon. Larger boulders lay in this direction, strewn along the wall of the canyon. When she reached one, she rose to her feet and stepped behind it, then peered around its left side and back up the canyon.

Myra just then triggered a shot.

Balldinger and his men returned fire, Balldinger cursing loudly and yelling, "Dead, Jay! You hear me? You have no way out of this! Braddock's gonna be one lonely widower!"

One of the other men laughed and howled.

Jay could see the smoke from their rifles maybe fifty yards to her right, rising above their covered positions.

Quickly, but stepping carefully so as not to fall, she made her way down the steep slope, grabbing rocks and shrubs to break her descent, wending her way through the rocks and boulders. As she descended the ridge, she heard Myra occasionally snapping off sporadic shots, drawing more fire from Balldinger's men.

As Jay gained the bottom of the canyon, she peered around a gnarled juniper and cast her gaze up the canyon. She could see only the occasional smoke puff marking a triggered rifle.

Good!

She crossed the trail bisecting the canyon floor, then hurried into the rocks and shrubs beyond for a good thirty feet before swinging around and walking just as quickly up the canyon, toward where Balldinger and the two ranch hands were hunkered down in the rocks. She made a beeline for the gunfire, heading for the two ranch hands first.

When she could hear the occasional shooting coming from her right, she turned and walked back toward the trail. She walked around a patch of evergreen shrubs and a wild berry thicket and stopped.

Both hands lay before her, one crouched behind a stout cedar, the other behind a flat-topped rock the size of a large tombstone.

"Devils," Jay snarled through gritted teeth as she dropped to a knee and quietly jacked a fresh round into the Henry's action.

Apparently, she hadn't cocked the weapon quietly enough, or maybe the man on her right, the man crouched behind the cedar, had just sensed her behind him. He turned his head to look over his left shoulder. Seeing her, his eyes widened in surprise, and then he jerked his entire body around, raising the carbine in his hands.

Jay shot him through the dead center of his chest. The man screamed and stumbled backward, triggering the carbine straight down before him and drilling a round into the toe of his left boot.

The other man cursed and swung toward Jay.

Jay pumped a fresh round into the Henry and flinched as

the man sent a round curling the air inches off her right ear. She punched a .44 round through his throat and another through his right cheek. He twisted around, giving a strangled wail, slammed into his covering rock, and then dropped straight back to the ground, tossing his rifle away, throwing his arms wide.

He lay on the gravel-strewn ground, jerking as he gave up the ghost.

Quickly, Jay levered another round and turned to peer to her left.

Balldinger . . .

She'd just started to move cautiously toward where she'd last seen the rancher crouched behind a boulder, when a gunshot and then a shrill scream rose from the shelf on which the cabin sat.

A cold stone dropped in Jay's gut.

That had been Myra's scream.

"Myra!" she cried and began running back toward the shelf, leaping over one of the dead men as she did.

A few minutes earlier, Myra had pressed her cheek up against the Winchester's stock and aimed down into the canyon, trying to find a target. But then she'd heard a man yell. On the heels of the yell, a rifle had thundered. There had been more yells and more shooting, and Myra's heart had raced. She'd hoped Jay had accomplished her task.

Myra had waited, staring down the Winchester's barrel into the canyon.

She had spied movement in the corner of her right eye and had lifted her head suddenly. She'd screamed when she saw a hatless, muddy-faced man poke his big head and a rifle out around the side of a boulder maybe fifty feet away on her right. Balldinger was hatless, and his face was mud streaked. He held the rifle a little awkwardly, as though his right arm or shoulder was injured. Myra gasped and jerked her head down, pressing her chin against the ground. As she did, the rancher's rifle barked.

Myra winced as she felt the bullet part the hair at the crown of her skull before it thudded into the ground a few feet away on her left.

Balldinger cursed. Myra heard him jacking a fresh round into his Winchester's breech. Myra rolled up closer to her covering rock, then pushed up onto her knees, raised the rifle, aimed at Balldinger, who was now aiming back at her around the side of the rock, and fired.

Click!

Her Winchester was empty. She'd left the cartridges inside! She pulled her head down behind the rock a half second before the rancher's own rifle barked. The bullet spanged shrilly as it slammed into the very top edge of Myra's rock, pelting her with stone shards.

Again, she screamed, then heaved herself to her feet and ran as hard and fast as she could for the cabin.

Balldinger laughed menacingly behind her. "Nowhere to run, Miss Myra. Your trail ends *here*!"

Myra glanced over her shoulder to see Balldinger step down from his perch in the rocks and stride toward her, limping slightly, wincing against the pain in one or maybe both hips.

"No!" Myra cried as she approached the cabin.

She fumbled the door open, ran inside, saw a box of .44 cartridges on the table before her. Someone up high was looking out for them. She slammed the door, then hurried to the table. She set the rifle on the table and picked up the cartridge box. Her hands shook so bad that just as she opened the box, she dropped it, spilling the entire box partly on the table and partly on the floor.

She gave a frustrated wail and reached for a cartridge rolling around on the table, but she did not get the bullet into the

Winchester's loading gate before she heard loud footsteps and raking, angry breaths just outside the cabin.

The cabin door exploded inward.

"No!" Myra cried, wheeling to see Balldinger's big frame fill the entire doorway, silhouetted against the gray light behind him.

He raised his Winchester to his shoulder, bellowing, "Death to you, little girl!" and tightened his gloved hand around the Winchester's neck, narrowing one eye as he aimed down the barrel.

Myra gave another wail and stumbled backward against the table, raising her hands and turning her face to one side, awaiting the bullet with the most profound dread imaginable.

The rifle roared.

Myra screamed, convulsed.

The rifle roared again.

Beneath the ringing in her ears, Myra was vaguely aware of no bullets having ripped into her.

She opened her eyes to see Balldinger stumbling back out the door, lowering his rifle to his side, his head wobbling on his shoulders, his eyes wide with shock and horror. Blood oozed from two ragged holes in his chest.

Suddenly, he stopped stumbling and stood still. Well, not still. His body sort of quivered in place.

Myra whipped her head around to see Del sitting up on the cot, his six-shooter clenched in his right fist and aimed over Myra's head at the open doorway. Smoke curled from the barrel.

"*Balldinger!*" Myra heard a woman yell from outside.

She turned her head to stare through the open door.

Balldinger shifted his feet, turning his big body awkwardly to face the opposite direction. As he did, Myra saw Jay striding up to him, holding her rifle down low by her right side. When she was ten feet away from the rancher, she stopped. Fury sparked in her eyes as she cocked and raised the Henry rifle and pressed the butt to her shoulder, then narrowed her right eye as she aimed down the barrel at the rancher's head.

The Henry roared.

Balldinger's head fairly exploded, jerking backward sharply, a fist-sized chunk of the back of his head, along with a good bit of brains and blood, spewing onto the ground behind him.

The rancher opened his right hand, dropped his rifle straight down to the ground. He rocked back and forth on the heels of his boots, and then, as though finally making a decision as to which way he wanted to go, he fell backward and struck the ground heavily without even breaking his fall.

Myra shuttled her shocked gaze from the rancher, who lay still, gazing sightlessly straight up at the sky, to Jay, who slowly lowered her smoking Henry.

She turned from Jay to Del, who slowly lowered his smoking six-shooter.

"Del . . . ," she whispered, heart still racing.

He gave a crooked smile. "How's my girl?"

Again, Myra looked at the dead rancher.

She looked at Jay, who stood smiling at her from the spot from which she'd shot Balldinger. Then Myra turned to Del and smiled, her heart only now beginning to slow.

"Better now." She choked out a sob of deep relief and went to her man.

Chapter 38

"Why the special interest?" Pecos asked Slash, keeping his voice low, though there was no way the six Talon Renfro men at the bar could overhear him with the din in the San Juan Hotel saloon as loud as it was. "S'pose they recognize us?"

"Nah," Slash said. "Maybe they know we're here to kill 'em." He smiled across the smoky saloon and pinched his hat brim at the two Renfro men who had turned to face him and Pecos and were scowling at them dubiously.

That the six were Renfro's men, there could be no mistake. True, there were six down here, not seven, which was the total number of men in the gang. But that just meant Talon Renfro himself was likely upstairs, doing only God knew what to Fannie Diamond.

No. Slash thought he knew what he was doing, all right.

Slash glanced at Pecos and beckoned with his head. "Come on. Let's have a seat, figure out a way for one of us to get upstairs."

They'd only just then taken a seat at a table roughly halfway between the front door and the bar when a pretty girl who'd been making the rounds, laughing with the men, enduring several slaps to her rear, and taking a few puffs off one of the patrons' long black cigarillos, stopped just off Slash's right elbow.

She tugged Slash's hat brim down over his eyes and said, "Hello, handsome! Where've you been all my life?" She spoke in a heavy Spanish accent, though she was as bubbly as any blonde.

Slash poked his hat brim back up away from his eyes and looked at the plump little gal—oval faced, dark skinned, brown eyed, and with long, coarse coal-black hair. Likely Mexican, with some Indian blood. She filled out her skimpy attire right well. She was too coarse featured to be called pretty, and she had a small scar on the nub of her chin as well as pimple scarring on her cheeks and forehead.

Still, she was not hard on the eyes. Even if she were, Slash would have still said exactly what he did now: "Darlin', I been wonderin' that same thing!" He shoved his chair back and rose, extending his right elbow. "What do you say we go upstairs and get to know each other?"

"*Mierda*!" she said, chuckling, hooking her arm through his. "You don't take much coaxing. But you must pay at the bar first, handsome!"

"How much, li'l gal?"

"For me—ten dollars." She gave a slow, seductive blink of her eyes and then reached up to straighten Slash's crooked ribbon tie. "And I am worth every penny. Soon, you shall see, and you will remember this night forever!"

Slash glanced at Pecos, who regarded him with lines of deep incredulity corrugating his forehead. "Hold down the fort, partner."

"Slash, what's the plan here?"

"We done talked about my feelin's about plans. Life's too short," Slash said as he let the girl direct him over to the bar, where he tossed a silver cartwheel to a beefy, mustached gent—one of several aproned bartenders—behind the bar, who then nodded at the girl and tossed the coin into a tin coffee can perched on a backbar shelf.

"This way, handsome," the girl said, leading Slash on down the bar toward the stairs.

As Slash and the girl passed the two Talon Renfro men still studying him skeptically, Slash smiled and pinched his hat brim at them again, then gave Pecos a cautious look over his right shoulder. Pecos was then placing his order with another scantily clad young gal holding a tray—a drink server, most likely—but he caught Slash's look and returned it in kind.

With that look, they'd each agreed that if Pecos heard shooting upstairs, he'd better go to work fast down here.

Slash and the girl climbed the stairs. She smiled up at him, humming quietly, sonorously. Slash smiled back at her, but as soon as they reached the second-floor hall, he stopped, turned to the girl, and placed his hands on her shoulders.

"Did a man dressed like them six down at the bar come up here with a pretty blonde in a man's clothes?"

The doxie scowled up at Slash, deeply incredulous. "*What? I don't . . . know . . .*"

Just then, Slash heard footsteps on the stairs behind him. He swung around in time to see a fat, jowly blond man wearing an apron and steel-framed spectacles gain the second-floor landing. He was red faced and puffing from hauling two steaming steel buckets up the stairs. As he turned off the landing and trudged grimly past where Slash stood with the doxie, pale steam rose into the hall's murk from the buckets.

Slash turned his head to stare after the man. He frowned curiously at the two steaming buckets.

This time of the day, whores toil on their backs and don't take baths. Maybe ol' Talon Renfro wants his girl clean before he . . .

A strange suspicion crept into Slash's mind, set up a tingling in his palms. That girl was cagey, she purely was. . . .

"Stay here," he told the doxie and began following the beefy gent with the buckets.

The beefy gent stopped at the last door on the hall's left side. As Slash strode toward him, gradually increasing his pace, the beefy gent kicked the door and said, "Mr. Smith . . . Mrs. Smith . . . your bathwater . . . good an' hot, just like you asked!"

Slash frowned, suspicion building in him.

Mr. and Mrs. Smith . . . ?

As he walked toward the beefy gent with the two steaming buckets, he closed his hands over his .44s. He had both revolvers half out of their holsters when he heard footsteps in the hall behind him.

Ahead of him, the door in front of the beefy gent opened, and a man's tall shadow filled the doorway. A handsome fella in a rakish sort of way, with long, thick dark brown hair and a handlebar mustache. He was clad only in long handles, and a fat cigar protruded from the right corner of his mouth.

Talon Renfro . . . ?

Behind Slash, a man yelled, "Hey, Talon!"

The man in the long handles had just started to step back to let the beefy gent with the water enter his room. Now he stopped and cast his gaze down the hall, his eyes flickering curiously at Slash.

Slash glanced behind him to see three of the duster-clad men from downstairs walking toward him side by side, dusters whipping back in the wind of their passage to show holstered six-shooters residing on their hips or thonged on their thighs.

"Trouble, Talon. *Trouble!*" the duster-clad man in the middle of the trio yelled as he and the others stopped and stretched their lips back from their mustached upper lips and reached for their guns.

Ahead of Slash, Talon Renfro slammed the door closed in the face of the beefy gent with the water buckets. The beefy gent gave a yowl of exasperation as he stumbled backward, hot water slopping over the sides of his buckets.

The old refrain rang through Slash's head—*If it weren't for bad luck, we'd have no luck at all!*—as he whipped around, filling his hands with his own .44s. Before him, guns flashed, barked, and smoked in the hall's murk. Behind Slash, the beefy gent yowled again as a bullet meant for Slash tore into him and threw him back against the wall at the hall's end.

More bullets caromed around Slash, one slicing an icy burn across the side of his neck as he dropped to a knee, raised both of his pretty poppers straight out before him, and returned fire, the Colts bucking and roaring in his hands. The man in the middle of the trio went down first but not before triggering one last round, which slammed into Slash's upper left arm. The bullet jerked Slash sharply left and backward over his left hip.

Good thing it had, too, or a bullet fired by the man on the left would have likely cored him just above his left eye. Instead, it hammered into the wailing beefy gent, who yowled again and then wailed even louder where he lolled on the carpeted hall floor, soaked with the steaming water.

Slash sat back on his butt, wincing against the pain in his left arm, but extended that left-hand gun and arm straight out before him once more and drilled a round through the chest of the man on his left, then quickly sighted down the smoking barrel of his right-hand gun on the third man, whom he was surprised to see stumbling back against the wall on the right side of the hall, cursing.

Slash hadn't realized he'd struck the man with one of his first volleys.

"Right impressive, if I do say so myself!" he bit out and fired at the man again.

That bullet missed and carved a hole in the wall to his right.

"That wasn't!" Slash barked at himself.

The third man went down on one knee and swung toward Slash, raising the six-shooter remaining in his left hand. Fortunately, he must have been right-handed; that round fired from his left-hand gun sailed wide of Slash and silenced once and for all the wails of the beefy gent behind him.

Slash cut loose with both of his Colts at the same time; one bullet punched a hole in the third man's chest, and the other one ripped into the man's right, upraised knee and shredded his broadcloth pants. That bullet was from Slash's left-hand Colt, understandably not as steady, what with the bullet kicking up a white-hot agony in that arm.

Suddenly, silence filled the hall.

Slash froze, a frozen hand of apprehension splayed across the dead center of his back.

He turned his head slowly right to see Talon Renfro aiming two silver-chased, long-barreled Smith & Wessons at him, grinning, showing a full set of pearly white teeth.

"You're about to saddle a golden cloud, you son of a buck!" Talon cried, eyes glittering devilishly as he drew his index fingers back against his Smithys' triggers.

Slash tightened, awaiting the bullet that was about to make his beloved Jay a widow once again. . . .

A few minutes ago, Pecos was sitting downstairs, taking a sip of the frothy ale the saloon girl had brought him.

As he sipped the not bad-tasting but lukewarm beer, he locked gazes with the six train robbers standing at the bar. The two who had faced him and Slash before Slash and the doxie headed for the hogpens upstairs were still staring at him, but now the other four had joined in the entertainment. They studied him, too, guardedly, holding a beer or shot glass in one hand, resting the elbow of the other arm back atop the bar behind them.

Keeping their free hands free.

After swallowing his beer and setting the mug back down on the table, Pecos growled under his breath, "Sure, Slash, you go up to find the one with Fannie an' leave me with the other *six* . . ."

If that wasn't just like his owly former train-robbing partner!

The man on the right end of the six said something to the man standing to *his* right while keeping his eyes on Pecos. While keeping his eyes on Pecos, the man to the first one's right relayed the message to the man on *his* right, who did likewise, keeping his gaze on Pecos, until the message was conveyed to all five of the owlhoots standing with their backs to the bar, giving Pecos the woolly eyeball and keeping him from more thoroughly enjoying his beer.

Suddenly, the three men on the left side of the pack pushed away from the bar, turned, and filed off down the bar toward the stairs.

"Now, that's more like it," Pecos muttered before taking another sip of his beer and enjoying it a little more this time. Nothing like better odds for making a man enjoy a frothy ale, even a lukewarm one . . .

Fair's fair, partner!

While Pecos had been sharing stares with the six train robbers, he'd noted out of the corners of his eyes that the tables around him had very gradually been vacated. Apparently, it had been all too apparent—what with the six men at the bar giving the stink eye to Pecos, who had a sawed-off double-bore hanging from a lanyard off his right shoulder—that remaining in their original positions was growing more and more less than healthy.

Now that the other three had ventured toward the stairs, where Pecos's partner had ventured less than two minutes ago, it must have become even more apparent that a foofaraw between the remaining four men giving each other the eye cabbage was imminent. Pecos wasn't about to take his eyes off the three remaining at the bar, but he was fairly certain from a few brief eye-shuttling glimpses to his left and right that the once-rollicking saloon was now damn near vacated, with maybe only a handful of interested onlookers looking on from the room's peripheries.

Only one of the former three barmen remained, and that man just now slid his bleak gaze between Pecos and the three owlhoots one last time, gave a sigh, and ducked down behind the bar.

From upstairs, and clearly heard in the saloon's now-funereal silence, a man shouted, "Trouble, Talon. *Trouble!*"

That kicked Pecos and the three men before him into motion.

As the three slapped leather, Pecos leapt up from his chair, kicking it back behind him and aiming the double-bore straight out across the table as he rocked both rabbit-ear hammers back.

He triggered the right barrel between the two men on the trio's right a quarter blink before both men triggered their revolvers. The widely spread buckshot tore into both men's chest high, shredding one sleeve of each man's duster, as well as the brown wool vests under the dusters, and tearing into the hands that triggered the revolvers, nudging one shot down into the table before Pecos and the other over his right shoulder, close enough to tickle his earlobe.

The roar of the shotgun and the two revolvers hadn't even begun to fade before Pecos threw himself to his right just as the man on the trio's far left triggered his own Bisley .44. The bullet split the air where Pecos had been standing a sixteenth of a second earlier. Pecos struck the floor on his left shoulder, and as the owlhoot tracked him with his smoking Bisley and tightened his finger around the hogleg's trigger, Pecos raised the twelve-gauge and triggered the left barrel.

He gave that owlhoot the full benefit of the blast, the buckshot ripping into his chest and lifting him up and over the bar behind him as he screamed like a leg-trapped banshee.

Nothing hurt like a heart and lungs shredded by a ten-gauge buck. . . .

Pecos let the shotgun sag down against the floor as he shucked his Russian from the holster thonged on his right thigh. The two others were yelling as they flopped back against the bar, but they were still in commission, despite the agony the single load of twelve-gauge buck had evoked in each howling scoundrel, and just then they bore down on Pecos with their hoglegs. With his left hand, Pecos pulled a chair down in front of him. One bullet slammed into the seat of the chair just in time to keep from drilling Pecos a third eye. The bullet fired by the second yowling train robber clipped the end of a wooden leg.

Pecos dropped the chair, aimed the Russian over it, then shot the man on the right first, the man on the left second. While they fell back against the bar again, bellowing, one triggering his next round into the ceiling and the other one triggering his next round into a window at the front of the saloon, Pecos shot the man on the right again and then the man on the left again.

In turn, the men bounced off the bar and fell in two separate, quivering, bloody heaps along the bar's brass footrail.

In the sudden silence down here in the main saloon hall, Pecos could hear the monsoon storm–like thunder on the second floor above his head. He heaved himself heavily to his feet, kicked the chair out of his way, and ran to the stairs, yelling, "*Slash!*"

Amazing how big and black a .44 maw appeared when it was staring down at you, within a half a second of sending you to the pearly gates . . . or, in Slash's case, likely the smoking gates, Slash vaguely pondered.

He closed his eyes. No point in watching.

The gun roared. Every tensed bone in Slash's body jerked so hard he thought they'd shatter.

Slash grunted, drew a breath.

Wait. How could he draw a breath? He was dead.

Wasn't he . . . ?

He opened his eyes, found himself staring up at Talon Renfro, who looked as puzzled as Slash felt. Renfro beetled his brows, lowered his .44, and triggered it into the hall floor just right of his right foot, clad in a white wool sock. He stepped forward, taking a halting step with his left foot. As he did, blood oozed from the large, round hole in the center of his chest, at the bottom of the V formed by his unbuttoned balbriggan top.

He took another halting step forward, this time with his right foot. He got that foot caught on Slash's right boot. He gave a forlorn wail, as though tripping over Slash's boot was the final insult, and fell to the floor flat on his face to lie as motionless as the fat blond gent, whose only sin had been hauling hot water to Mrs. Smith for a bath.

Running footsteps thundered down the hall in the direction of the stairs. As they grew louder, Pecos shouted, "Slash! You all right, Slash?"

Suddenly, Pecos stopped in the hall before reaching Slash, who did not turn toward him.

Slash was staring at the open doorway of Mr. and Mrs. Smith's room just as Mrs. Smith herself, aka Fannie Diamond, emerged holding a .44 revolver straight out in both hands. As she slowly stepped out of the room, looking as befuddled as Talon Renfro had, she just as slowly lowered the smoking popper, then dropped it to the floor.

She stared down in befuddlement and horror at the dead outlaw she'd shot in the back. She slid her gaze to Slash and started sobbing, falling to her knees.

"Oh, God. What have I done?" she wailed. "Oh, God. What have I done?" She looked in sudden disgust at Slash and yelled, "I killed Talon to save *your* life. Scalawag! Oh, God. What have I *done*?" Again, she sobbed, and lowering her head and pounding her fists against her temples, she cried, "Oh, Fannie, what have you *done*?"

Pecos walked over to Slash and stared down at him. "You're hit, partner."

Slash winced, only now feeling the pain in his wounded left arm again. As he closed his right hand over the arm, he glanced at the howling and self-flagellating actress, then turned back to Pecos and said, "Yeah, but I don't feel half as bad as she does about savin' my life!"

Pecos laughed, pulled a handkerchief from his coat pocket, and knelt down to wrap his partner's arm. "Don't worry. She'll get over it."

"I doubt it."

Pecos looked at the bawling girl once more. "No, prob'ly not," he conceded, then gave a dry chuckle.

Epilogue

Slash and Pecos felt so bad about how bad Fannie felt about having saved Slash's life, by killing the man it turned out had helped her shake free of them, that they considered turning her loose.

In the end, however, they decided they'd come too far to turn back now. Besides, when you got right down to it, why turn loose a so-called actress who felt so consarned *bad* about saving your life? Slash appreciated that she *had* saved his life and all, but there were limits to his sympathy. She berated both men as well as herself nearly all the way to Denver, which they reached a week later—a week late for the trial, no doubt, but trials could be rescheduled.

So could hangings, and a hanging was what they figured would befall them both if they failed to bring the actress to Luther T. "Bleed-'Em-So" Bledsoe.

Speaking of hangings . . .

As it turned out—and much to Slash's and Pecos's everlasting exasperation—they learned from Bledsoe that Chaz "the Knife" Lutz had hanged himself in prison.

Yeah.

"Happened the day after you boys left Denver," Bledsoe said, chuckling around the cigar in his teeth. "I was up in the mountains on that extended working vacation with my mine owner friend, so I didn't learn about it in time to stop you . . . nor Quarles and Thomas . . . so . . . well . . ." He looked at the pretty actress standing before him, suddenly appearing happier than she had since Slash and Pecos had first laid eyes on her. "You can turn her loose. And now if you boys and lady will forgive me . . . I got work to do."

They'd already informed the man they'd taken down the entire Duke Winter gang, Slash sharing credit with Pecos.

Do you think that got them a single word of thanks from the nasty old, cotton-headed gent in the push chair? Hell, no! He simply said curtly that despite sending Quarles and Thomas as backup, he'd expected nothing less for the money he paid them and for his keeping the hangman from playing cat's cradle with their heads. The nasty old man chuckled again, thoroughly delighted with himself, and told them he'd send them their money in Camp Collins "when he got around to it."

He dismissed them with a veiny old paw.

Now they were left wondering what to do with Fannie.

They discussed the matter out on the street before the federal building after Pecos and Bledsoe's alluring secretary, Miss Abigail Langdon, had exchanged mooncalf gazes, of course.

"Don't worry, Fannie. We'll buy you a train ticket back to Frisco," Slash assured her.

"And send the bill to Bleed-'Em-So," Pecos added.

Fannie pondered the matter, tucking her upper lip under her bottom teeth.

Then she looked at the two men who'd kidnapped her and said, "Hmmm . . . I've heard Camp Collins is nice. More civilized than the mountain gold camps. And now that Duke and Boone are dead, and I have no one left to manage or protect me, maybe I'll head there with you two old scalawags. You'll introduce me around, won't you?"

She flicked her fingers against each man's hat in turn and flounced on one hip. "I think it's the least you could do."

Slash and Pecos shared a conferring glance.

Pecos shrugged, arched a brow. "Jay might know what to do with her."

"I reckon she would at that," Slash said, giving a shrug of his own. He turned to Fannie. "I reckon Fannie Diamond's ready for Camp Collins and maybe even the Thousand Delights. The question is," he added, turning to Pecos, "is Camp Collins ready for Fannie Diamond!"

"Scoundrel!" Fannie said and elbowed Slash in the ribs.

She turned to her horse, throwing her hair back, and said, "Come along, boys. My future is waiting!"

She climbed into the saddle.

Pecos turned to Slash, whose ribs still hurt from the elbow she'd given him. At least she'd left his wounded arm alone this time.

"Do we know what we're getting into here, Slash?" Pecos asked softly as the girl reined her mount out into the bustling Denver street.

"Oh, I think by now we know exactly what we're getting into here, partner!"

They laughed—a little uneasily—and mounted up.

They rode to Camp Collins, with Slash having one hell of a story to entertain his recent bride with, only to find out once reaching home that the former Jaycee Breckenridge, Myra Thompson, and Delbert Thayer had an interesting tale of their own. . . .